NISHIKATA

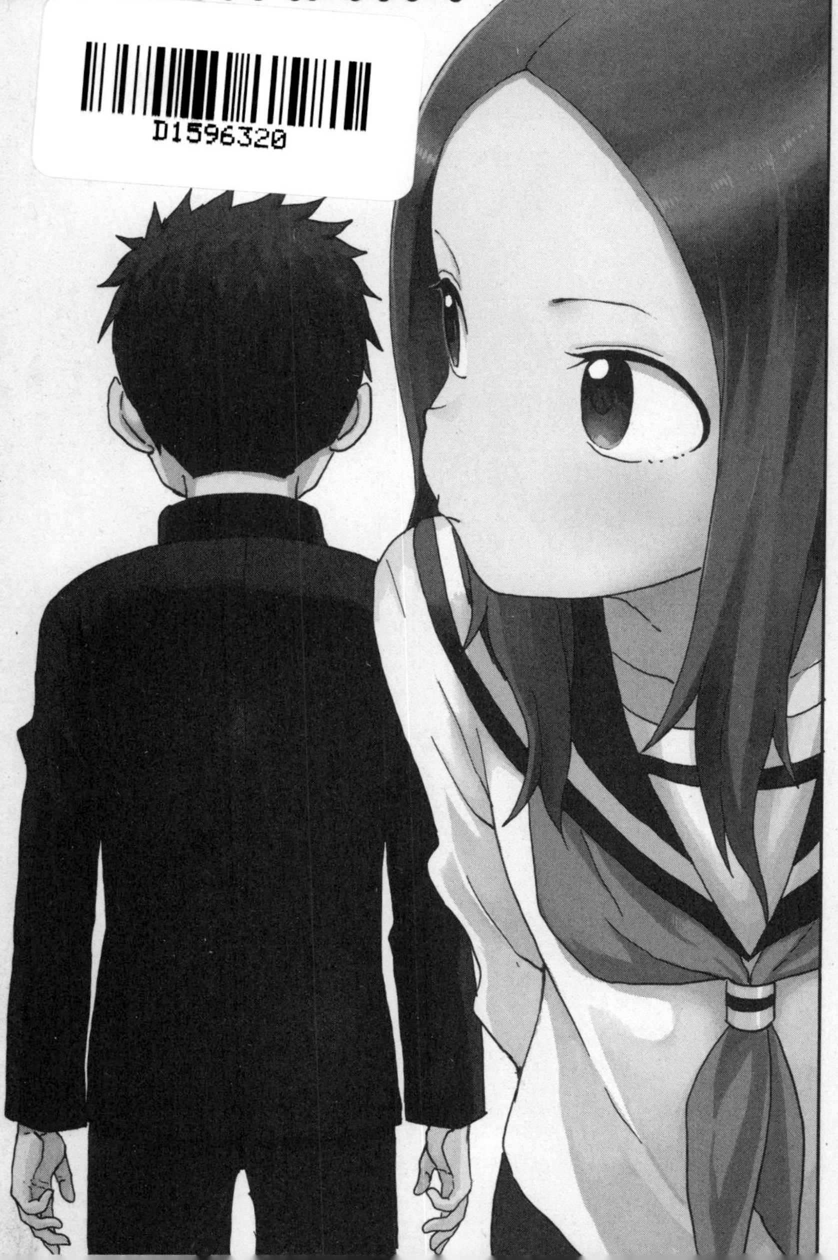

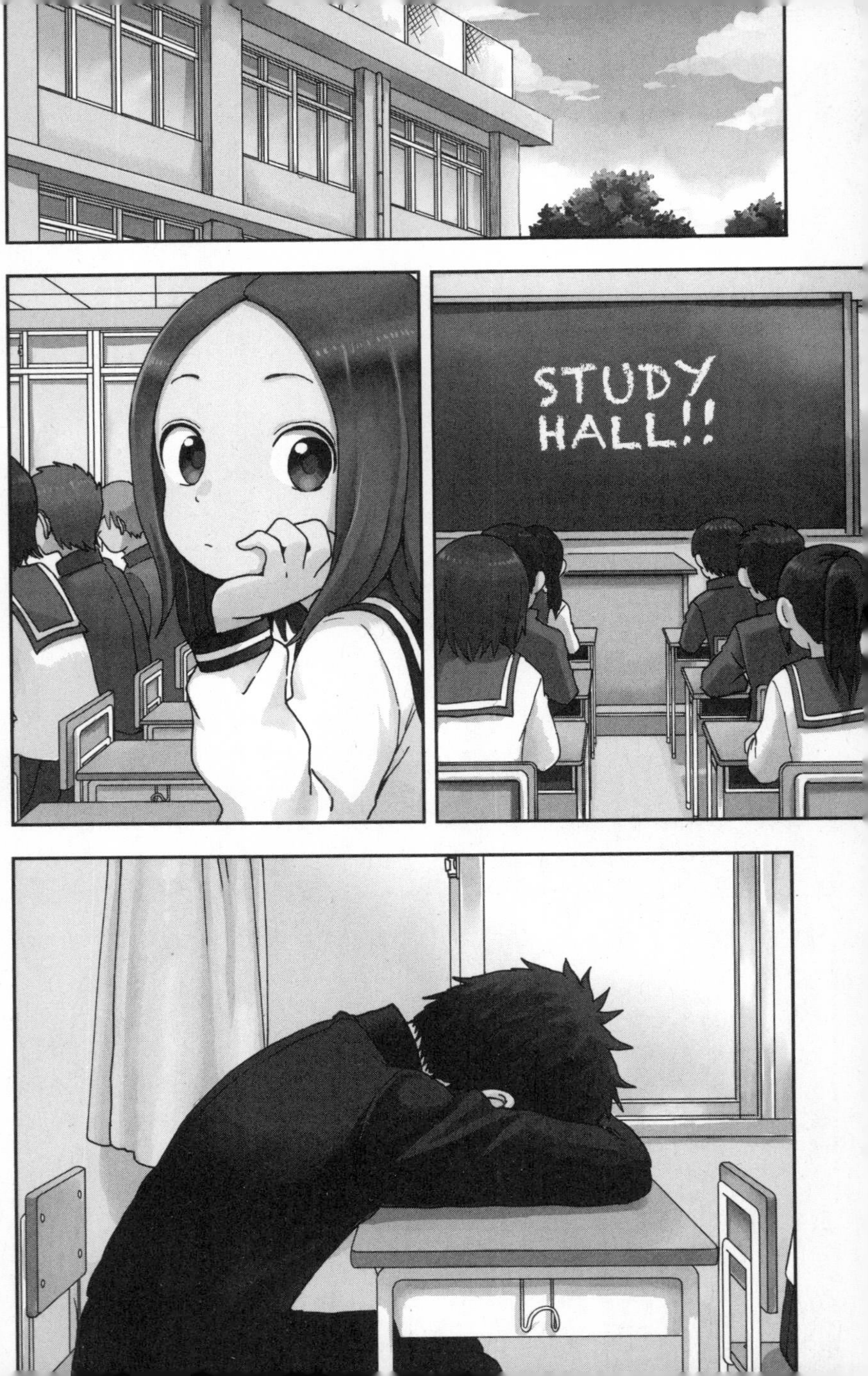
STUDY HALL!!

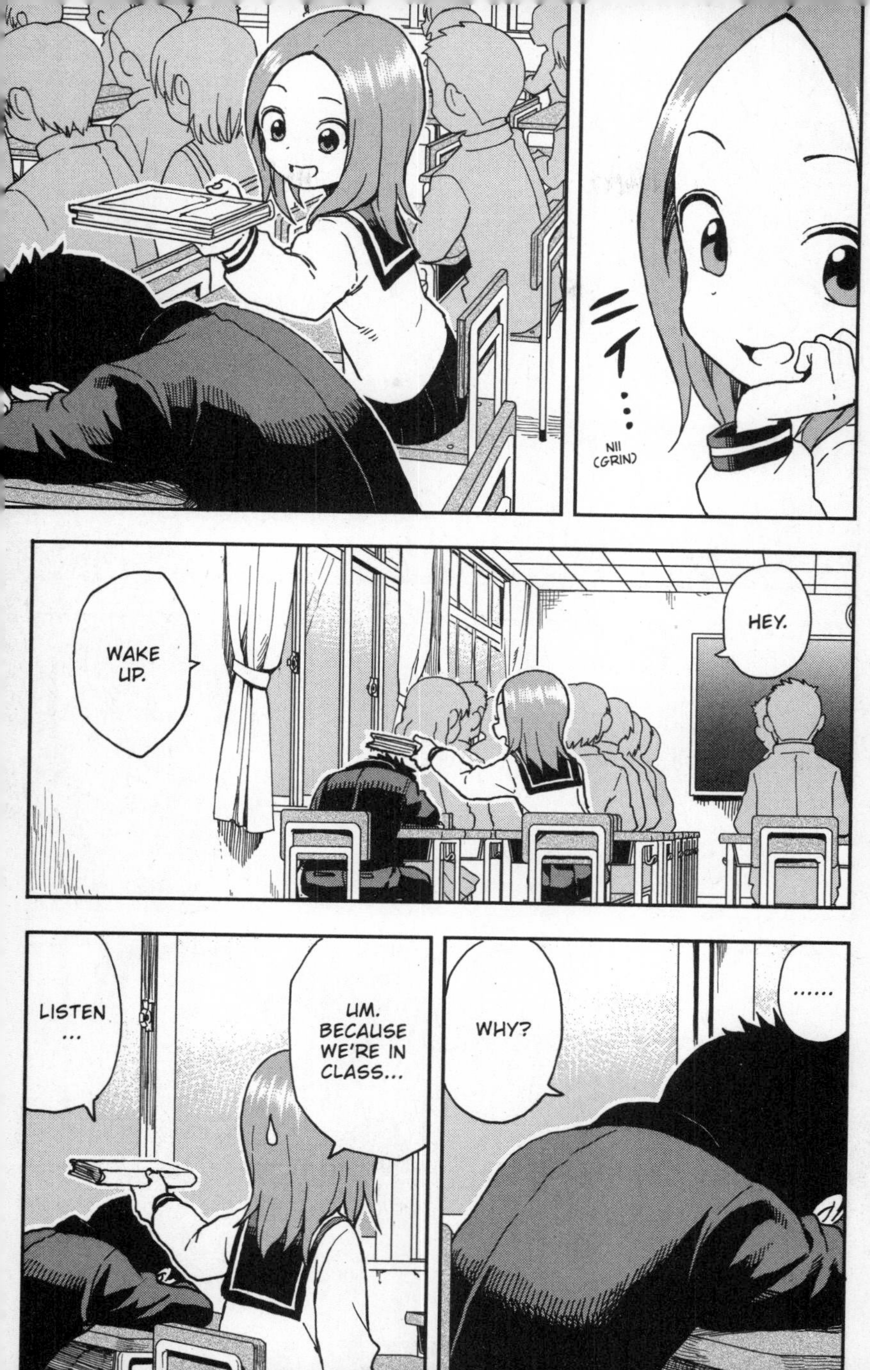
ニイ…
NII (GRIN)
HEY.
WAKE UP.
......
WHY?
UM. BECAUSE WE'RE IN CLASS...
LISTEN ...

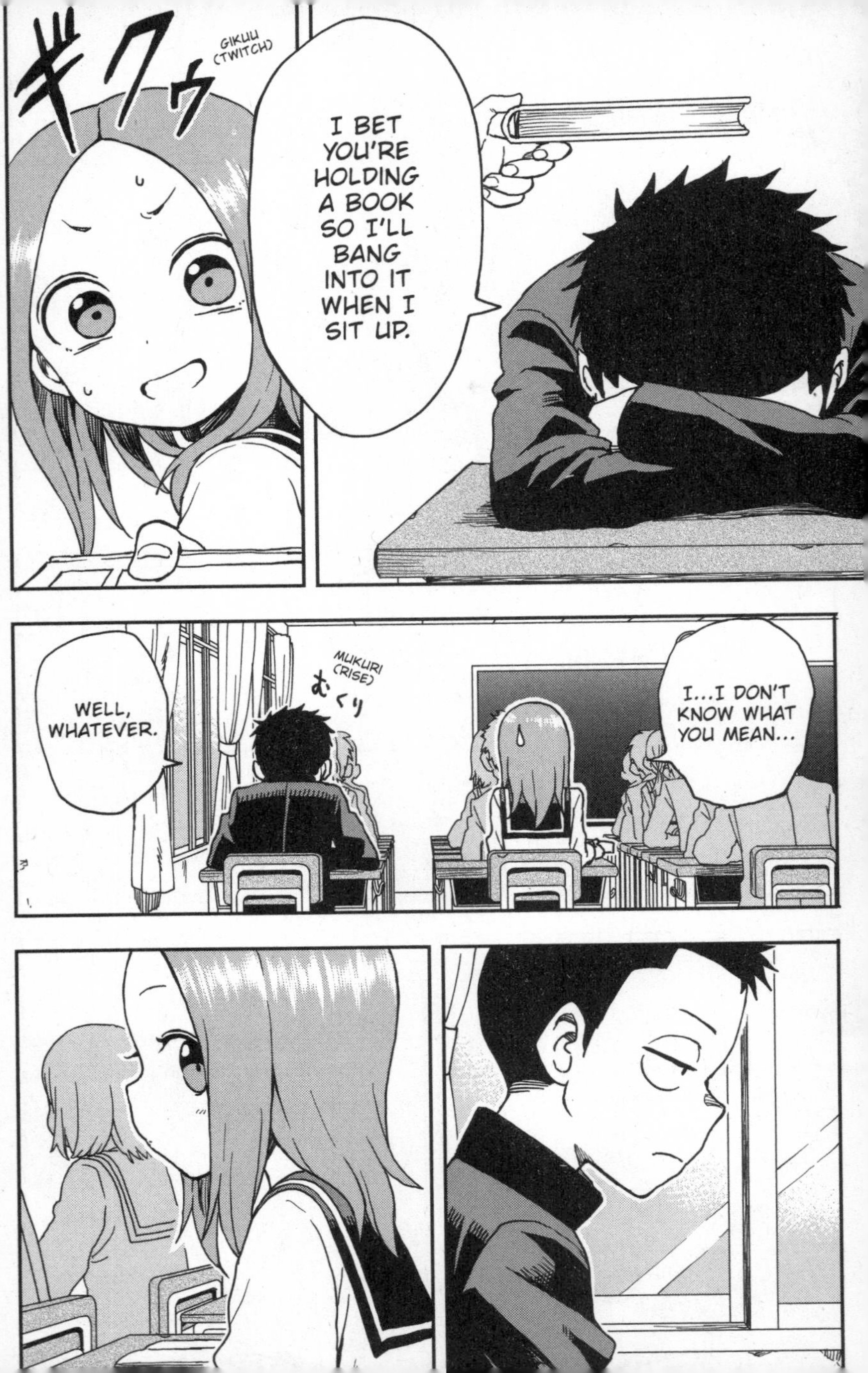
I BET YOU'RE HOLDING A BOOK SO I'LL BANG INTO IT WHEN I SIT UP.
ギクゥ
GIKUU (TWITCH)
I...I DON'T KNOW WHAT YOU MEAN...
MUKURI (RISE)
むくり
WELL, WHATEVER.

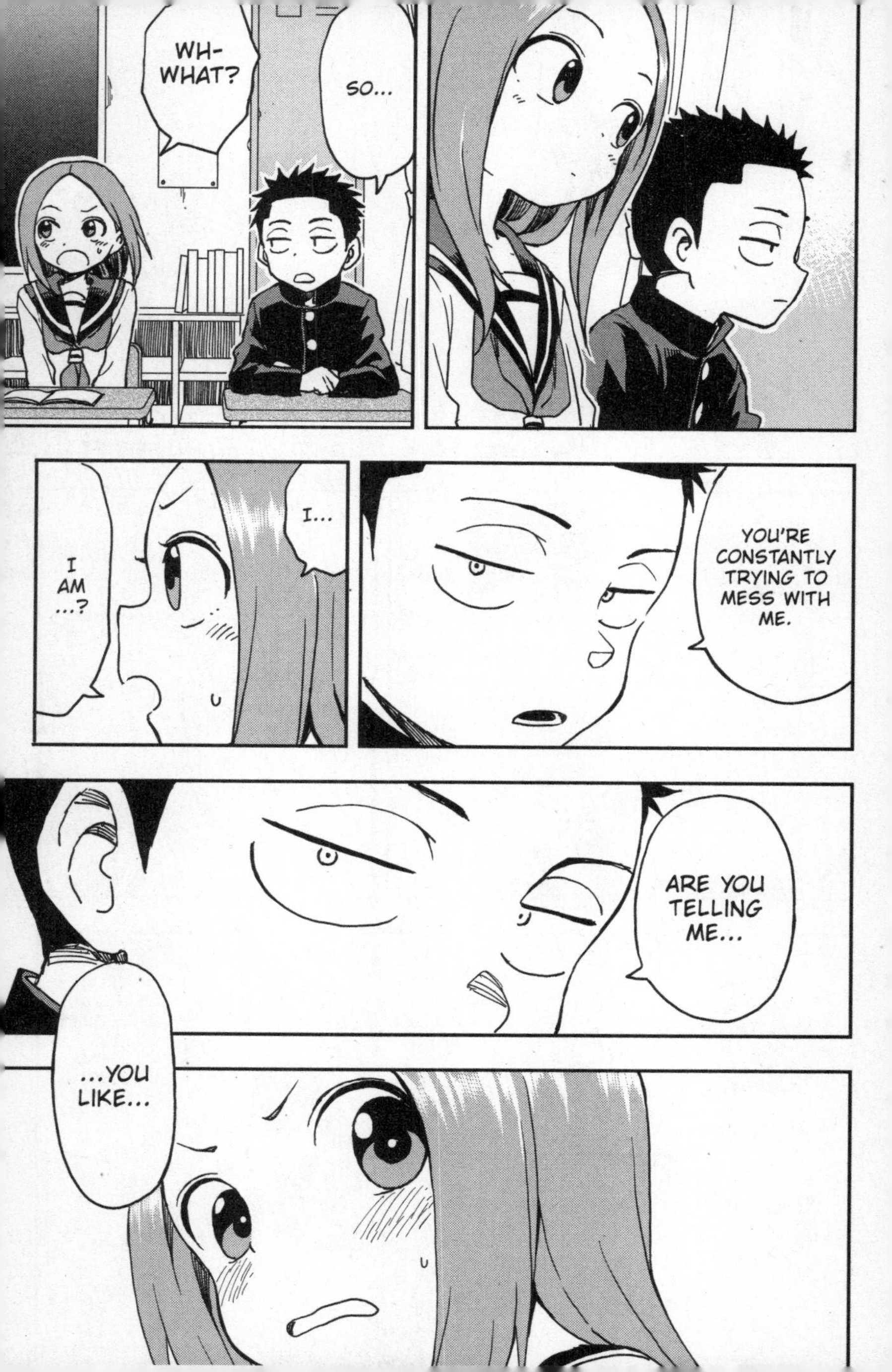
SO...
WH-WHAT?
YOU'RE CONSTANTLY TRYING TO MESS WITH ME.
I...
I AM ...?
ARE YOU TELLING ME...
...YOU LIKE...

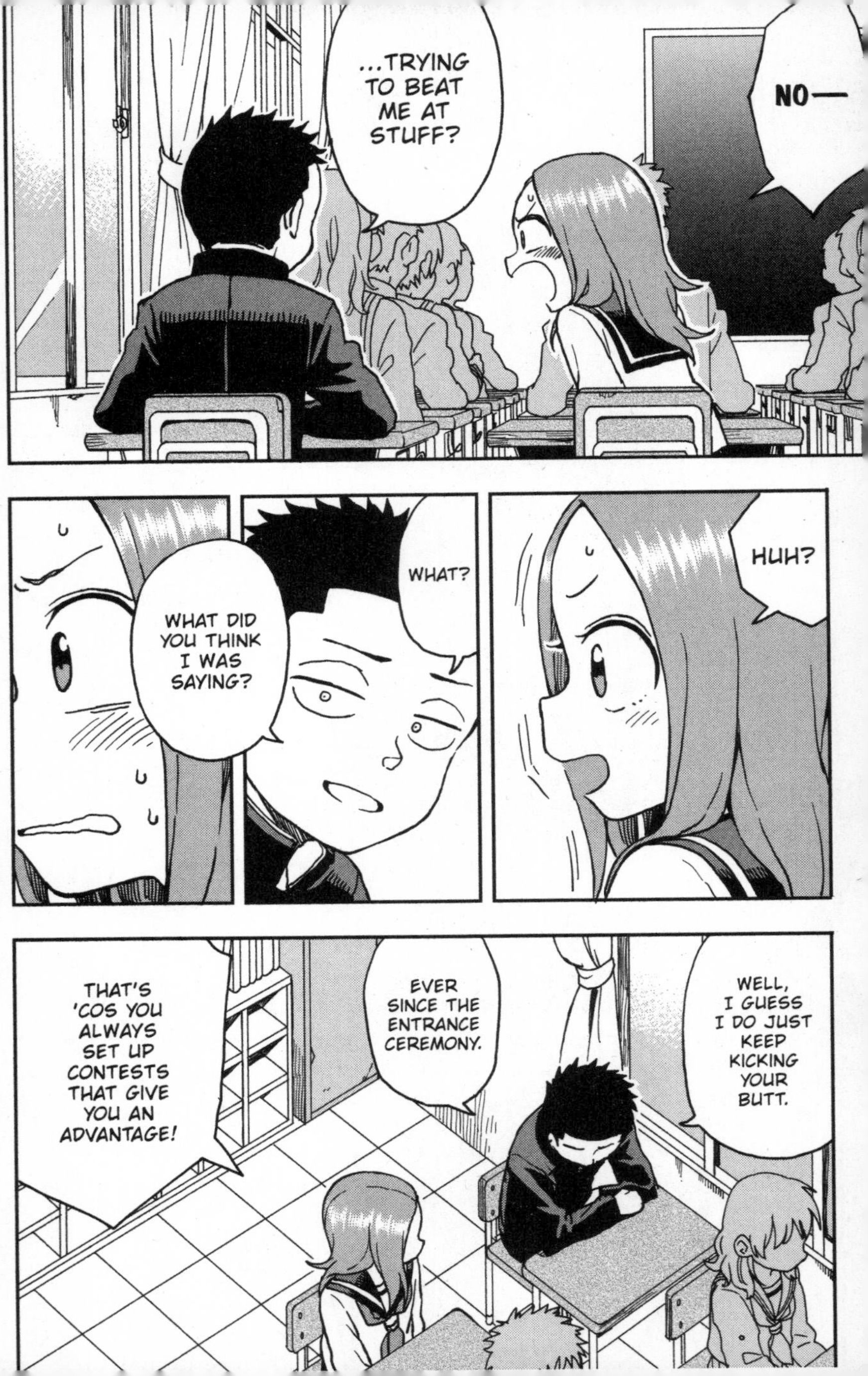
NO—
...TRYING TO BEAT ME AT STUFF?
HUH?
WHAT?
WHAT DID YOU THINK I WAS SAYING?
WELL, I GUESS I DO JUST KEEP KICKING YOUR BUTT.
EVER SINCE THE ENTRANCE CEREMONY.
THAT'S 'COS YOU ALWAYS SET UP CONTESTS THAT GIVE YOU AN ADVANTAGE!

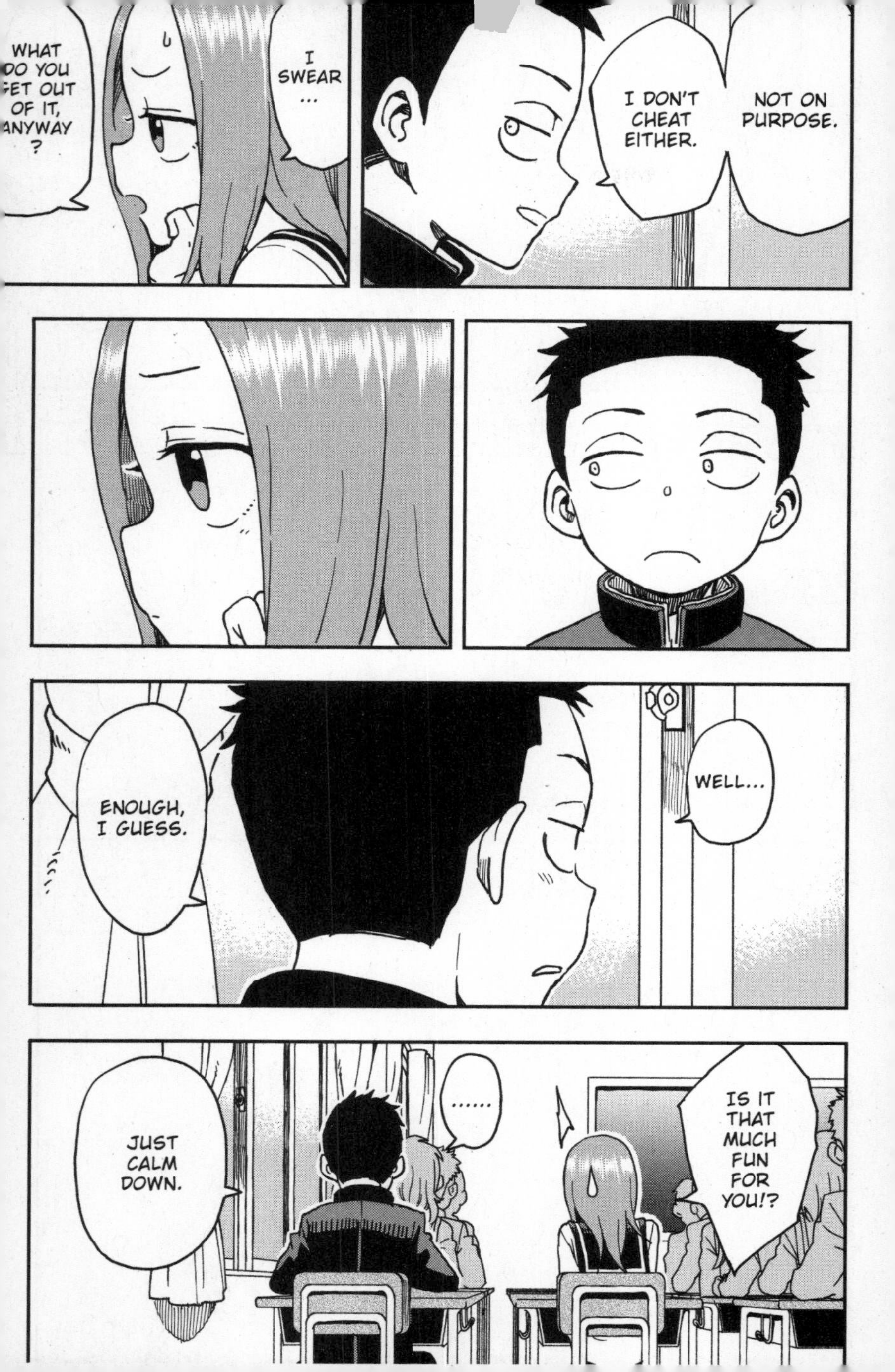
NOT ON PURPOSE.
I DON'T CHEAT EITHER.
I SWEAR...
WHAT DO YOU GET OUT OF IT, ANYWAY?
WELL...
ENOUGH, I GUESS.
IS IT THAT MUCH FUN FOR YOU!?
......
JUST CALM DOWN.

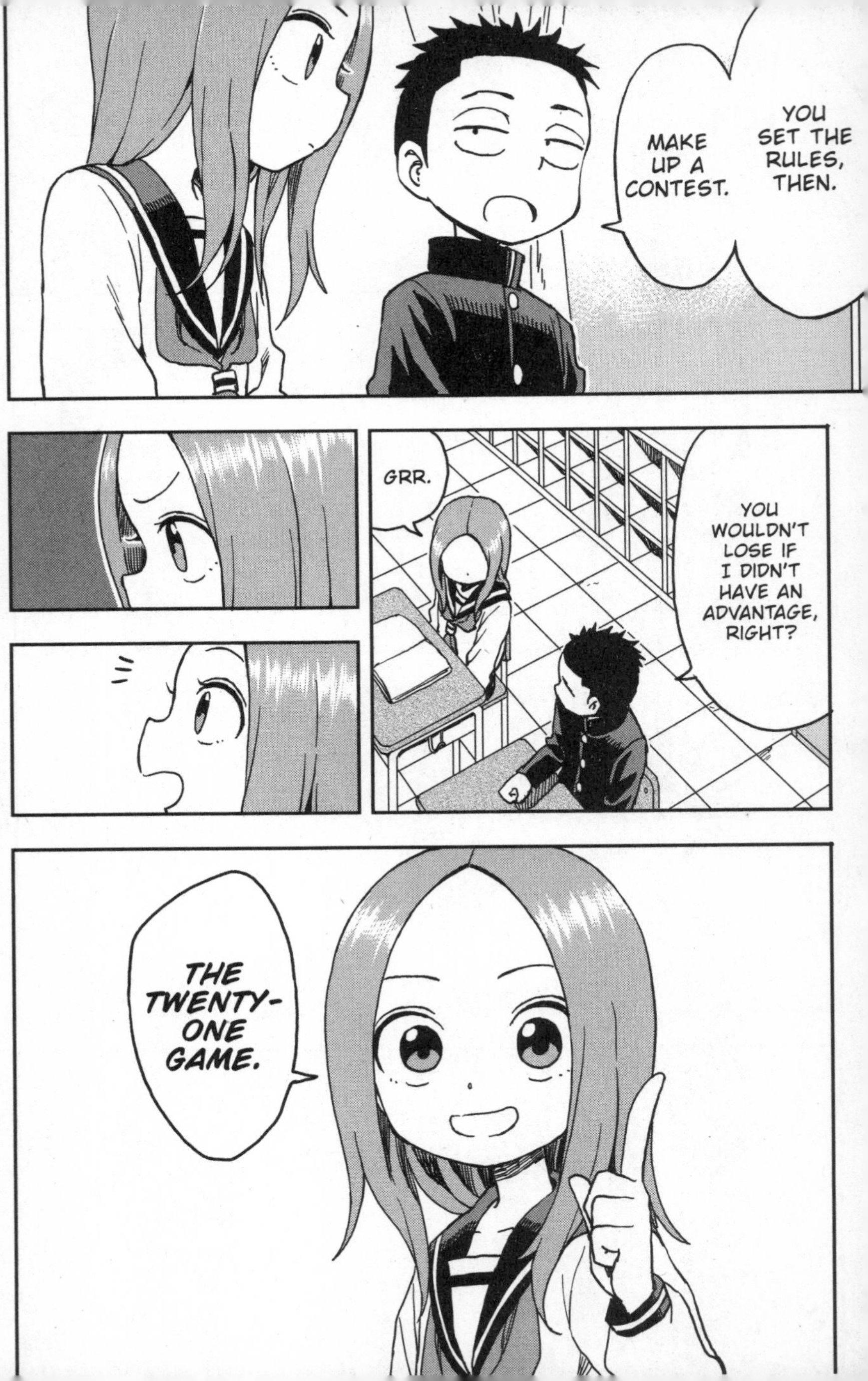
YOU SET THE RULES, THEN.
MAKE UP A CONTEST.
YOU WOULDN'T LOSE IF I DIDN'T HAVE AN ADVANTAGE, RIGHT?
GRR.
THE TWENTY-ONE GAME.

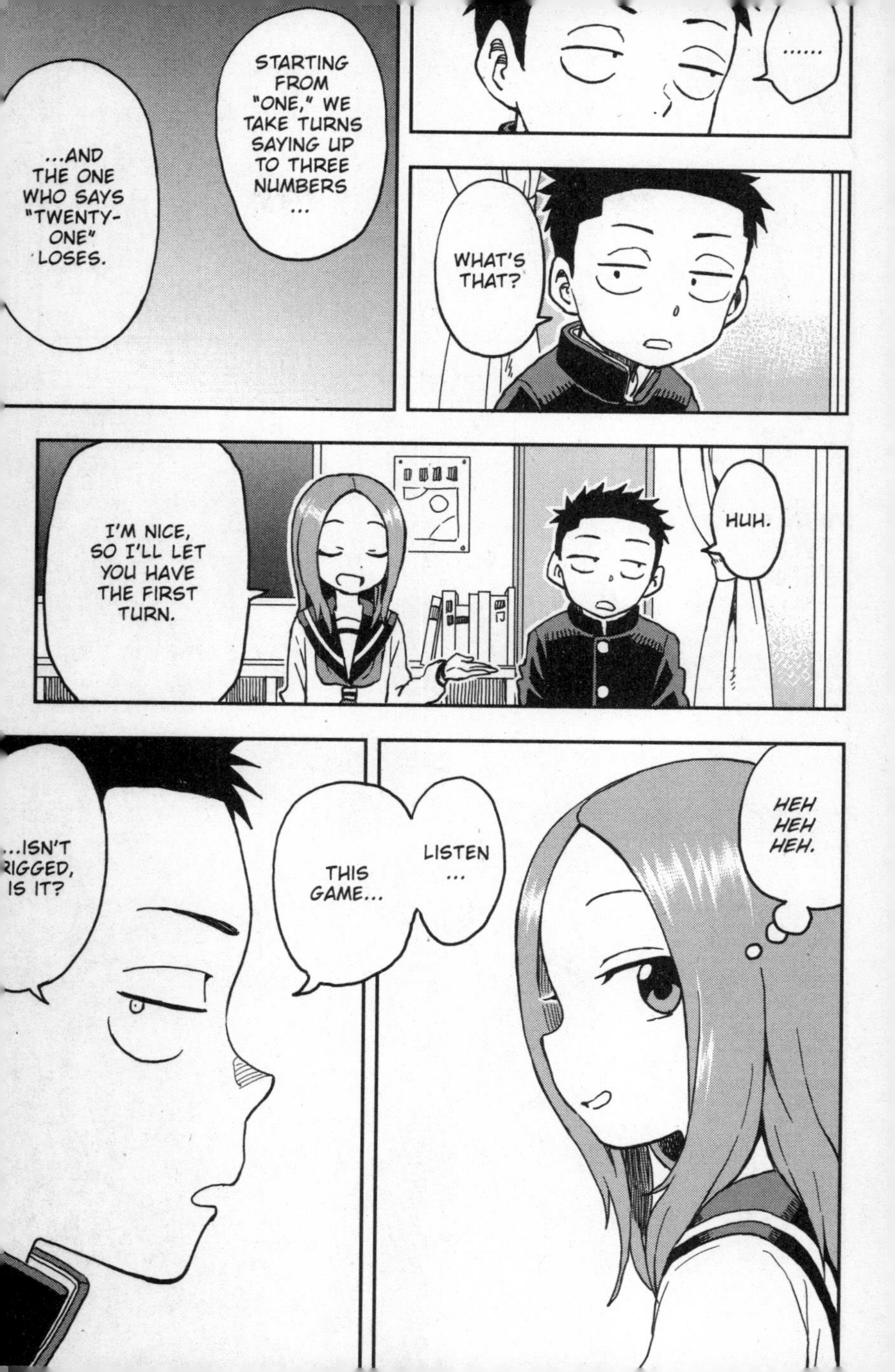
......
WHAT'S THAT?
STARTING FROM "ONE," WE TAKE TURNS SAYING UP TO THREE NUMBERS ...
...AND THE ONE WHO SAYS "TWENTY-ONE" LOSES.
HUH.
I'M NICE, SO I'LL LET YOU HAVE THE FIRST TURN.
HEH HEH HEH.
LISTEN ...
THIS GAME...
...ISN'T RIGGED, IS IT?

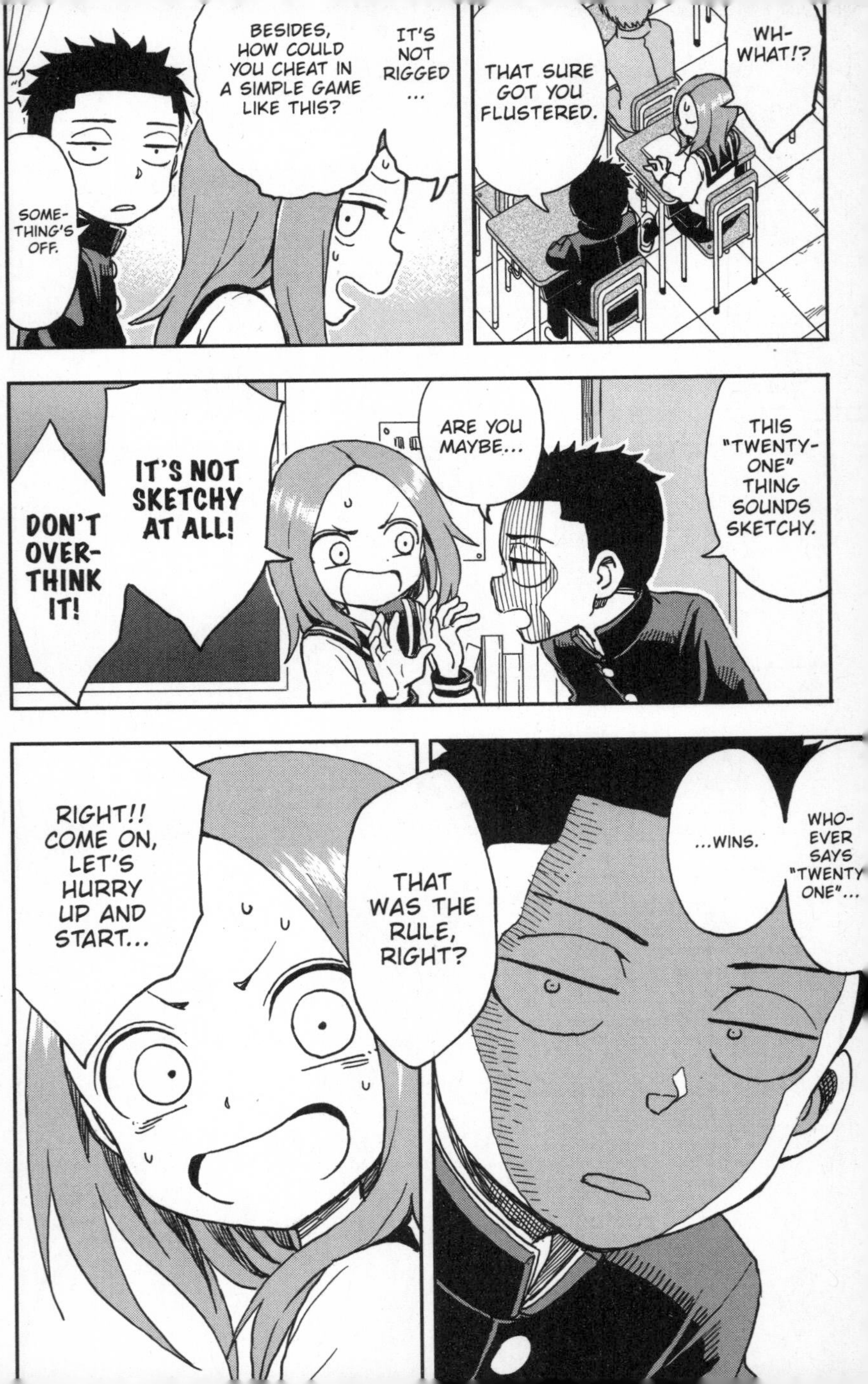
WH-WHAT!?
THAT SURE GOT YOU FLUSTERED.
IT'S NOT RIGGED ...
BESIDES, HOW COULD YOU CHEAT IN A SIMPLE GAME LIKE THIS?
SOME-THING'S OFF.
THIS "TWENTY-ONE" THING SOUNDS SKETCHY.
ARE YOU MAYBE...
IT'S NOT SKETCHY AT ALL!
DON'T OVER-THINK IT!
WHO-EVER SAYS "TWENTY ONE"...
...WINS.
THAT WAS THE RULE, RIGHT?
RIGHT!! COME ON, LET'S HURRY UP AND START...

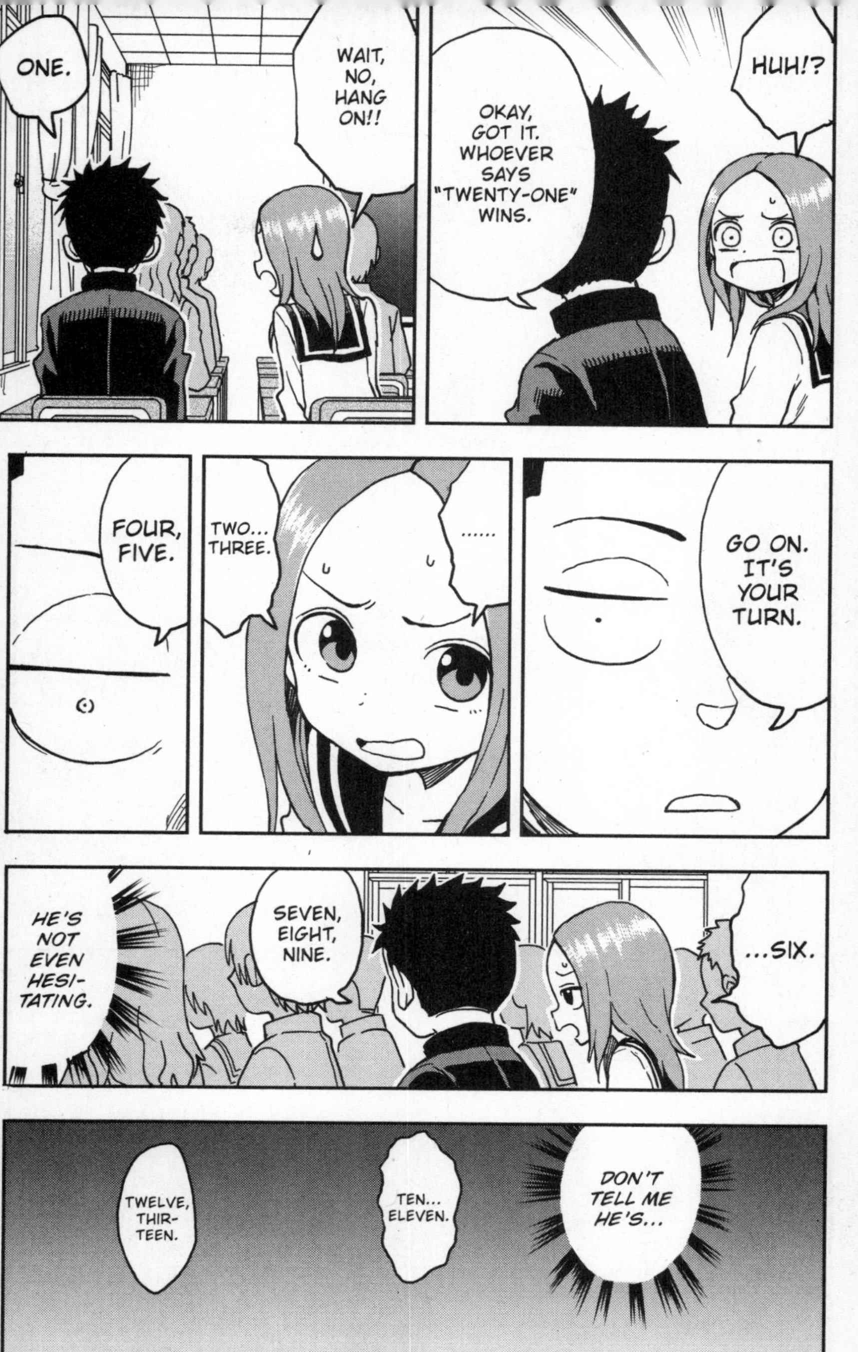
HUH!?
OKAY, GOT IT. WHOEVER SAYS "TWENTY-ONE" WINS.
WAIT, NO, HANG ON!!
ONE.
GO ON. IT'S YOUR TURN.
......
TWO... THREE.
FOUR, FIVE.
...SIX.
SEVEN, EIGHT, NINE.
HE'S NOT EVEN HESI-TATING.
DON'T TELL ME HE'S...
TEN... ELEVEN.
TWELVE, THIR-TEEN.

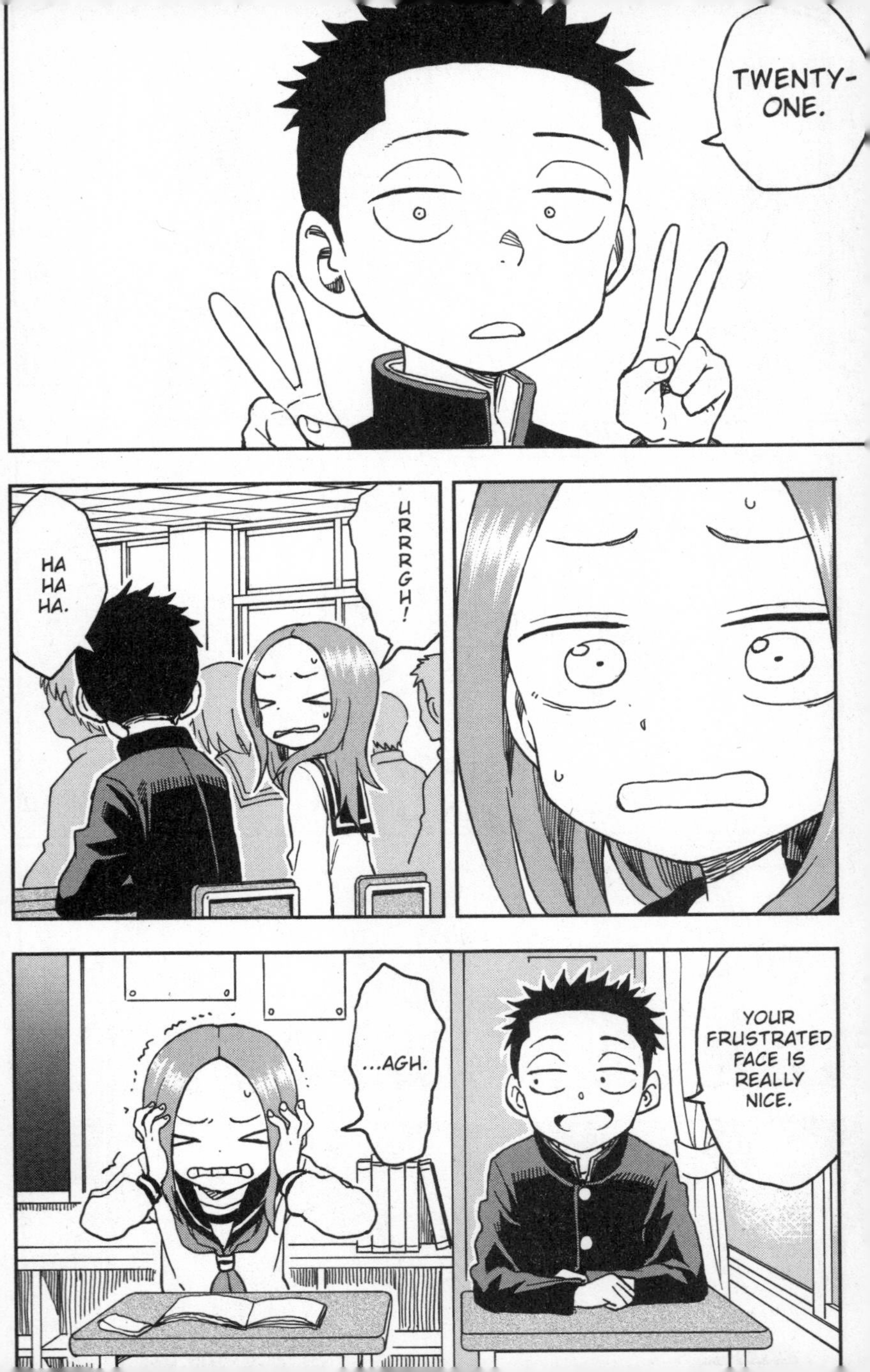
TWENTY-ONE.
URRRGH!
HA HA HA.
YOUR FRUSTRATED FACE IS REALLY NICE.
...AGH.

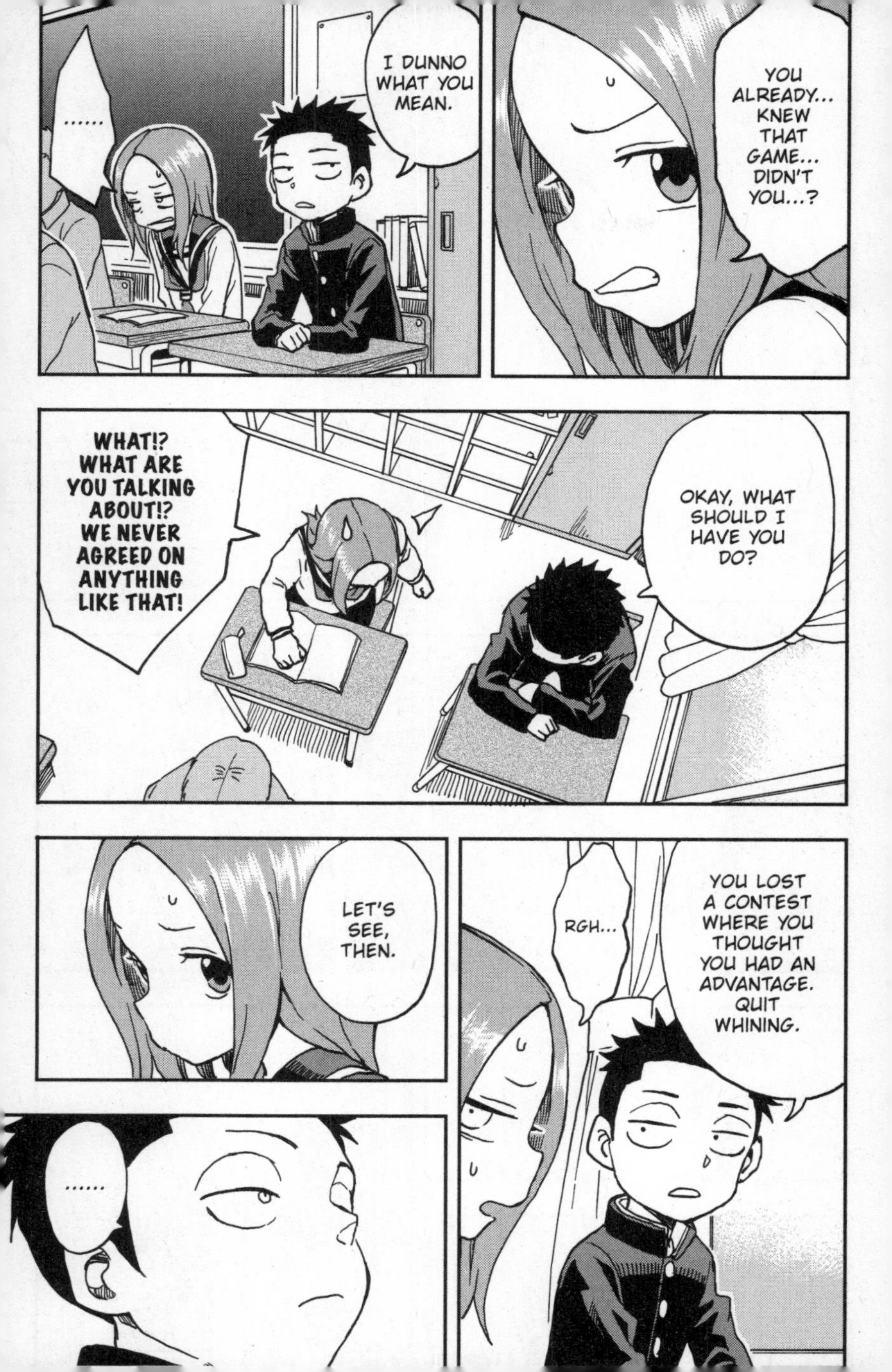
YOU ALREADY... KNEW THAT GAME... DIDN'T YOU...?
I DUNNO WHAT YOU MEAN.
......
OKAY, WHAT SHOULD I HAVE YOU DO?
WHAT!? WHAT ARE YOU TALKING ABOUT!? WE NEVER AGREED ON ANYTHING LIKE THAT!
YOU LOST A CONTEST WHERE YOU THOUGHT YOU HAD AN ADVANTAGE. QUIT WHINING.
RGH...
LET'S SEE, THEN.
......

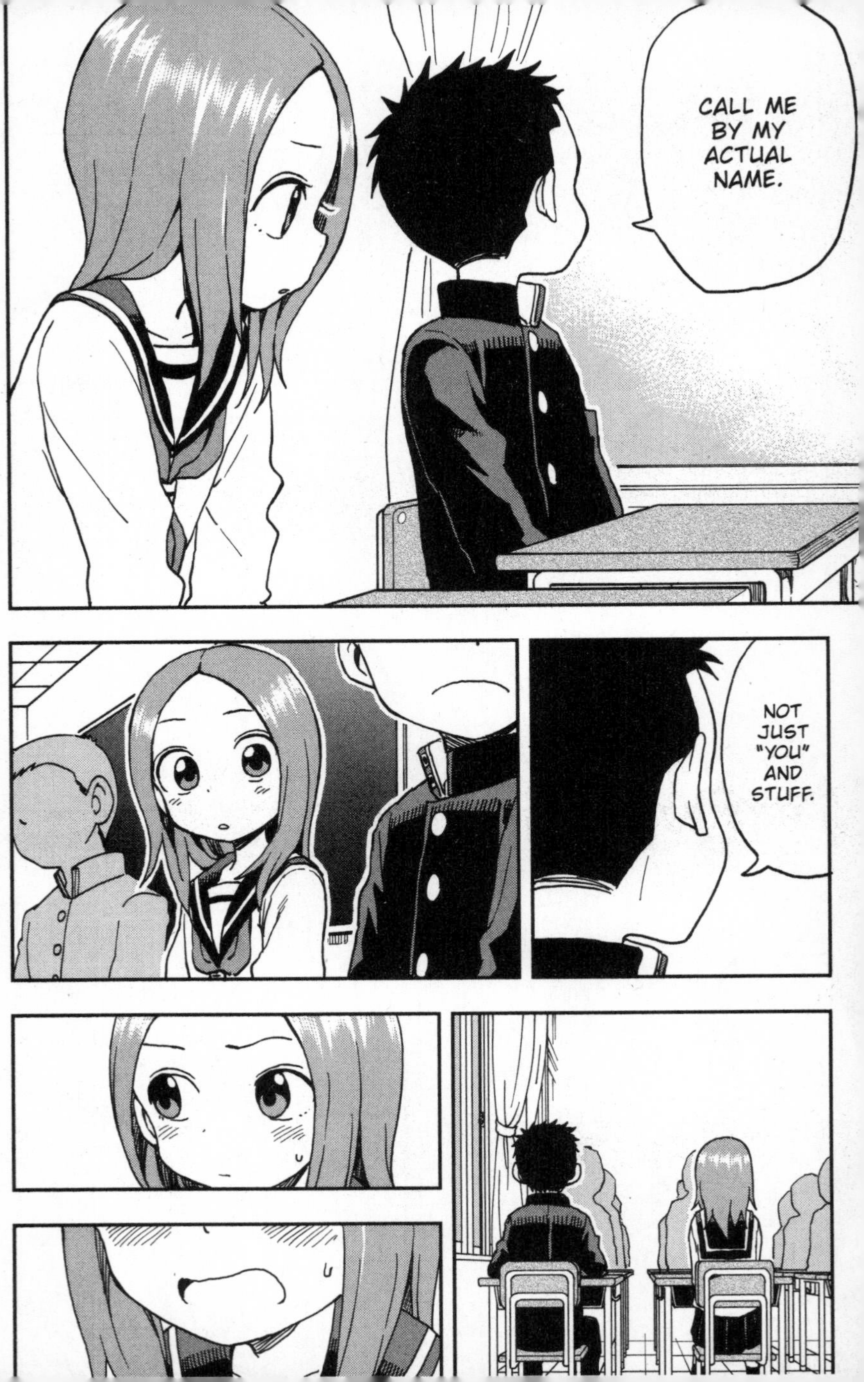
CALL ME BY MY ACTUAL NAME.
NOT JUST "YOU" AND STUFF.

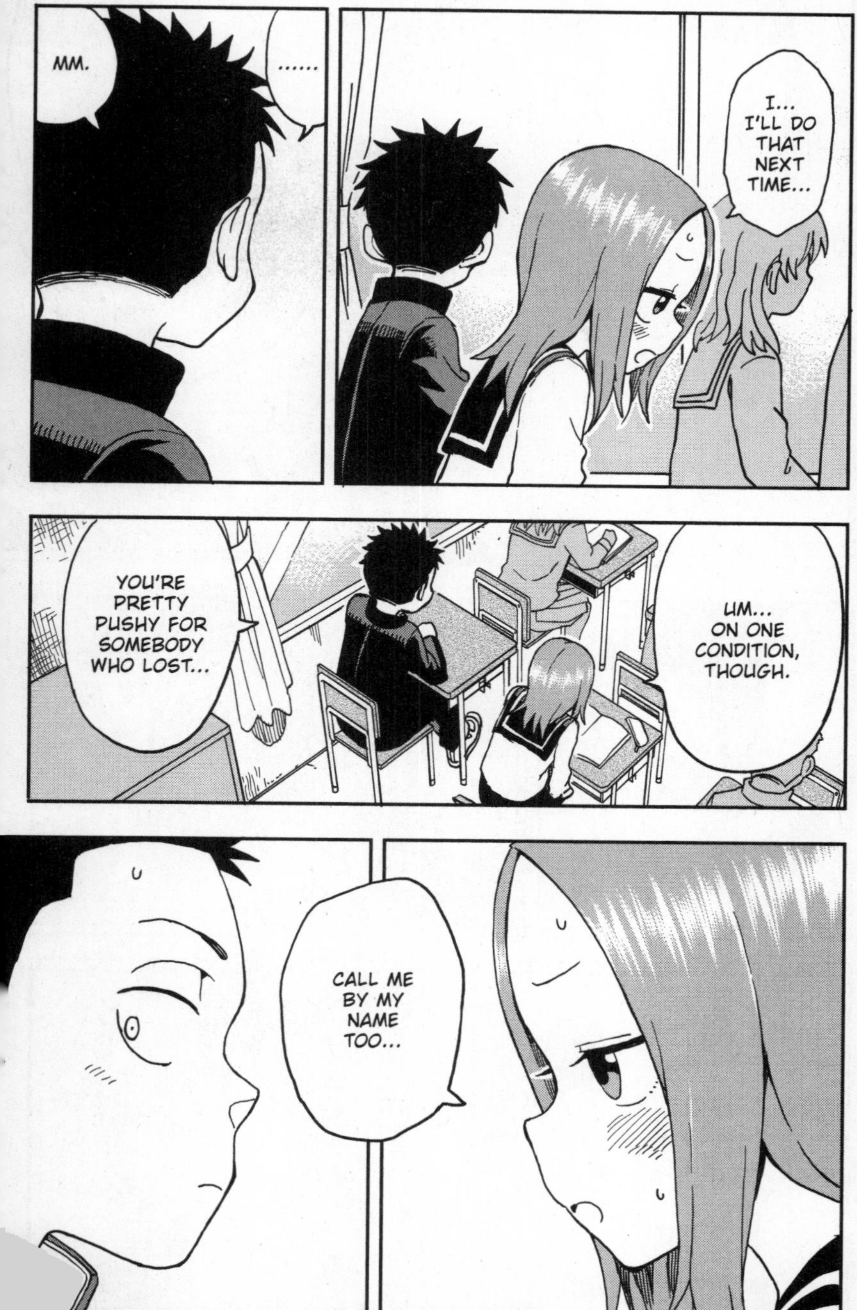
I... I'LL DO THAT NEXT TIME...
......
MM.
UM... ON ONE CONDITION, THOUGH.
YOU'RE PRETTY PUSHY FOR SOMEBODY WHO LOST...
CALL ME BY MY NAME TOO...

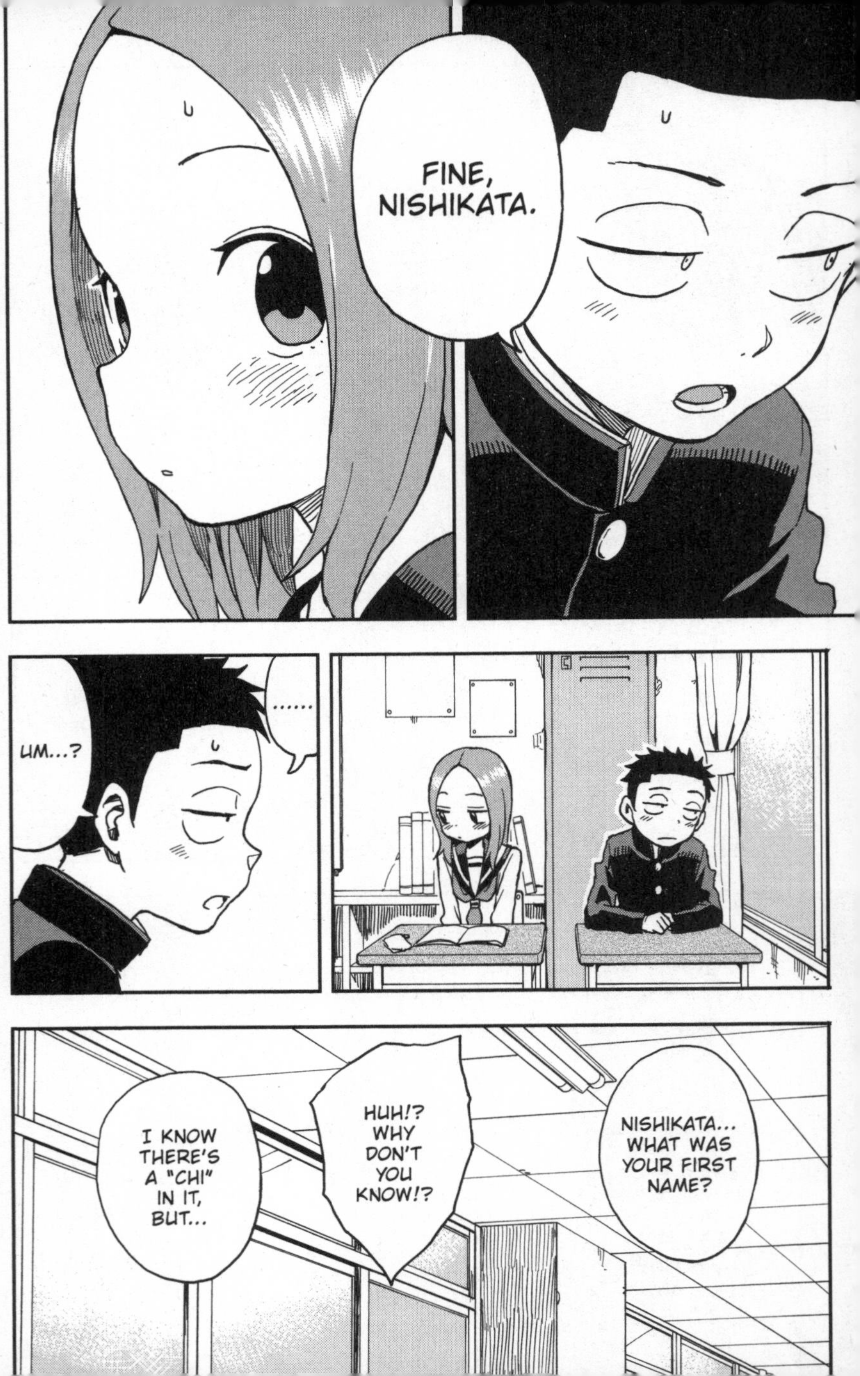
FINE, NISHIKATA.
......
UM...?
NISHIKATA... WHAT WAS YOUR FIRST NAME?
HUH!? WHY DON'T YOU KNOW!?
I KNOW THERE'S A "CHI" IN IT, BUT...

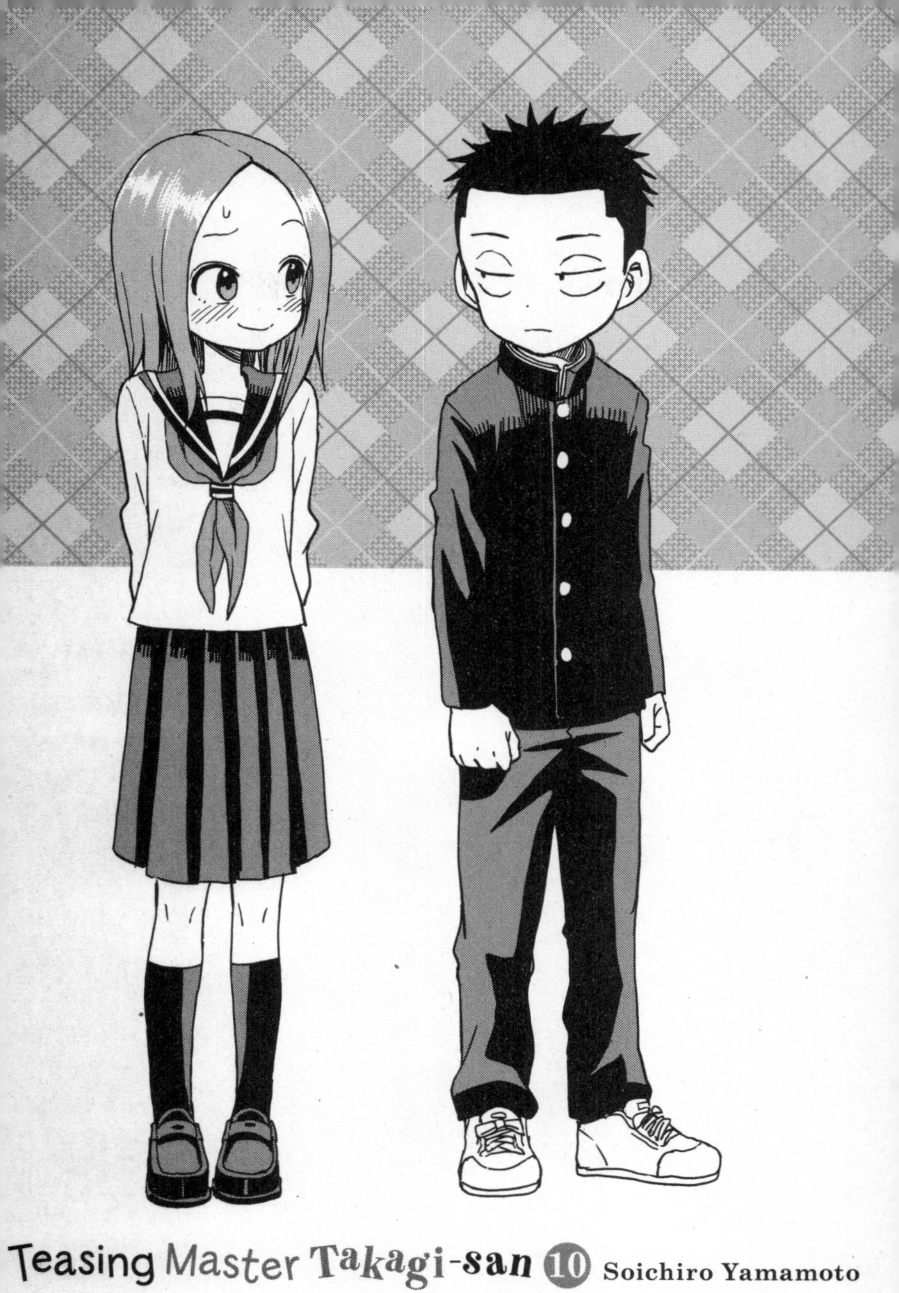

Teasing Master Takagi-san 10 Soichiro Yamamoto

Contents

APRIL FOOLS' DAY
67

COOKIES
51

DOG
35

VERTICAL MESSAGES
19

NISHIKATA
1

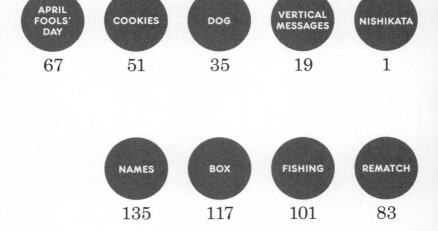

NAMES
135

BOX
117

FISHING
101

REMATCH
83

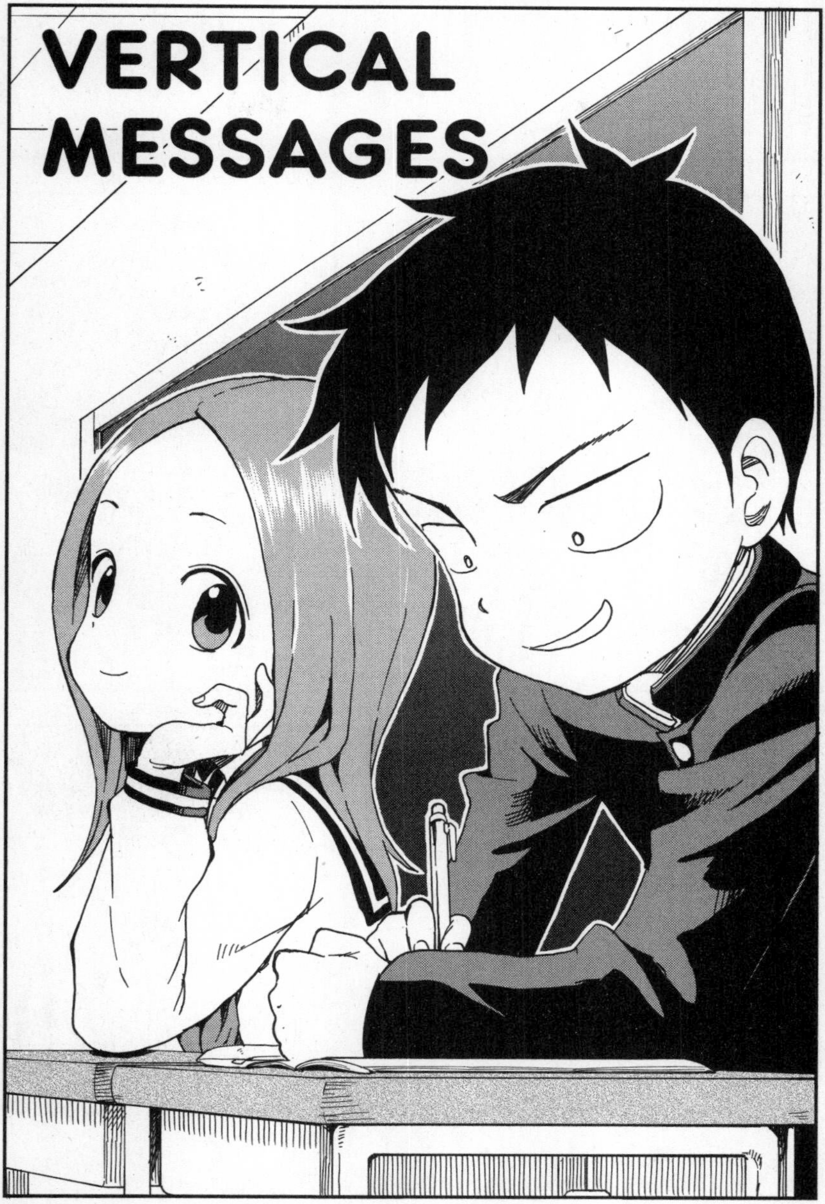
VERTICAL
MESSAGES

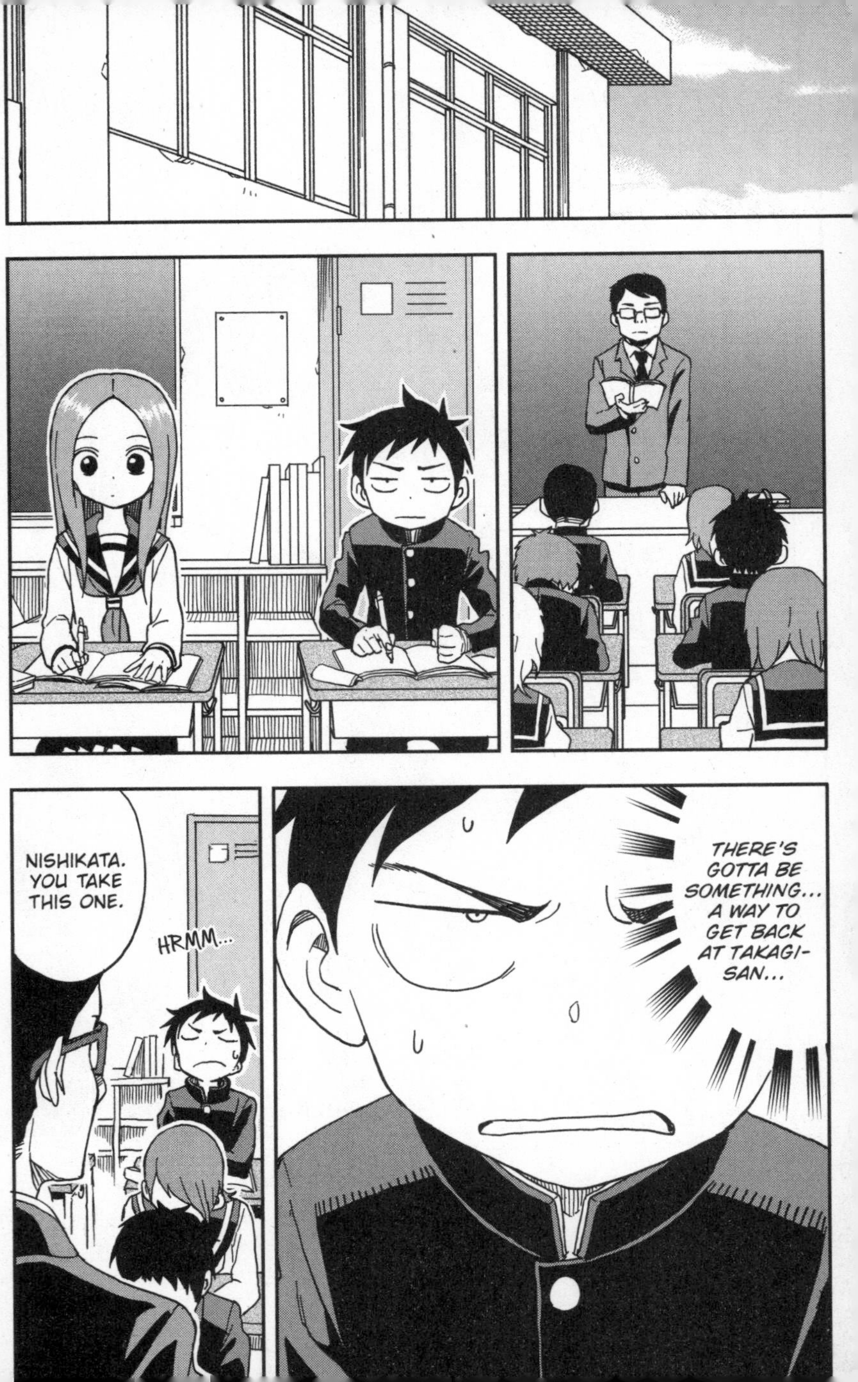
THERE'S GOTTA BE SOMETHING... A WAY TO GET BACK AT TAKAGI-SAN...
NISHIKATA. YOU TAKE THIS ONE.
HRMM...

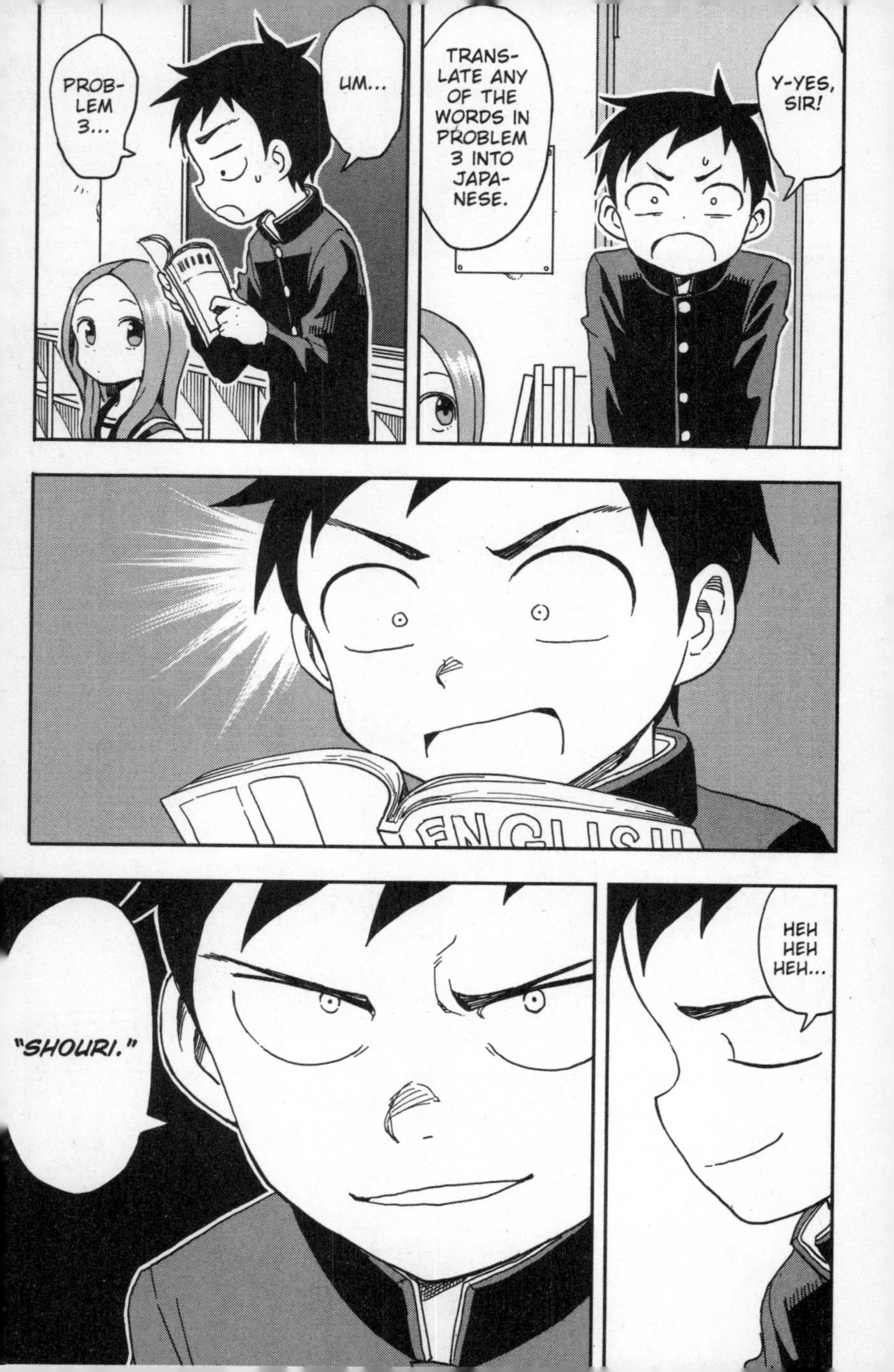
Y-YES, SIR!
TRANS-LATE ANY OF THE WORDS IN PROBLEM 3 INTO JAPA-NESE.
UM...
PROB-LEM 3...
ENGLISH
HEH HEH HEH...
"SHOURI."

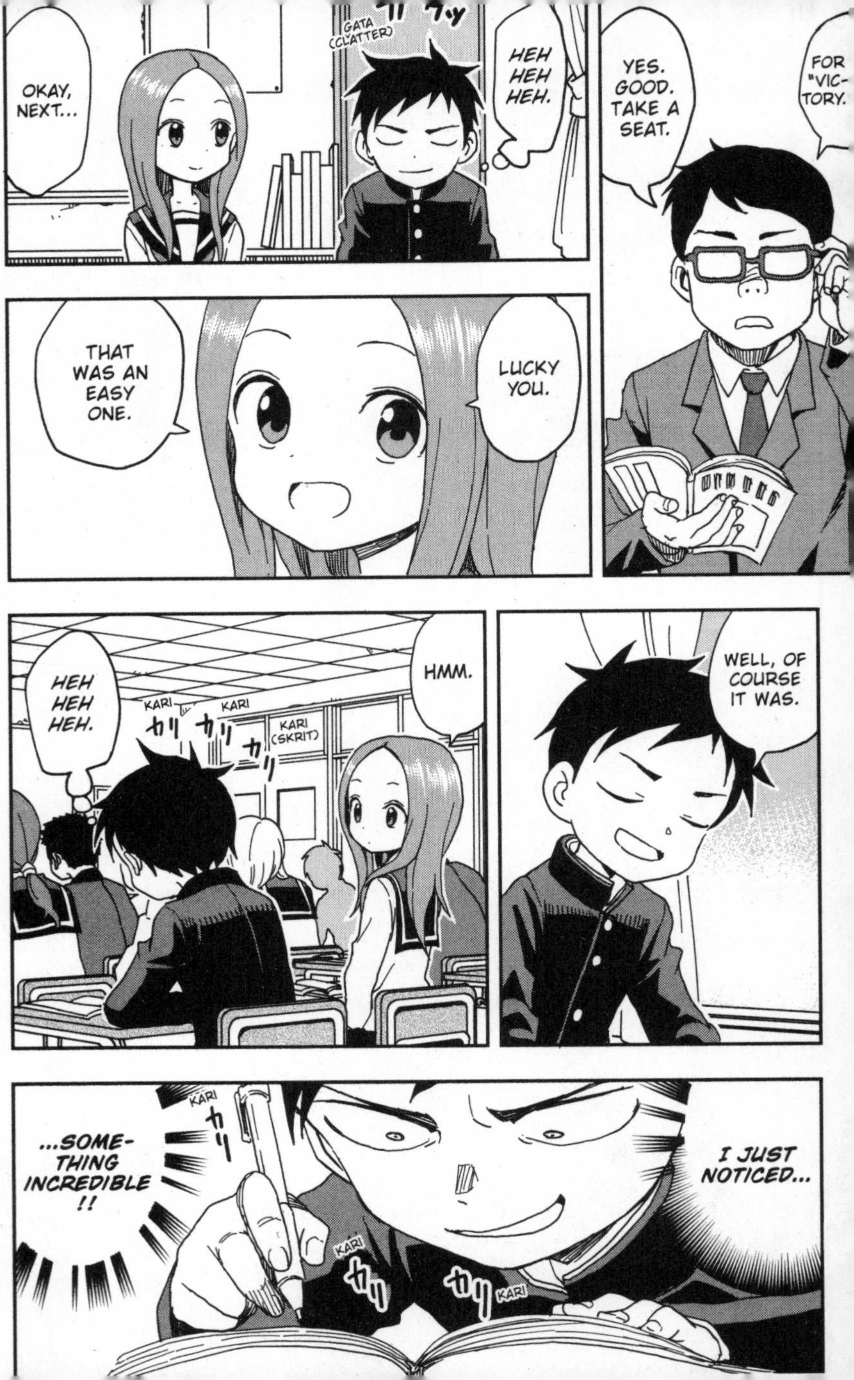
FOR "VIC-TORY."
YES. GOOD. TAKE A SEAT.
HEH HEH HEH.
GATA (CLATTER)
OKAY, NEXT...
LUCKY YOU.
THAT WAS AN EASY ONE.
WELL, OF COURSE IT WAS.
HMM.
KARI (SKRIT)
KARI
KARI
HEH HEH HEH.
I JUST NOTICED...
KARI
...SOME-THING INCREDIBLE!!
KARI
KARI

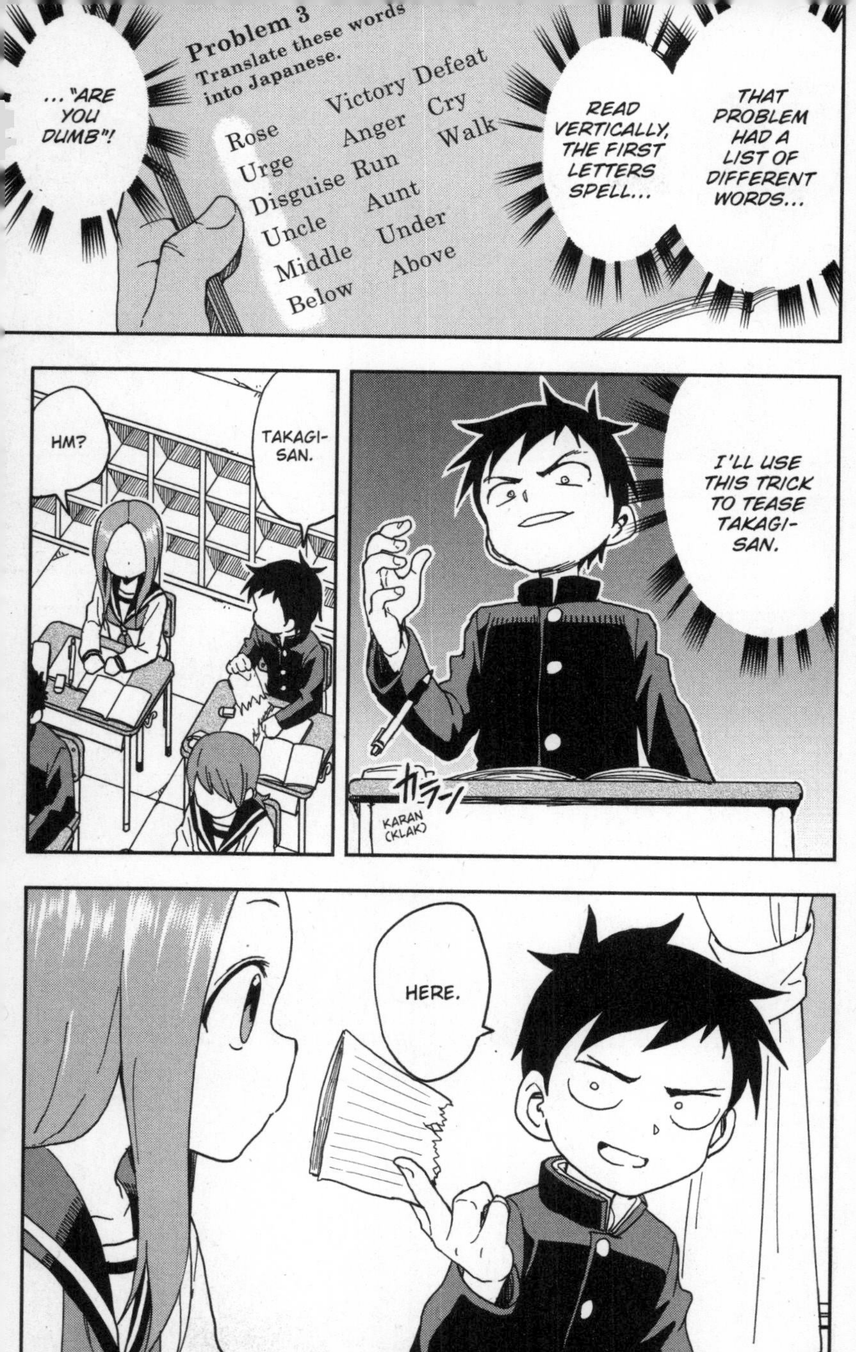
THAT PROBLEM HAD A LIST OF DIFFERENT WORDS...
READ VERTICALLY, THE FIRST LETTERS SPELL...
Problem 3
Translate these words into Japanese.
Rose Victory Defeat
Urge Anger Cry
Disguise Run Walk
Uncle Aunt
Middle Under
Below Above
..."ARE YOU DUMB"!
I'LL USE THIS TRICK TO TEASE TAKAGI-SAN.
カラーン
KARAN (KLAK)
TAKAGI-SAN.
HM?
HERE.

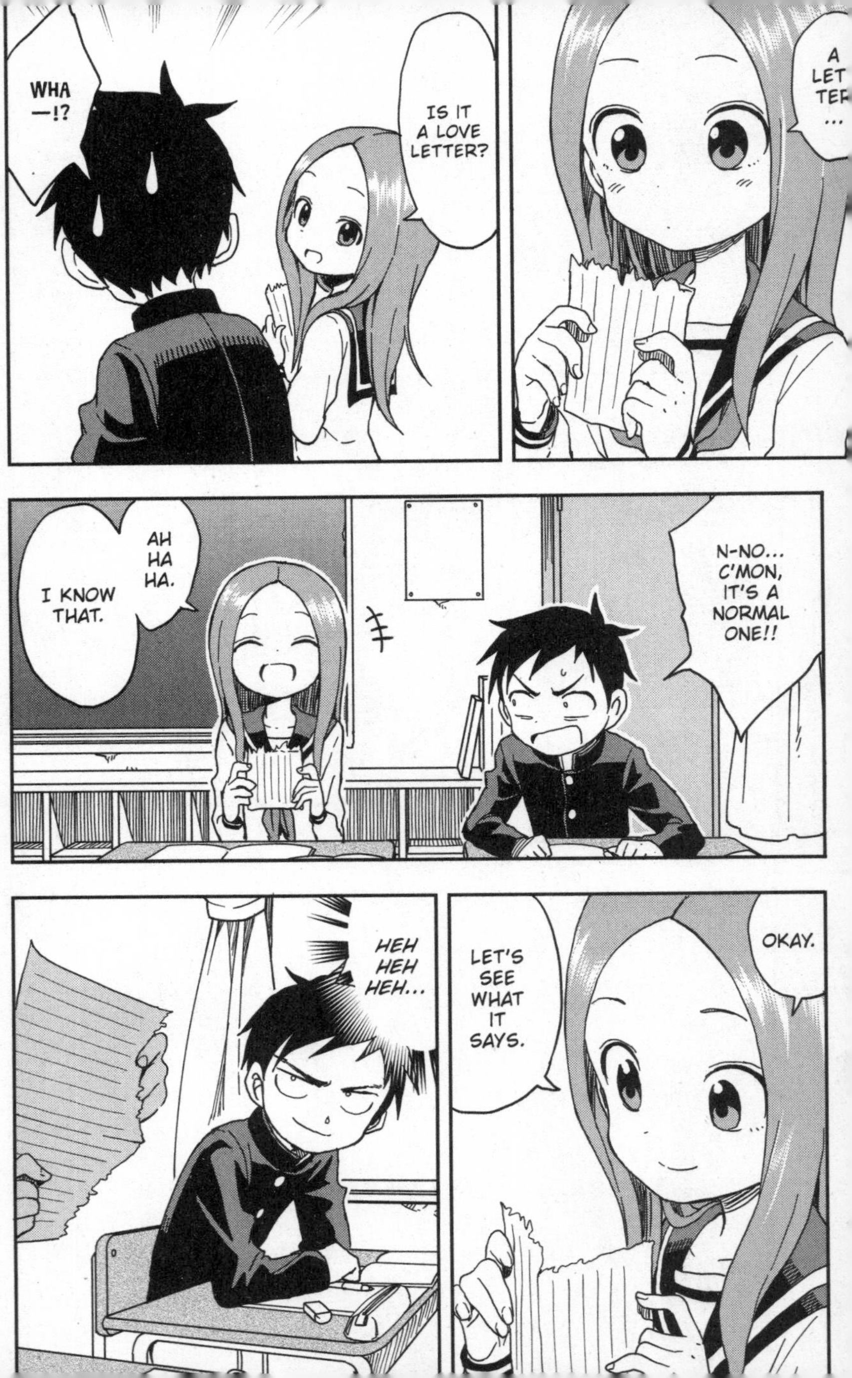
A LETTER...
IS IT A LOVE LETTER?
WHA—!?
N-NO... C'MON, IT'S A NORMAL ONE!!
AH HA HA.
I KNOW THAT.
OKAY.
LET'S SEE WHAT IT SAYS.
HEH HEH HEH...

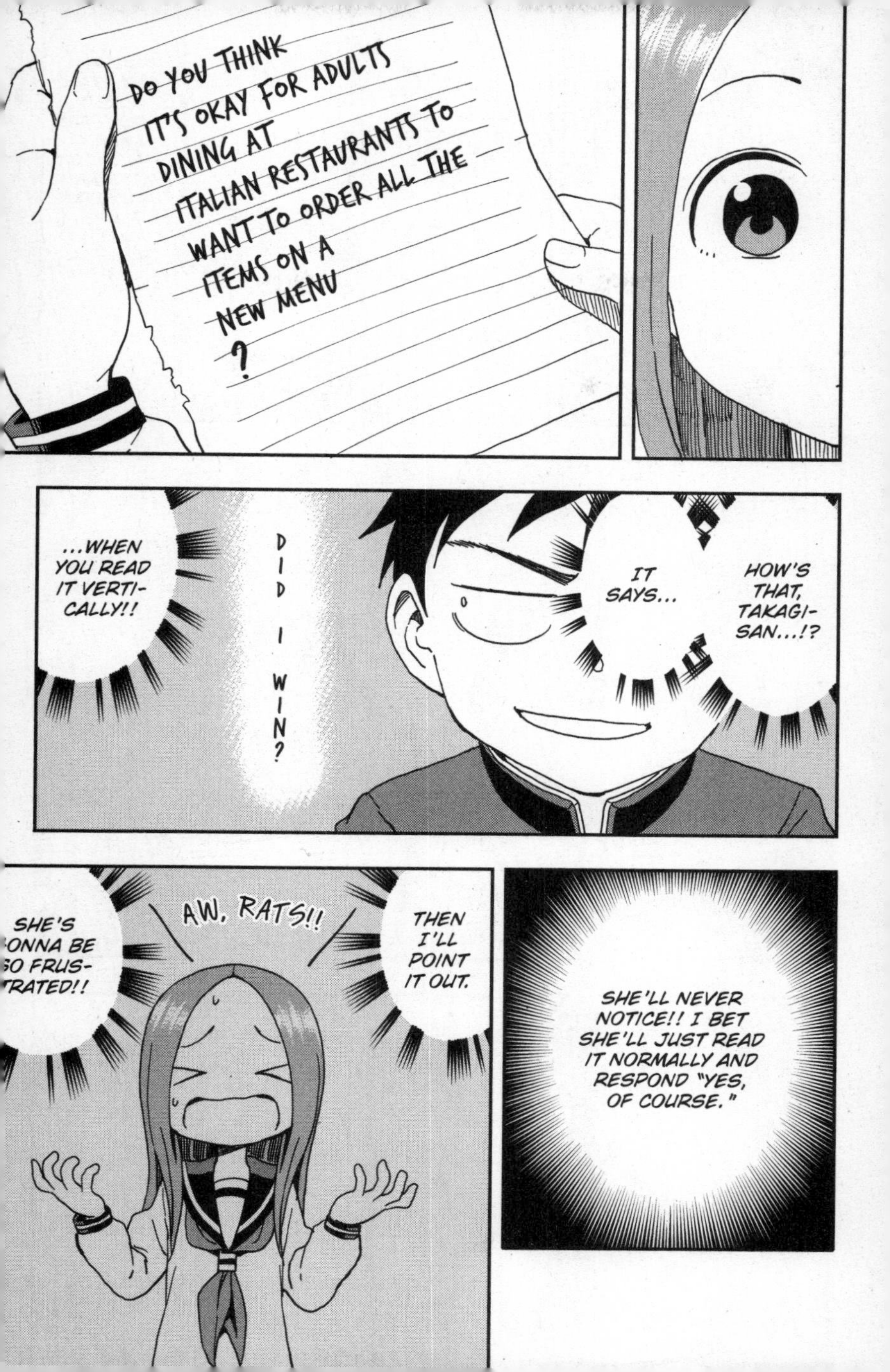
DO YOU THINK
IT'S OKAY FOR ADULTS
DINING AT
ITALIAN RESTAURANTS TO
WANT TO ORDER ALL THE
ITEMS ON A
NEW MENU
?
HOW'S THAT, TAKAGI-SAN...!?
IT SAYS...
DID I WIN?
...WHEN YOU READ IT VERTICALLY!!
SHE'LL NEVER NOTICE!! I BET SHE'LL JUST READ IT NORMALLY AND RESPOND "YES, OF COURSE."
THEN I'LL POINT IT OUT.
AW, RATS!!
SHE'S ONNA BE O FRUS-TRATED!!

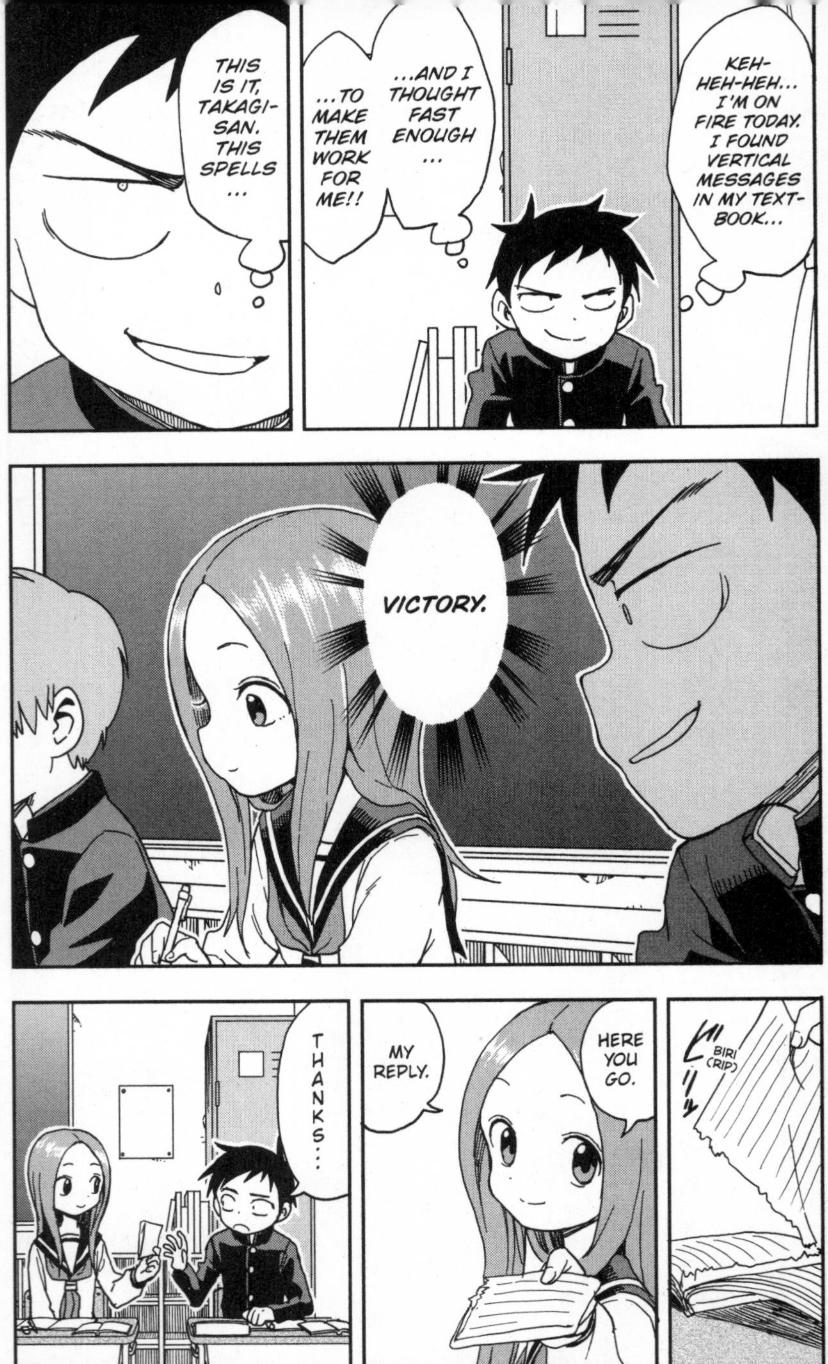

KEH-HEH-HEH... I'M ON FIRE TODAY. I FOUND VERTICAL MESSAGES IN MY TEXT-BOOK...
...AND I THOUGHT FAST ENOUGH...
...TO MAKE THEM WORK FOR ME!!
THIS IS IT, TAKAGI-SAN. THIS SPELLS...
VICTORY.
BIRI (RIP)
HERE YOU GO.
MY REPLY.
THANKS...

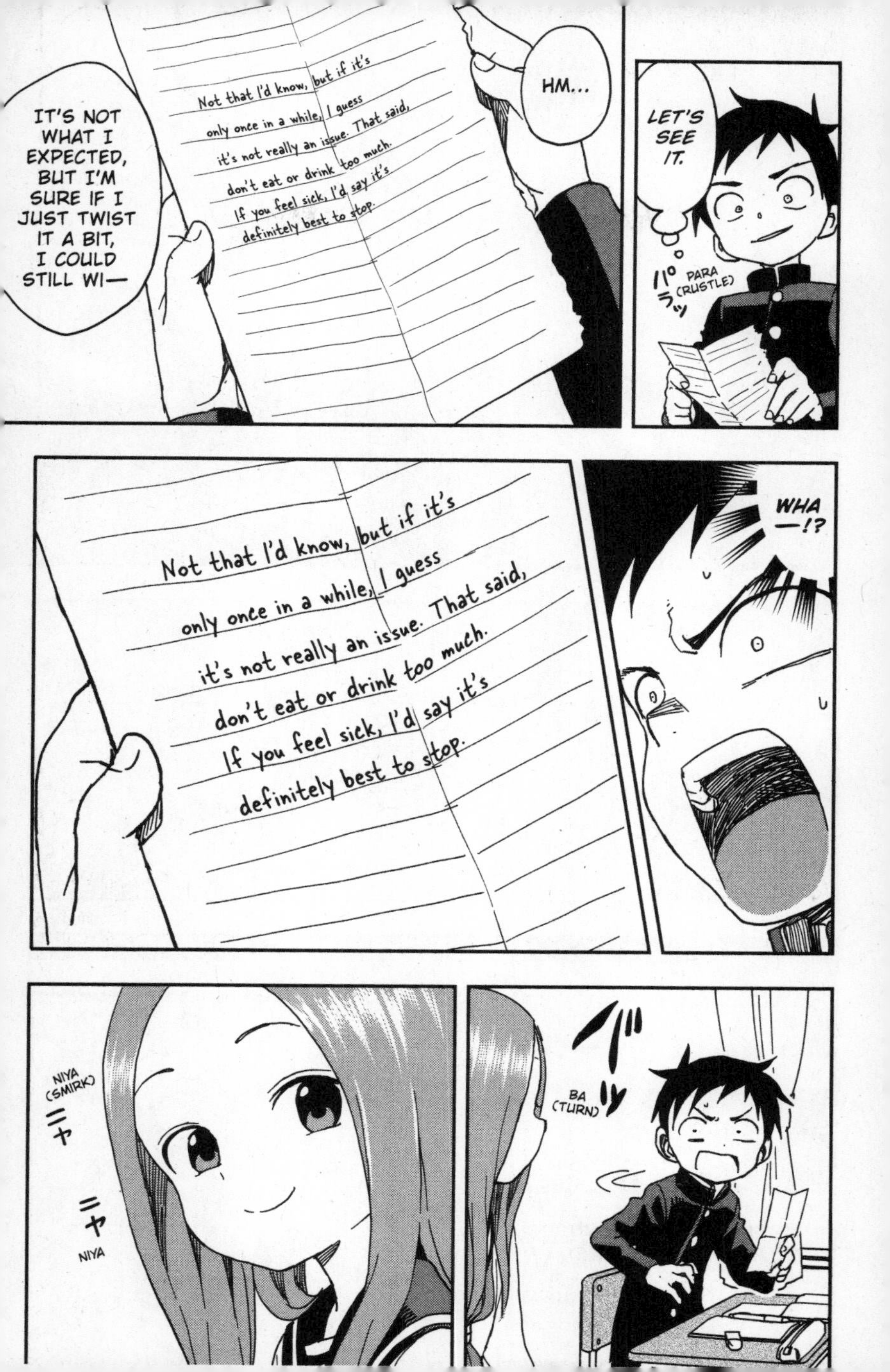
LET'S SEE IT.
パラッ
PARA (RUSTLE)
HM...
IT'S NOT WHAT I EXPECTED, BUT I'M SURE IF I JUST TWIST IT A BIT, I COULD STILL WI—
Not that I'd know, but if it's only once in a while, I guess it's not really an issue. That said, don't eat or drink too much. If you feel sick, I'd say it's definitely best to stop.
WHA—!?
Not that I'd know, but if it's only once in a while, I guess it's not really an issue. That said, don't eat or drink too much. If you feel sick, I'd say it's definitely best to stop.
バッ
BA (TURN)
ニヤ
NIYA (SMIRK)
ニヤ
NIYA

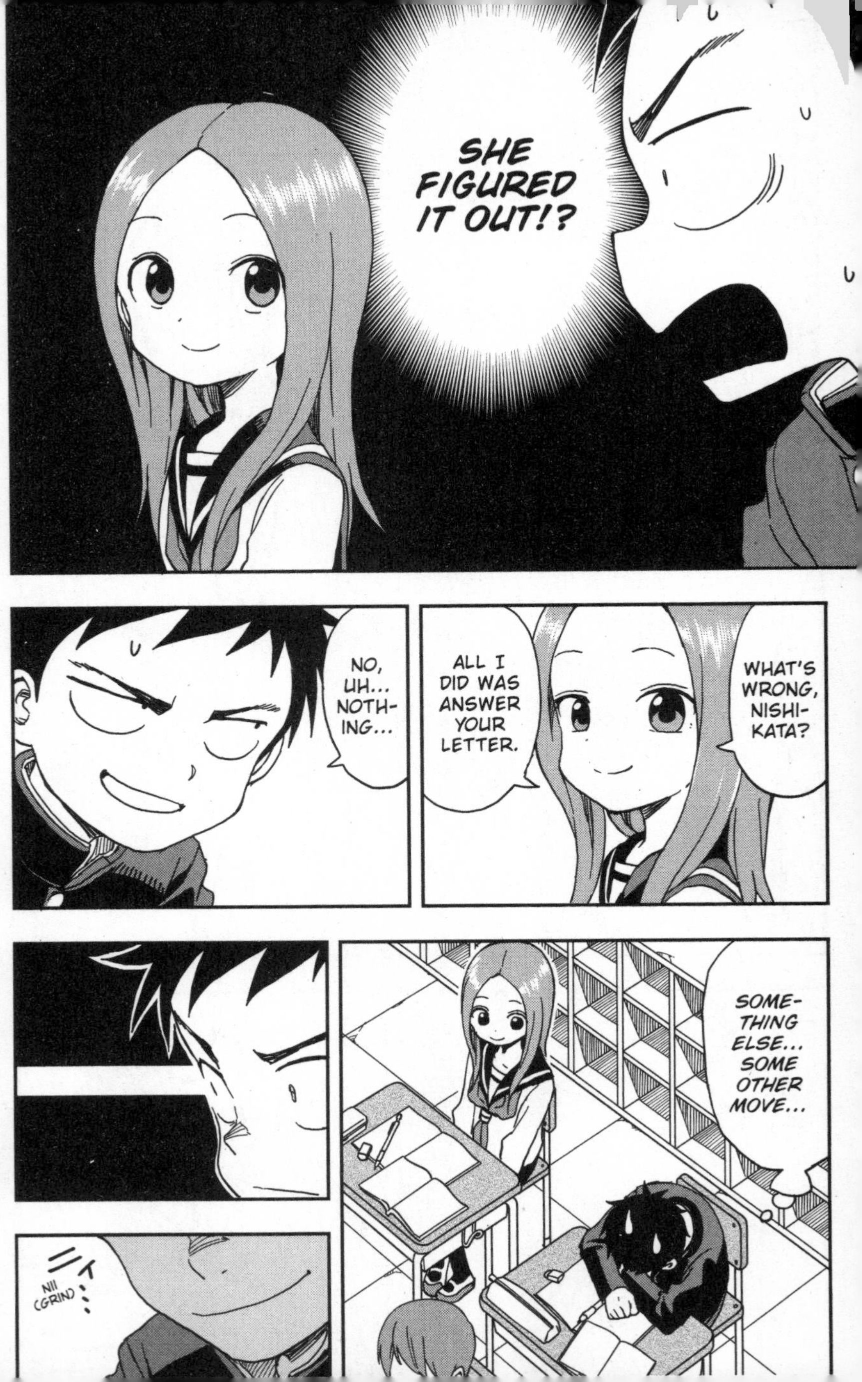
SHE FIGURED IT OUT!?
WHAT'S WRONG, NISHI-KATA?
ALL I DID WAS ANSWER YOUR LETTER.
NO, UH... NOTH-ING...
SOME-THING ELSE... SOME OTHER MOVE...
ニィ…
NII (GRIN)

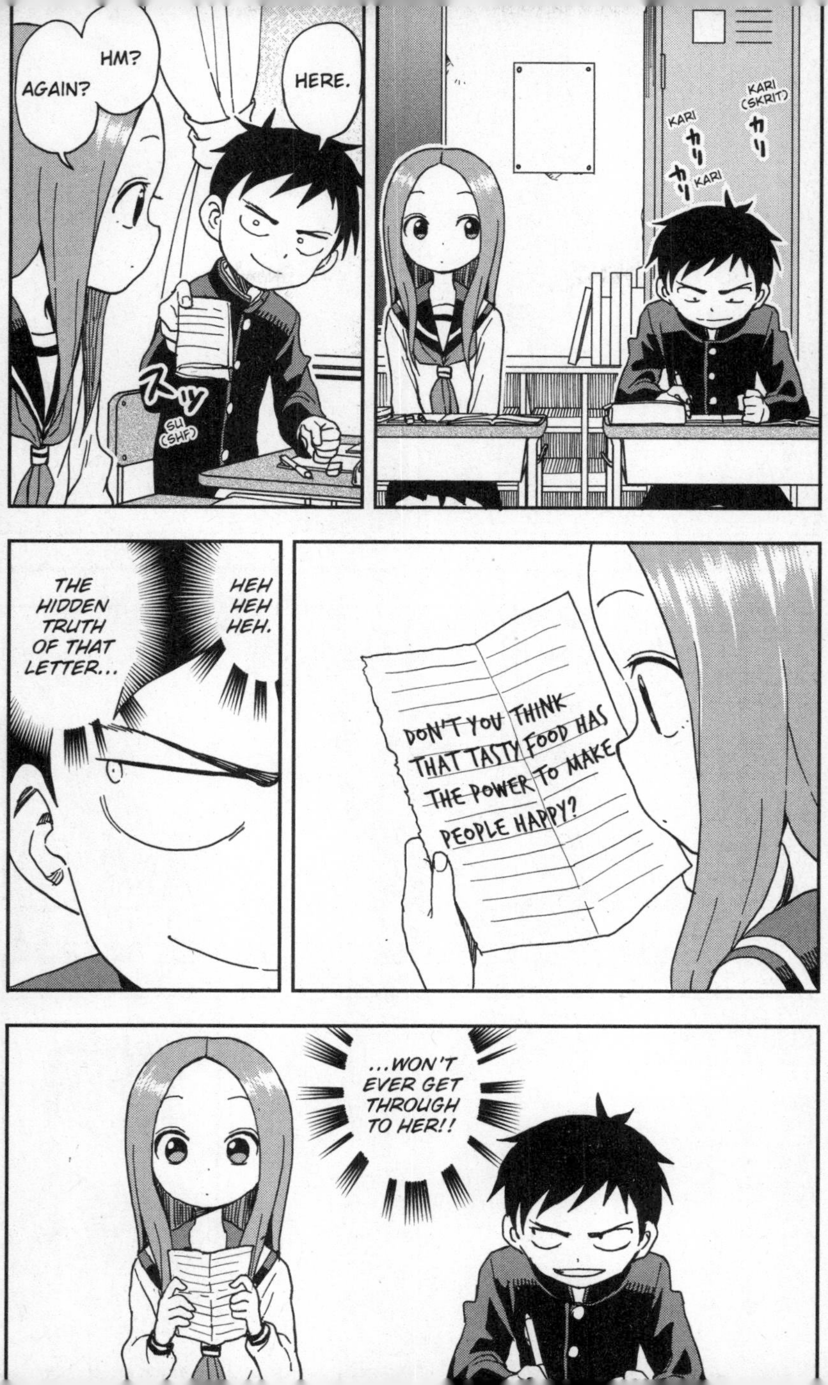
KARI (SKRIT)
カリ
KARI
カリ
カリ
KARI
HERE.
HM? AGAIN?
スッ
SU (SHF)
DON'T YOU THINK THAT TASTY FOOD HAS THE POWER TO MAKE PEOPLE HAPPY?
HEH HEH HEH.
THE HIDDEN TRUTH OF THAT LETTER...
...WON'T EVER GET THROUGH TO HER!!

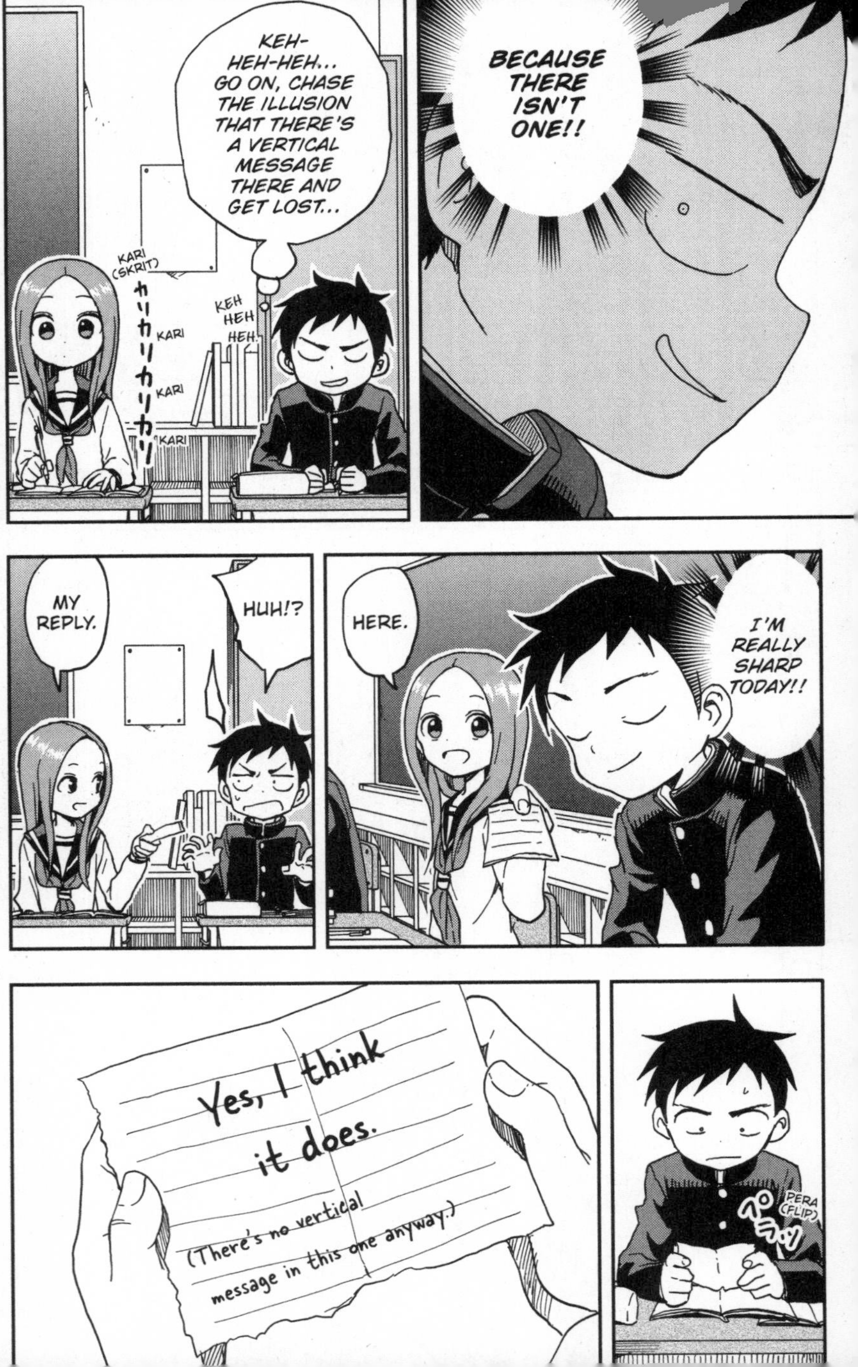
BECAUSE THERE ISN'T ONE!!
KEH-HEH-HEH... GO ON, CHASE THE ILLUSION THAT THERE'S A VERTICAL MESSAGE THERE AND GET LOST...
KEH HEH HEH.
カリカリカリカリ
KARI (SKRIT)
KARI
KARI
KARI
HERE.
I'M REALLY SHARP TODAY!!
MY REPLY.
HUH!?
ペラッ
PERA (FLIP)
Yes, I think it does.
(There's no vertical message in this one anyway.)

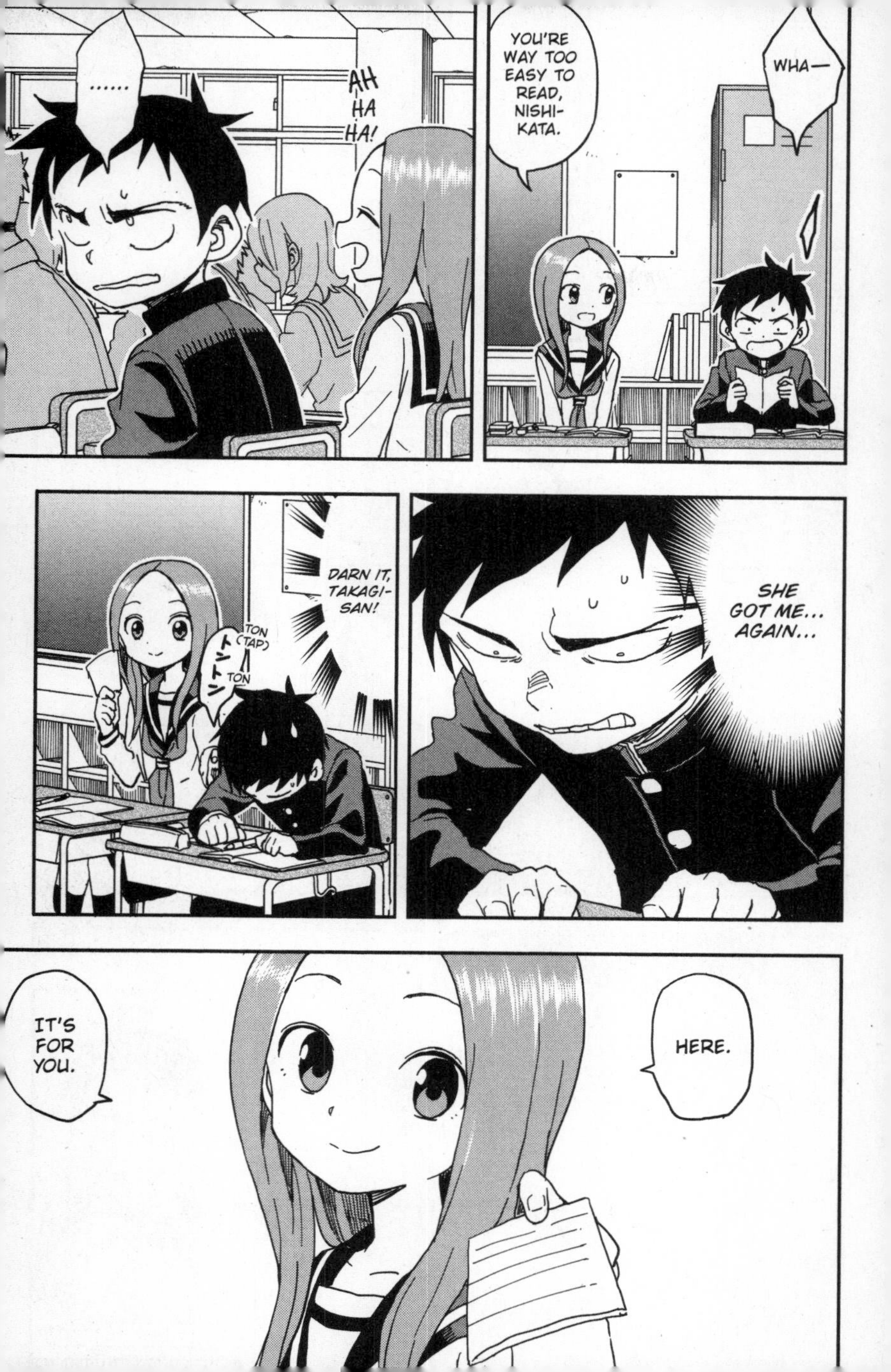
WHA—
YOU'RE WAY TOO EASY TO READ, NISHI-KATA.
AH HA HA!
......
SHE GOT ME... AGAIN...
DARN IT, TAKAGI-SAN!
TON (TAP) TON
HERE.
IT'S FOR YOU.

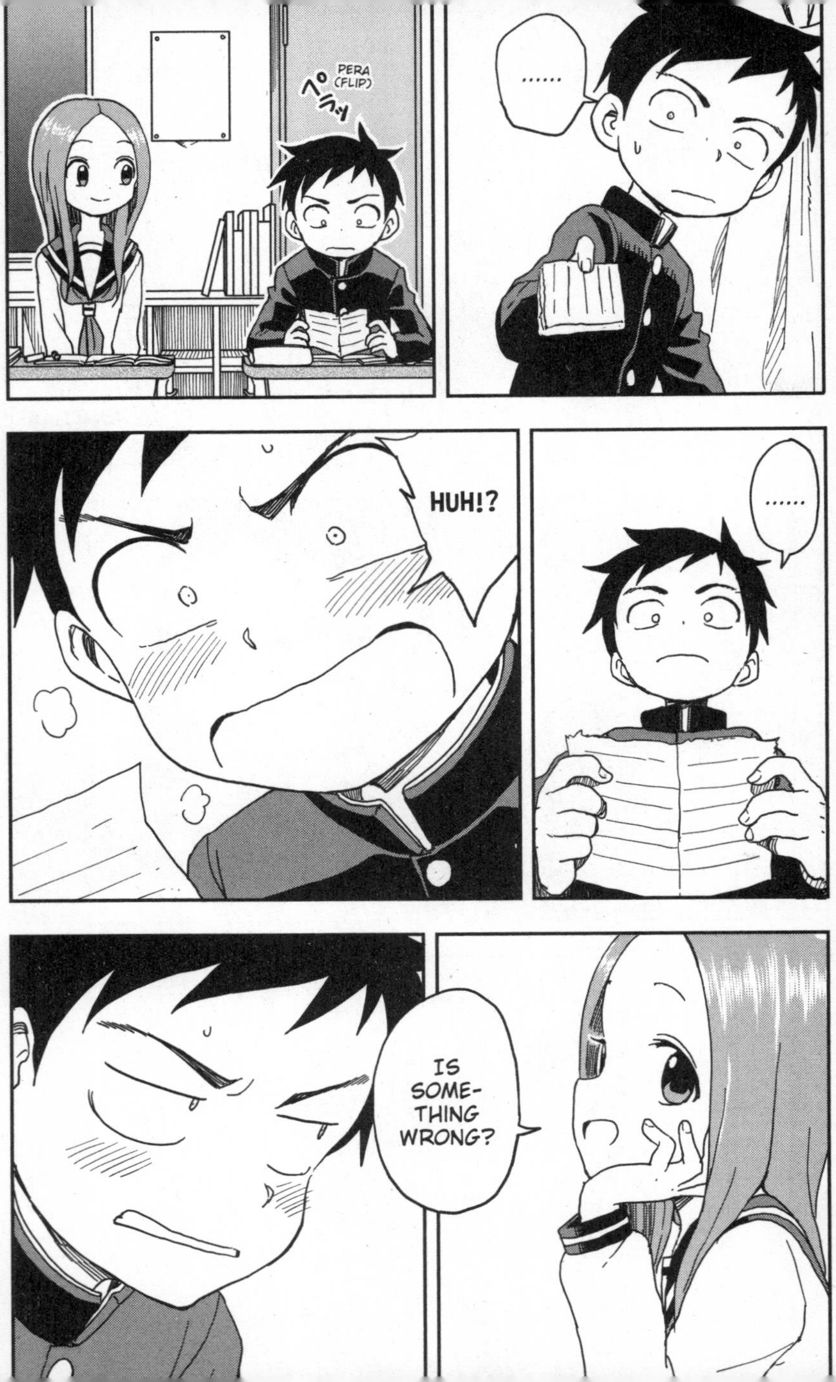
......
ペラッ
PERA (FLIP)
......
HUH!?
IS SOME-THING WRONG?

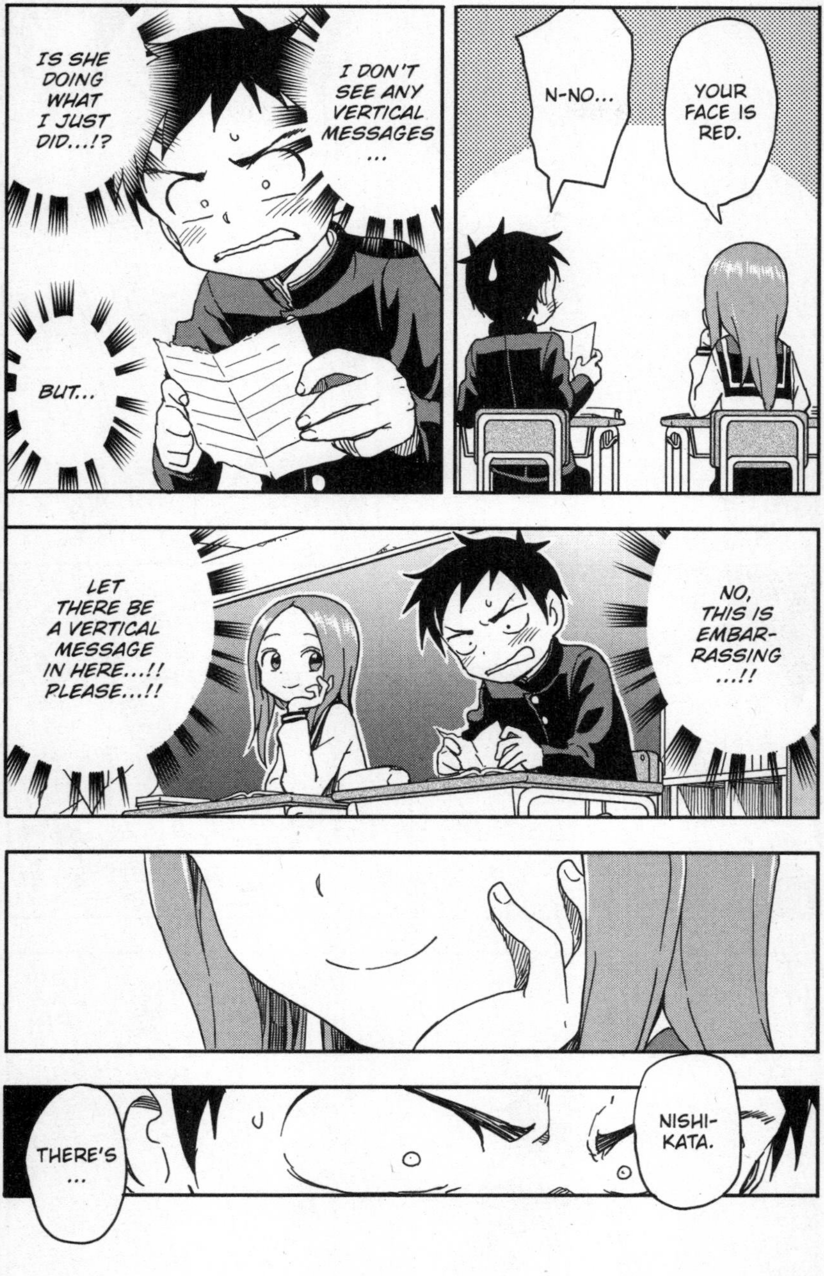
YOUR FACE IS RED.
N-NO...
I DON'T SEE ANY VERTICAL MESSAGES ...
IS SHE DOING WHAT I JUST DID...!?
BUT...
NO, THIS IS EMBARRASSING ...!!
LET THERE BE A VERTICAL MESSAGE IN HERE...!! PLEASE...!!
NISHI-KATA.
THERE'S ...

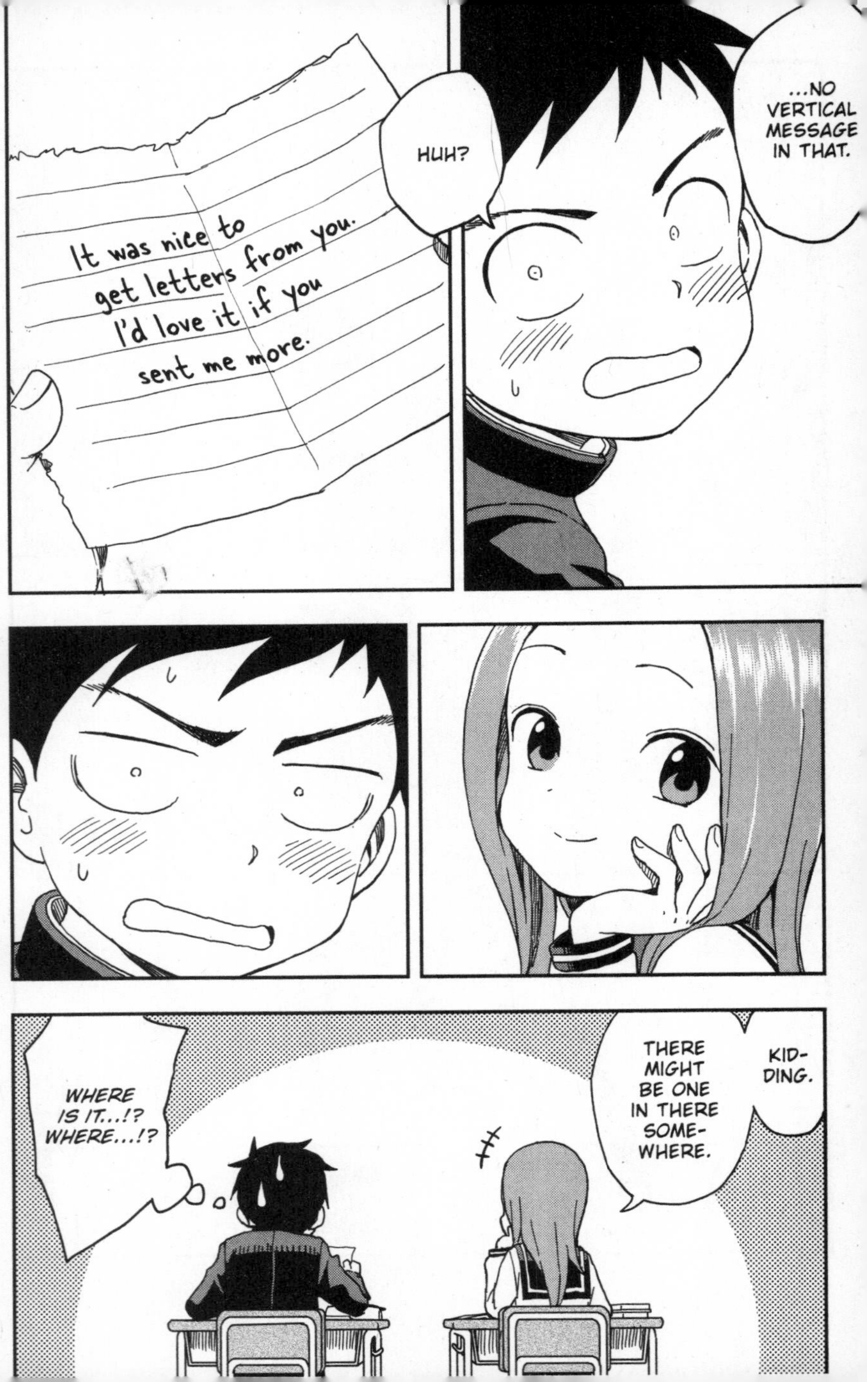
...NO VERTICAL MESSAGE IN THAT.
HUH?
It was nice to get letters from you. I'd love it if you sent me more.
KID-DING.
THERE MIGHT BE ONE IN THERE SOME-WHERE.
WHERE IS IT...!? WHERE...!?

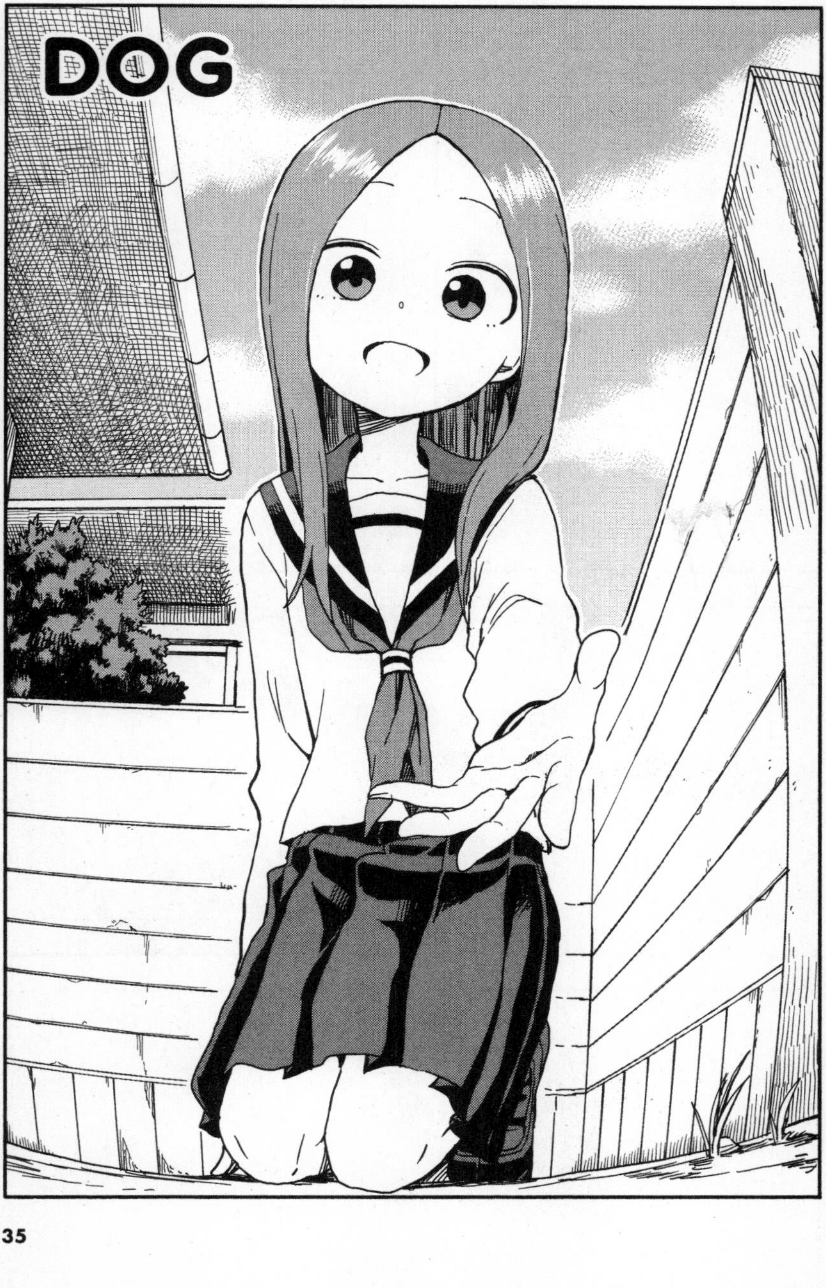
DOG

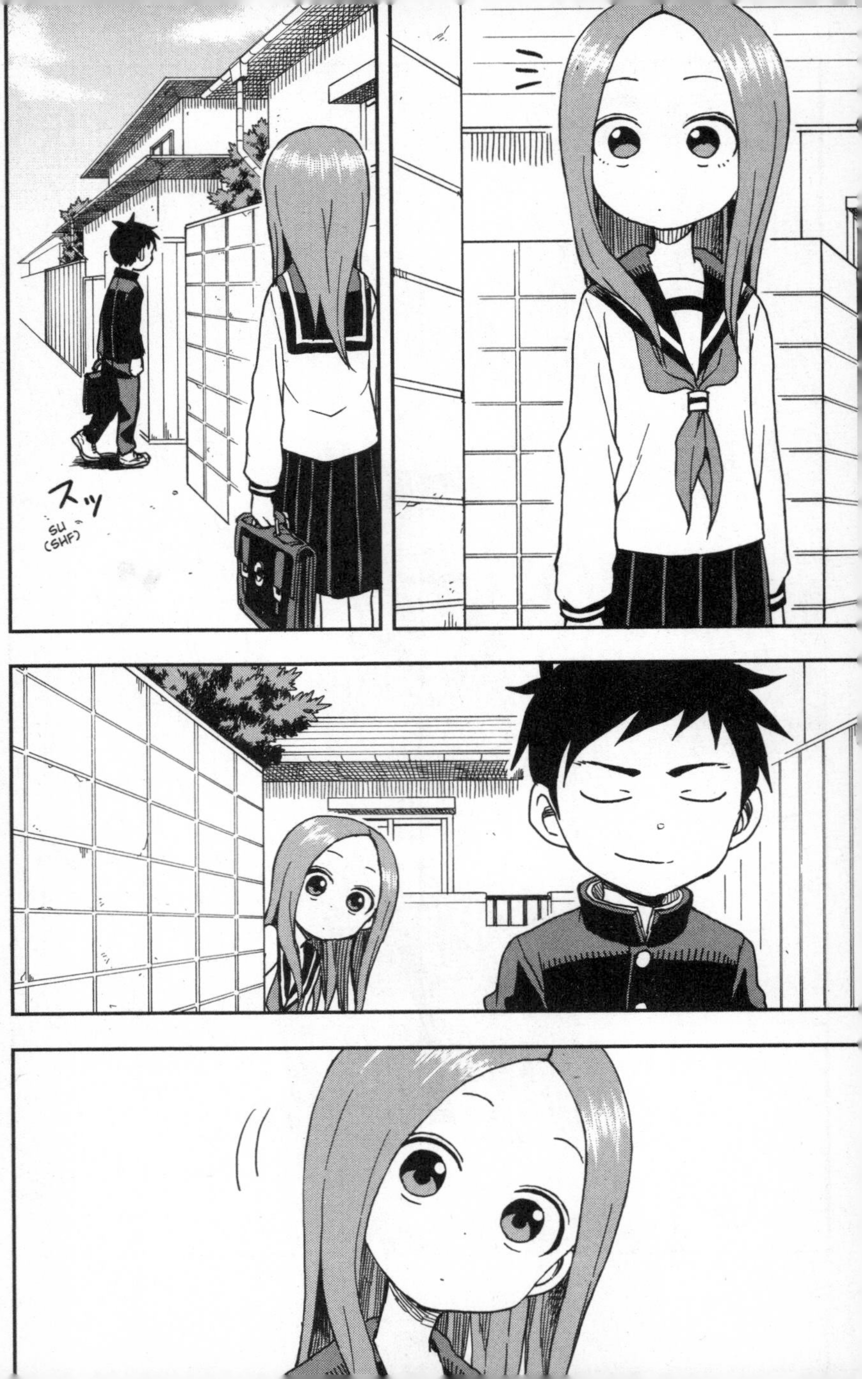
スッ
SU (SHF)

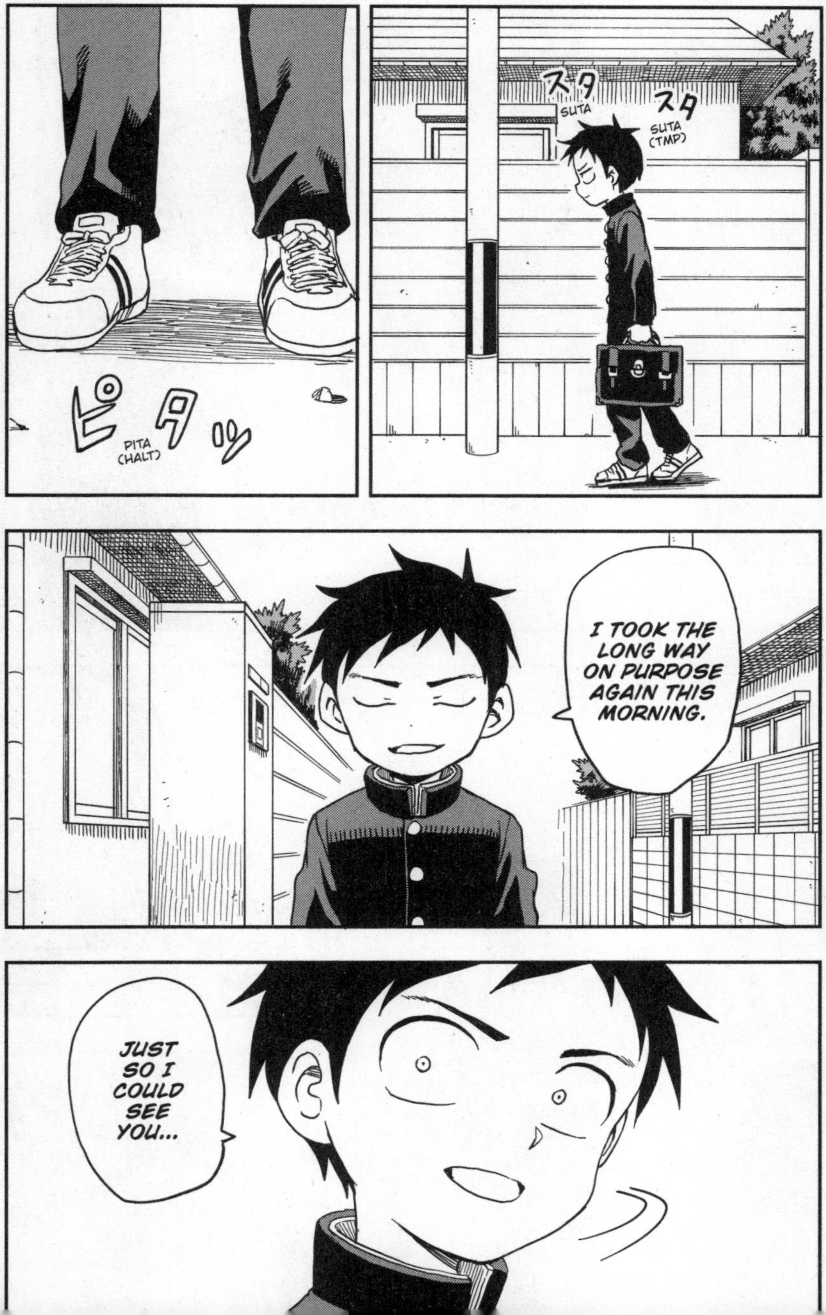
スタ
SUTA
スタ
SUTA (TMP)
ピタッ
PITA (HALT)
I TOOK THE LONG WAY ON PURPOSE AGAIN THIS MORNING.
JUST SO I COULD SEE YOU...

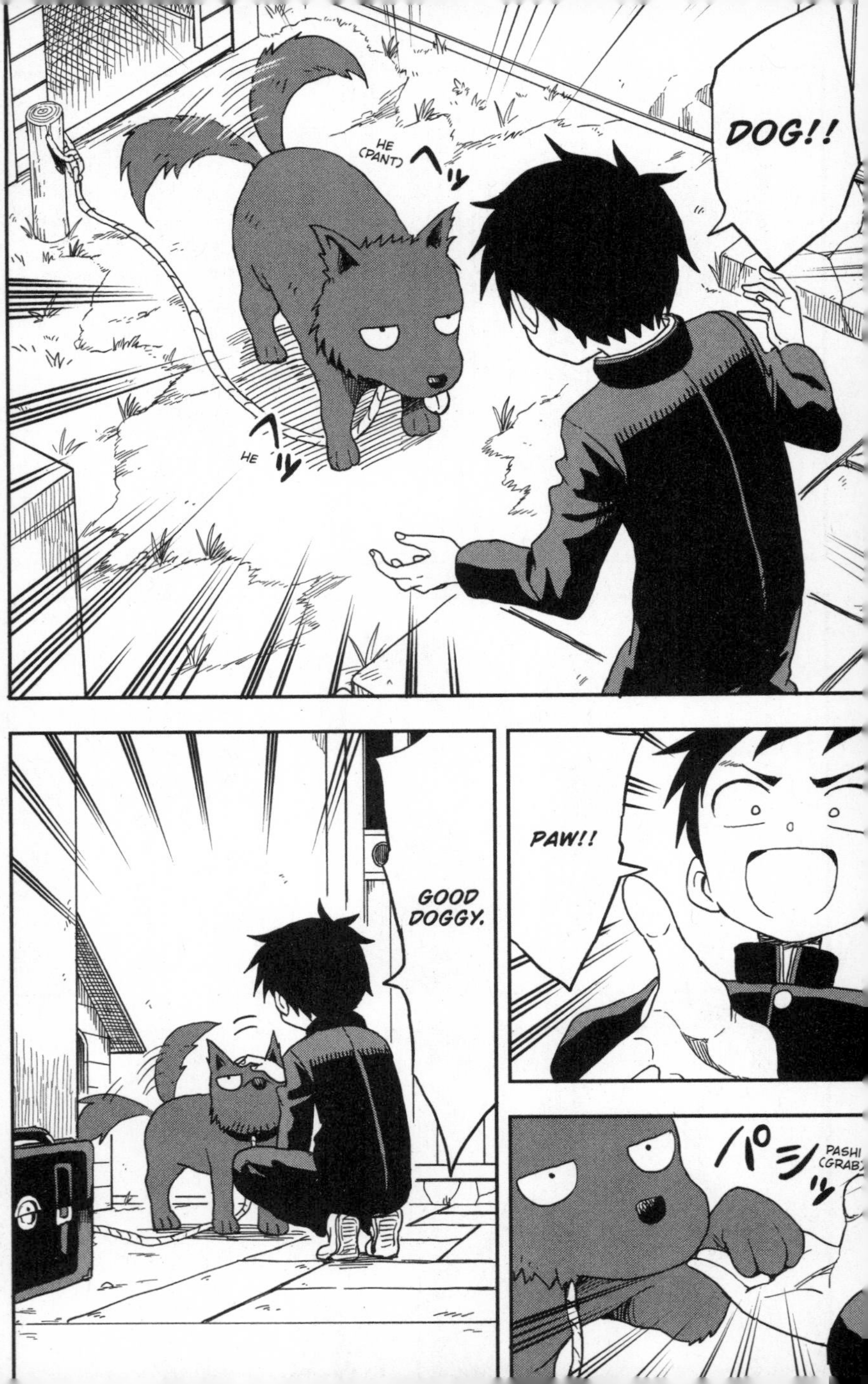

DOG!!
ヘッ
HE (PANT)
ヘッ
HE
PAW!!
パシッ
PASHI (GRAB)
GOOD DOGGY.

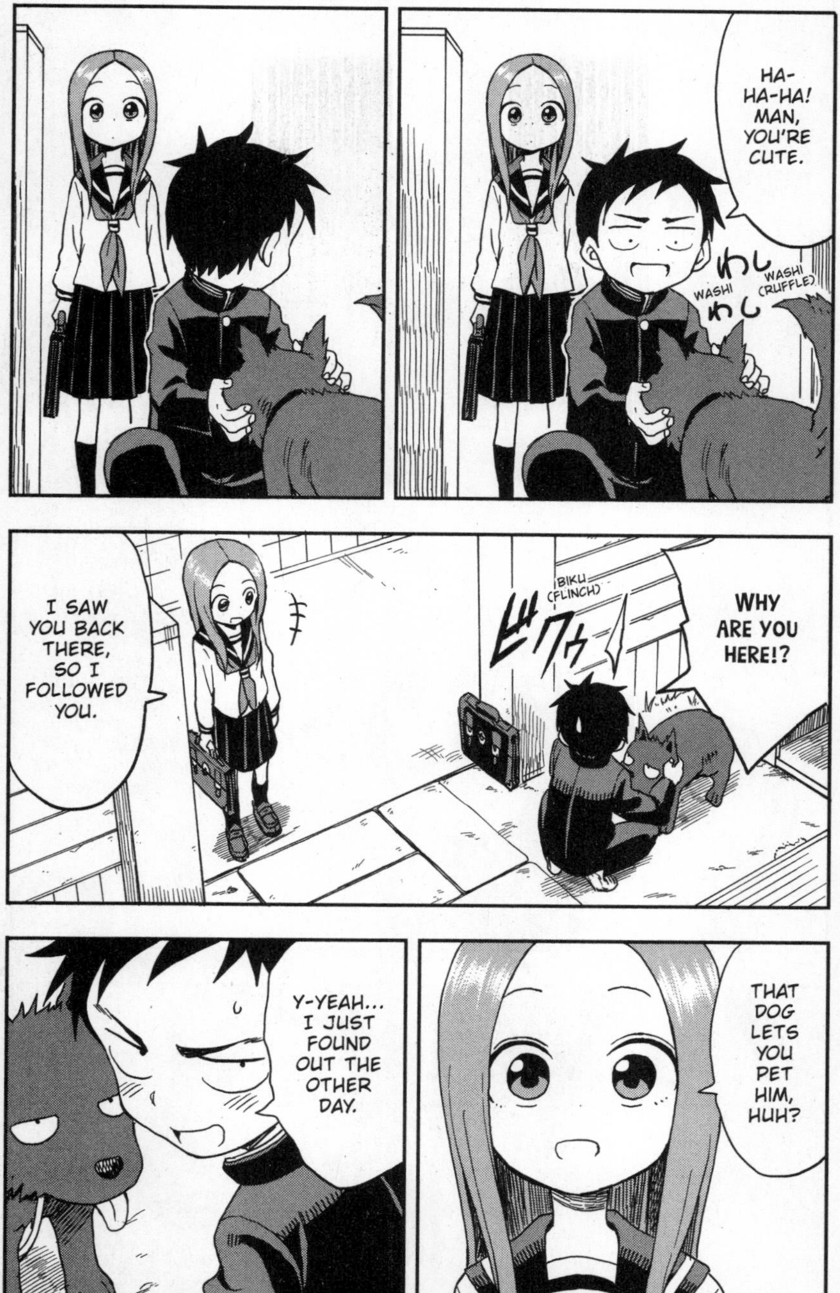
HA-HA-HA! MAN, YOU'RE CUTE.
わし
WASHI
わし
WASHI (RUFFLE)
WHY ARE YOU HERE!?
ビクゥ
BIKU (FLINCH)
I SAW YOU BACK THERE, SO I FOLLOWED YOU.
THAT DOG LETS YOU PET HIM, HUH?
Y-YEAH... I JUST FOUND OUT THE OTHER DAY.

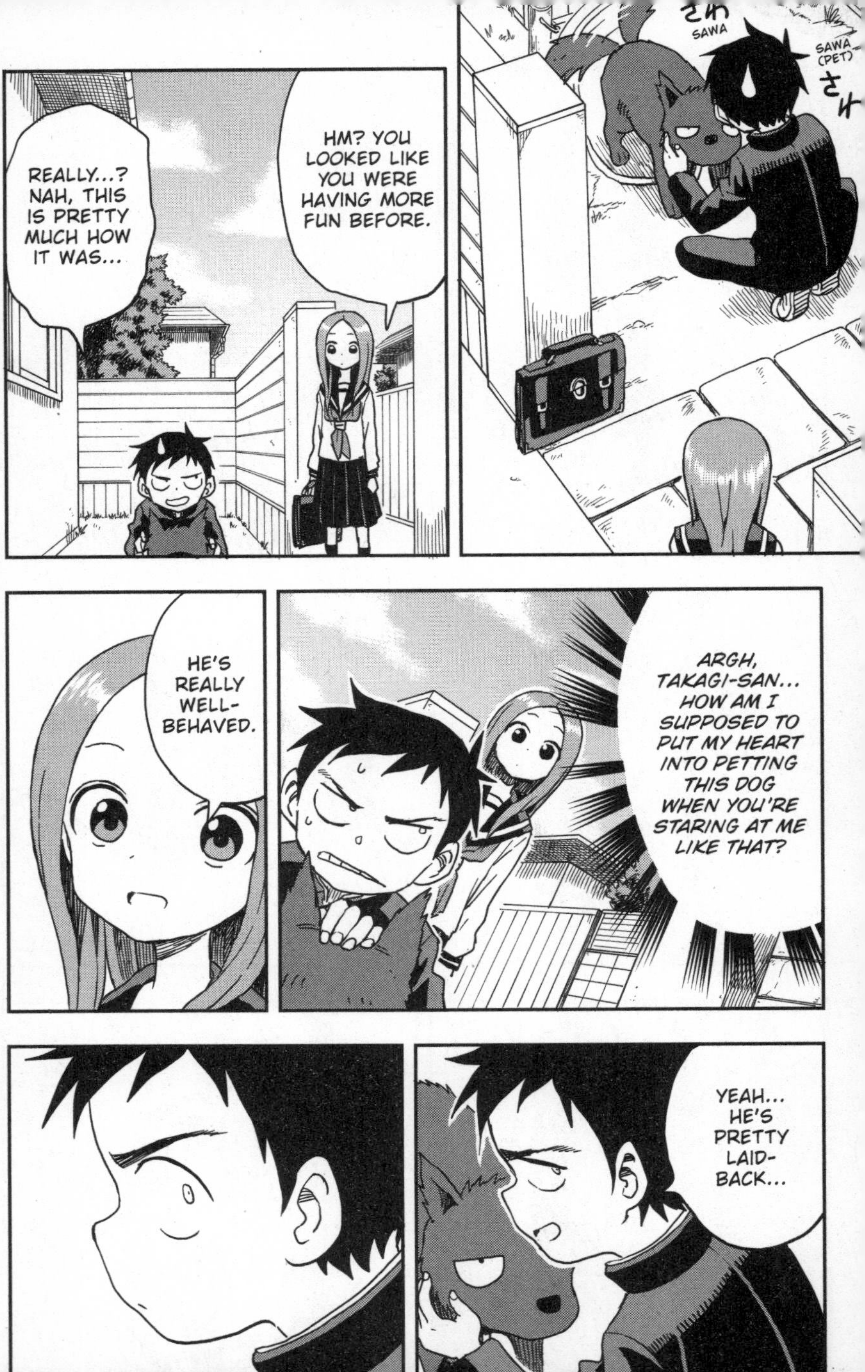
さわ
SAWA
SAWA (PET)
さわ
HM? YOU LOOKED LIKE YOU WERE HAVING MORE FUN BEFORE.
REALLY...? NAH, THIS IS PRETTY MUCH HOW IT WAS...
ARGH, TAKAGI-SAN... HOW AM I SUPPOSED TO PUT MY HEART INTO PETTING THIS DOG WHEN YOU'RE STARING AT ME LIKE THAT?
HE'S REALLY WELL-BEHAVED.
YEAH... HE'S PRETTY LAID-BACK...

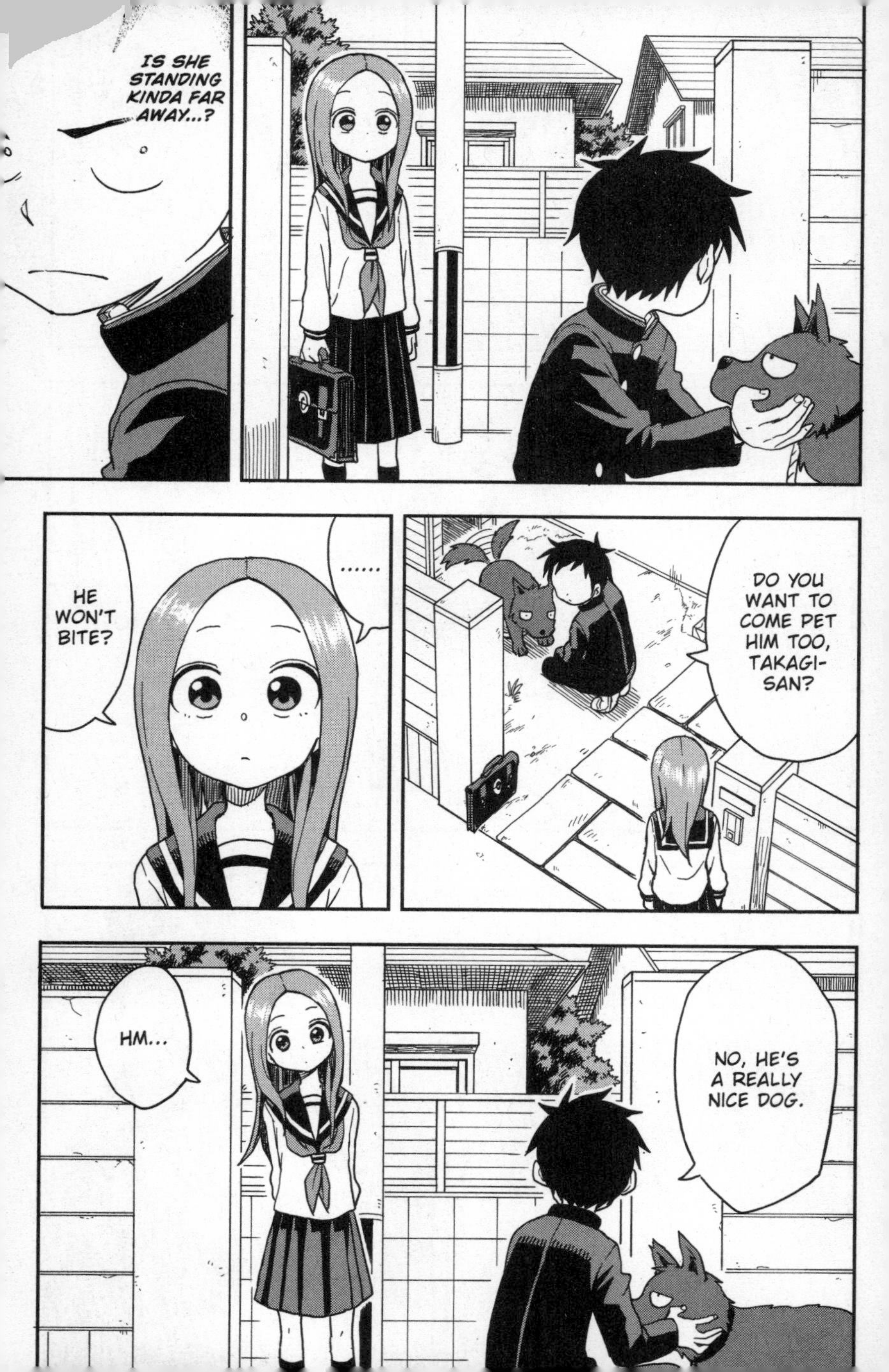
IS SHE STANDING KINDA FAR AWAY...?
DO YOU WANT TO COME PET HIM TOO, TAKAGI-SAN?
......
HE WON'T BITE?
NO, HE'S A REALLY NICE DOG.
HM...

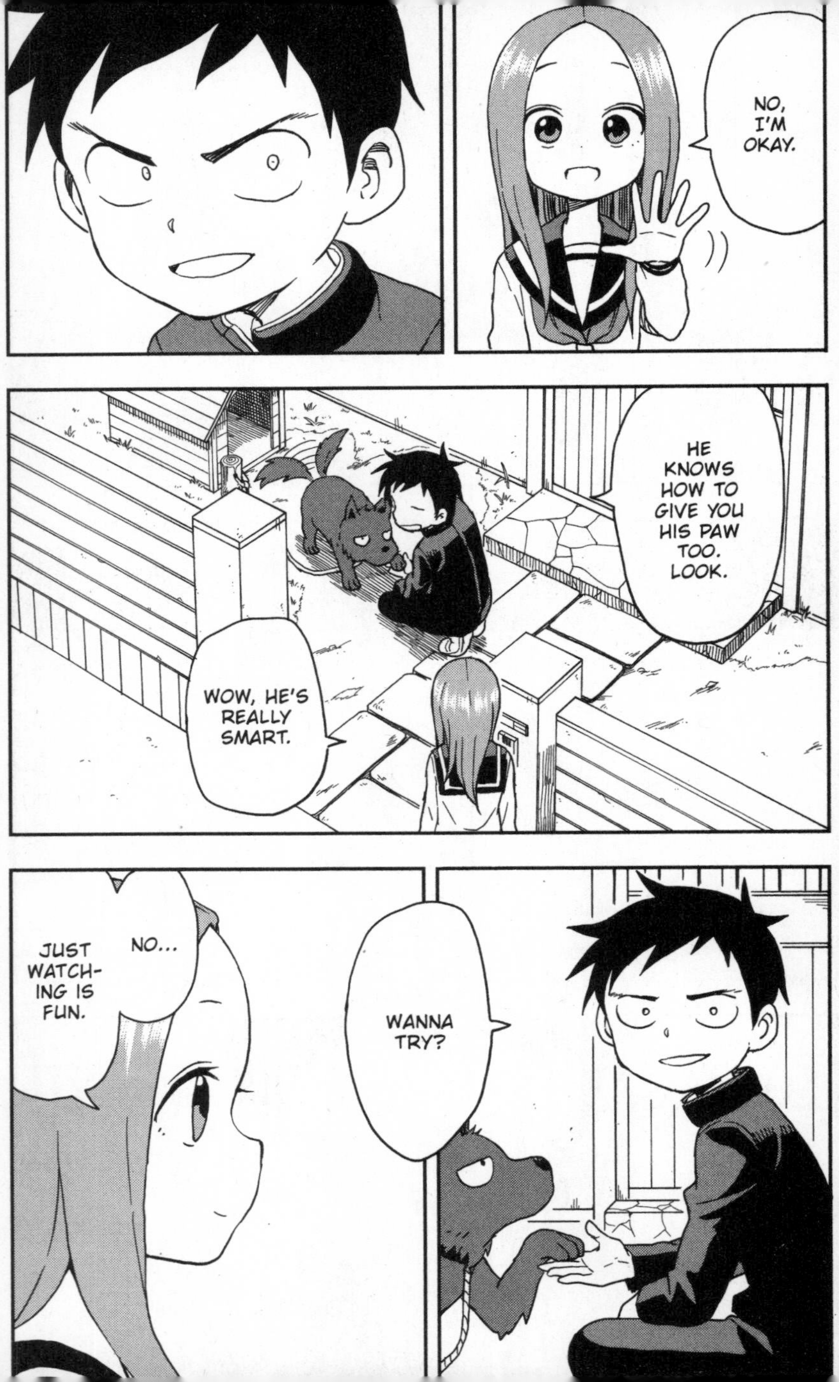
NO, I'M OKAY.
HE KNOWS HOW TO GIVE YOU HIS PAW TOO. LOOK.
WOW, HE'S REALLY SMART.
WANNA TRY?
NO...
JUST WATCHING-ING IS FUN.

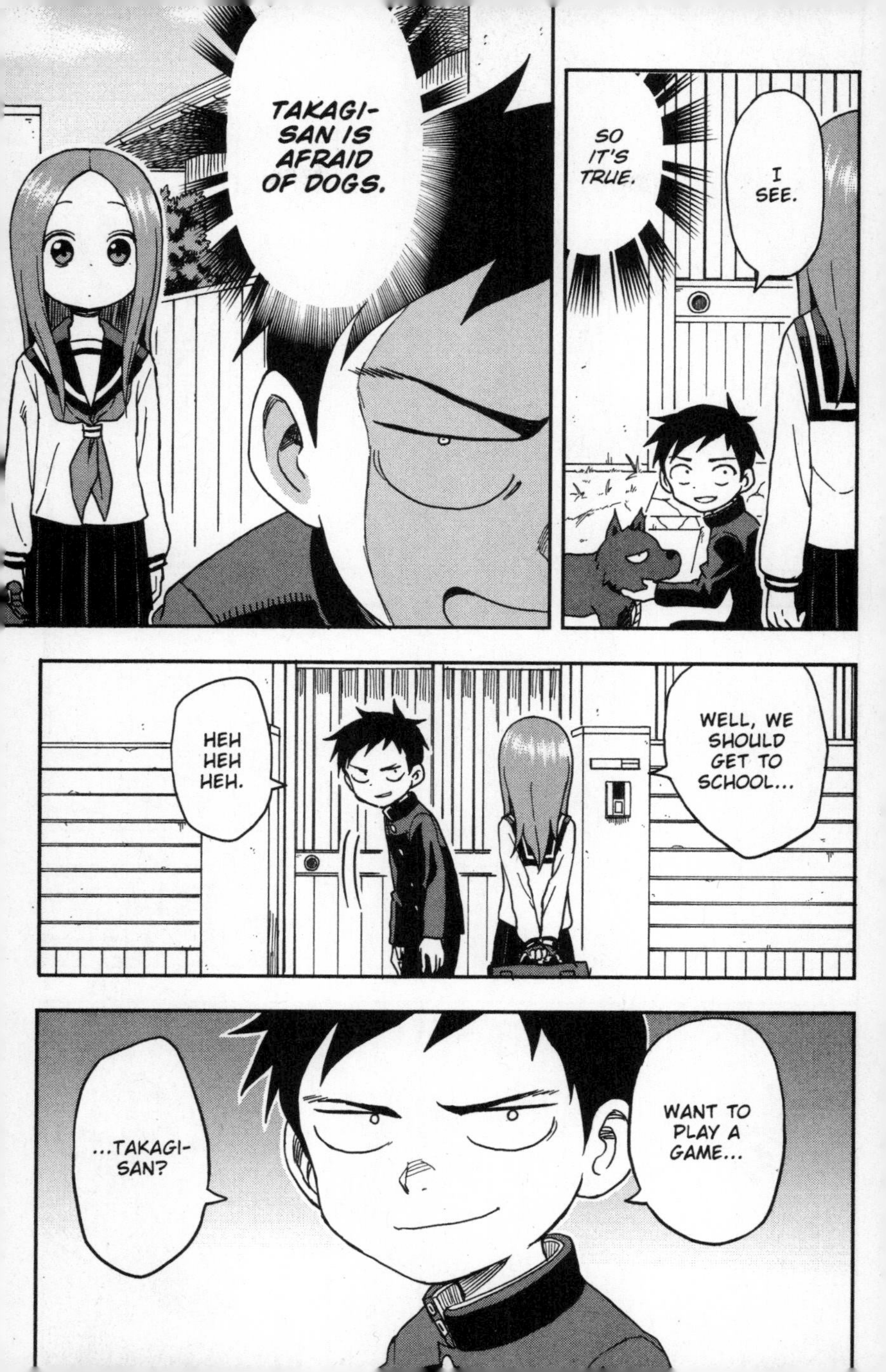
I SEE.
SO IT'S TRUE.
TAKAGI-SAN IS AFRAID OF DOGS.
WELL, WE SHOULD GET TO SCHOOL...
HEH HEH HEH.
WANT TO PLAY A GAME...
...TAKAGI-SAN?

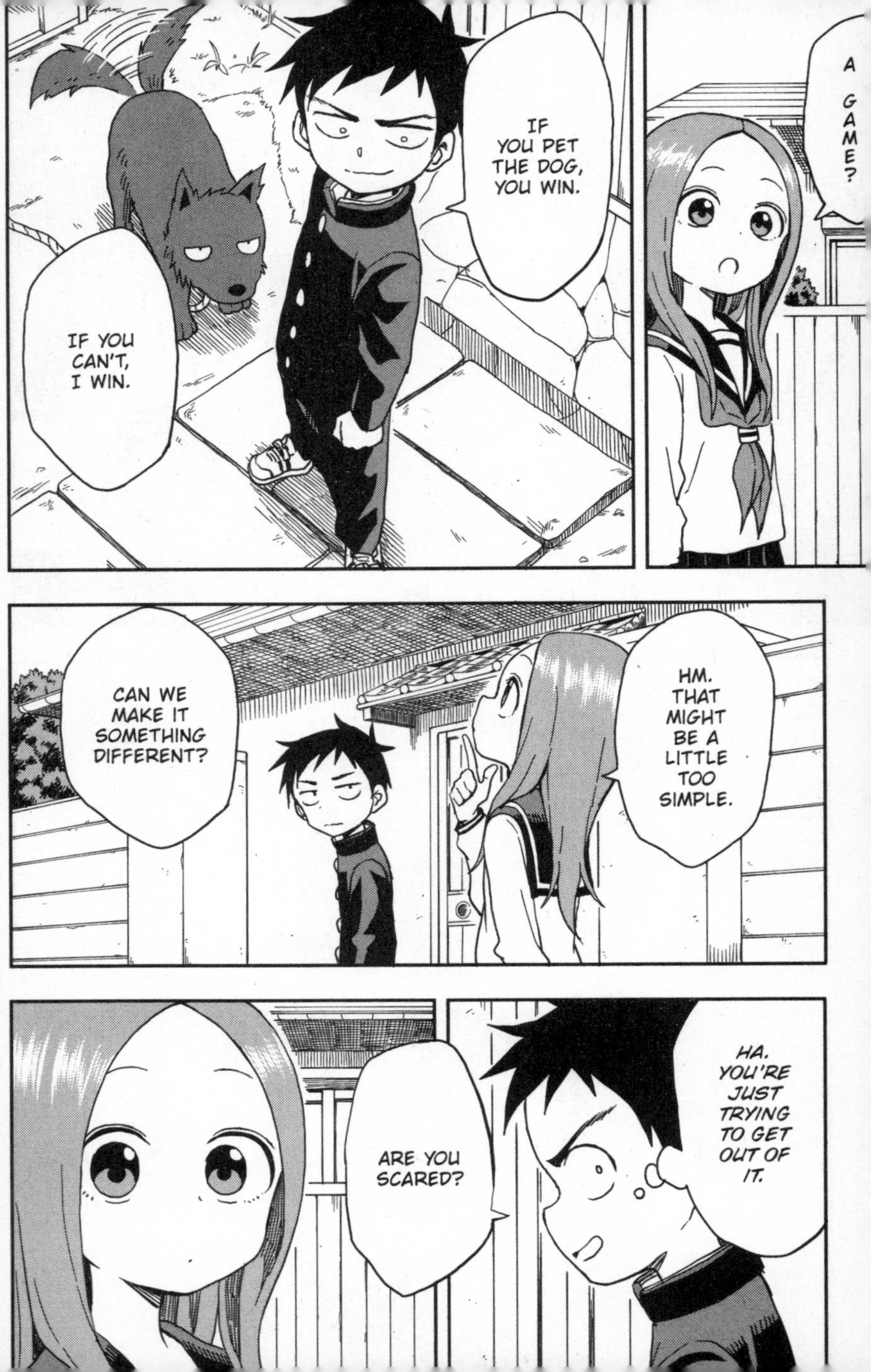
A GAME?
IF YOU PET THE DOG, YOU WIN.
IF YOU CAN'T, I WIN.
HM. THAT MIGHT BE A LITTLE TOO SIMPLE.
CAN WE MAKE IT SOMETHING DIFFERENT?
HA. YOU'RE JUST TRYING TO GET OUT OF IT.
ARE YOU SCARED?

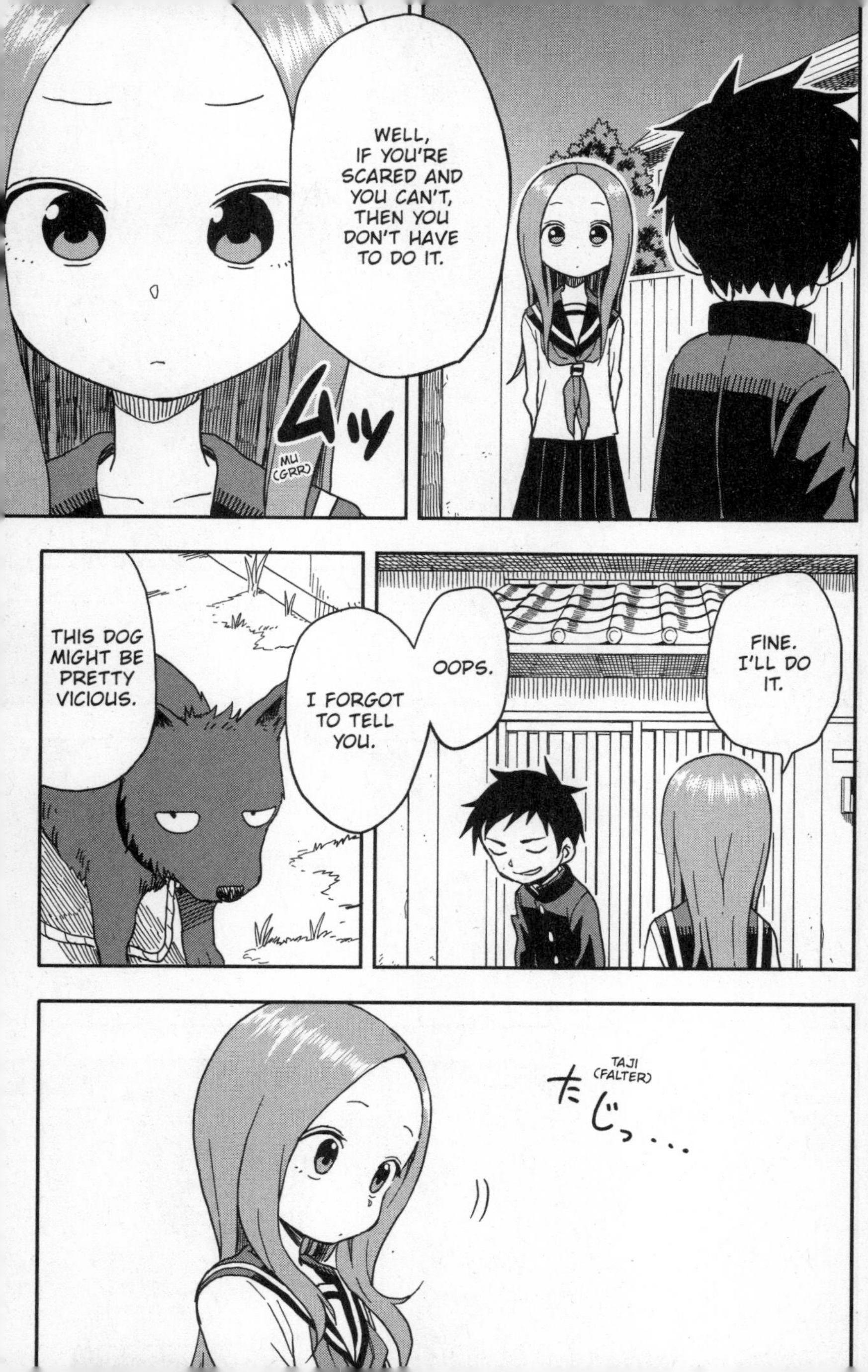
WELL, IF YOU'RE SCARED AND YOU CAN'T, THEN YOU DON'T HAVE TO DO IT.
ムッ
MU (GRR)
FINE. I'LL DO IT.
OOPS.
I FORGOT TO TELL YOU.
THIS DOG MIGHT BE PRETTY VICIOUS.
TAJI (FALTER)
たじっ...

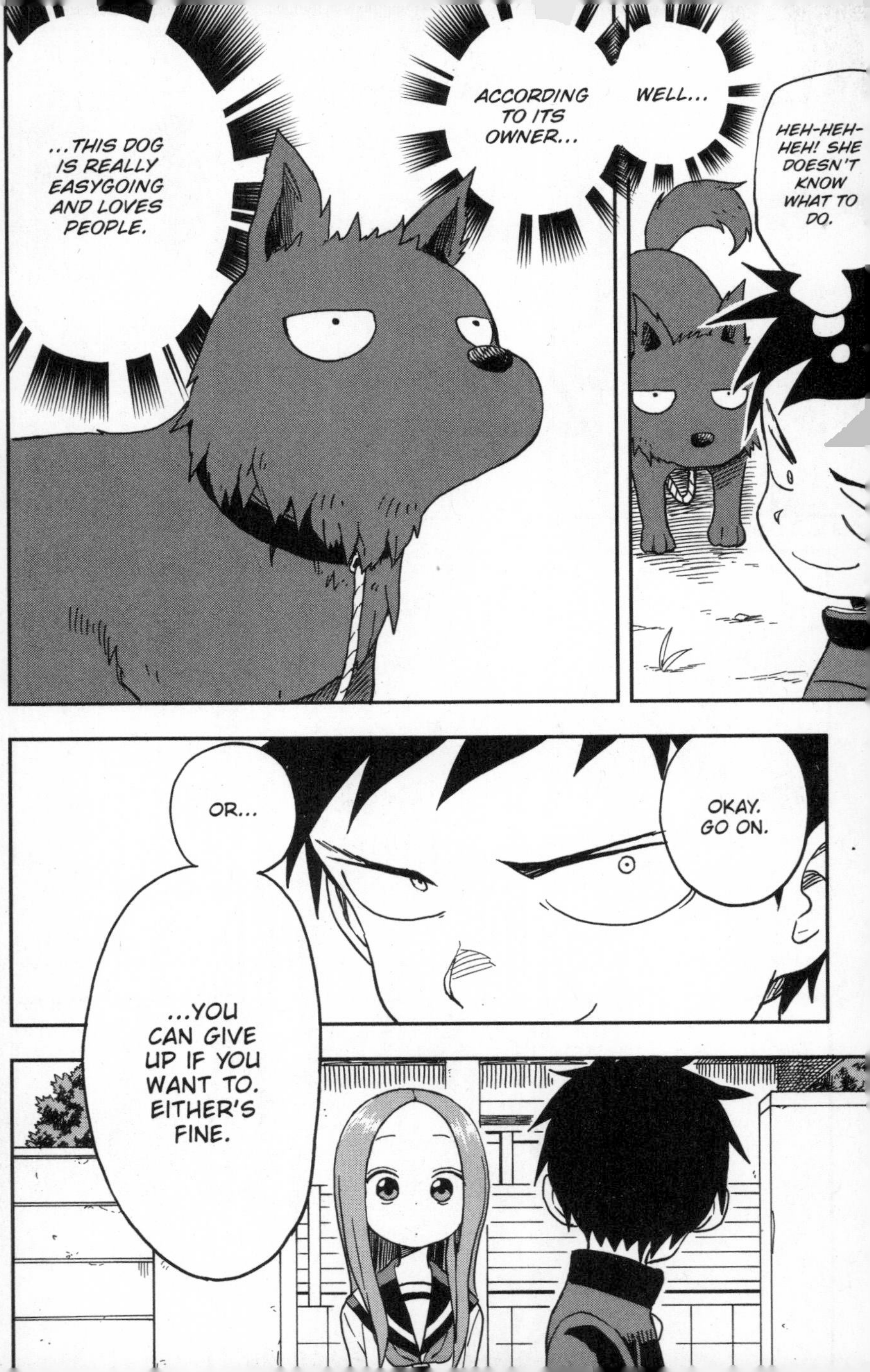
HEH-HEH-HEH! SHE DOESN'T KNOW WHAT TO DO.
WELL...
ACCORDING TO ITS OWNER...
...THIS DOG IS REALLY EASYGOING AND LOVES PEOPLE.
OKAY. GO ON.
OR...
...YOU CAN GIVE UP IF YOU WANT TO. EITHER'S FINE.

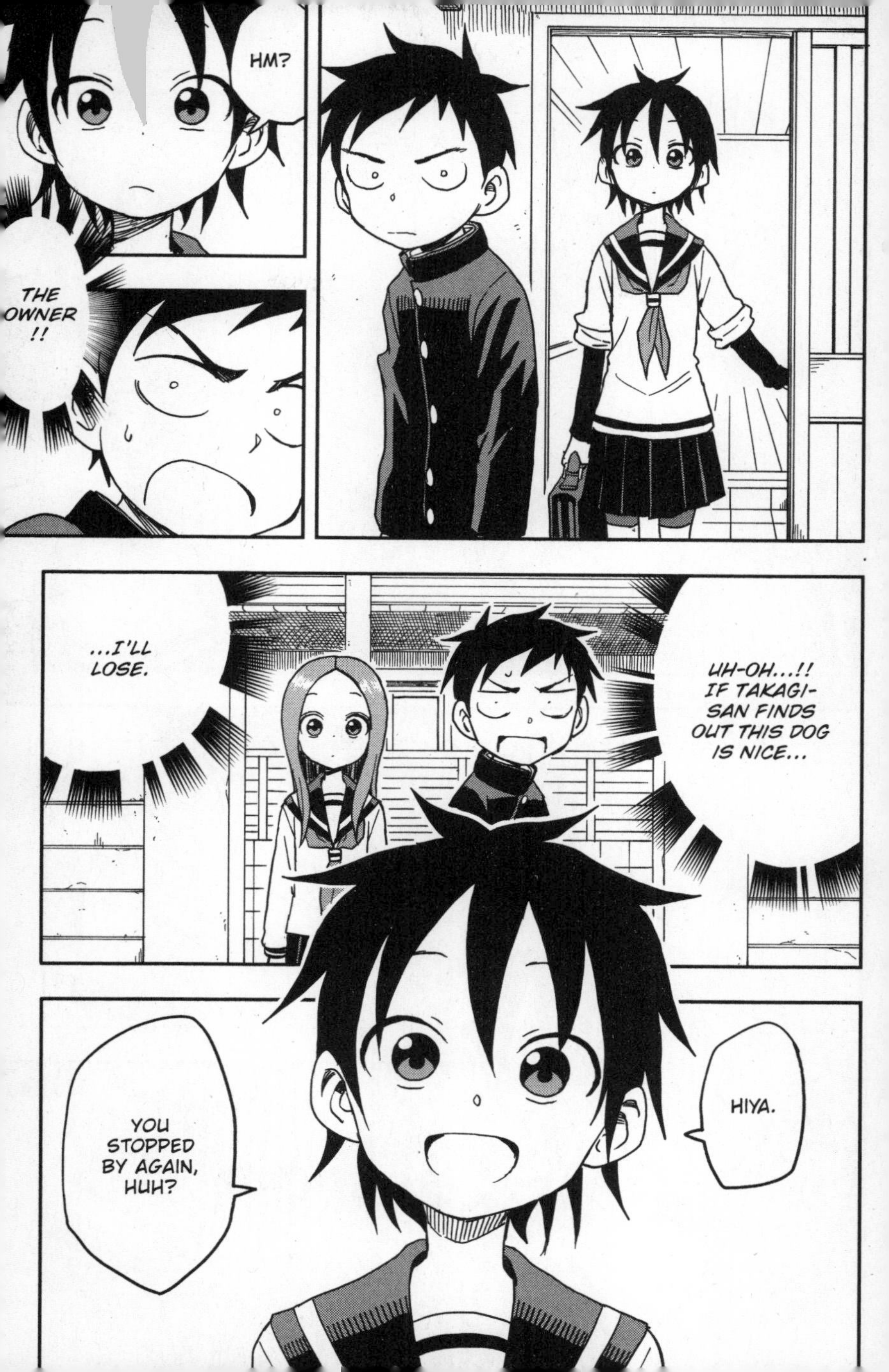
HM?
THE OWNER !!
UH-OH...!! IF TAKAGI-SAN FINDS OUT THIS DOG IS NICE...
...I'LL LOSE.
HIYA.
YOU STOPPED BY AGAIN, HUH?

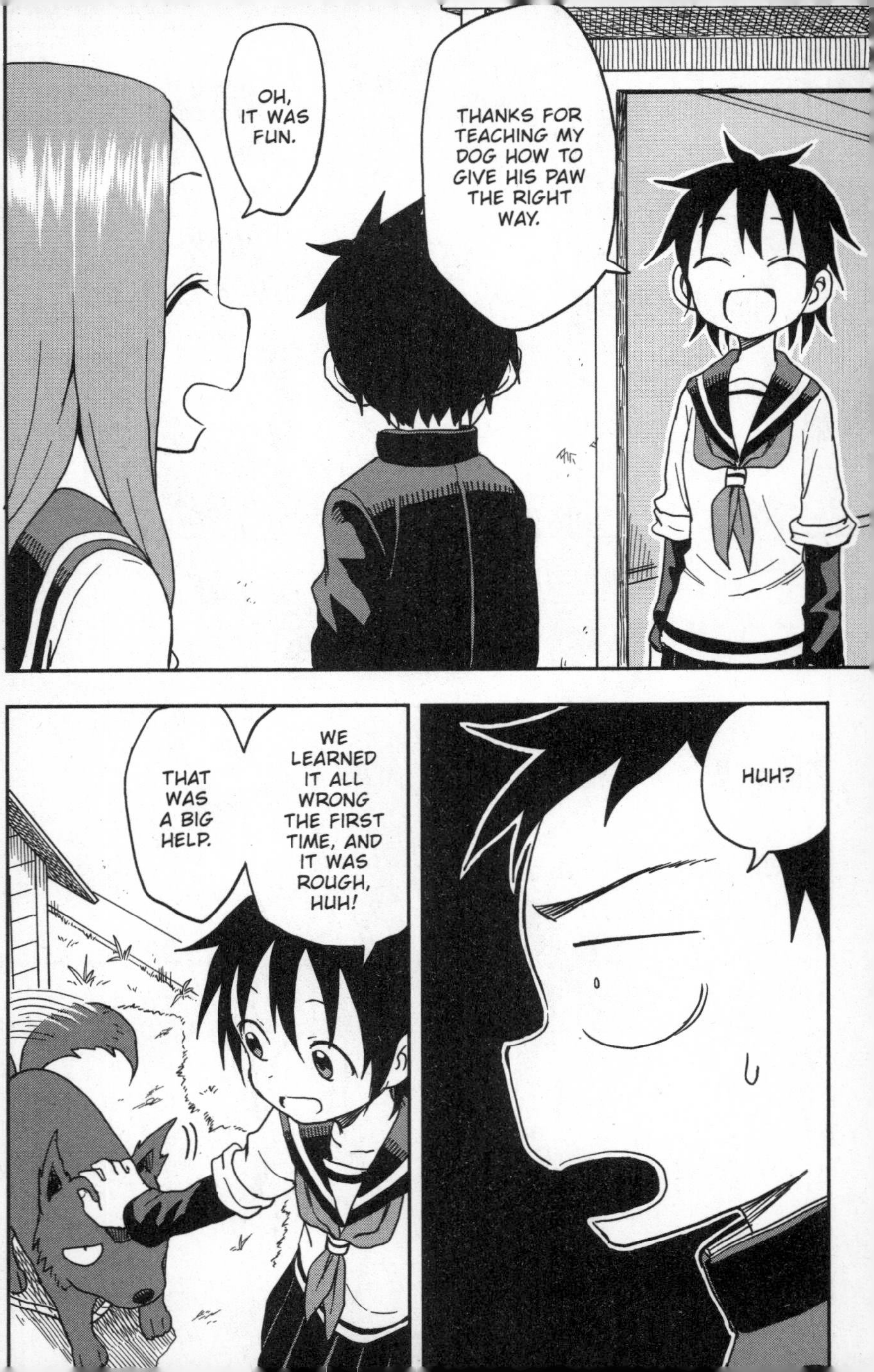
THANKS FOR TEACHING MY DOG HOW TO GIVE HIS PAW THE RIGHT WAY.
OH, IT WAS FUN.
HUH?
WE LEARNED IT ALL WRONG THE FIRST TIME, AND IT WAS ROUGH, HUH!
THAT WAS A BIG HELP.

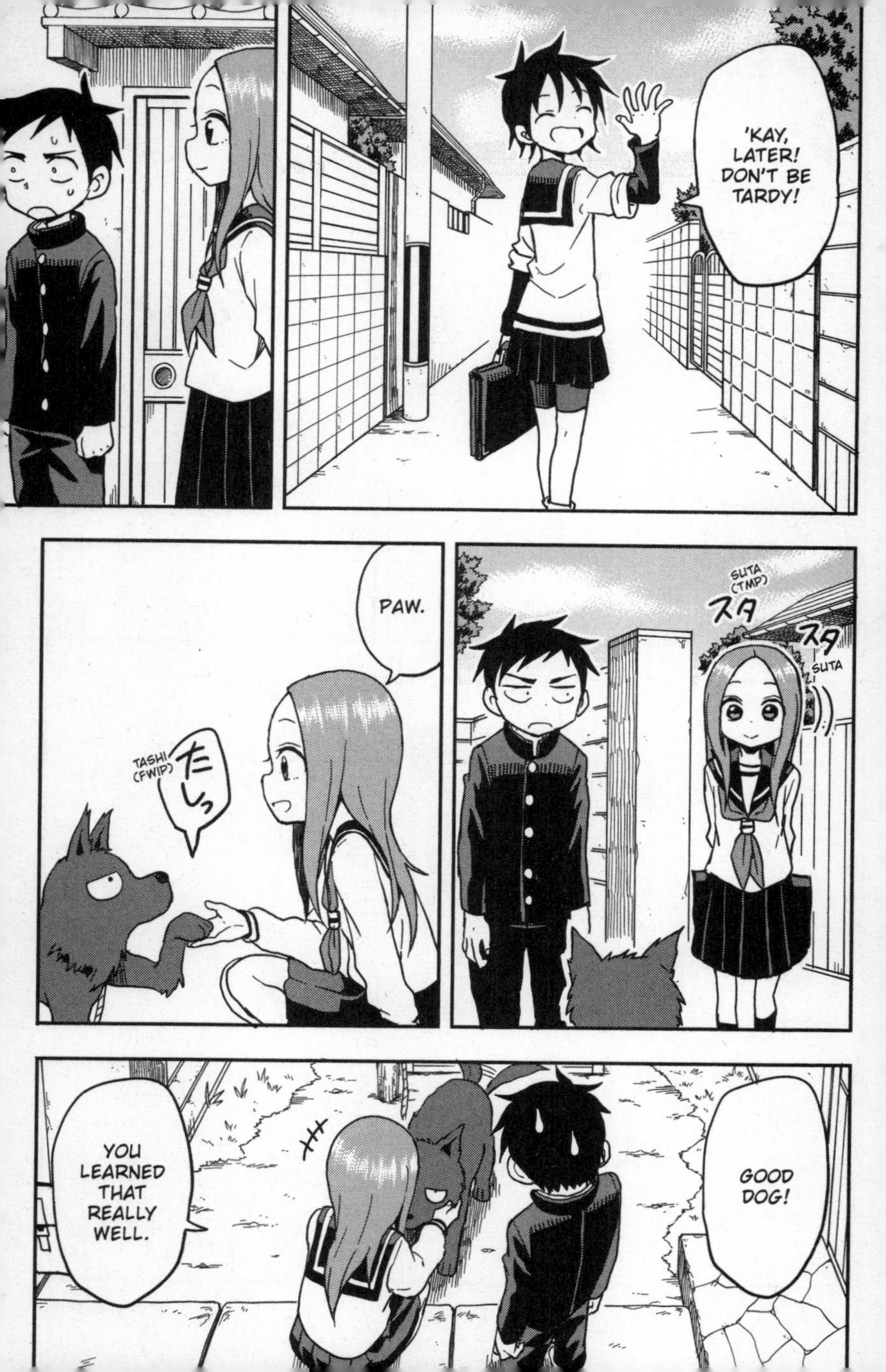
'KAY, LATER! DON'T BE TARDY!
スタ SUTA (TMP)
スタ SUTA
PAW.
たしっ TASHI (FWIP)
GOOD DOG!
YOU LEARNED THAT REALLY WELL.

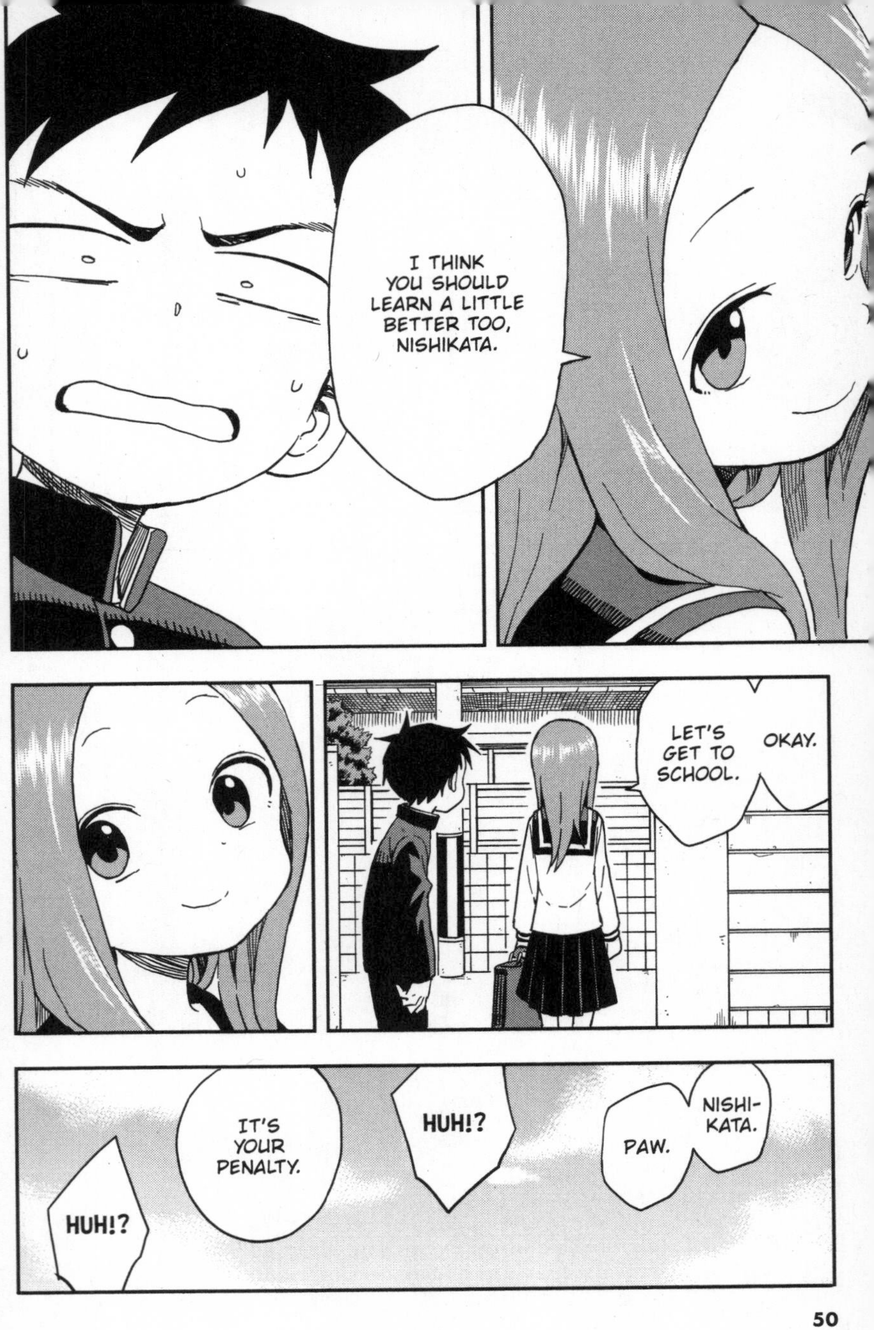
I THINK YOU SHOULD LEARN A LITTLE BETTER TOO, NISHIKATA.
OKAY.
LET'S GET TO SCHOOL.
NISHI-KATA.
PAW.
HUH!?
IT'S YOUR PENALTY.
HUH!?

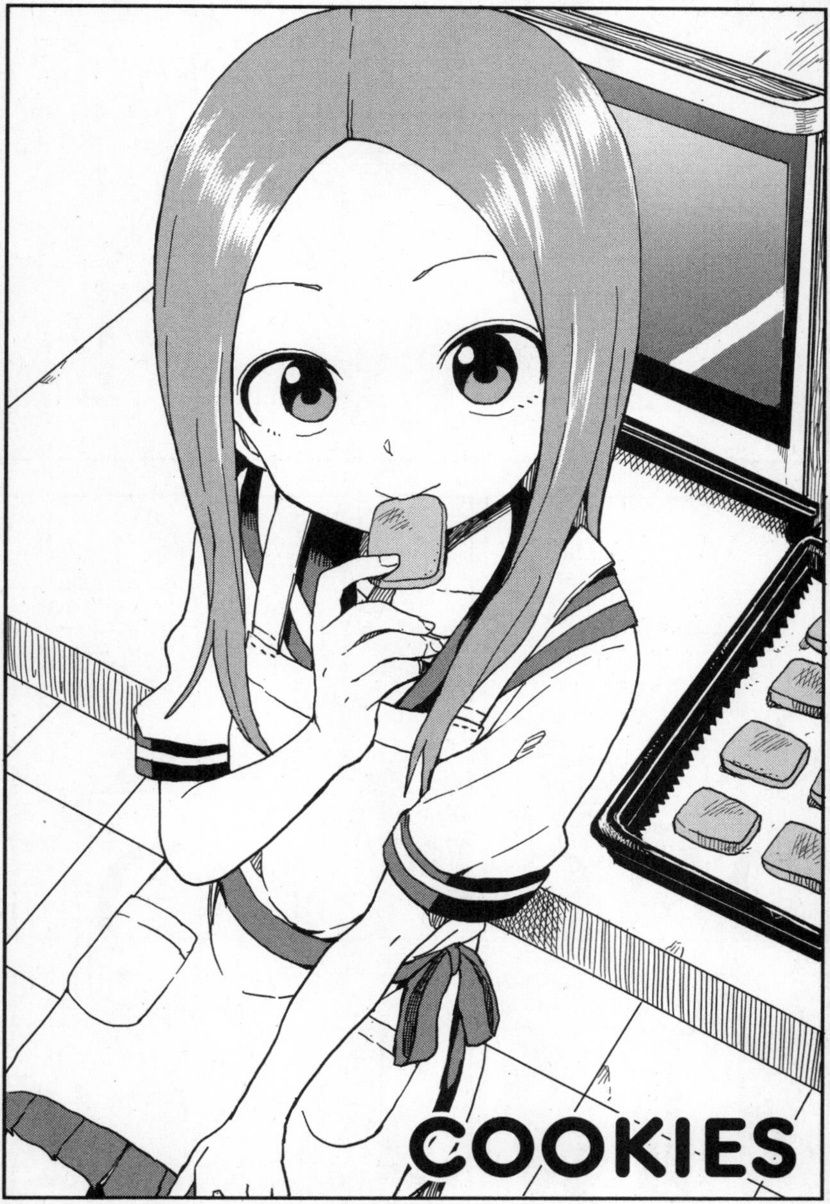
COOKIES

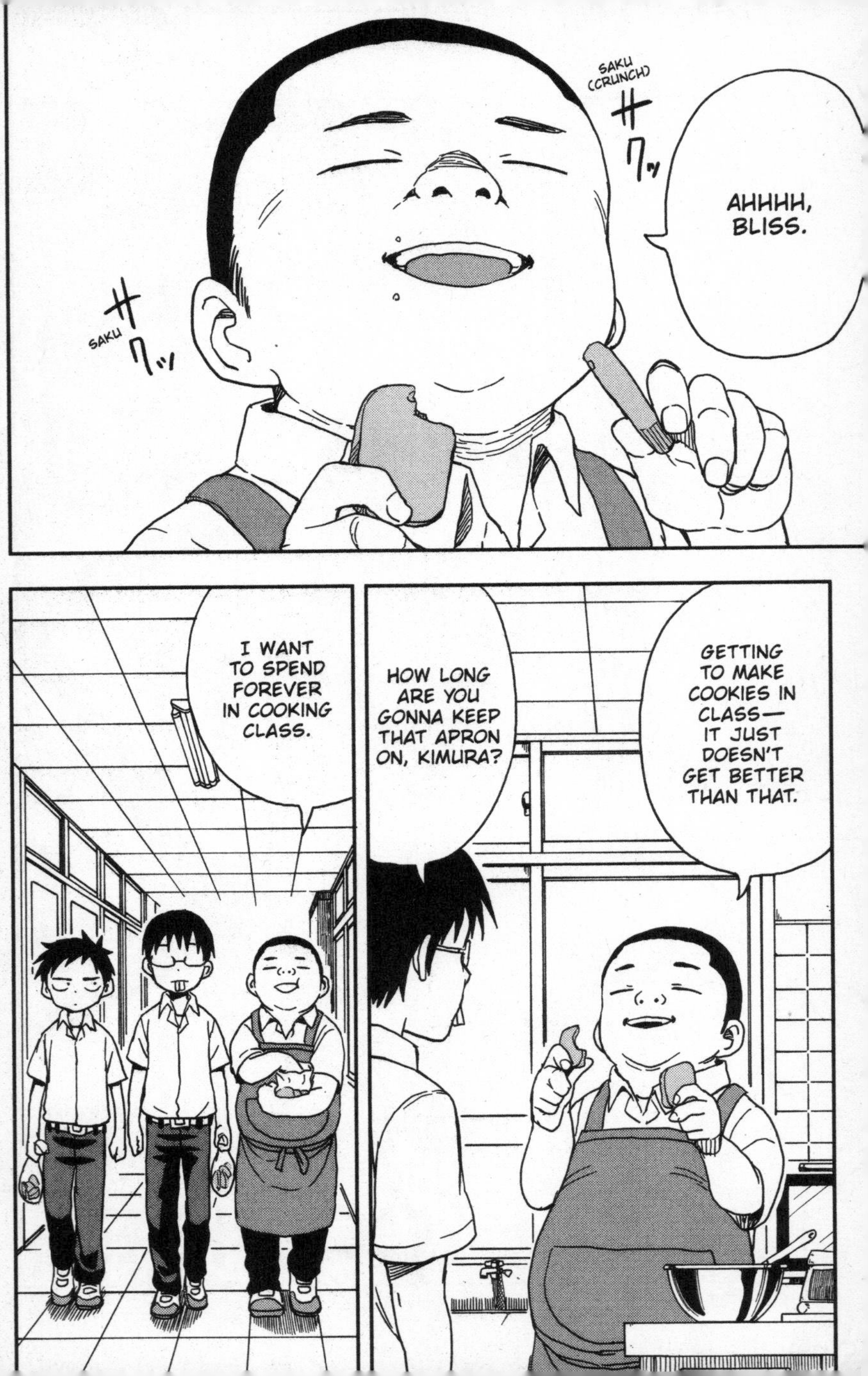
SAKU (CRUNCH)
AHHHH, BLISS.
SAKU
GETTING TO MAKE COOKIES IN CLASS— IT JUST DOESN'T GET BETTER THAN THAT.
HOW LONG ARE YOU GONNA KEEP THAT APRON ON, KIMURA?
I WANT TO SPEND FOREVER IN COOKING CLASS.

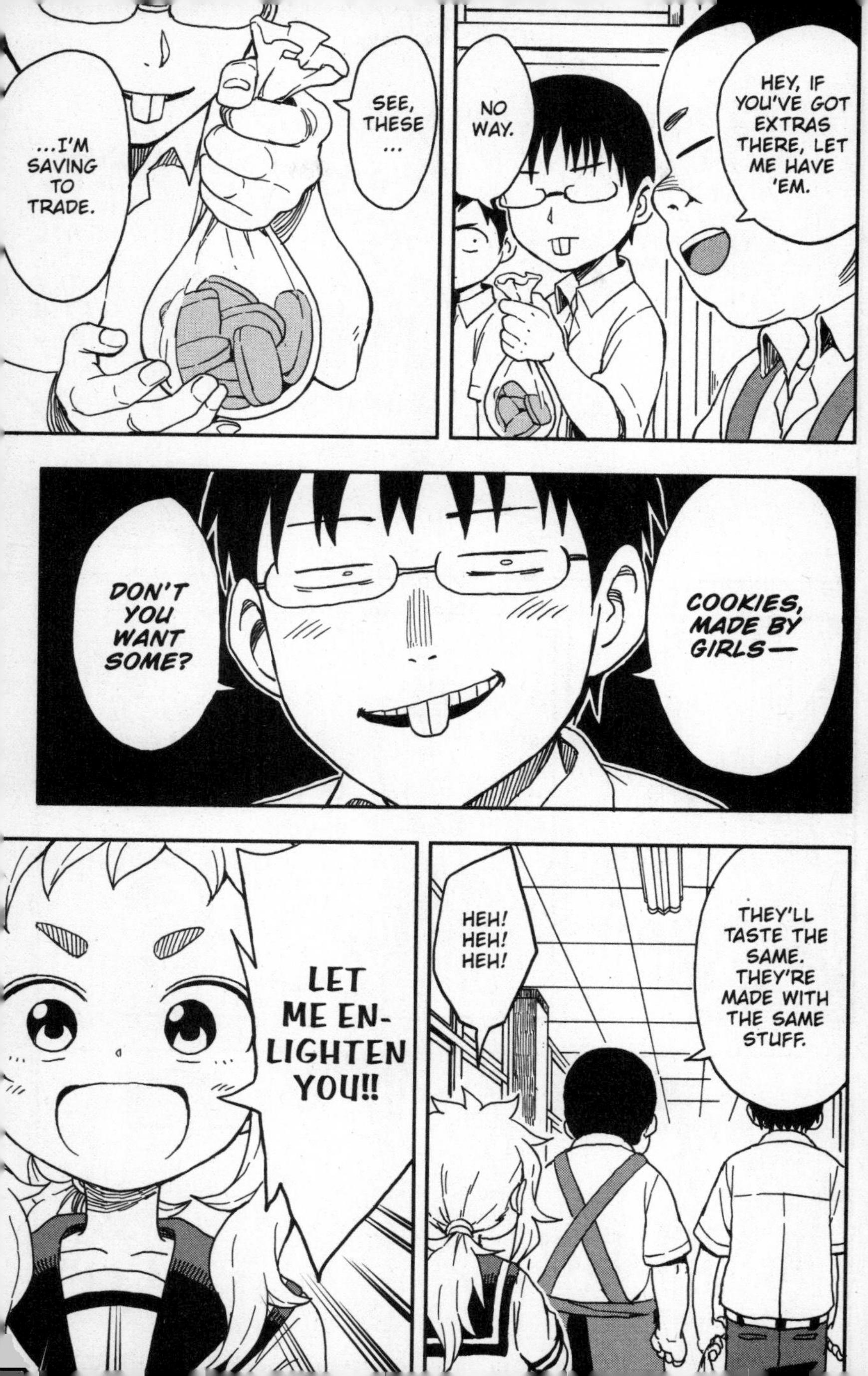
HEY, IF YOU'VE GOT EXTRAS THERE, LET ME HAVE 'EM.
NO WAY.
SEE, THESE ...
...I'M SAVING TO TRADE.
COOKIES, MADE BY GIRLS—
DON'T YOU WANT SOME?
THEY'LL TASTE THE SAME. THEY'RE MADE WITH THE SAME STUFF.
HEH! HEH! HEH!
LET ME EN-LIGHTEN YOU!!

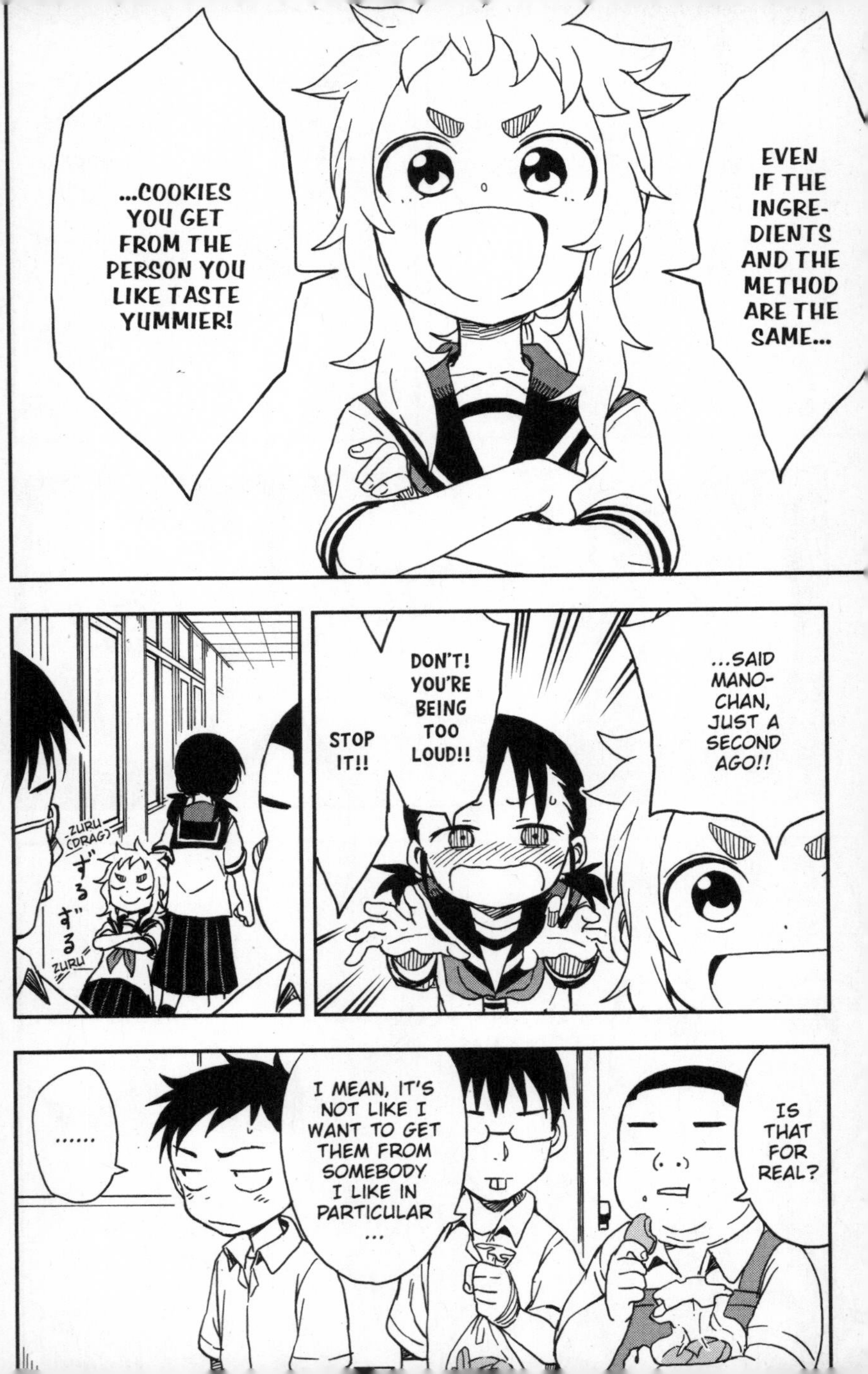
EVEN IF THE INGRE-DIENTS AND THE METHOD ARE THE SAME...
...COOKIES YOU GET FROM THE PERSON YOU LIKE TASTE YUMMIER!
...SAID MANO-CHAN, JUST A SECOND AGO!!
DON'T! YOU'RE BEING TOO LOUD!!
STOP IT!!
ずるずる
ZURU (DRAG)
ZURU
IS THAT FOR REAL?
I MEAN, IT'S NOT LIKE I WANT TO GET THEM FROM SOMEBODY I LIKE IN PARTICULAR ...
......

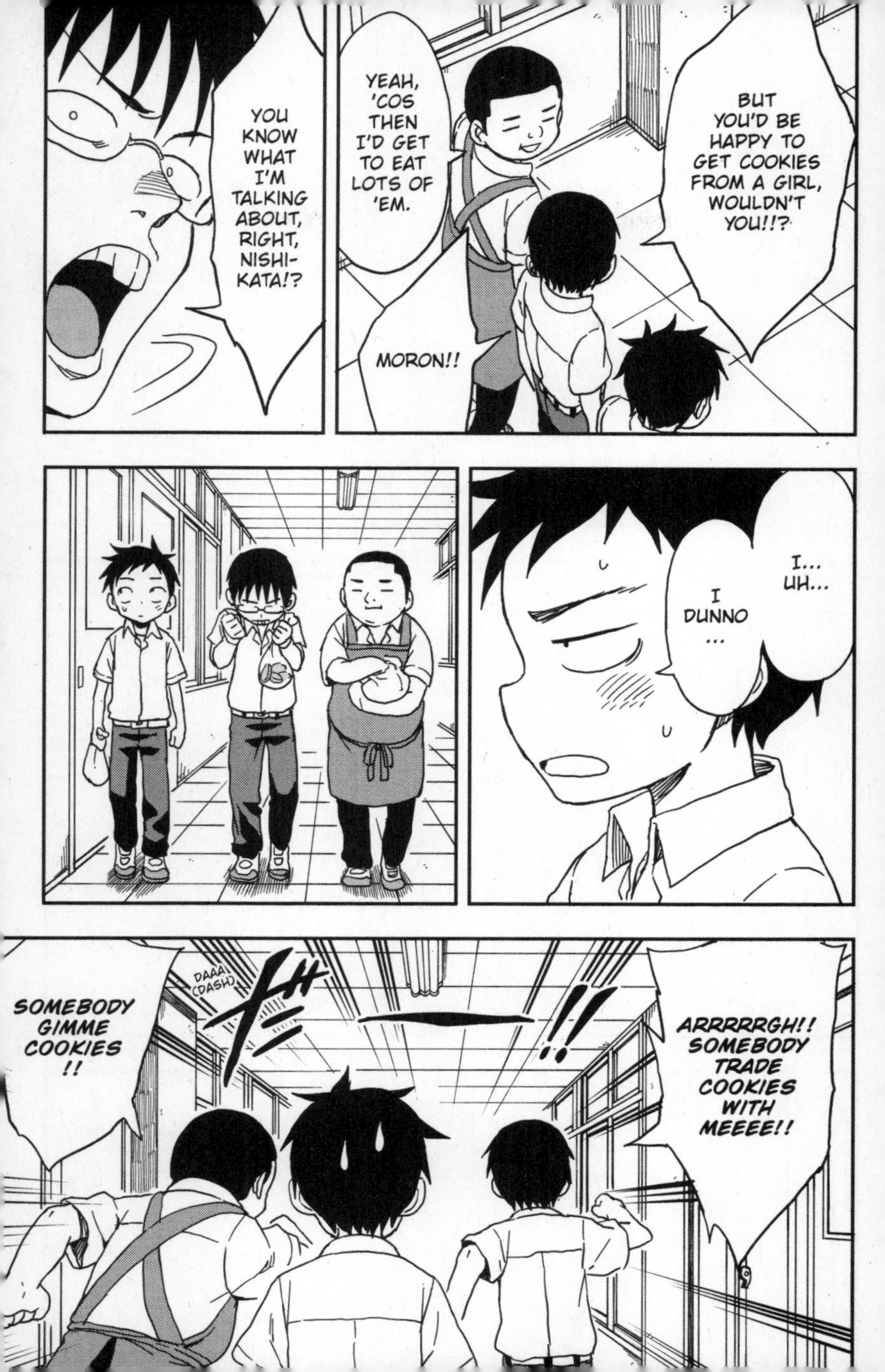
BUT YOU'D BE HAPPY TO GET COOKIES FROM A GIRL, WOULDN'T YOU!!?
YEAH, 'COS THEN I'D GET TO EAT LOTS OF 'EM.
MORON!!
YOU KNOW WHAT I'M TALKING ABOUT, RIGHT, NISHI-KATA!?
I... UH...
I DUNNO ...
ARRRRRGH!! SOMEBODY TRADE COOKIES WITH MEEEE!!
!!
DAAA (DASH)
SOMEBODY GIMME COOKIES !!

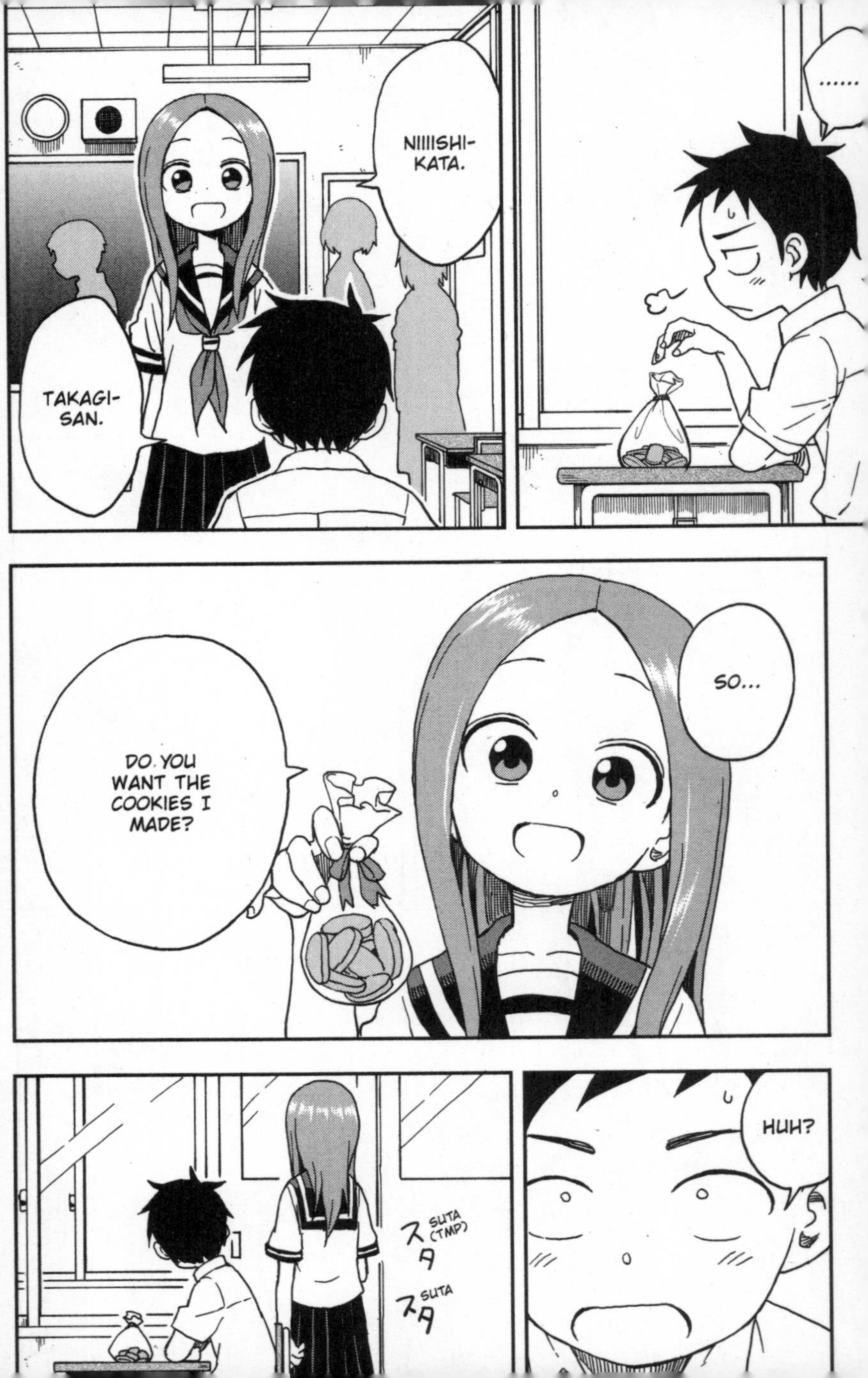
......
NIIIISHI-KATA.
TAKAGI-SAN.
SO...
DO YOU WANT THE COOKIES I MADE?
HUH?
スタ SUTA (TMP)
スタ SUTA

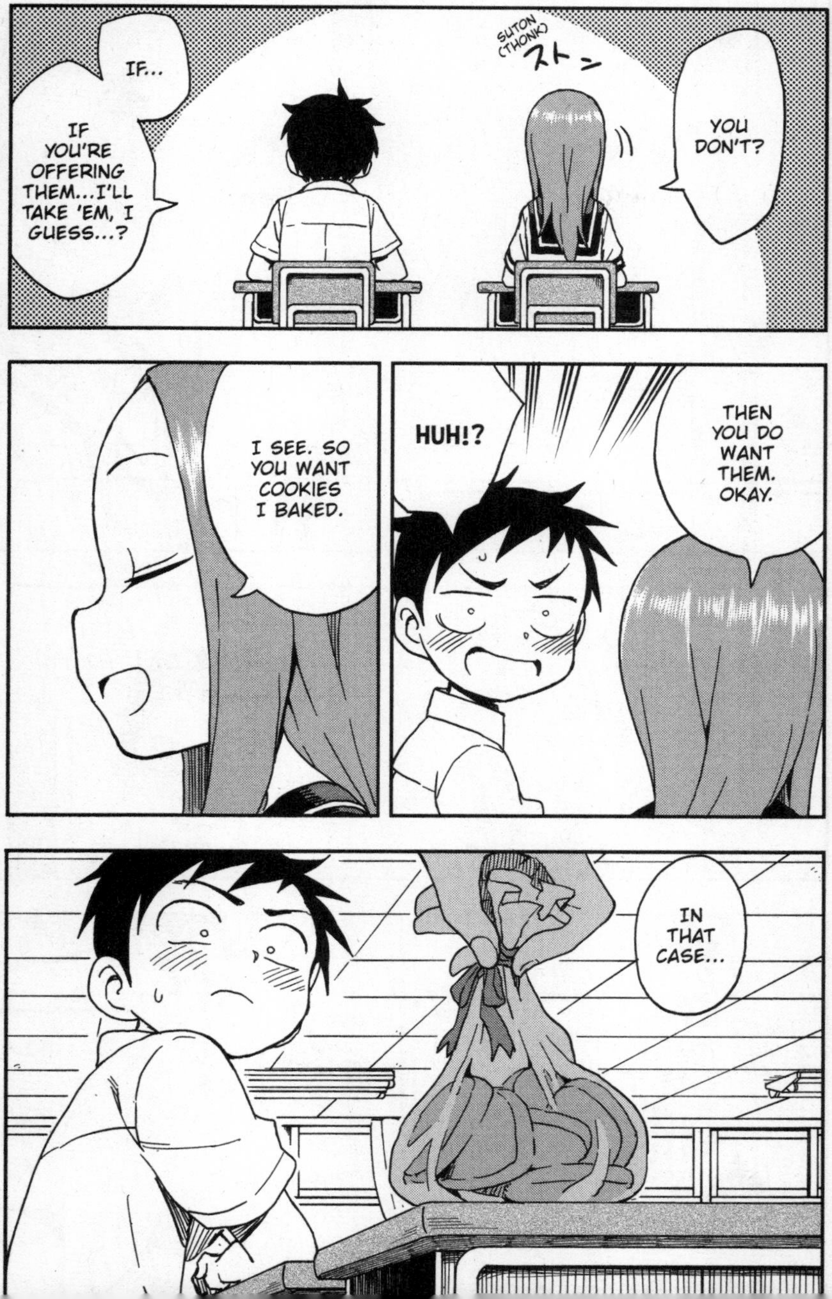
SUTON (THONK)
ストン
YOU DON'T?
IF...
IF YOU'RE OFFERING THEM...I'LL TAKE 'EM, I GUESS...?
THEN YOU DO WANT THEM. OKAY.
HUH!?
I SEE. SO YOU WANT COOKIES I BAKED.
IN THAT CASE...

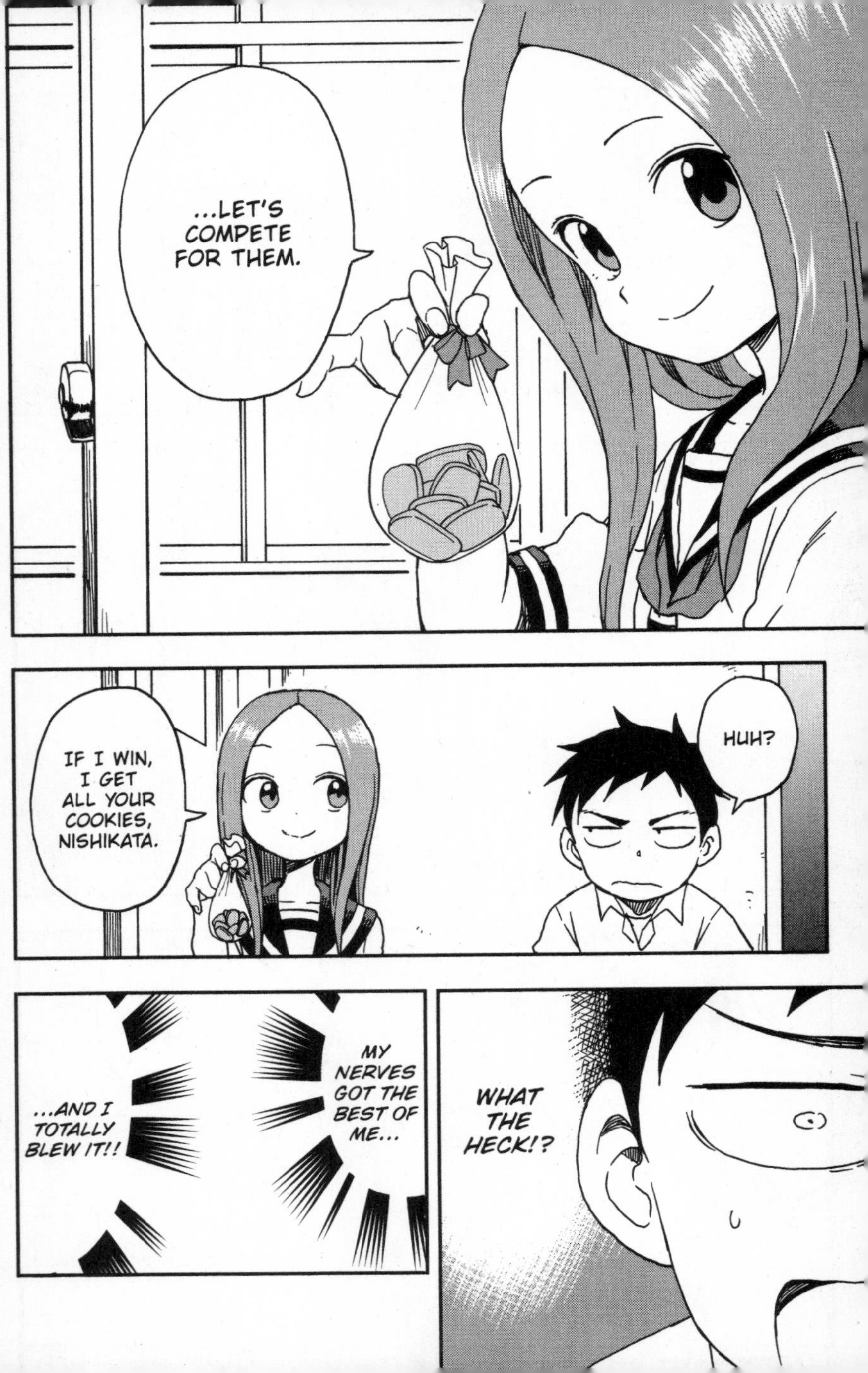
...LET'S COMPETE FOR THEM.
HUH?
IF I WIN, I GET ALL YOUR COOKIES, NISHIKATA.
WHAT THE HECK!?
MY NERVES GOT THE BEST OF ME...
...AND I TOTALLY BLEW IT!!

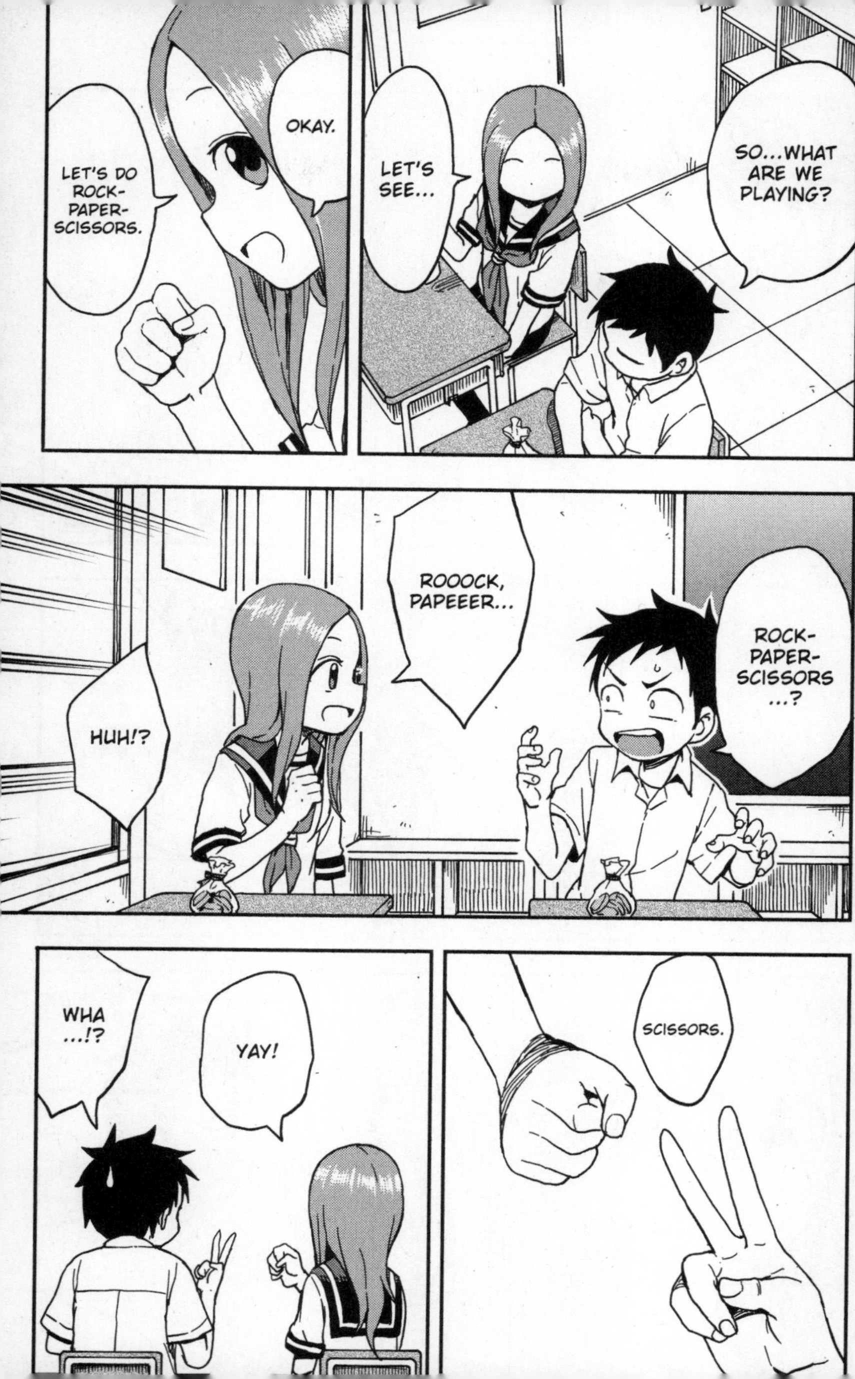
SO...WHAT ARE WE PLAYING?
LET'S SEE...
OKAY.
LET'S DO ROCK-PAPER-SCISSORS.
ROCK-PAPER-SCISSORS ...?
ROOOCK, PAPEEER...
HUH!?
SCISSORS.
YAY!
WHA ...!?

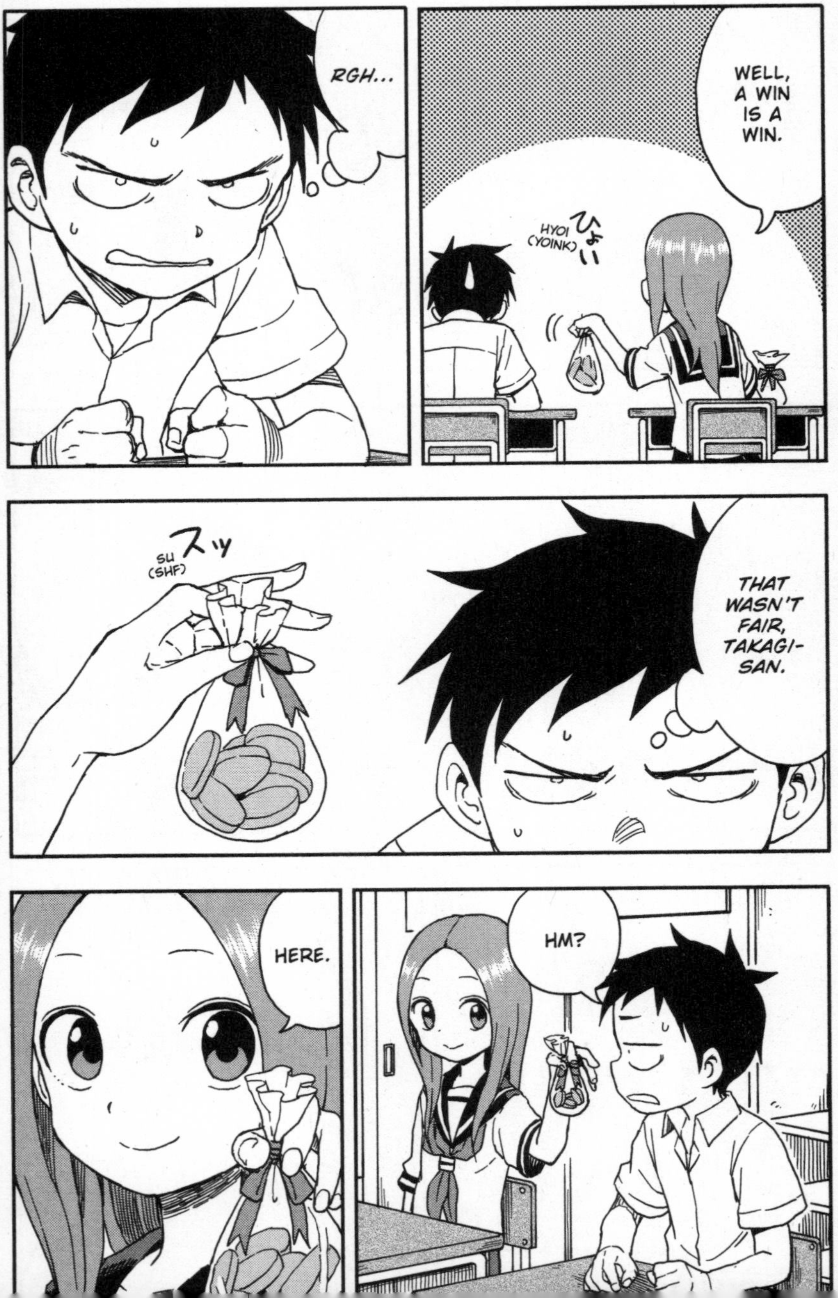
WELL, A WIN IS A WIN.
HYOI (YOINK) ひょい
RGH...
THAT WASN'T FAIR, TAKAGI-SAN.
SU (SHF) スッ
HM?
HERE.

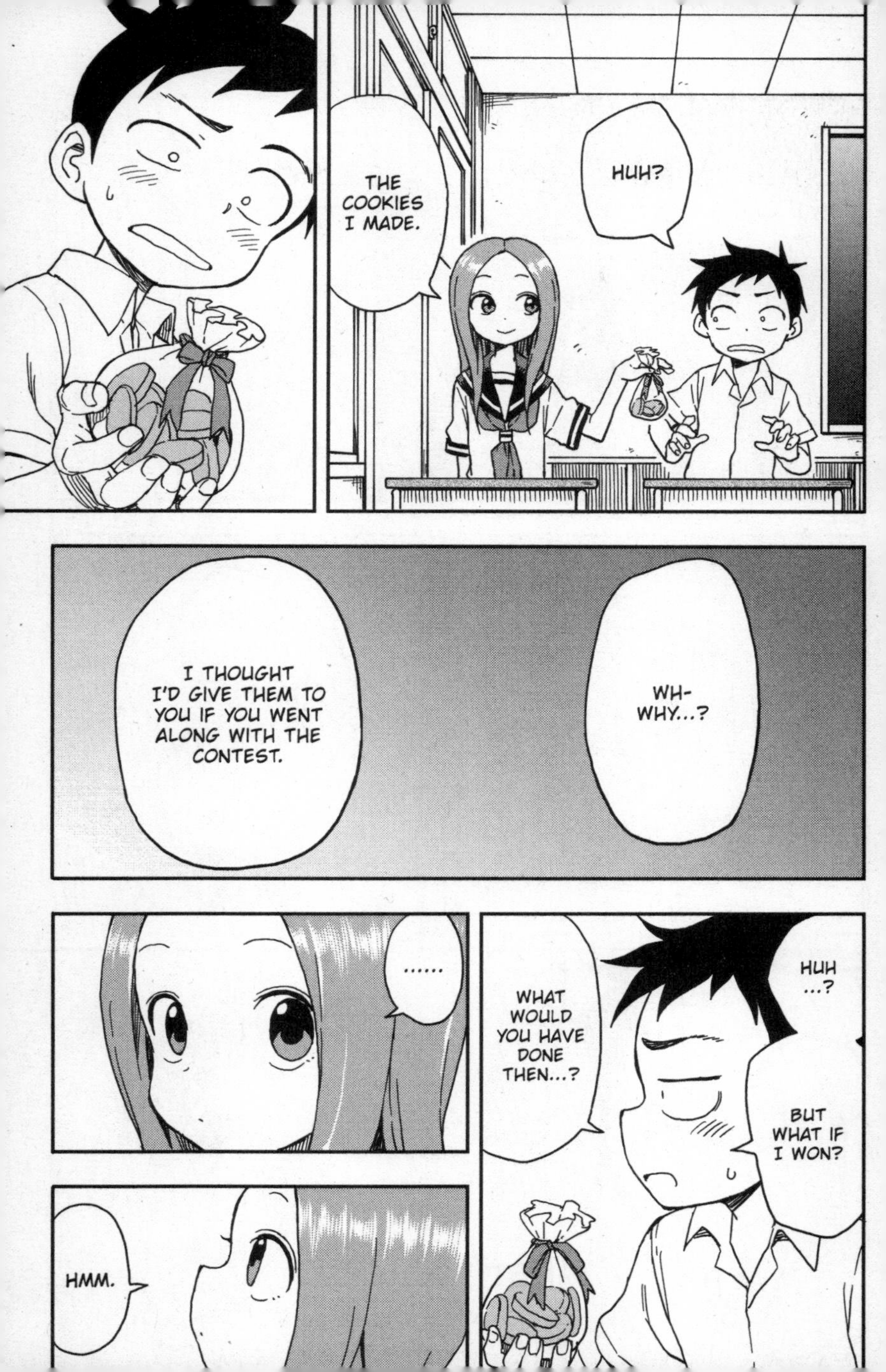
HUH?
THE COOKIES I MADE.
WH- WHY...?
I THOUGHT I'D GIVE THEM TO YOU IF YOU WENT ALONG WITH THE CONTEST.
HUH ...?
BUT WHAT IF I WON?
WHAT WOULD YOU HAVE DONE THEN...?
......
HMM.

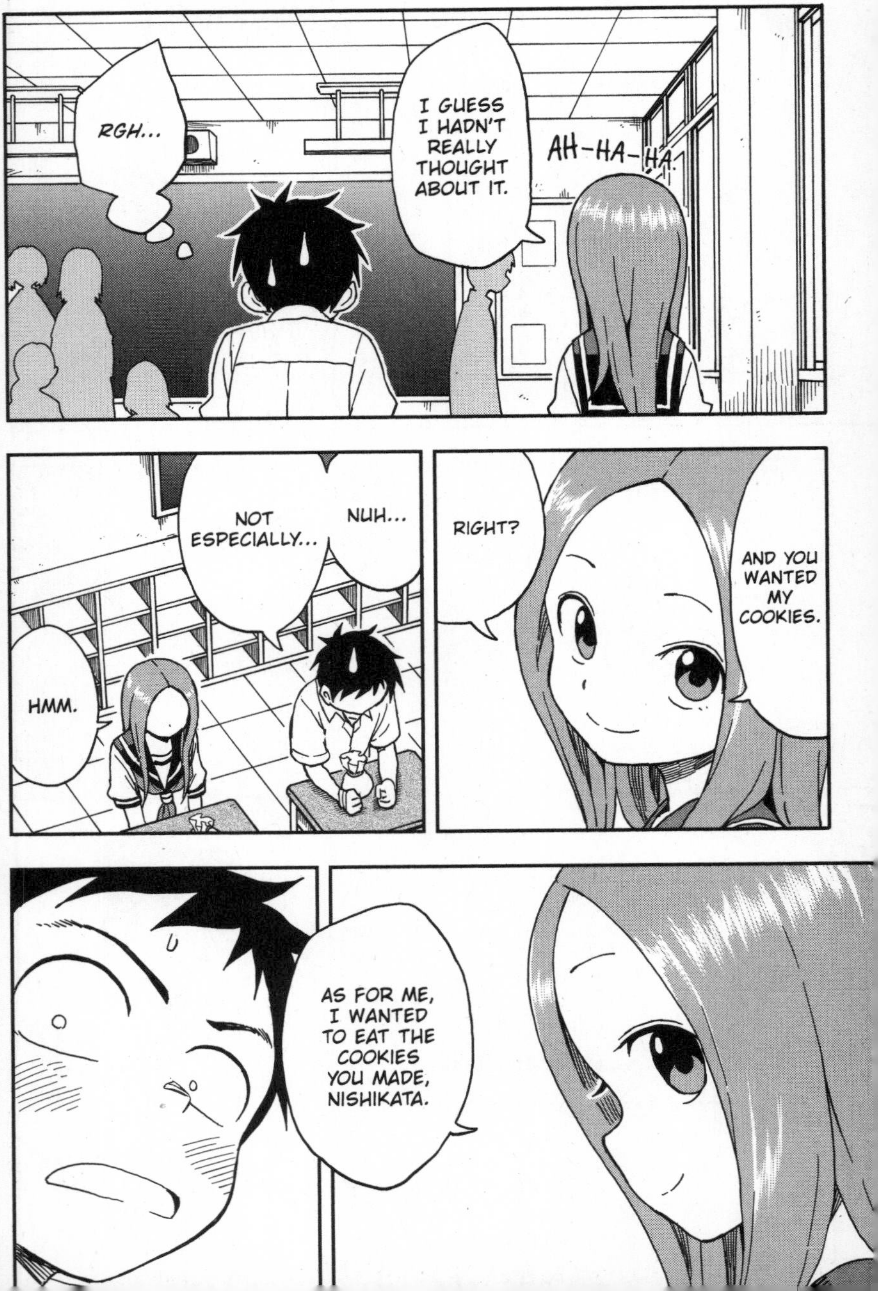

AH-HA-HA.
I GUESS I HADN'T REALLY THOUGHT ABOUT IT.
RGH...
AND YOU WANTED MY COOKIES.
RIGHT?
NUH...
NOT ESPECIALLY...
HMM.
AS FOR ME, I WANTED TO EAT THE COOKIES YOU MADE, NISHIKATA.

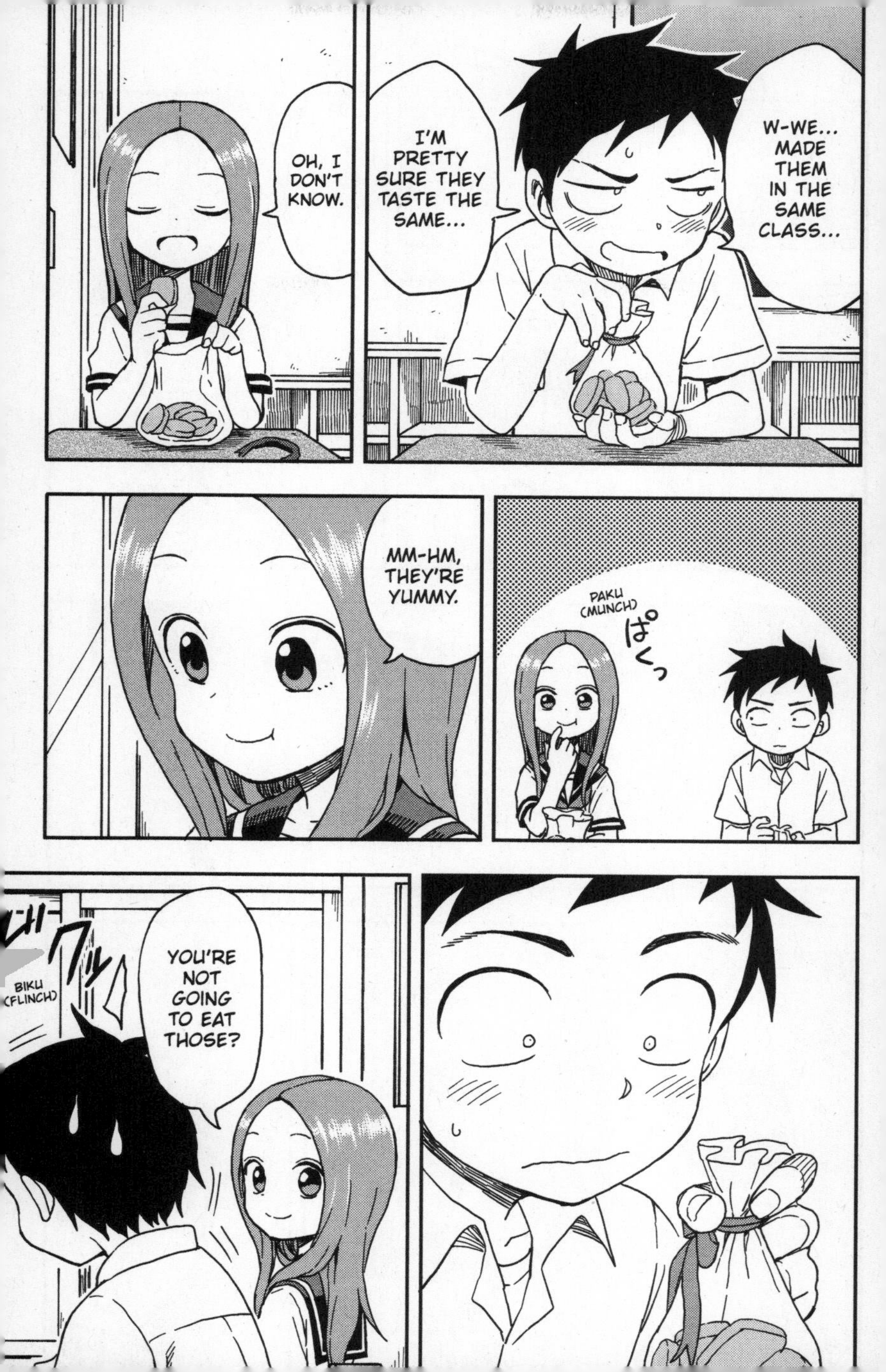
W-WE... MADE THEM IN THE SAME CLASS...
I'M PRETTY SURE THEY TASTE THE SAME...
OH, I DON'T KNOW.
PAKU (MUNCH)
ぱくっ
MM-HM, THEY'RE YUMMY.
YOU'RE NOT GOING TO EAT THOSE?
BIKU (FLINCH)

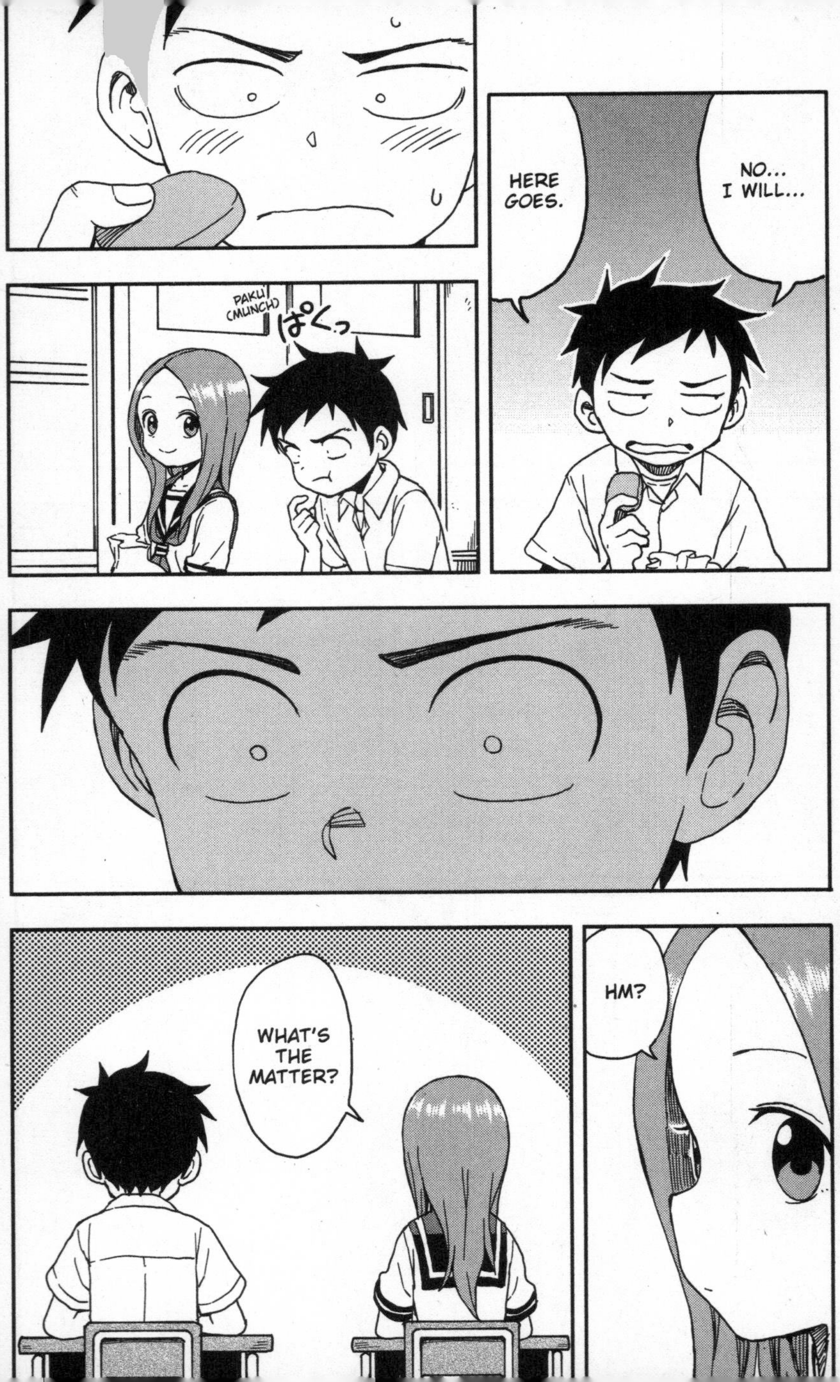
NO… I WILL…
HERE GOES.
PAKU (MUNCH)
ぱくっ
HM?
WHAT'S THE MATTER?

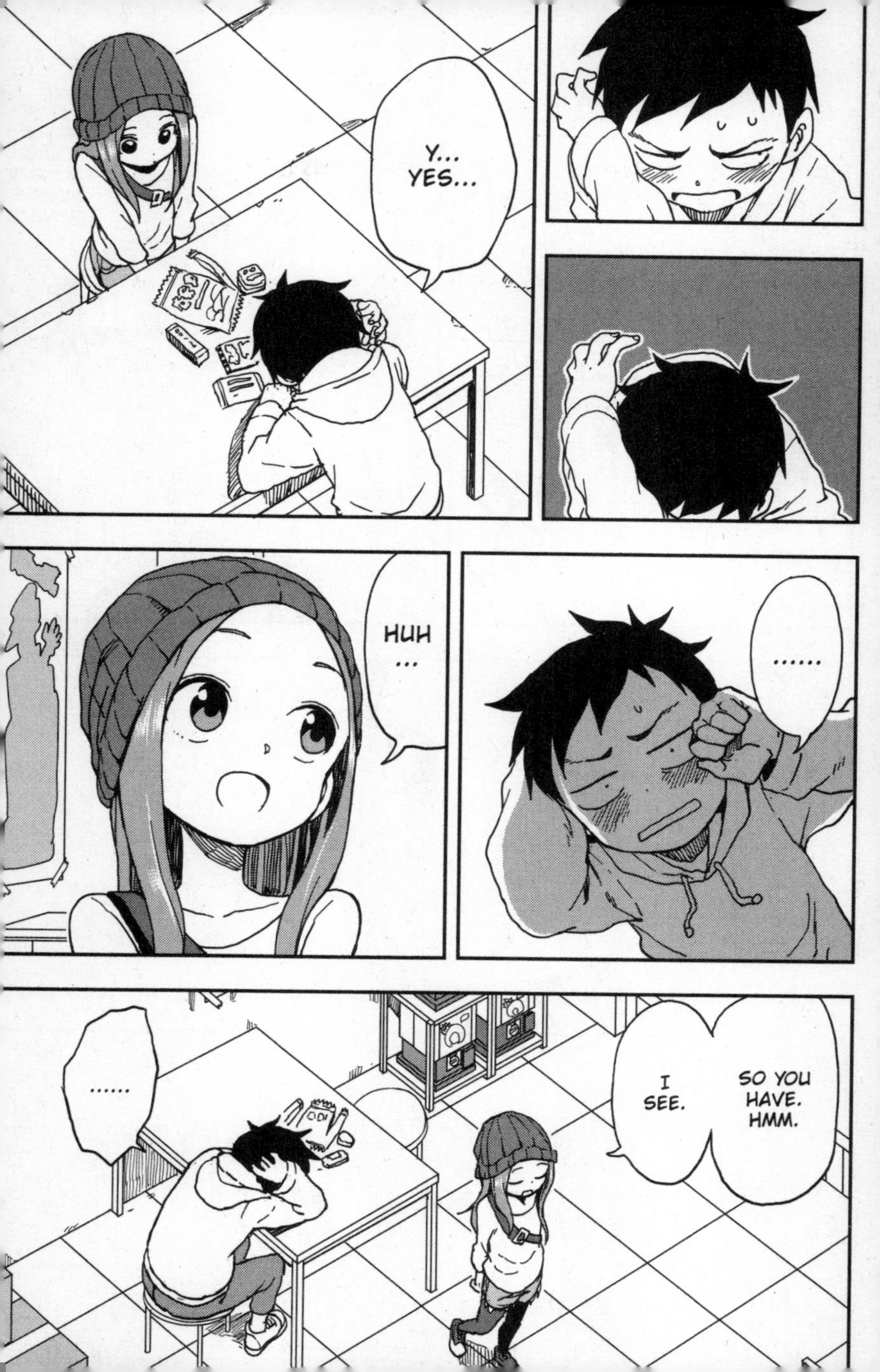
Y... YES...
......
HUH ...
SO YOU HAVE. HMM.
I SEE.
......

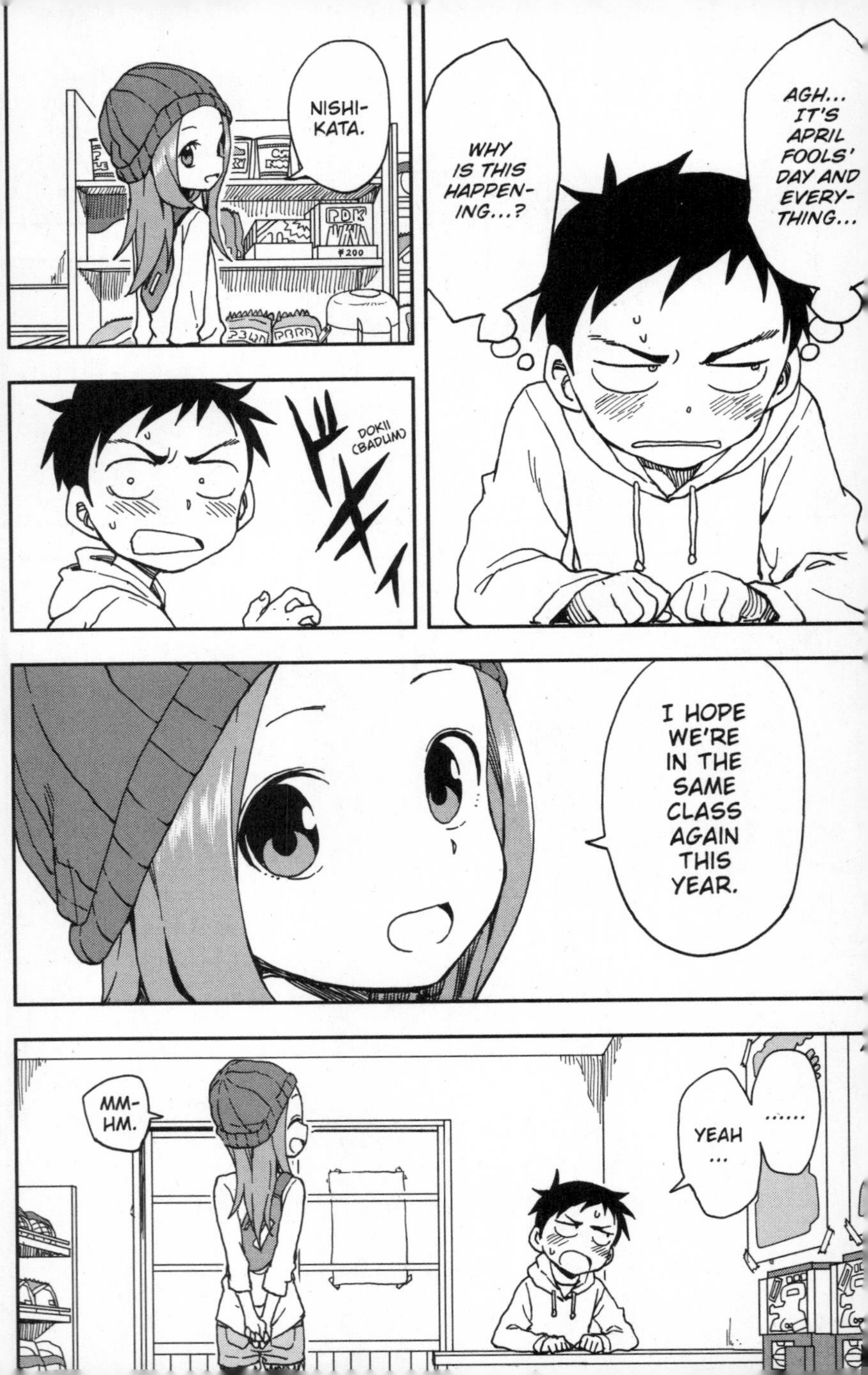
AGH... IT'S APRIL FOOLS' DAY AND EVERYTHING...
WHY IS THIS HAPPENING...?
NISHI-KATA.
DOKII (BADUM)
I HOPE WE'RE IN THE SAME CLASS AGAIN THIS YEAR.
......
YEAH ...
MM-HM.

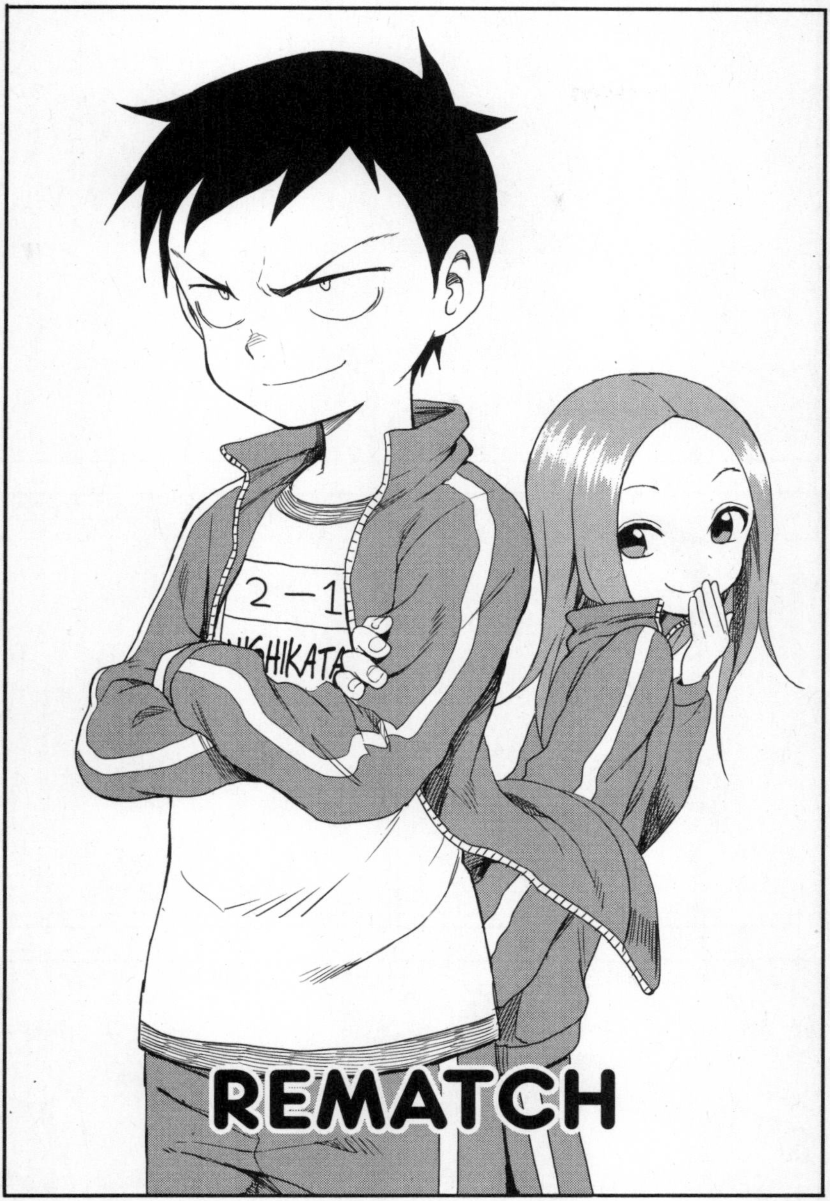
2—1
REMATCH

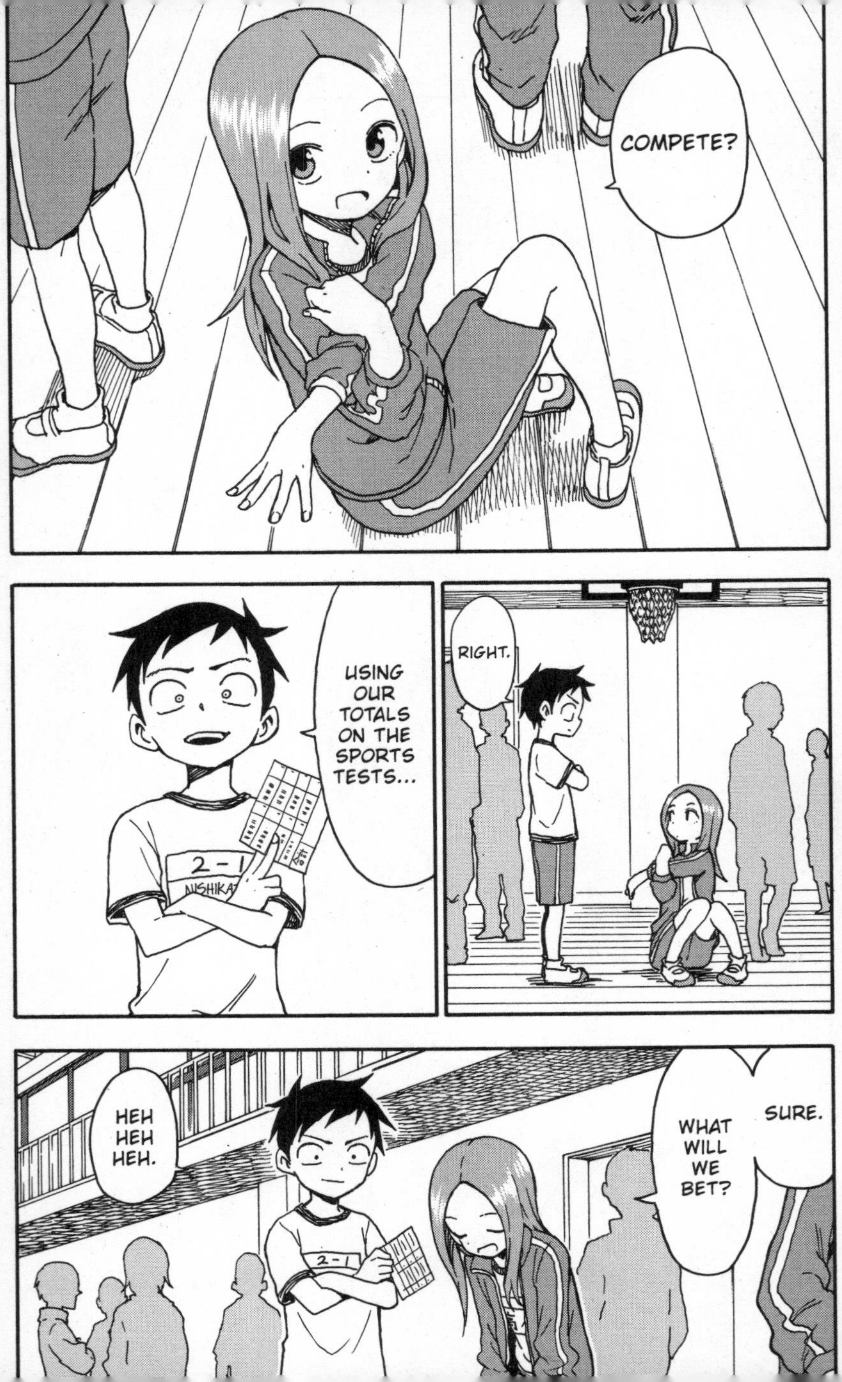
COMPETE?
RIGHT.
USING OUR TOTALS ON THE SPORTS TESTS...
SURE.
WHAT WILL WE BET?
HEH HEH HEH.

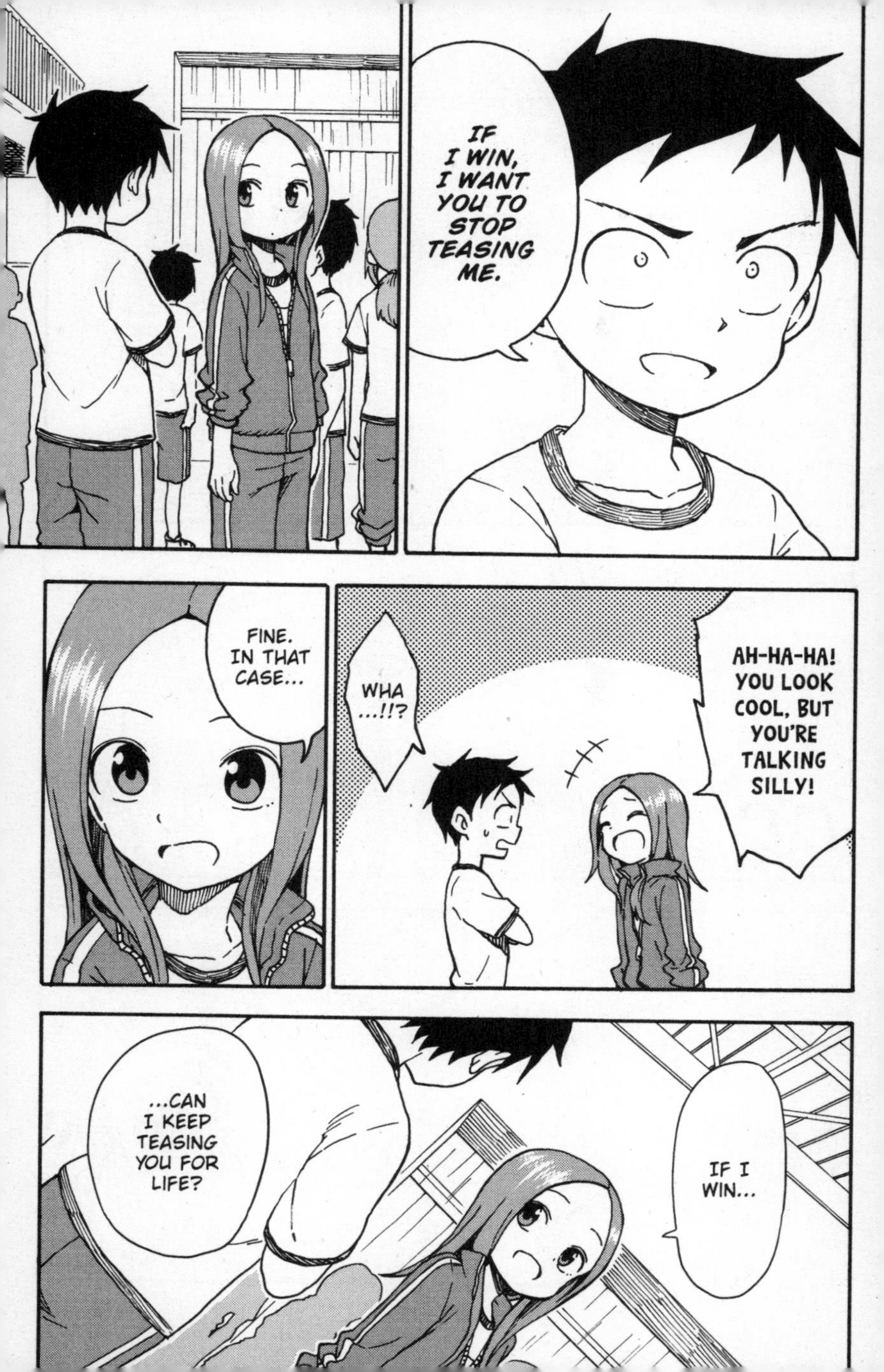
IF I WIN, I WANT YOU TO STOP TEASING ME.
AH-HA-HA! YOU LOOK COOL, BUT YOU'RE TALKING SILLY!
WHA...!!?
FINE. IN THAT CASE...
IF I WIN...
...CAN I KEEP TEASING YOU FOR LIFE?

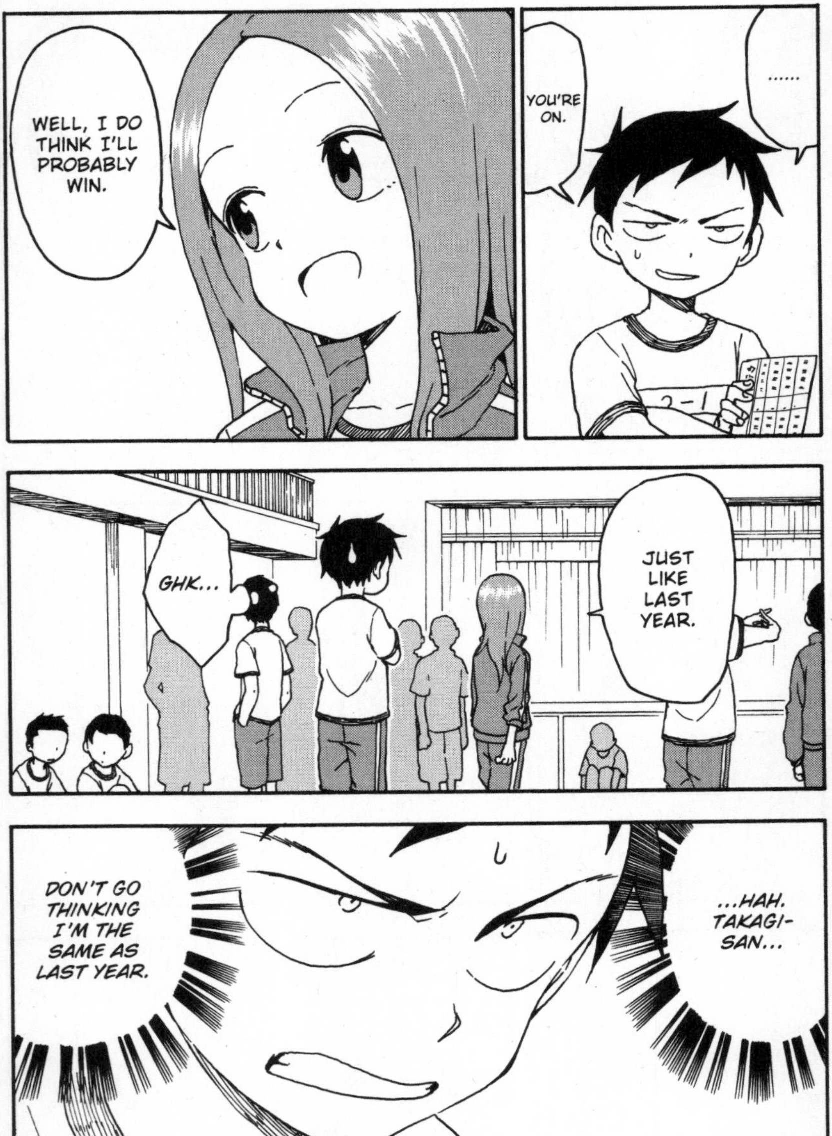
......
YOU'RE ON.
WELL, I DO THINK I'LL PROBABLY WIN.
JUST LIKE LAST YEAR.
GHK...
...HAH. TAKAGI-SAN...
DON'T GO THINKING I'M THE SAME AS LAST YEAR.

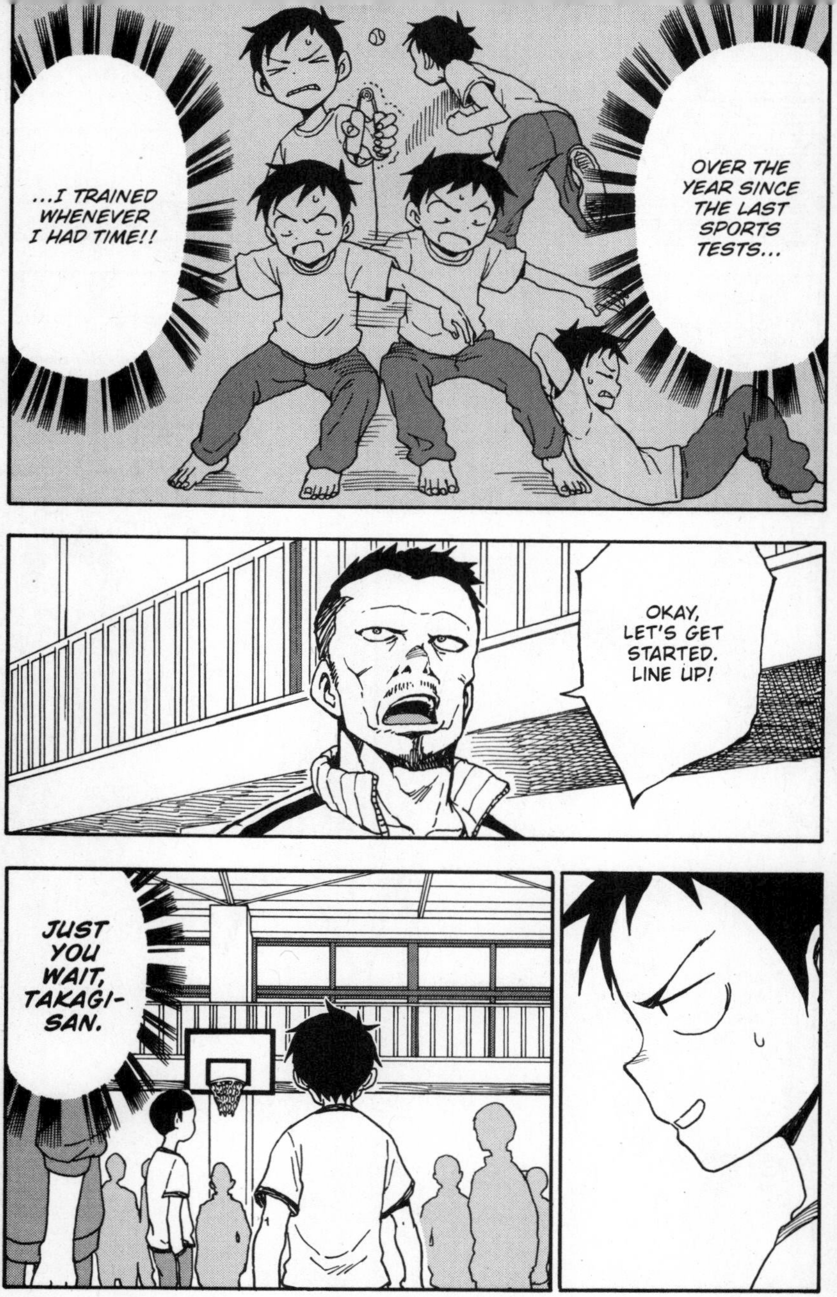
OVER THE YEAR SINCE THE LAST SPORTS TESTS...
...I TRAINED WHENEVER I HAD TIME!!
OKAY, LET'S GET STARTED. LINE UP!
JUST YOU WAIT, TAKAGI-SAN.

YOUR SCORES ARE PRETTY GOOD, NISHIKATA.

UH, THAT WAS FIFTY-THREE TIMES, SO...

HFF!

HFF!

2-1 NISHIKATA

YEAH...

HEH.

IT LOOKS LIKE MY TRAINING PAID OFF!

NICE, VERY NICE...!!

STANDING LONG JUMP	6 PTS	50	FRC STC	
LATERAL LINE JUMP	7 PTS		H	
20m SHUTTLE RUN	8 PTS		GRIP STRENGTH	
SIT-UPS	PTS			
TOTAL				

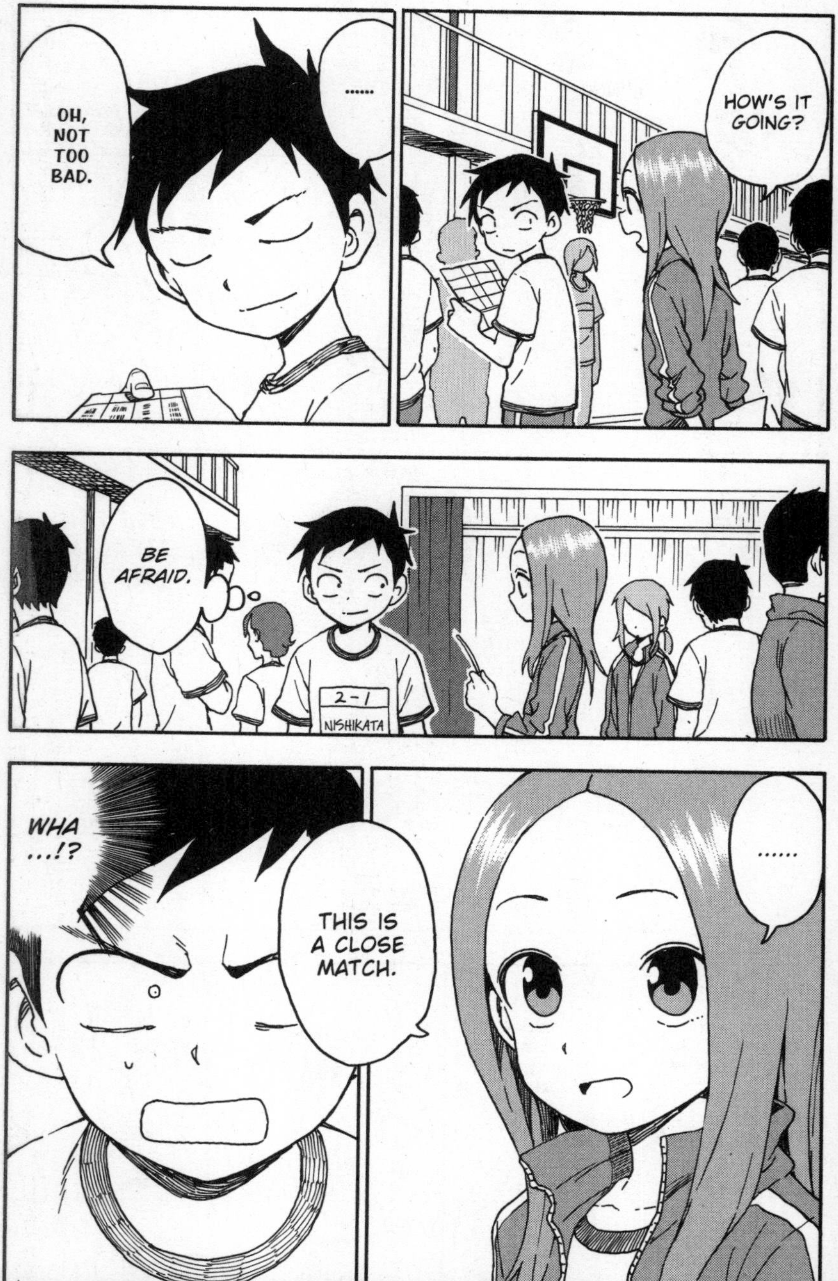
HOW'S IT GOING?
......
OH, NOT TOO BAD.
BE AFRAID.
2-1
NISHIKATA
......
THIS IS A CLOSE MATCH.
WHA ...!?

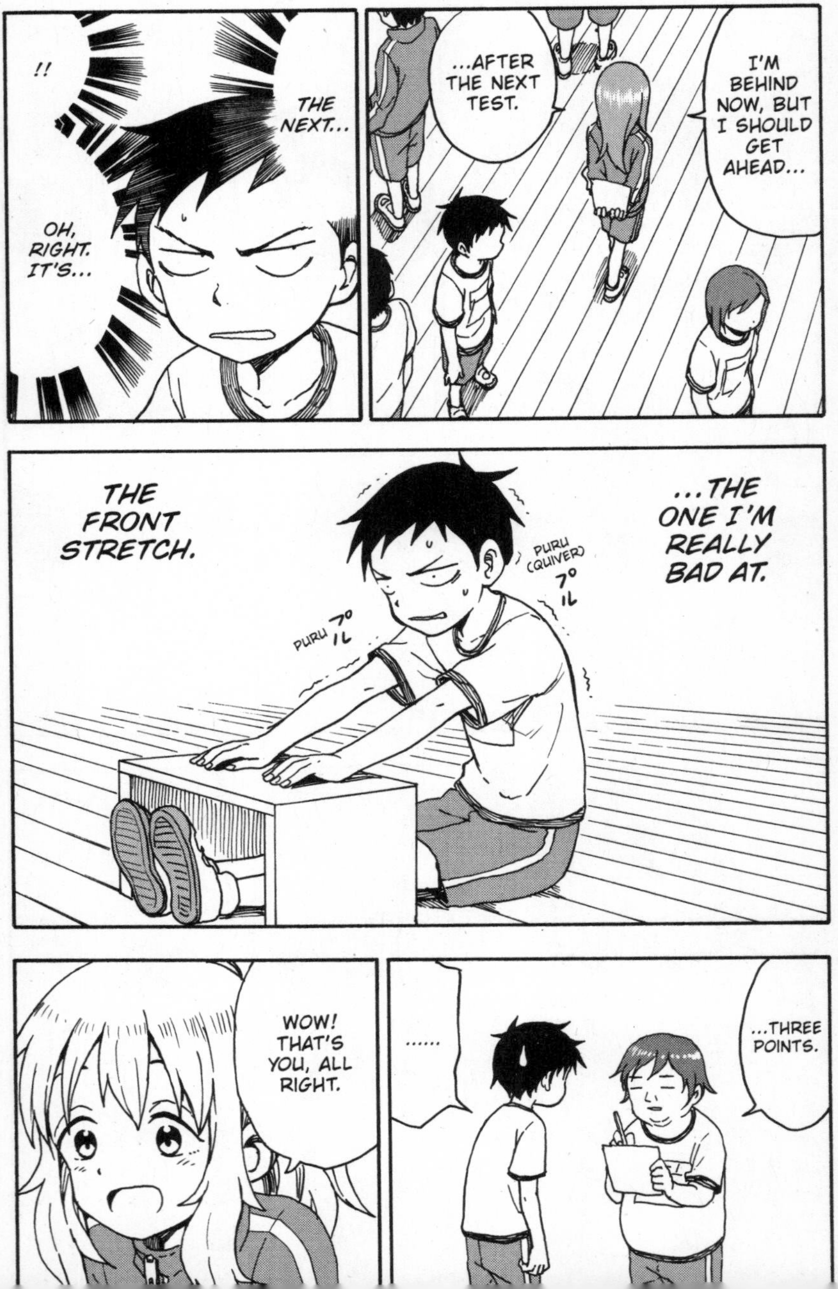
I'M BEHIND NOW, BUT I SHOULD GET AHEAD...
...AFTER THE NEXT TEST.
!!
THE NEXT...
OH, RIGHT. IT'S...
...THE ONE I'M REALLY BAD AT.
PURU (QUIVER) プル
THE FRONT STRETCH.
PURU プル
...THREE POINTS.
......
WOW! THAT'S YOU, ALL RIGHT.

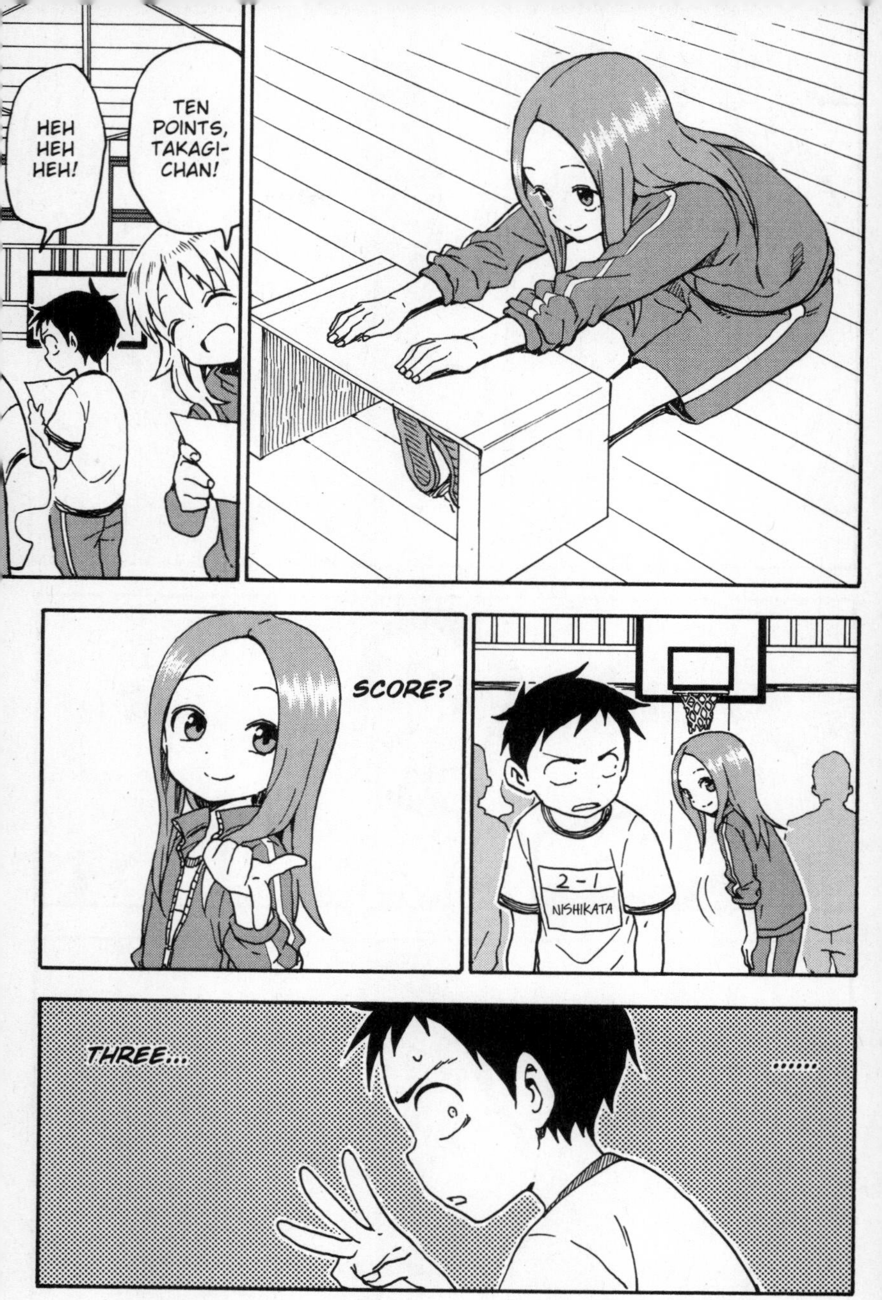
TEN POINTS, TAKAGI-CHAN!
HEH HEH HEH!
SCORE?
THREE...
......

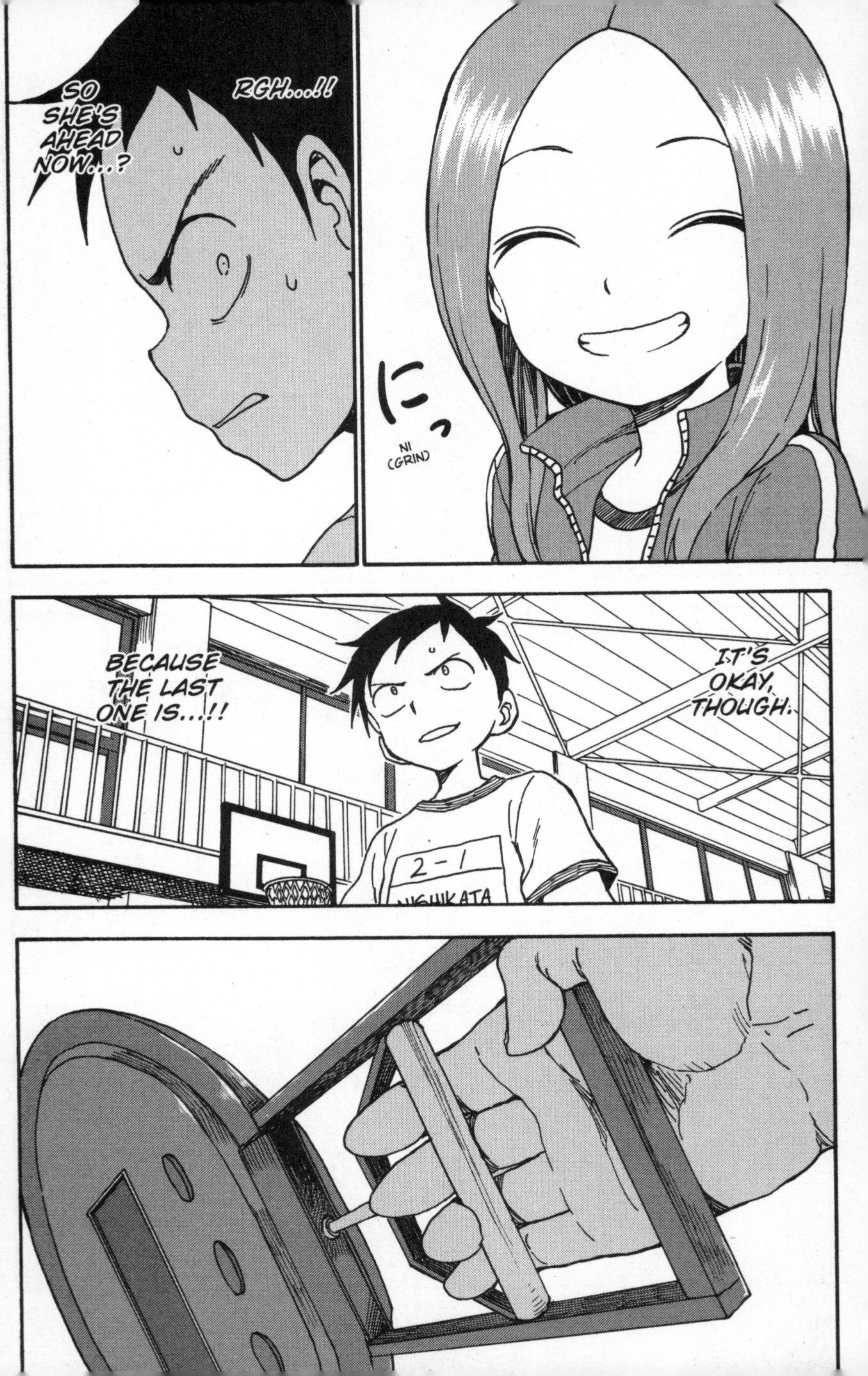
にっ
NI (GRIN)
RGH...!!
SO SHE'S AHEAD NOW...?
IT'S OKAY, THOUGH.
BECAUSE THE LAST ONE IS...!!
2-1

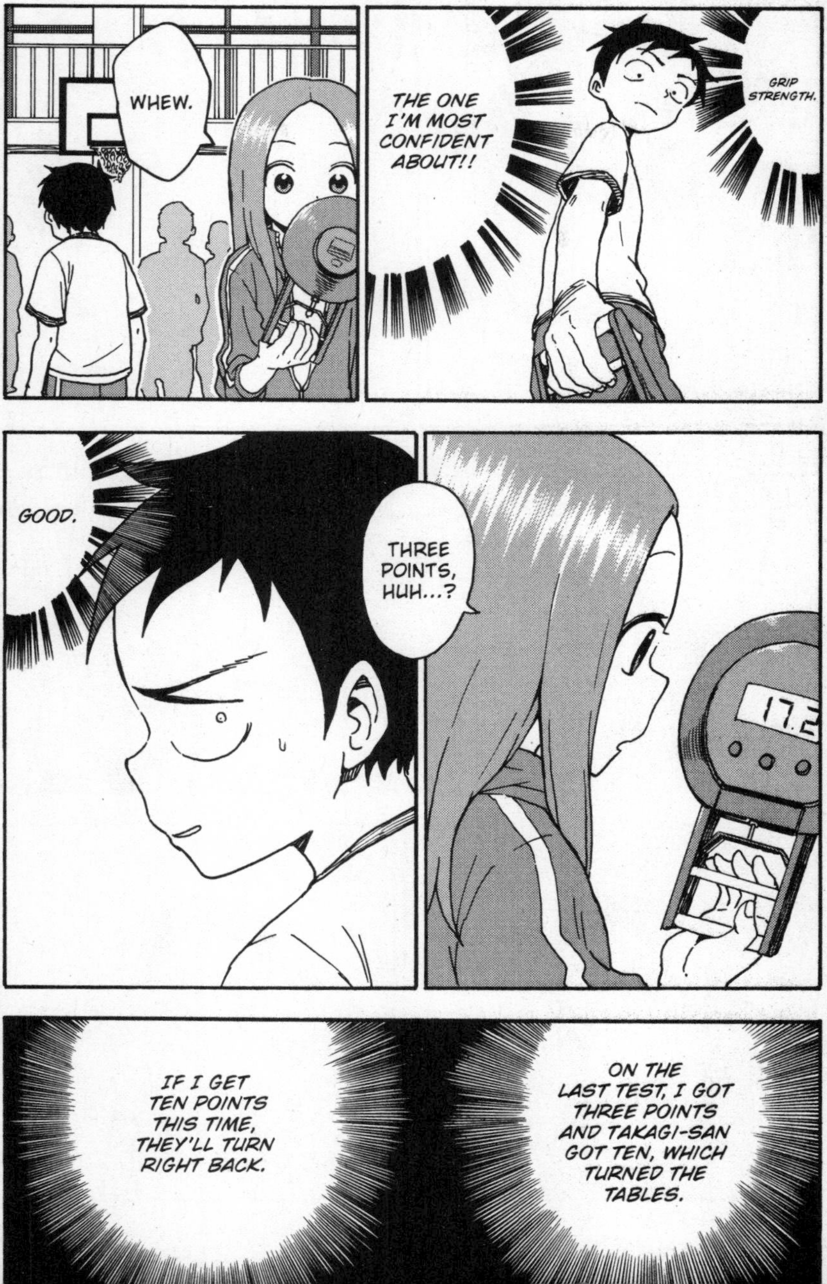
GRIP STRENGTH.
THE ONE I'M MOST CONFIDENT ABOUT!!
WHEW.
THREE POINTS, HUH...?
GOOD.
ON THE LAST TEST, I GOT THREE POINTS AND TAKAGI-SAN GOT TEN, WHICH TURNED THE TABLES.
IF I GET TEN POINTS THIS TIME, THEY'LL TURN RIGHT BACK.

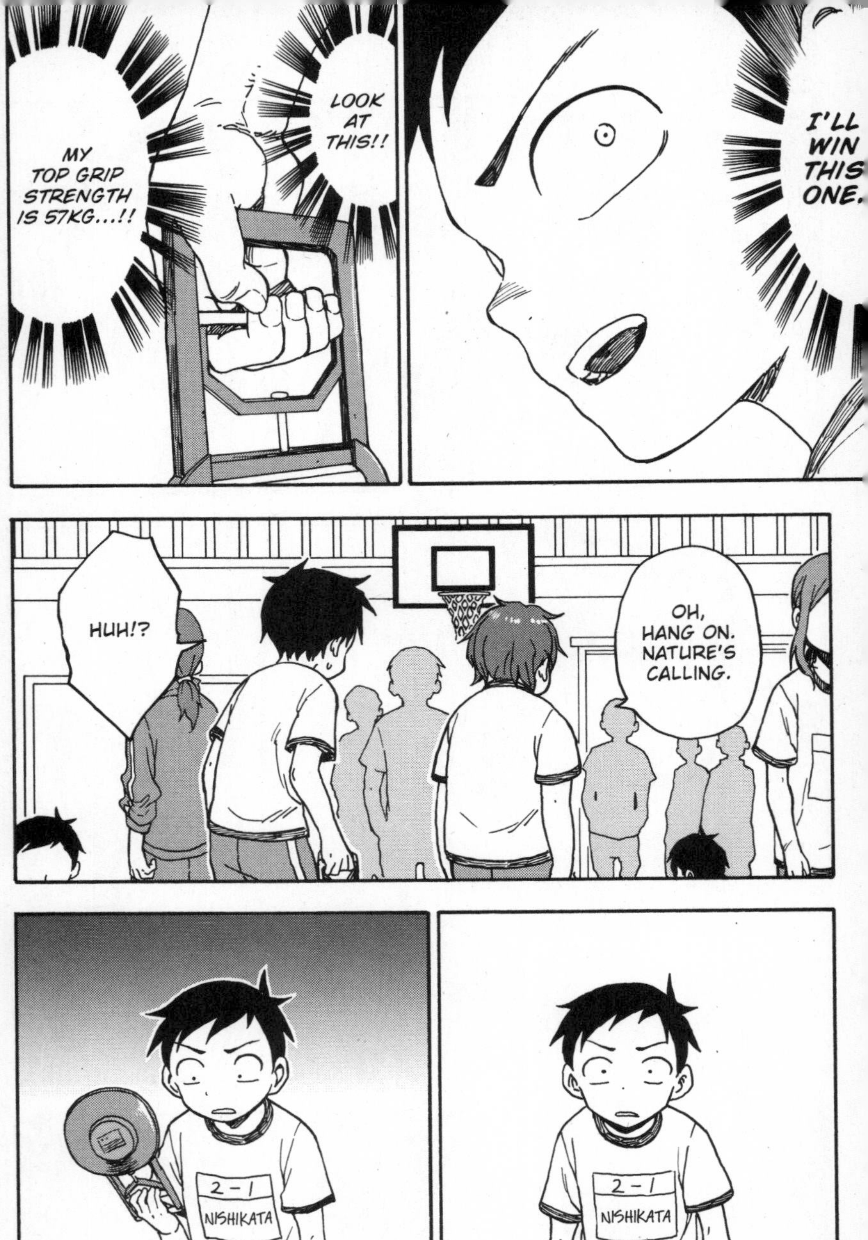
I'LL WIN THIS ONE.
LOOK AT THIS!!
MY TOP GRIP STRENGTH IS 57KG...!!
OH, HANG ON. NATURE'S CALLING.
HUH!?
2-1
NISHIKATA
2-1
NISHIKATA

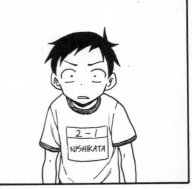

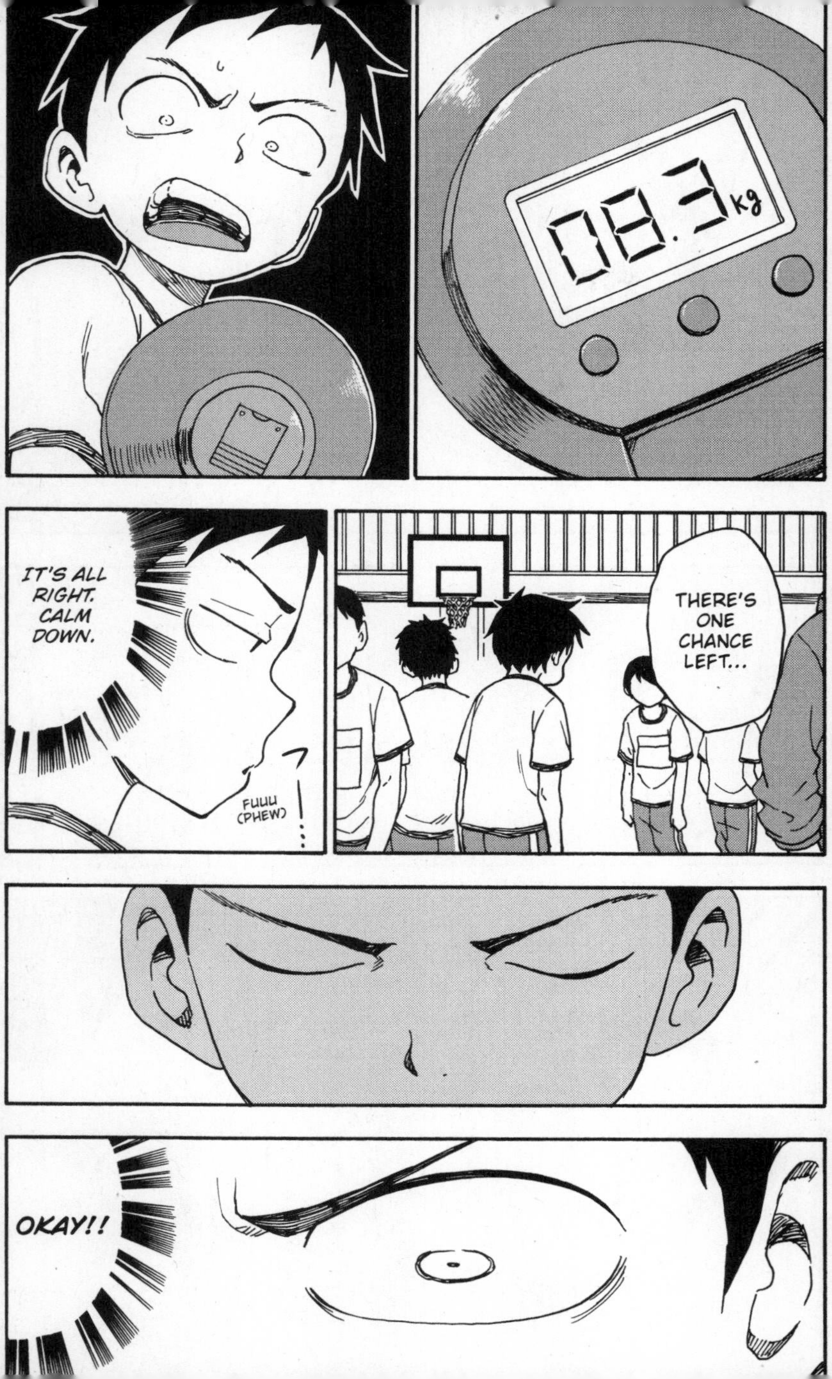
08.3 kg
THERE'S ONE CHANCE LEFT...
IT'S ALL RIGHT. CALM DOWN.
FUUU (PHEW)
OKAY!!

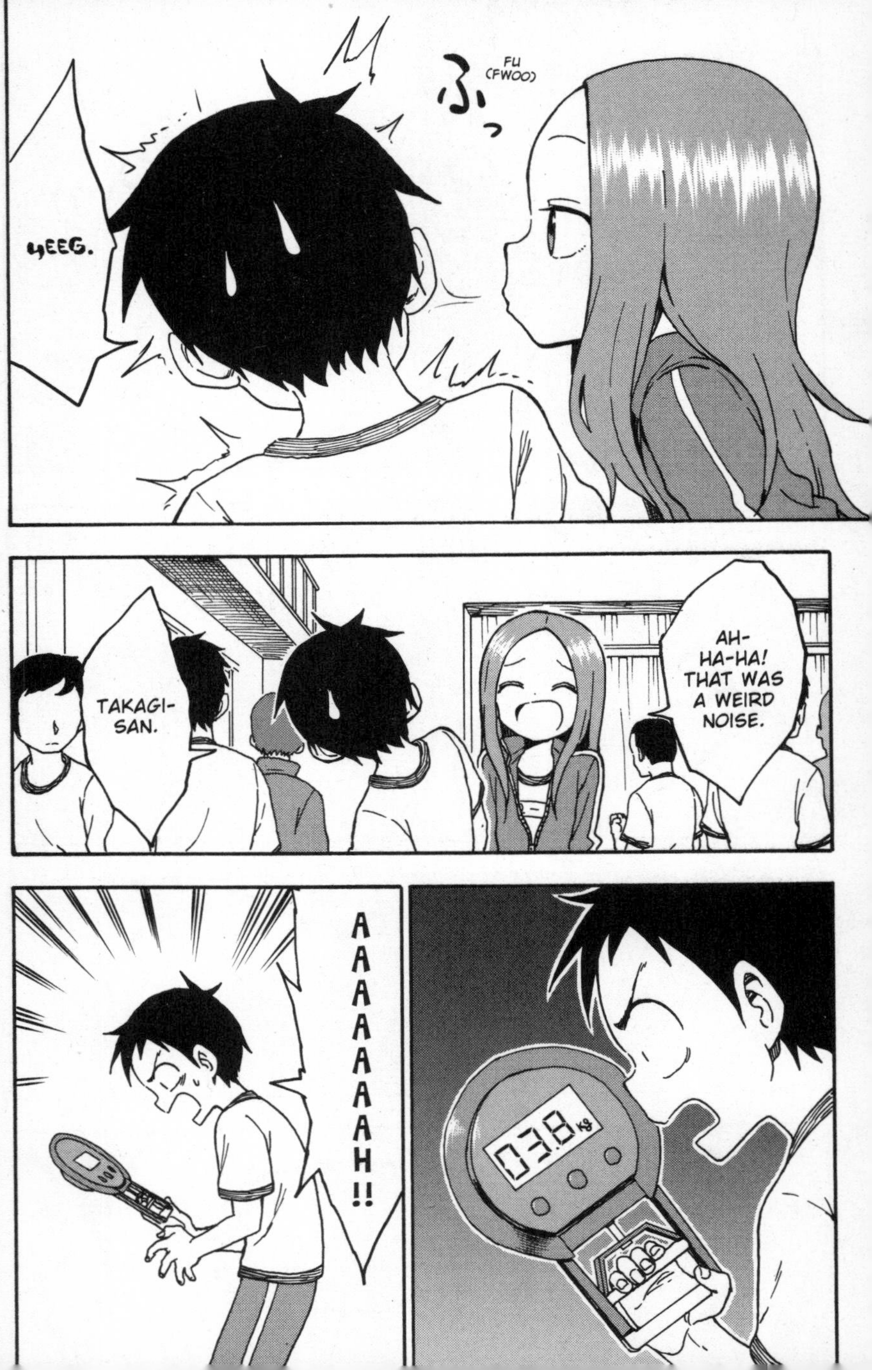
ふっ
FU (FWOO)
YEEG.
AH-HA-HA! THAT WAS A WEIRD NOISE.
TAKAGI-SAN.
03.8 kg
AAAAAAAAAAAH!!

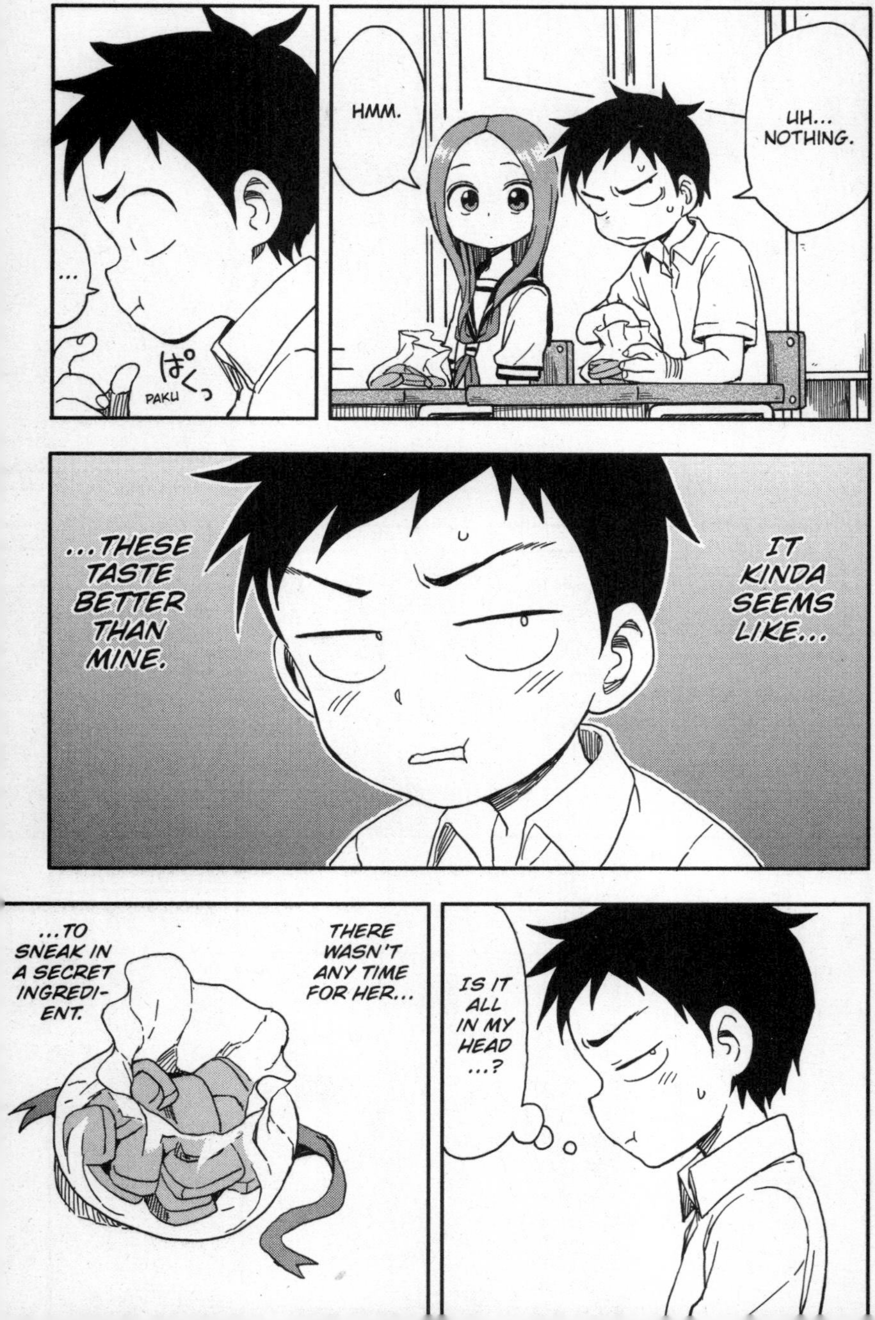
UH... NOTHING.
HMM.
...
ぱくっ
PAKU
IT KINDA SEEMS LIKE...
...THESE TASTE BETTER THAN MINE.
IS IT ALL IN MY HEAD ...?
THERE WASN'T ANY TIME FOR HER...
...TO SNEAK IN A SECRET INGREDI-ENT.

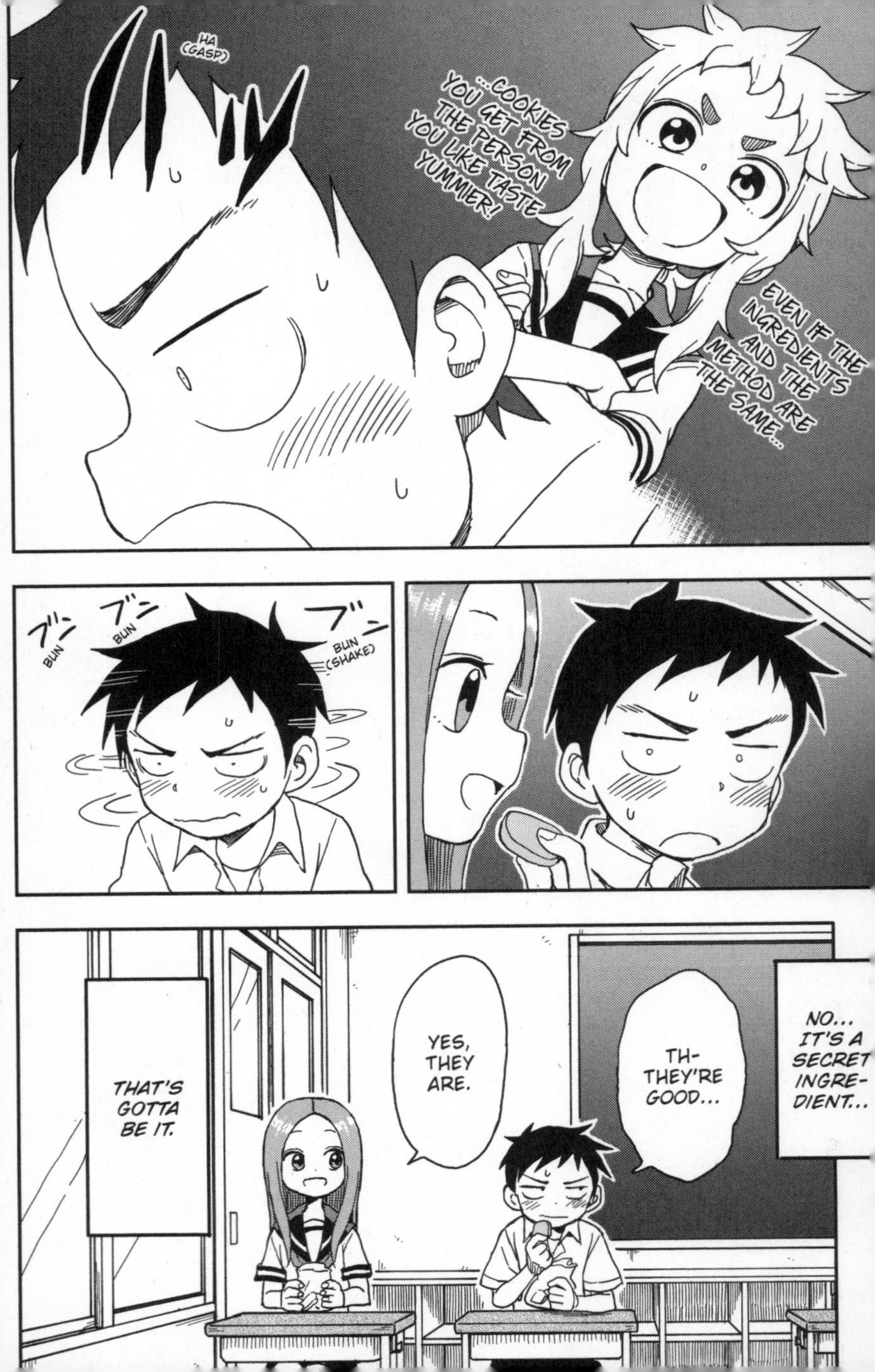
EVEN IF THE INGREDIENTS AND THE METHOD ARE THE SAME...
...COOKIES YOU GET FROM THE PERSON YOU LIKE TASTE YUMMIER!
HA (GASP)
ブン BUN (SHAKE)
ブン BUN
ブン BUN
NO... IT'S A SECRET INGREDIENT...
TH- THEY'RE GOOD...
YES, THEY ARE.
THAT'S GOTTA BE IT.

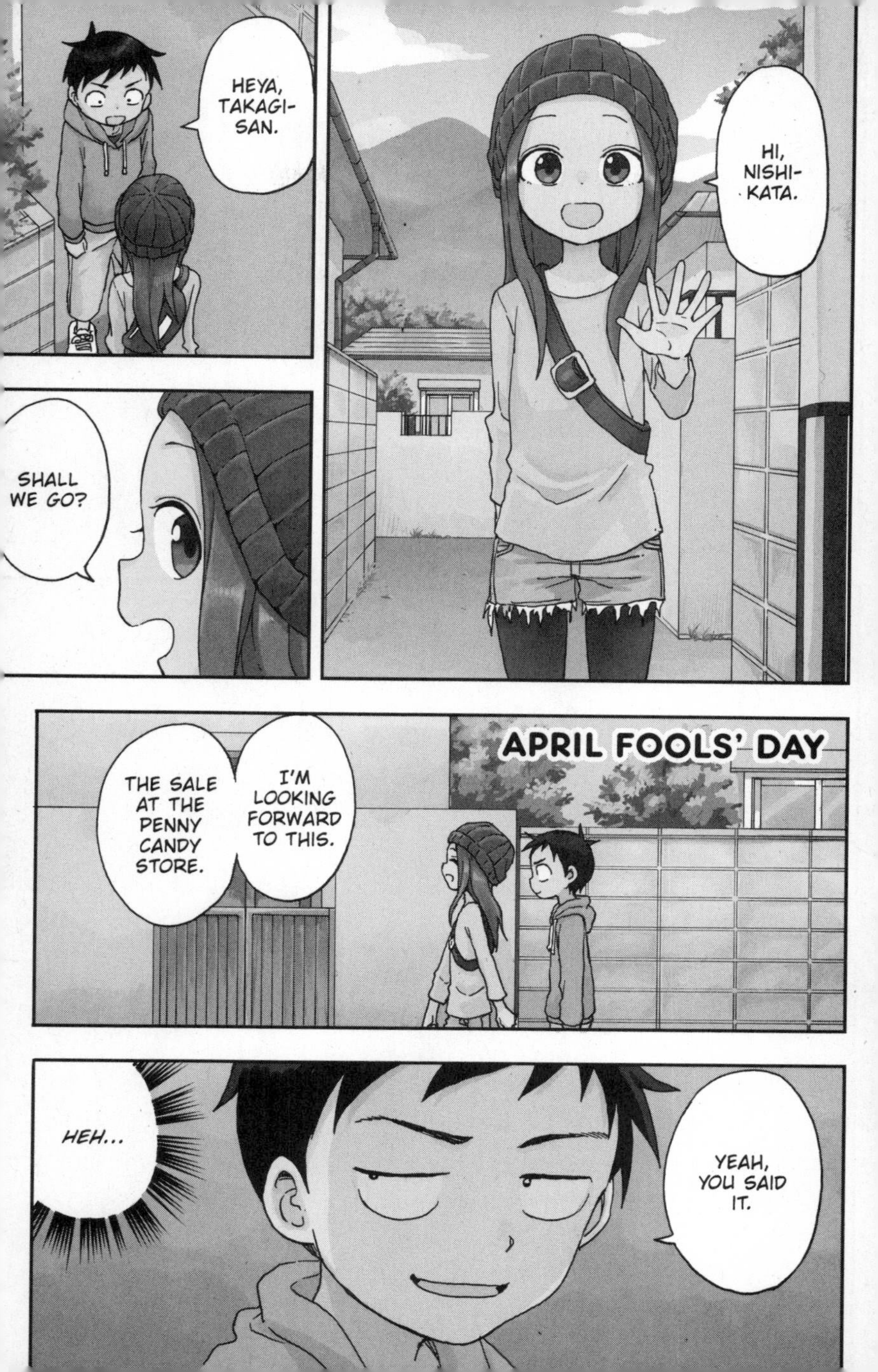
HI, NISHI-KATA.
HEYA, TAKAGI-SAN.
SHALL WE GO?
APRIL FOOLS' DAY
I'M LOOKING FORWARD TO THIS.
THE SALE AT THE PENNY CANDY STORE.
YEAH, YOU SAID IT.
HEH...

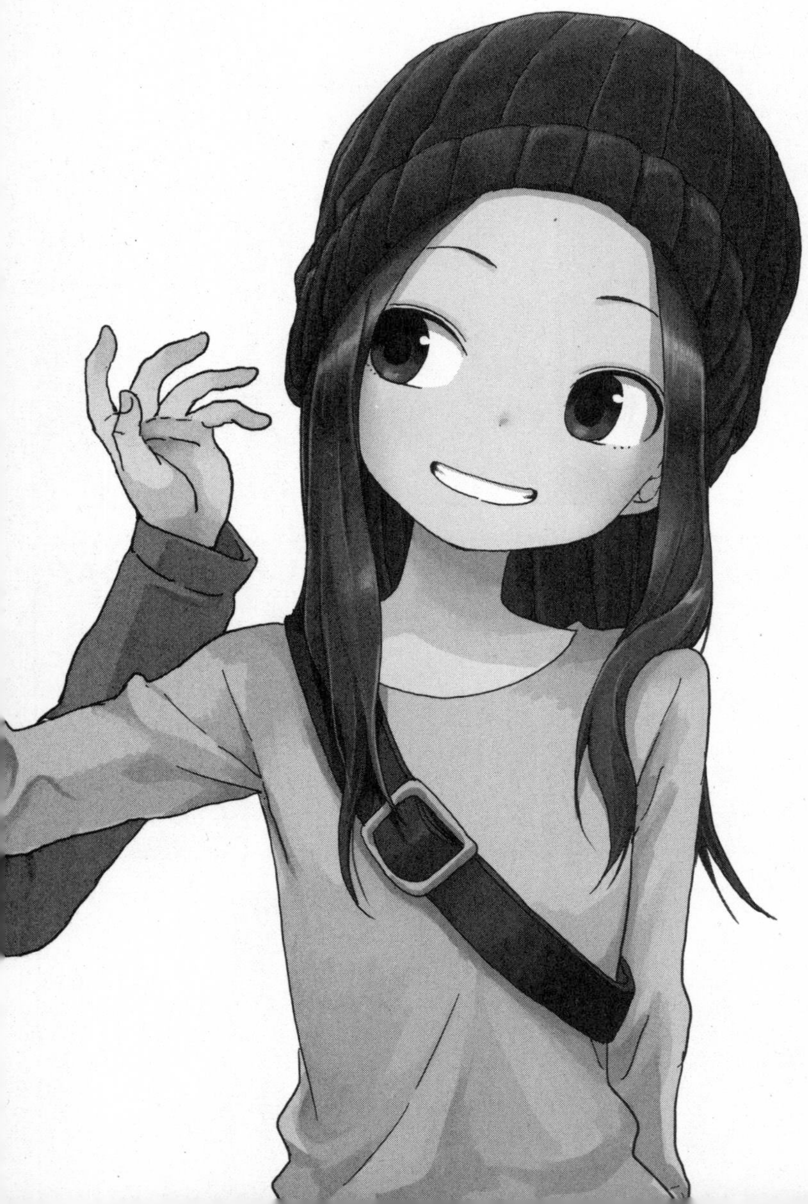

APRIL FOOLS' DAY

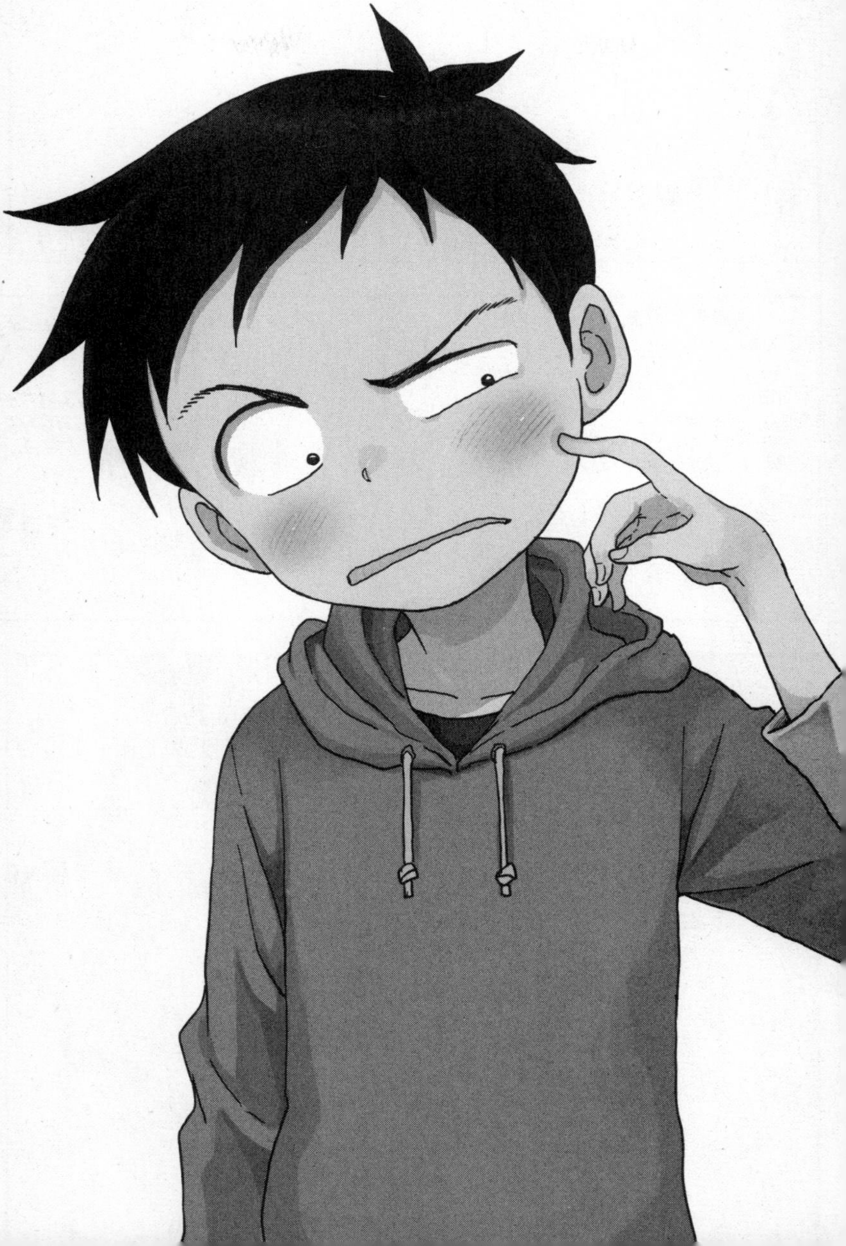

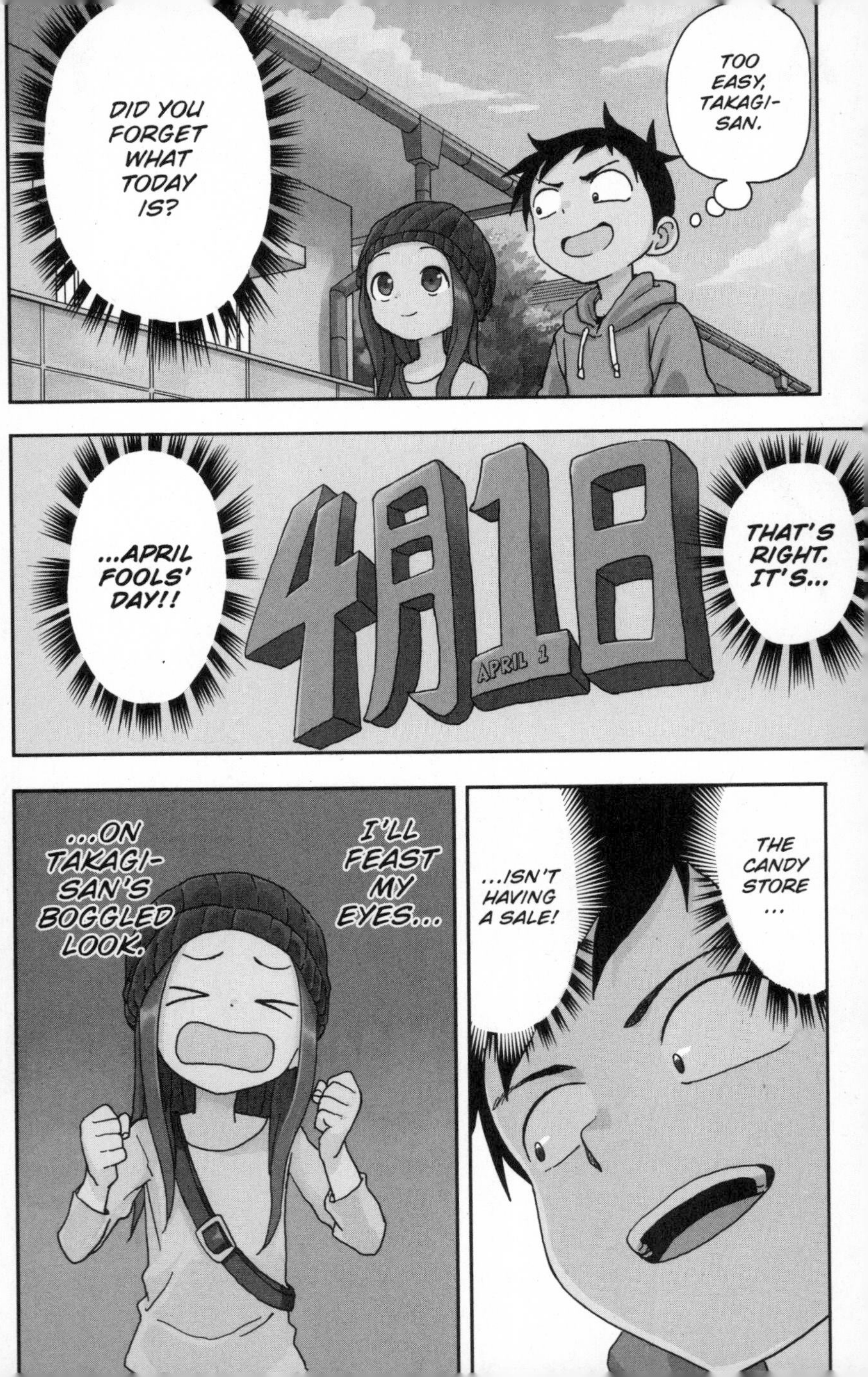
TOO EASY, TAKAGI-SAN.
DID YOU FORGET WHAT TODAY IS?
THAT'S RIGHT. IT'S...
4月1日
APRIL 1
...APRIL FOOLS' DAY!!
THE CANDY STORE...
...ISN'T HAVING A SALE!
I'LL FEAST MY EYES...
...ON TAKAGI-SAN'S BOGGLED LOOK.

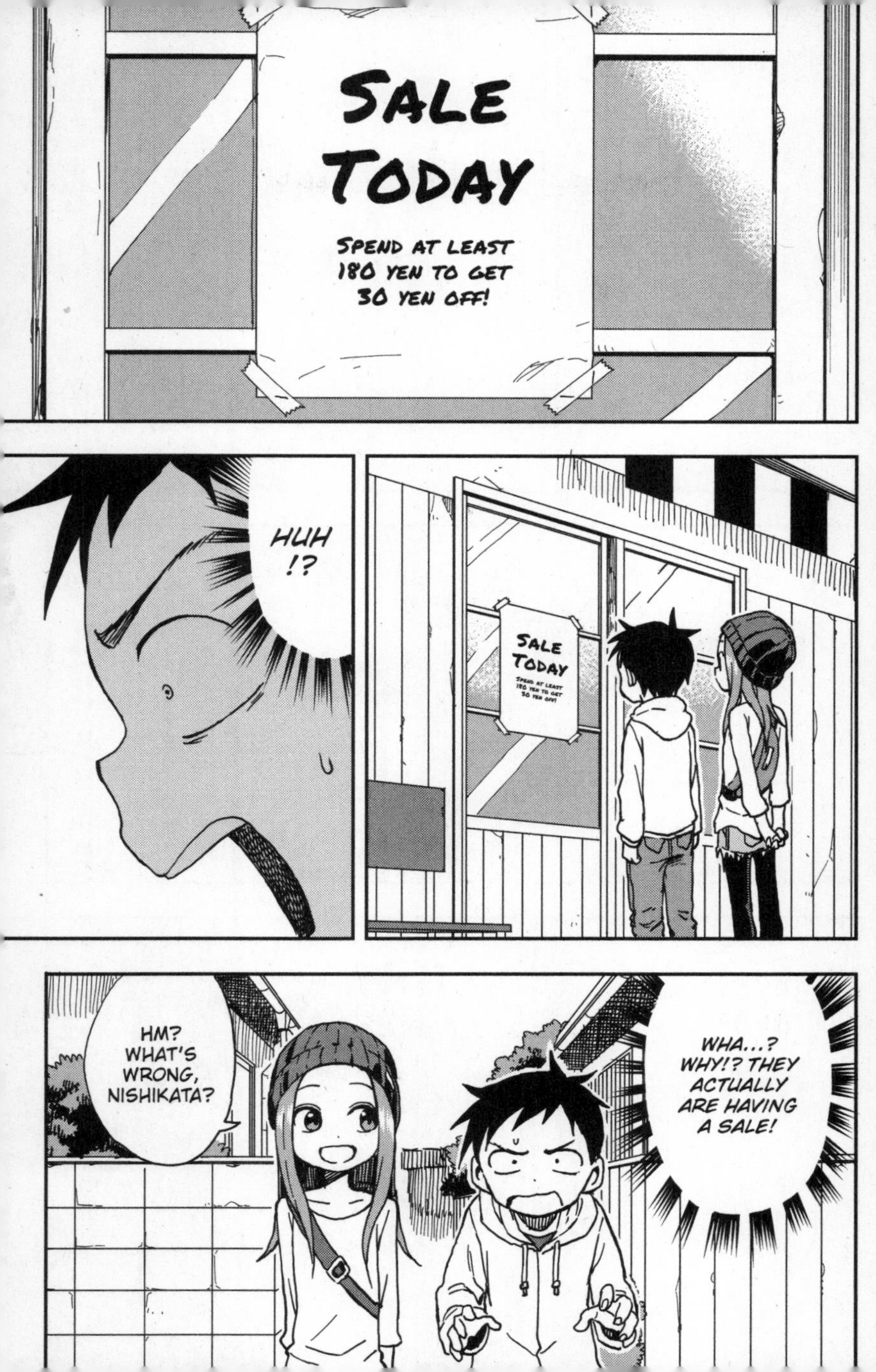
SALE
TODAY
SPEND AT LEAST
180 YEN TO GET
30 YEN OFF!
SALE
TODAY
SPEND AT LEAST
180 YEN TO GET
30 YEN OFF!
HUH
!?
WHA...? WHY!? THEY ACTUALLY ARE HAVING A SALE!
HM? WHAT'S WRONG, NISHIKATA?

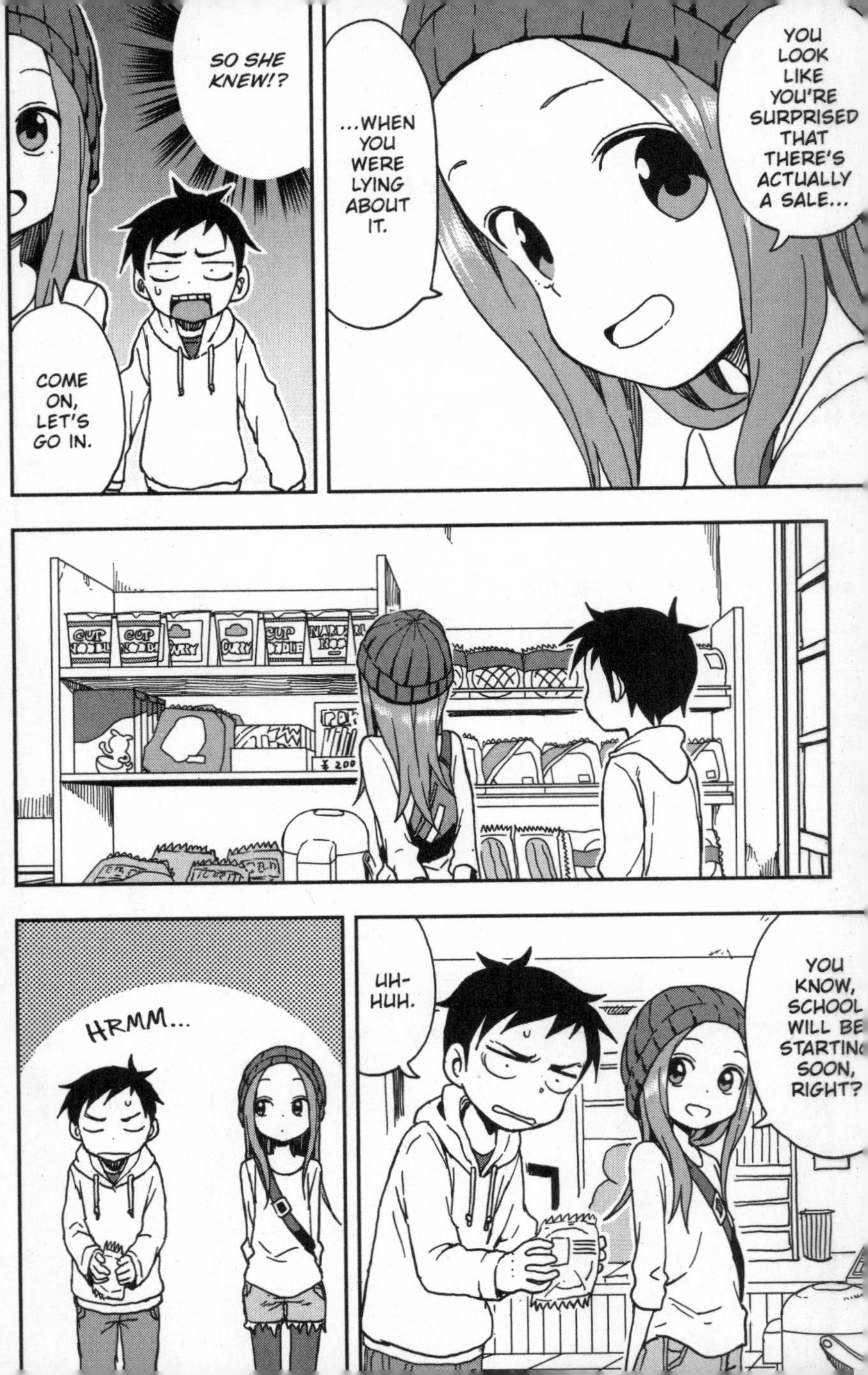
YOU LOOK LIKE YOU'RE SURPRISED THAT THERE'S ACTUALLY A SALE...
...WHEN YOU WERE LYING ABOUT IT.
SO SHE KNEW!?
COME ON, LET'S GO IN.
YOU KNOW, SCHOOL WILL BE STARTING SOON, RIGHT?
UH-HUH.
HRMM...

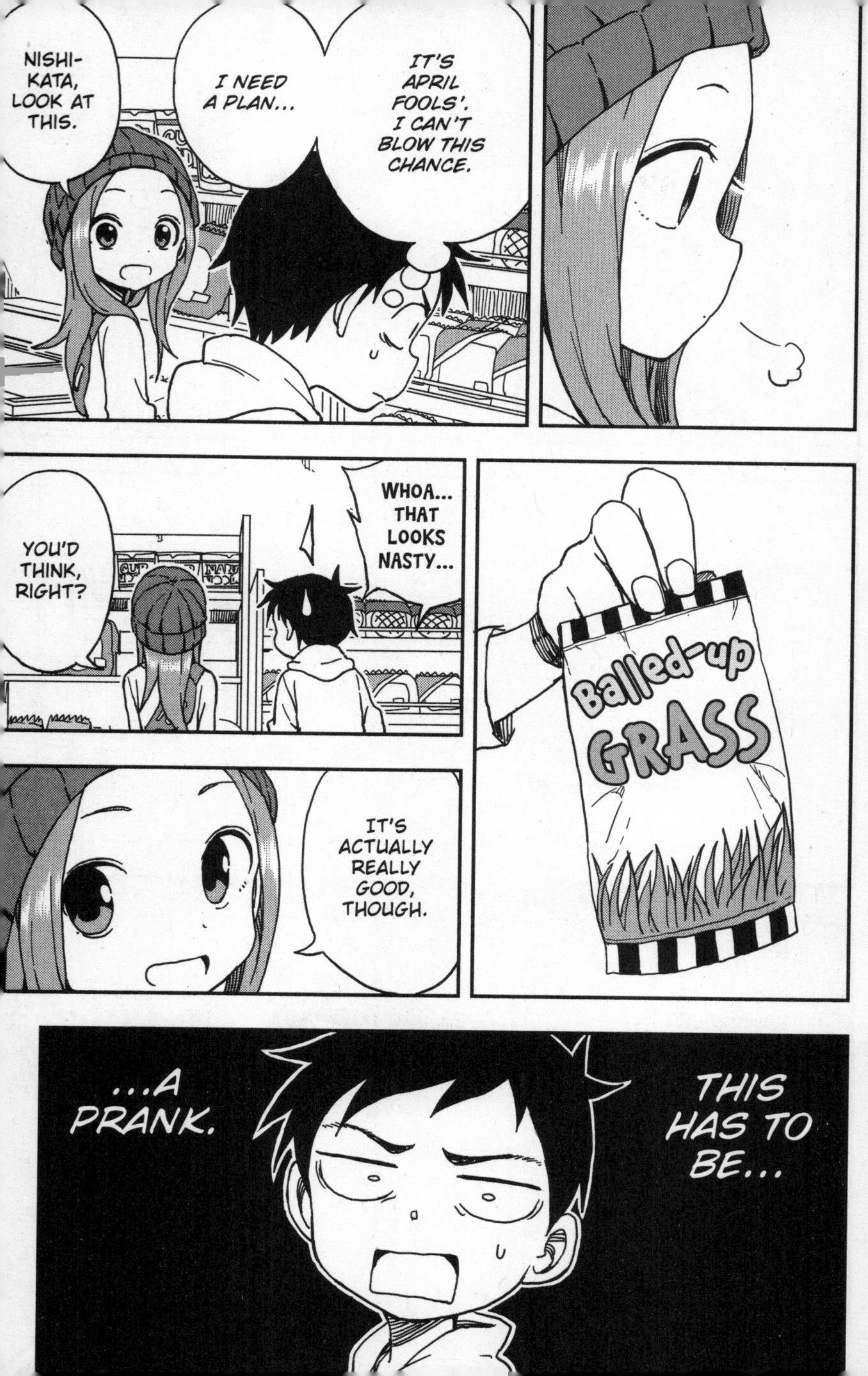
IT'S APRIL FOOLS'. I CAN'T BLOW THIS CHANCE.
I NEED A PLAN...
NISHI-KATA, LOOK AT THIS.
Balled-up GRASS
WHOA... THAT LOOKS NASTY...
YOU'D THINK, RIGHT?
IT'S ACTUALLY REALLY GOOD, THOUGH.
THIS HAS TO BE...
...A PRANK.

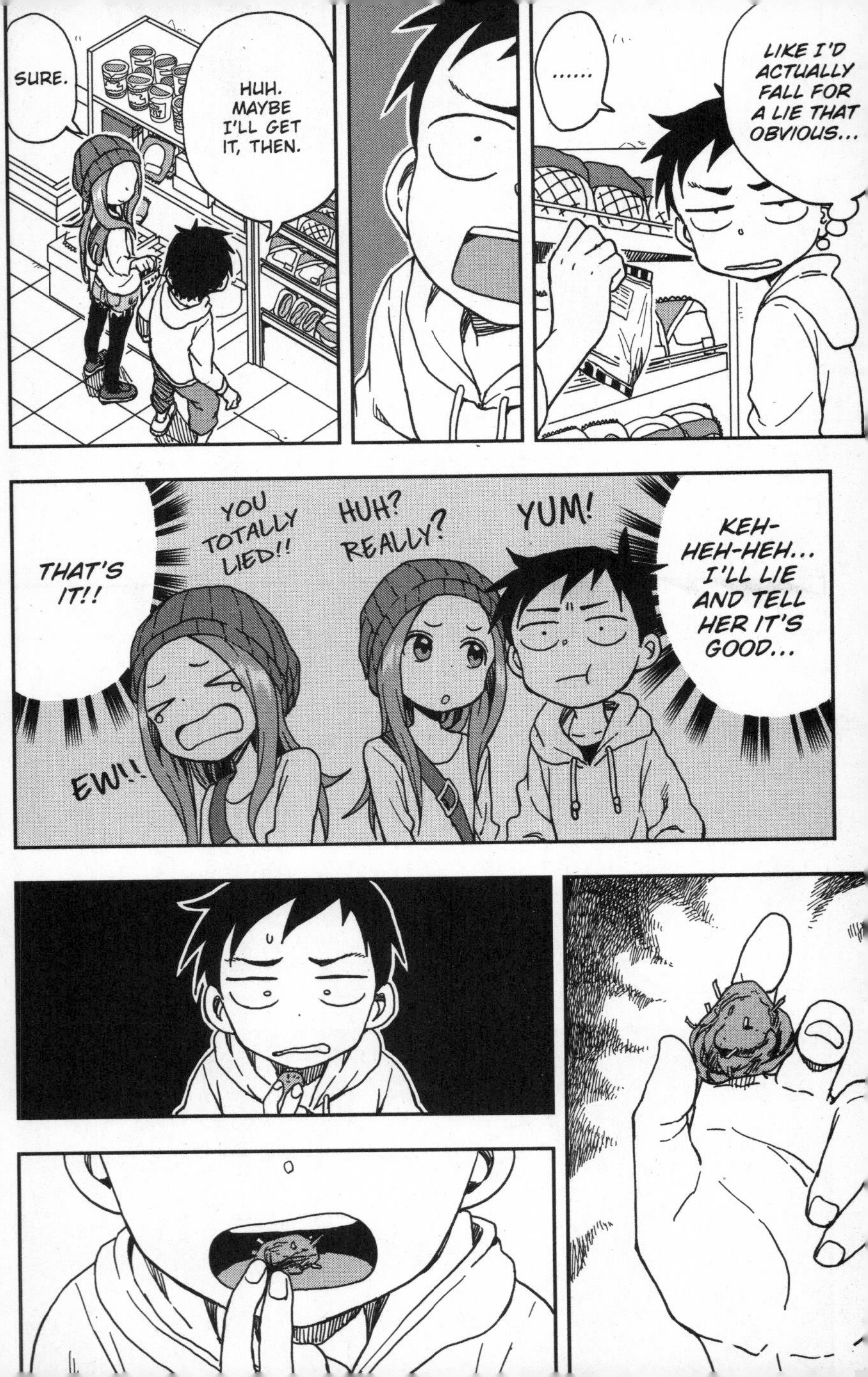
LIKE I'D ACTUALLY FALL FOR A LIE THAT OBVIOUS...
......
HUH. MAYBE I'LL GET IT, THEN.
SURE.
KEH-HEH-HEH... I'LL LIE AND TELL HER IT'S GOOD...
YUM!
HUH? REALLY?
YOU TOTALLY LIED!!
THAT'S IT!!
EW!!

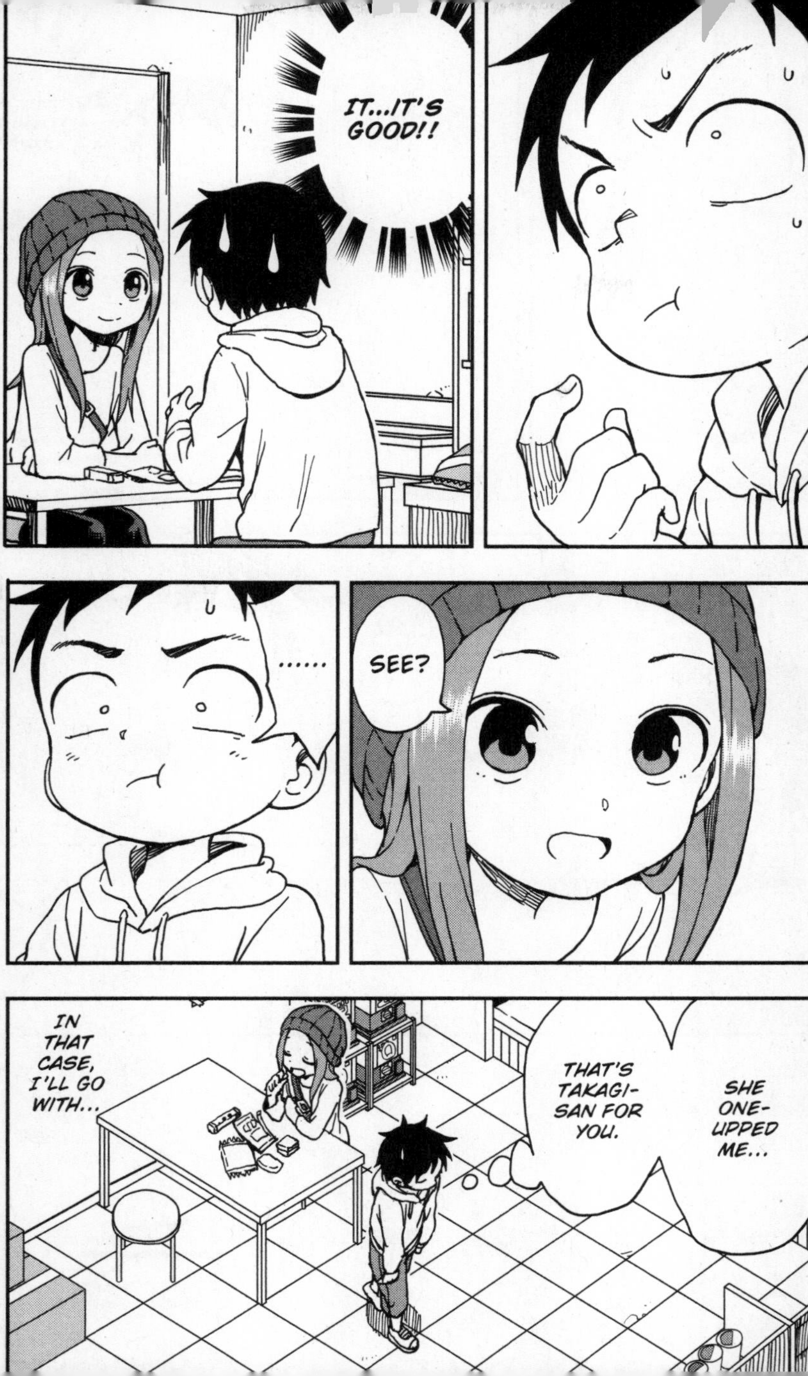
IT...IT'S GOOD!!
SEE?
......
SHE ONE-UPPED ME...
THAT'S TAKAGI-SAN FOR YOU.
IN THAT CASE, I'LL GO WITH...

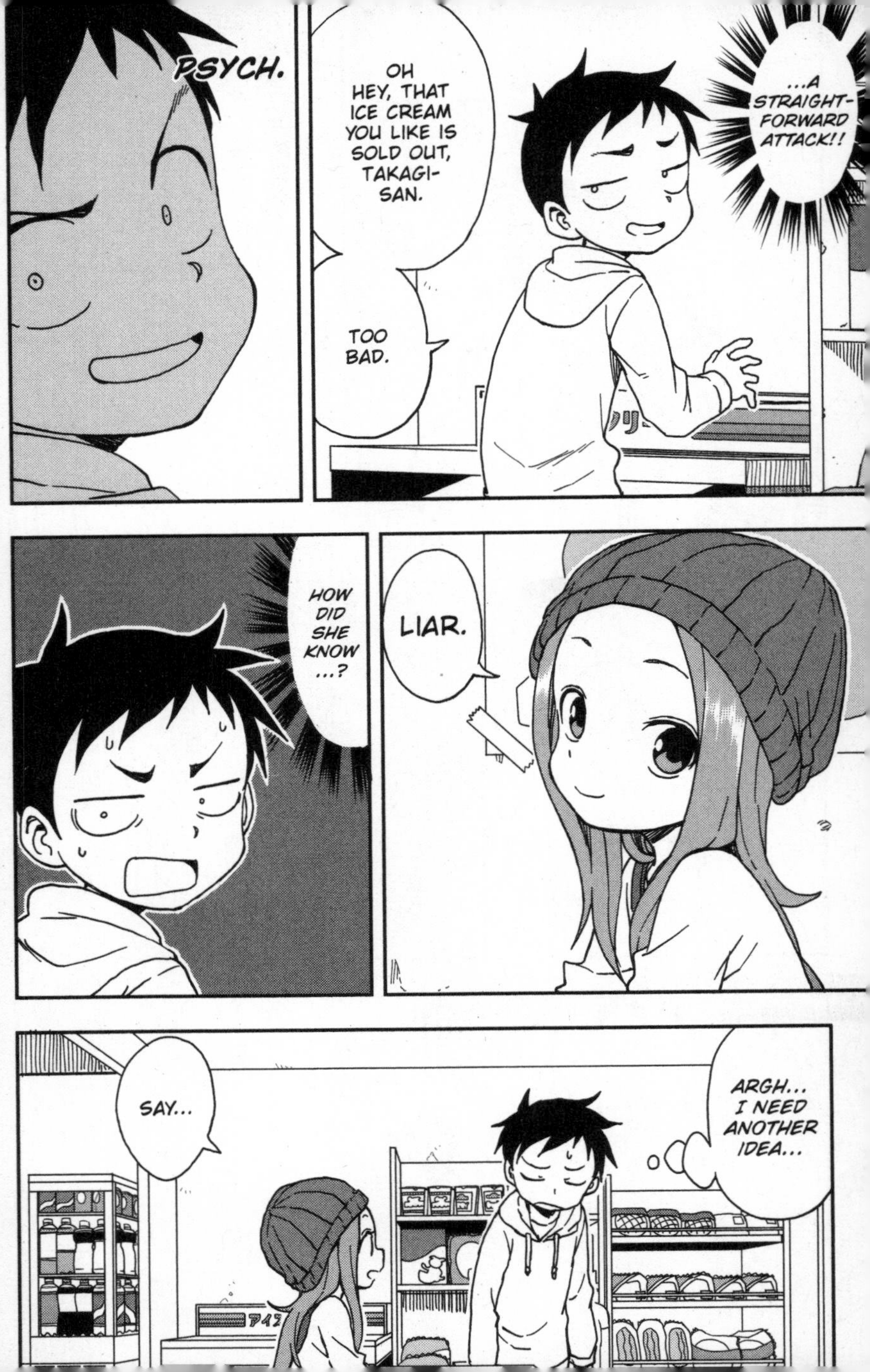
...A STRAIGHT-FORWARD ATTACK!!
OH HEY, THAT ICE CREAM YOU LIKE IS SOLD OUT, TAKAGI-SAN.
TOO BAD.
PSYCH.
LIAR.
HOW DID SHE KNOW...?
ARGH... I NEED ANOTHER IDEA...
SAY...

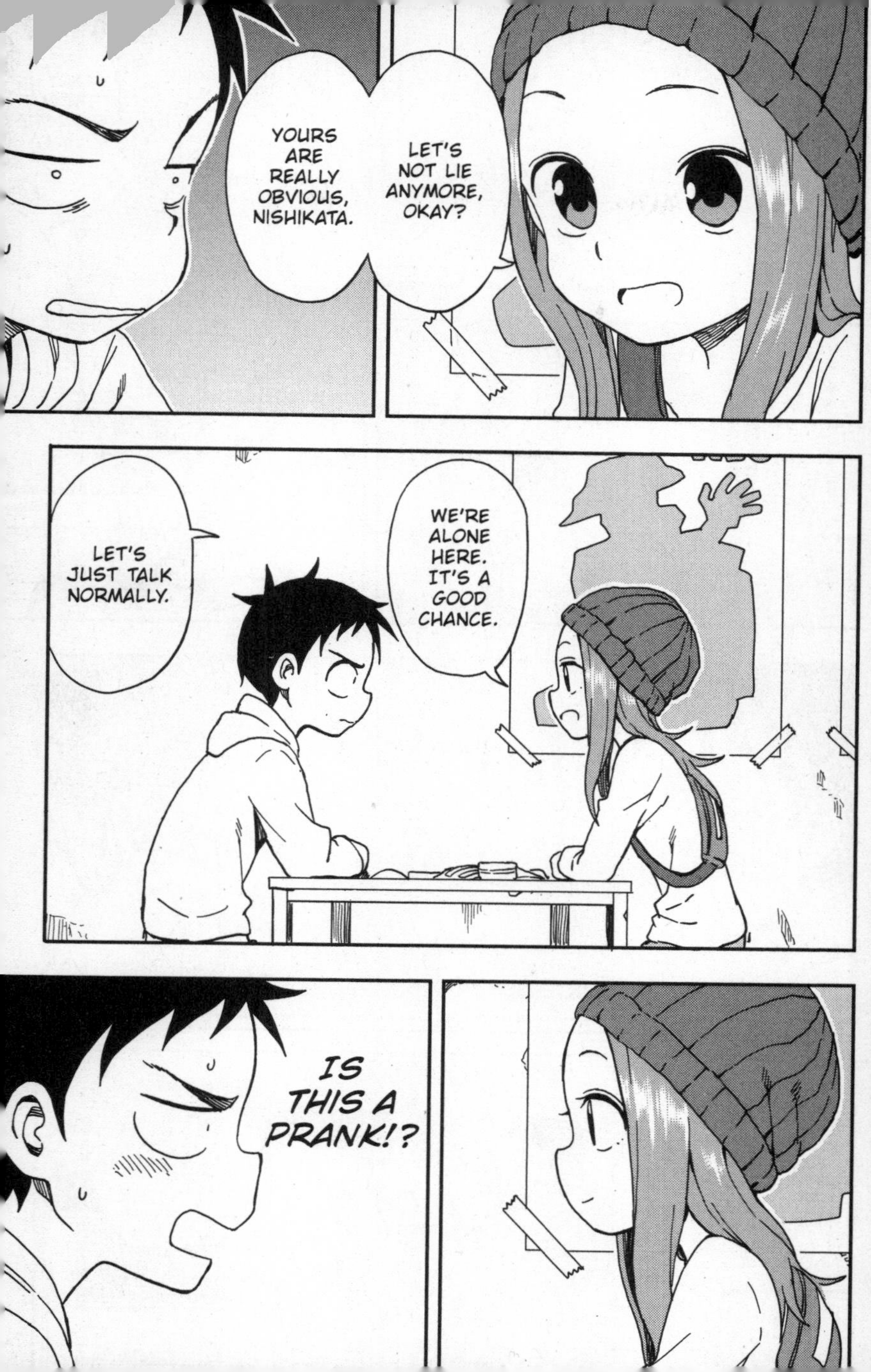
LET'S NOT LIE ANYMORE, OKAY?
YOURS ARE REALLY OBVIOUS, NISHIKATA.
WE'RE ALONE HERE. IT'S A GOOD CHANCE.
LET'S JUST TALK NORMALLY.
IS THIS A PRANK!?

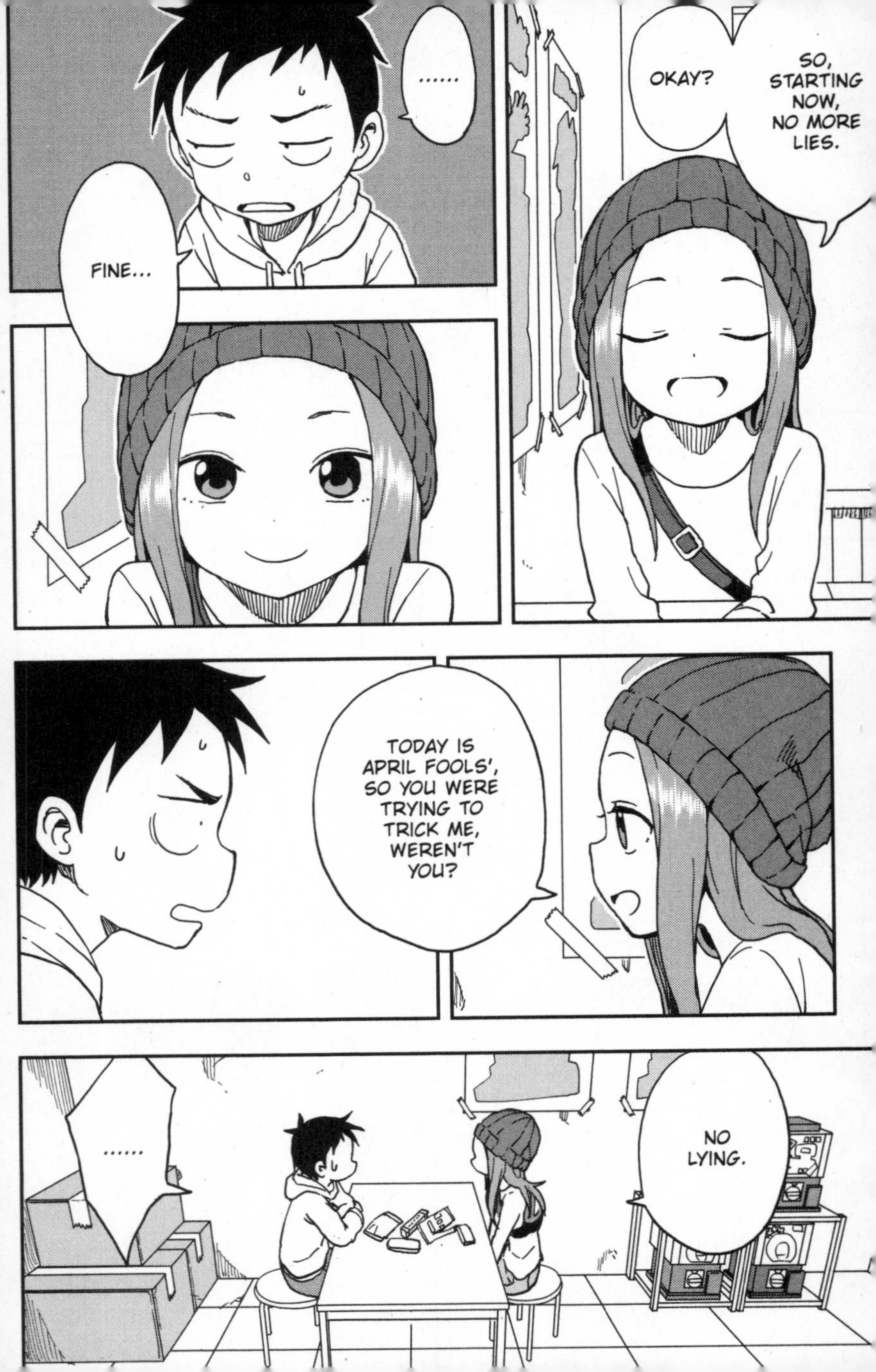
SO, STARTING NOW, NO MORE LIES.
OKAY?
......
FINE...
TODAY IS APRIL FOOLS', SO YOU WERE TRYING TO TRICK ME, WEREN'T YOU?
NO LYING.
......

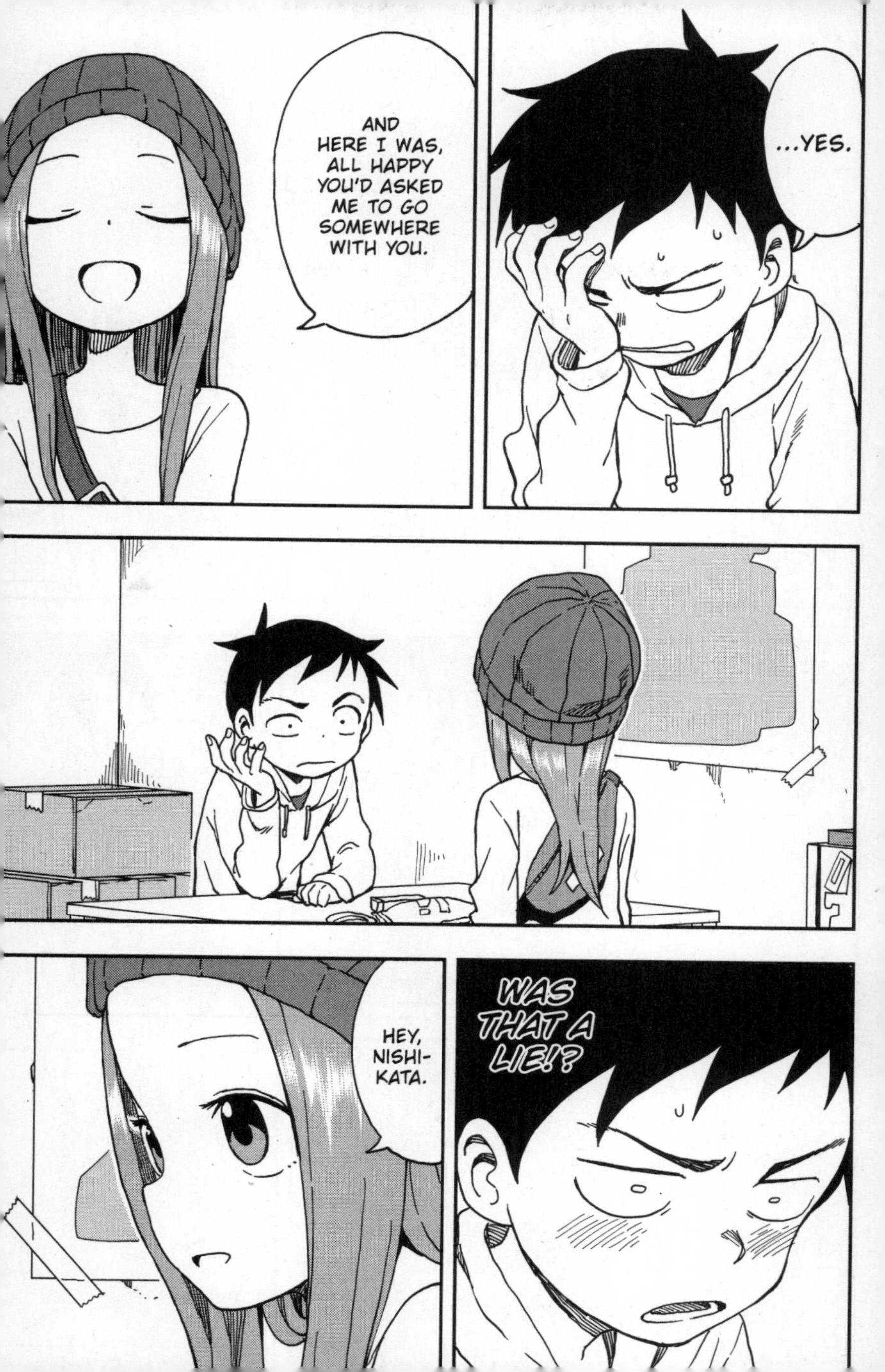
...YES.
AND HERE I WAS, ALL HAPPY YOU'D ASKED ME TO GO SOMEWHERE WITH YOU.
WAS THAT A LIE!?
HEY, NISHI-KATA.

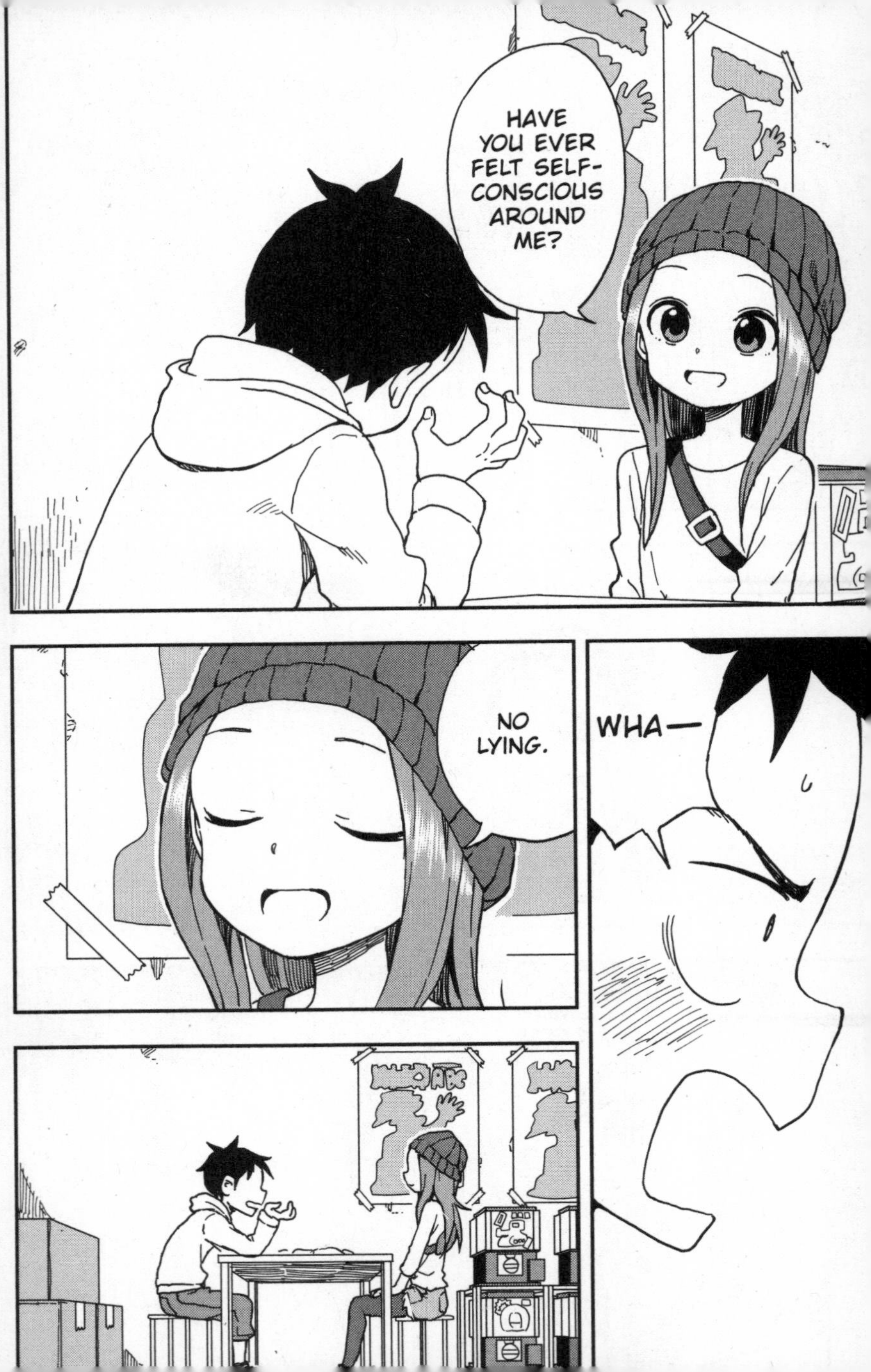
HAVE YOU EVER FELT SELF-CONSCIOUS AROUND ME?
WHA—
NO LYING.

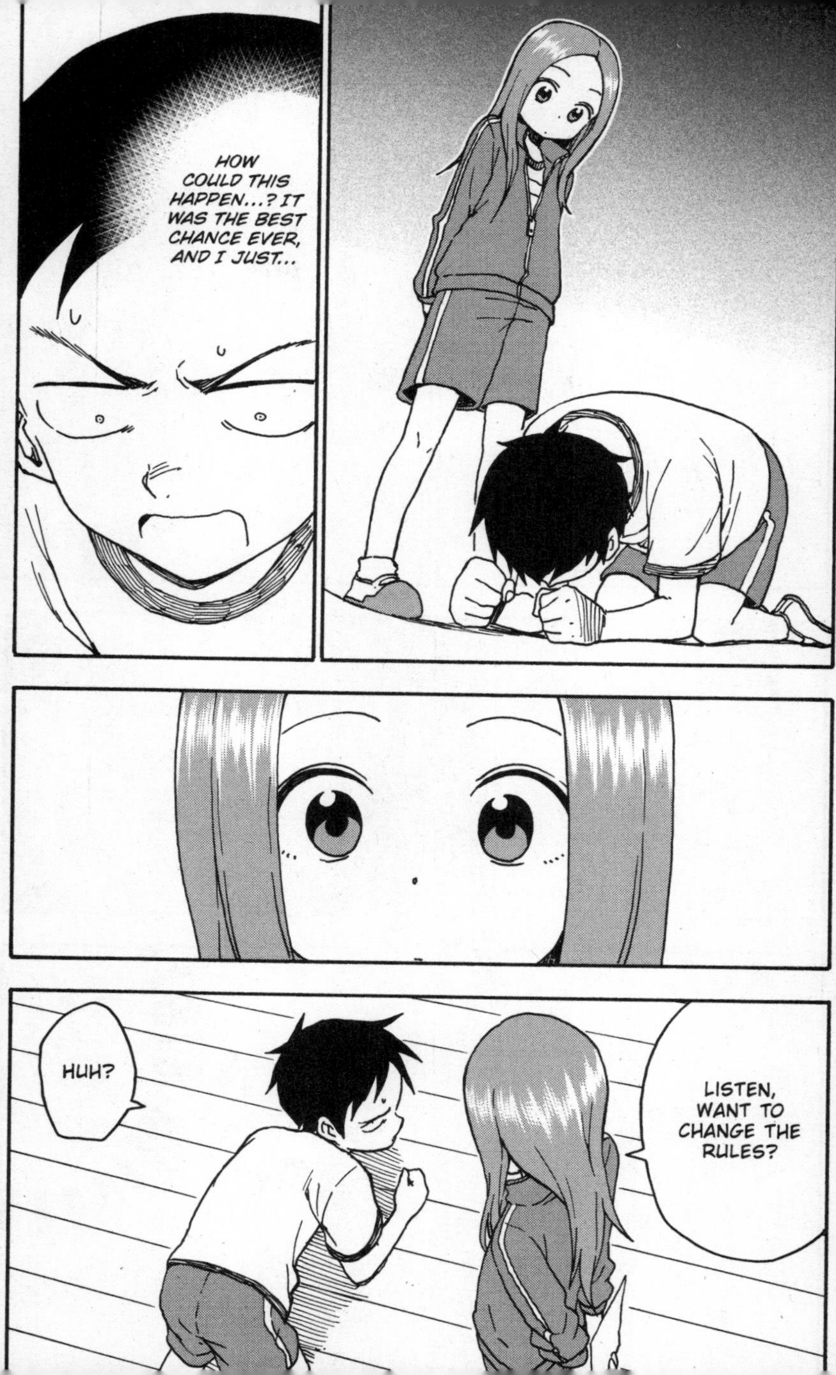
HOW COULD THIS HAPPEN...? IT WAS THE BEST CHANCE EVER, AND I JUST...
LISTEN, WANT TO CHANGE THE RULES?
HUH?

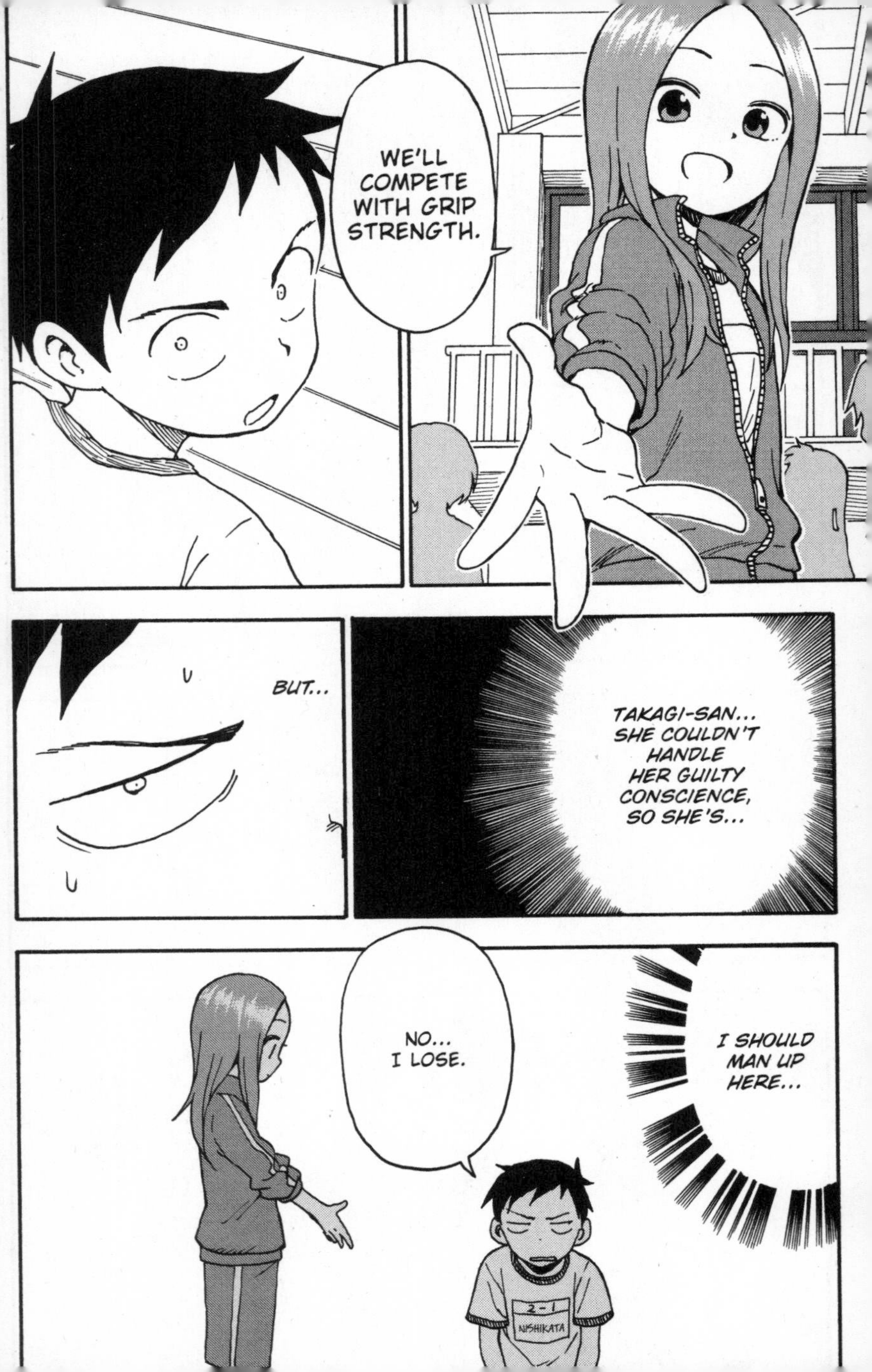
WE'LL COMPETE WITH GRIP STRENGTH.
TAKAGI-SAN... SHE COULDN'T HANDLE HER GUILTY CONSCIENCE, SO SHE'S...
BUT...
I SHOULD MAN UP HERE...
NO... I LOSE.
2-1
NISHIKATA

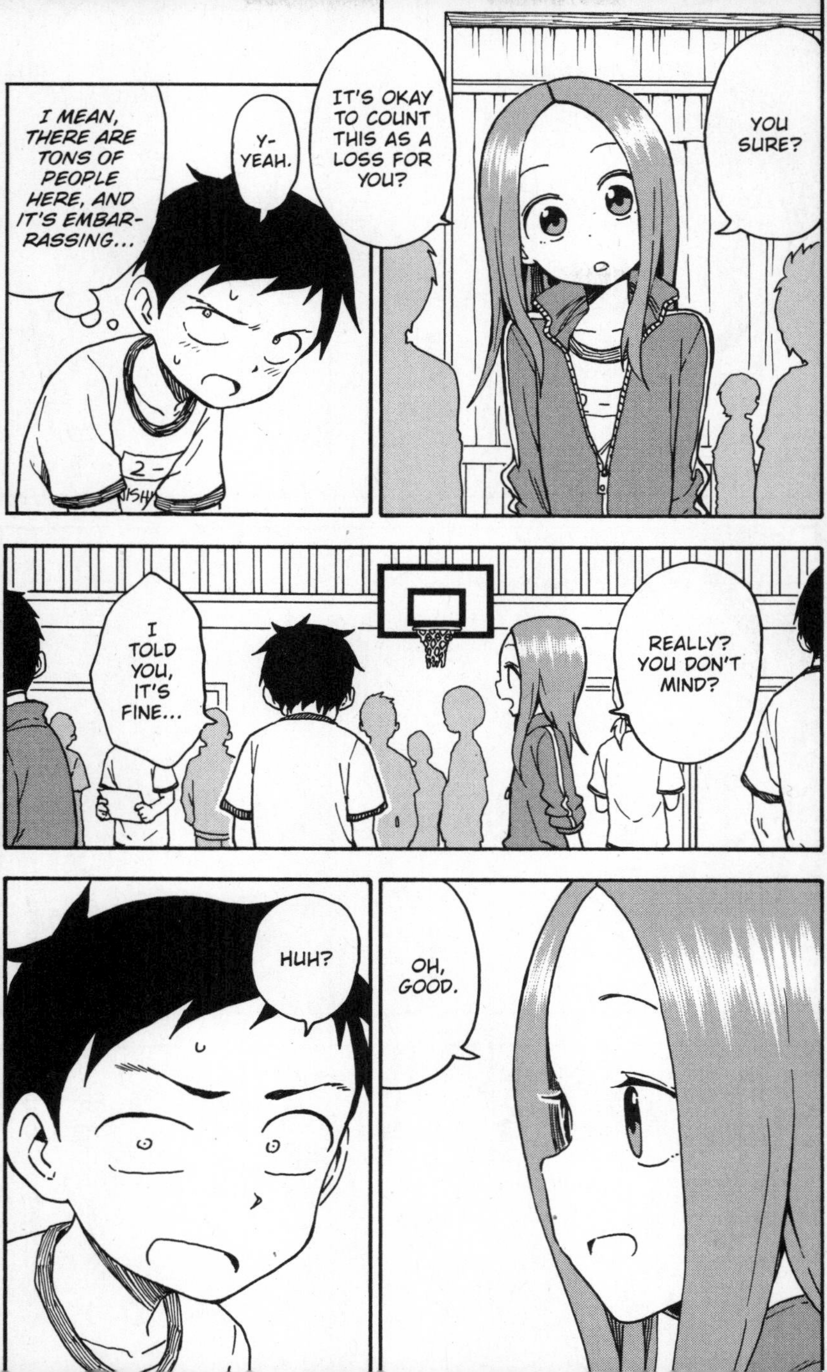
YOU SURE?
IT'S OKAY TO COUNT THIS AS A LOSS FOR YOU?
Y-YEAH.
I MEAN, THERE ARE TONS OF PEOPLE HERE, AND IT'S EMBARRASSING...
REALLY? YOU DON'T MIND?
I TOLD YOU, IT'S FINE...
OH, GOOD.
HUH?

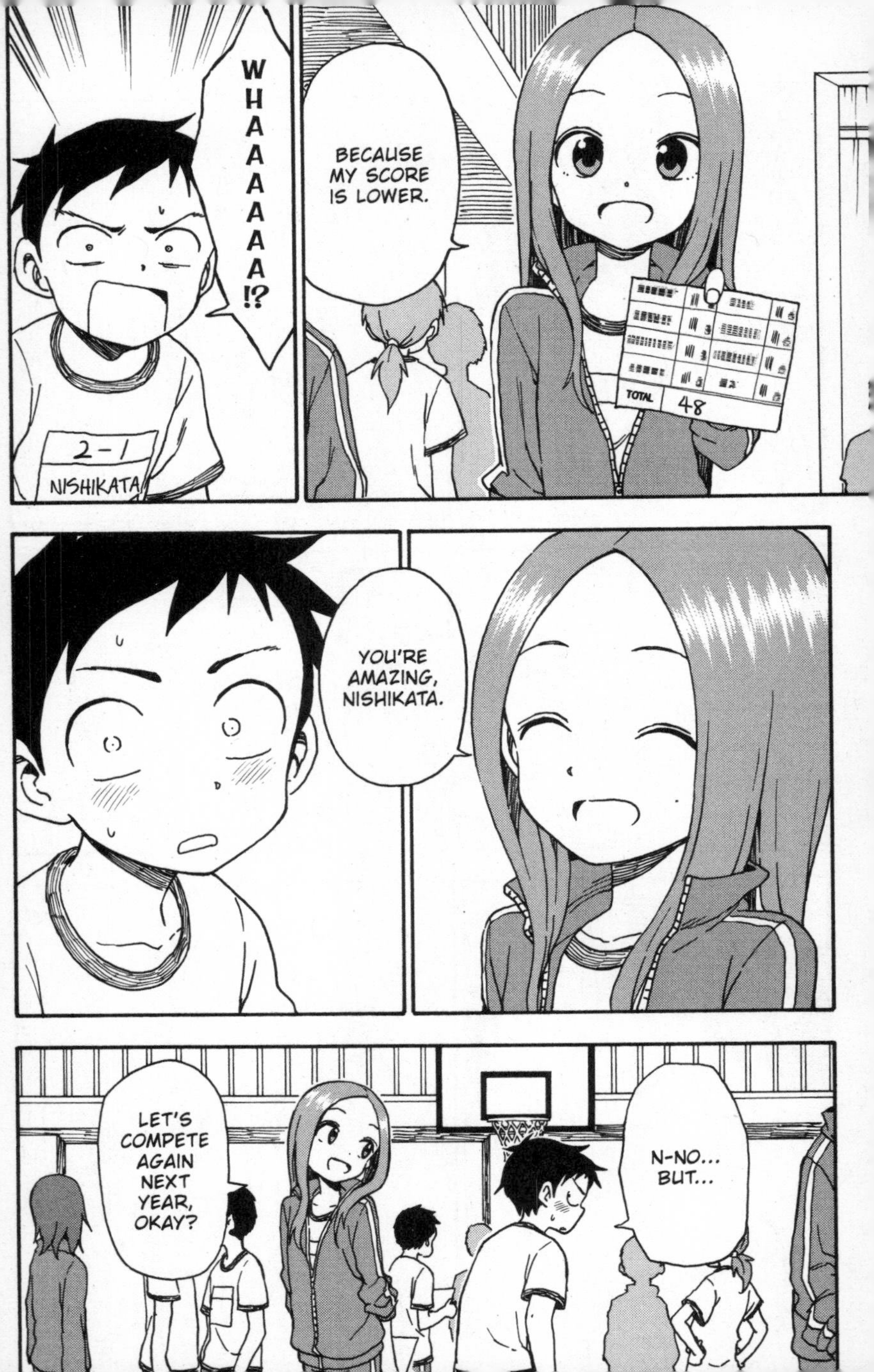
BECAUSE MY SCORE IS LOWER.
TOTAL 48
WHAAAAAA!?
2-1
NISHIKATA
YOU'RE AMAZING, NISHIKATA.
N-NO... BUT...
LET'S COMPETE AGAIN NEXT YEAR, OKAY?

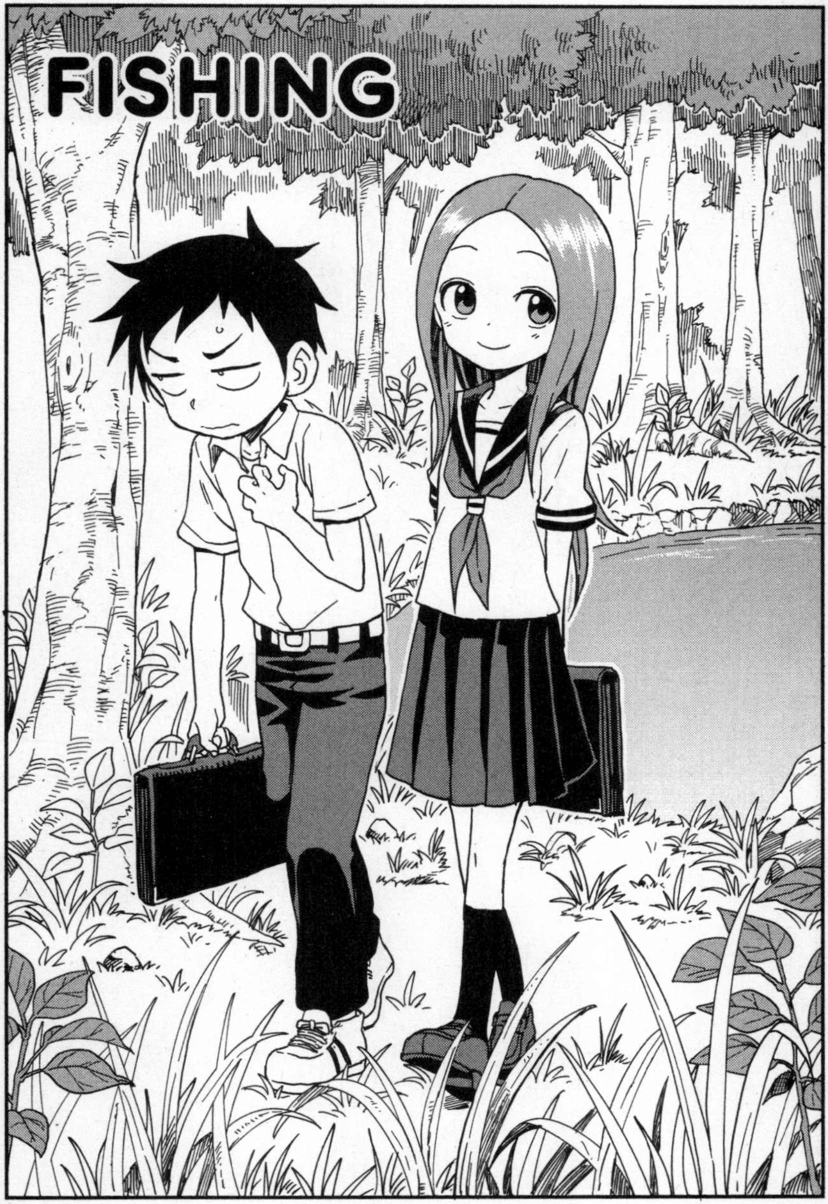
FISHING

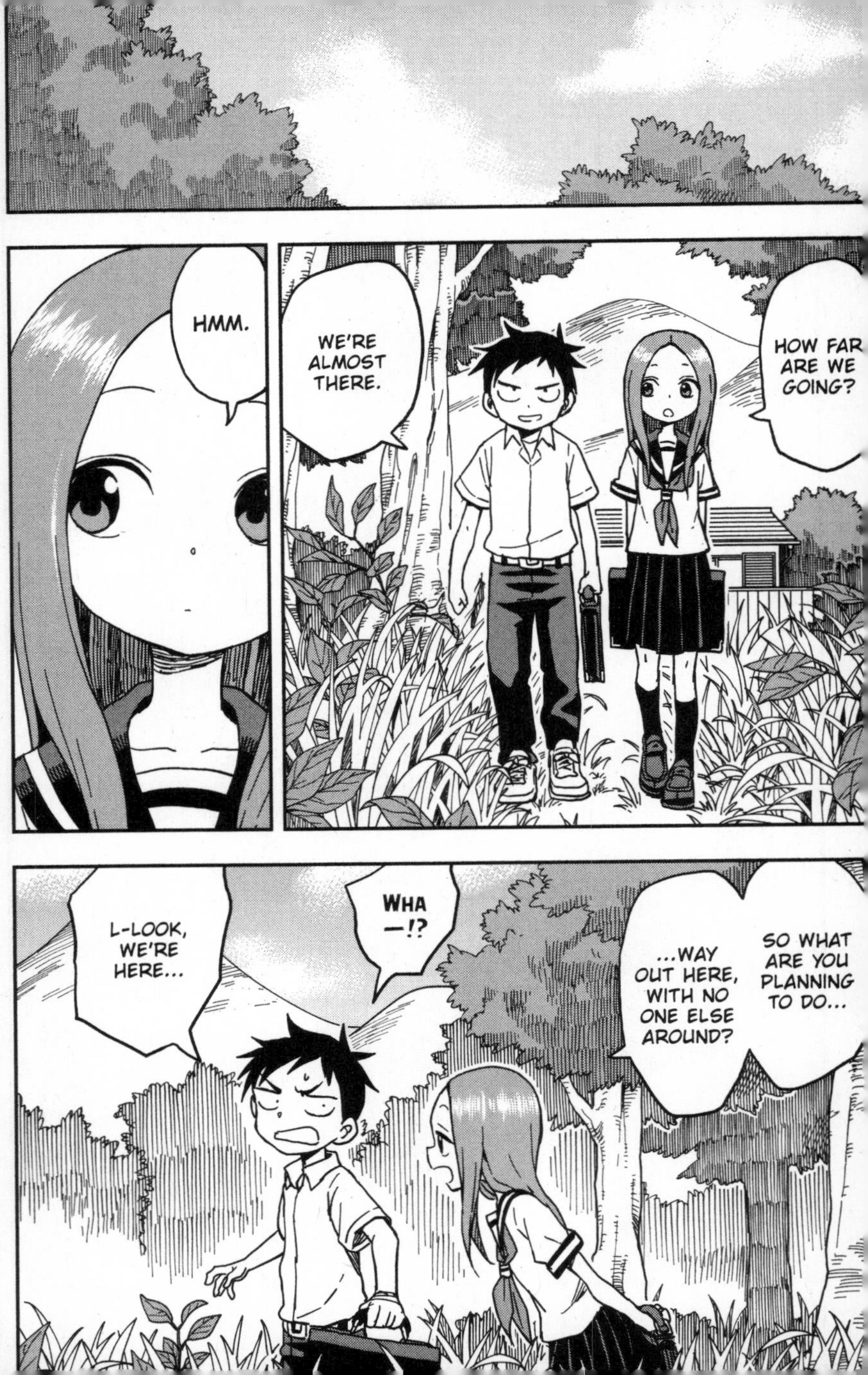
HOW FAR ARE WE GOING?
WE'RE ALMOST THERE.
HMM.
SO WHAT ARE YOU PLANNING TO DO...
...WAY OUT HERE, WITH NO ONE ELSE AROUND?
WHA—!?
L-LOOK, WE'RE HERE...

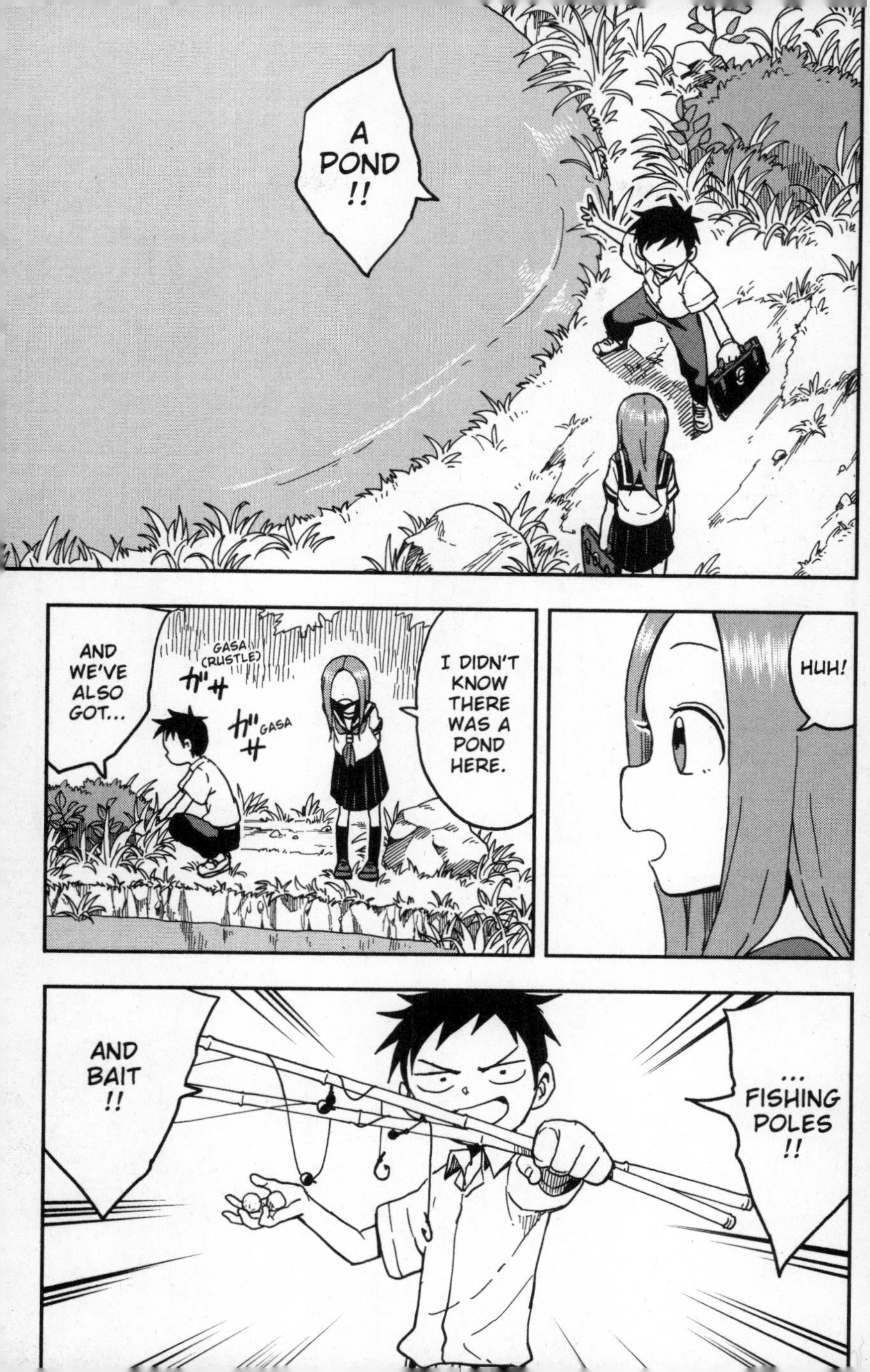
A POND !!
HUH!
I DIDN'T KNOW THERE WAS A POND HERE.
ガサ GASA (RUSTLE)
ガサ GASA
AND WE'VE ALSO GOT...
...FISHING POLES !!
AND BAIT !!

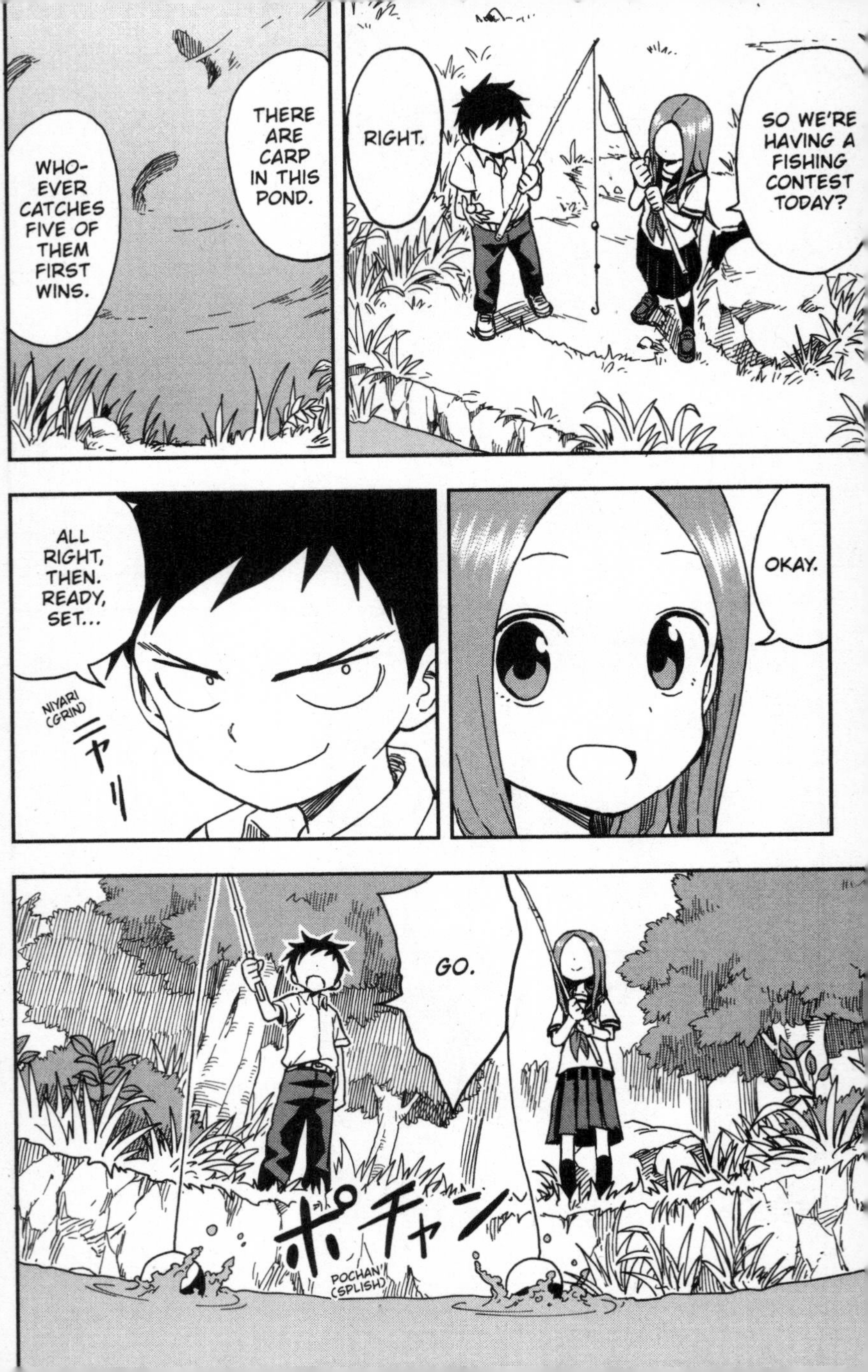
SO WE'RE HAVING A FISHING CONTEST TODAY?
RIGHT.
THERE ARE CARP IN THIS POND.
WHO-EVER CATCHES FIVE OF THEM FIRST WINS.
OKAY.
ALL RIGHT, THEN. READY, SET...
ニヤリ
NIYARI (GRIN)
GO.
ポチャン
POCHAN' (SPLISH)

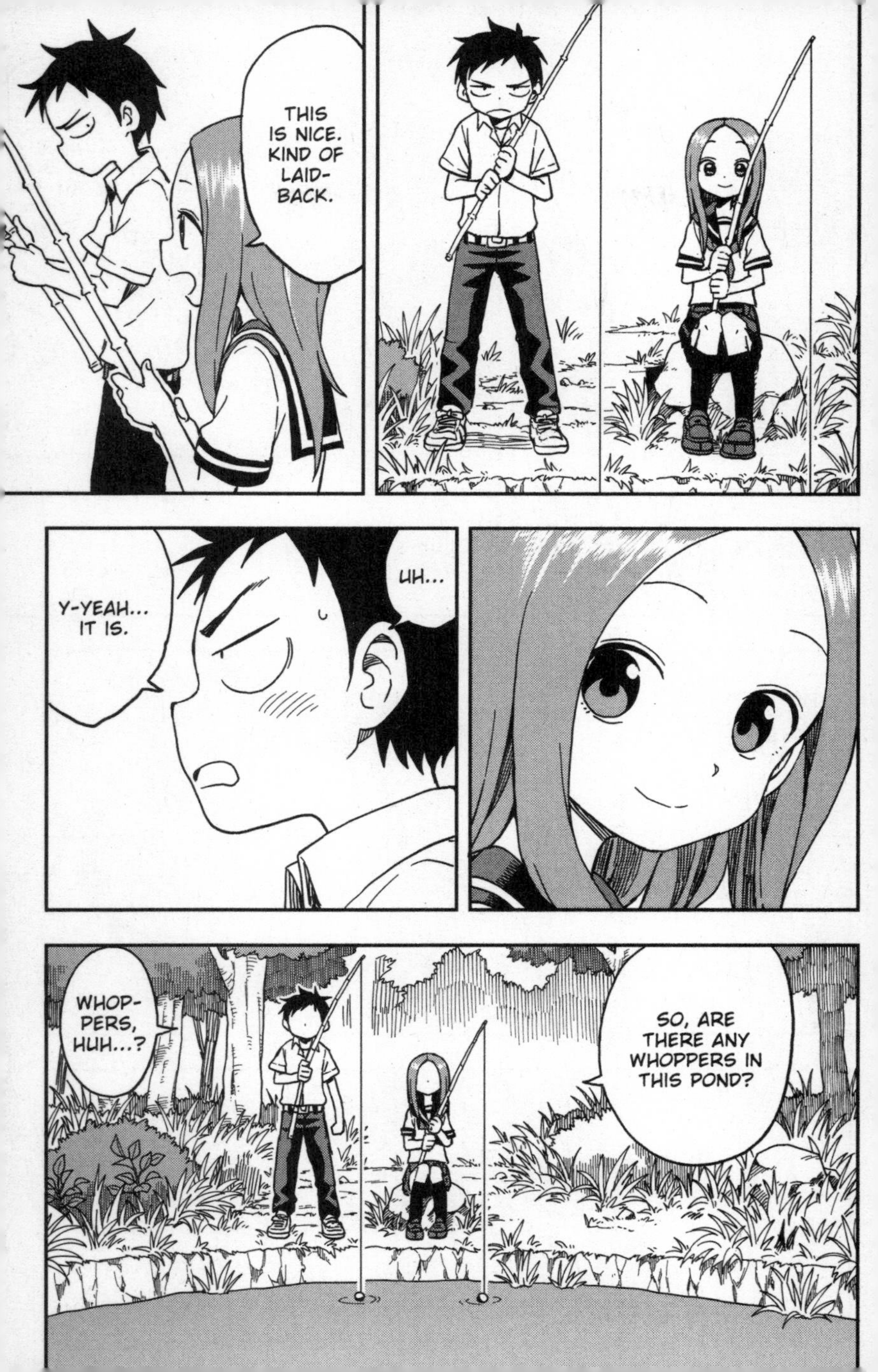
THIS IS NICE. KIND OF LAID-BACK.
UH...
Y-YEAH... IT IS.
SO, ARE THERE ANY WHOPPERS IN THIS POND?
WHOP-PERS, HUH...?

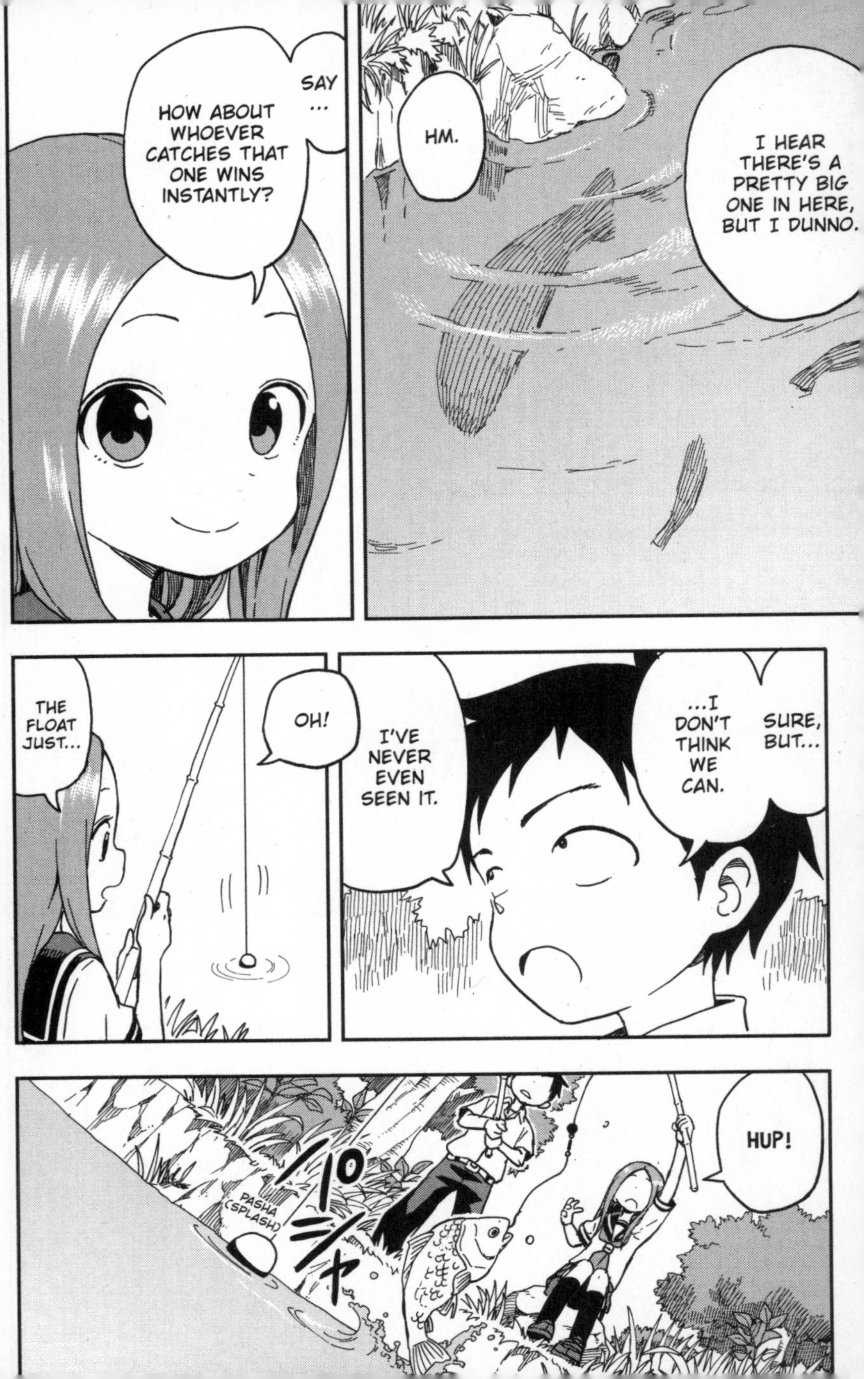
I HEAR THERE'S A PRETTY BIG ONE IN HERE, BUT I DUNNO.
HM.
SAY ...
HOW ABOUT WHOEVER CATCHES THAT ONE WINS INSTANTLY?
SURE, BUT...
...I DON'T THINK WE CAN.
I'VE NEVER EVEN SEEN IT.
OH!
THE FLOAT JUST...
HUP!
PASHA (SPLASH)

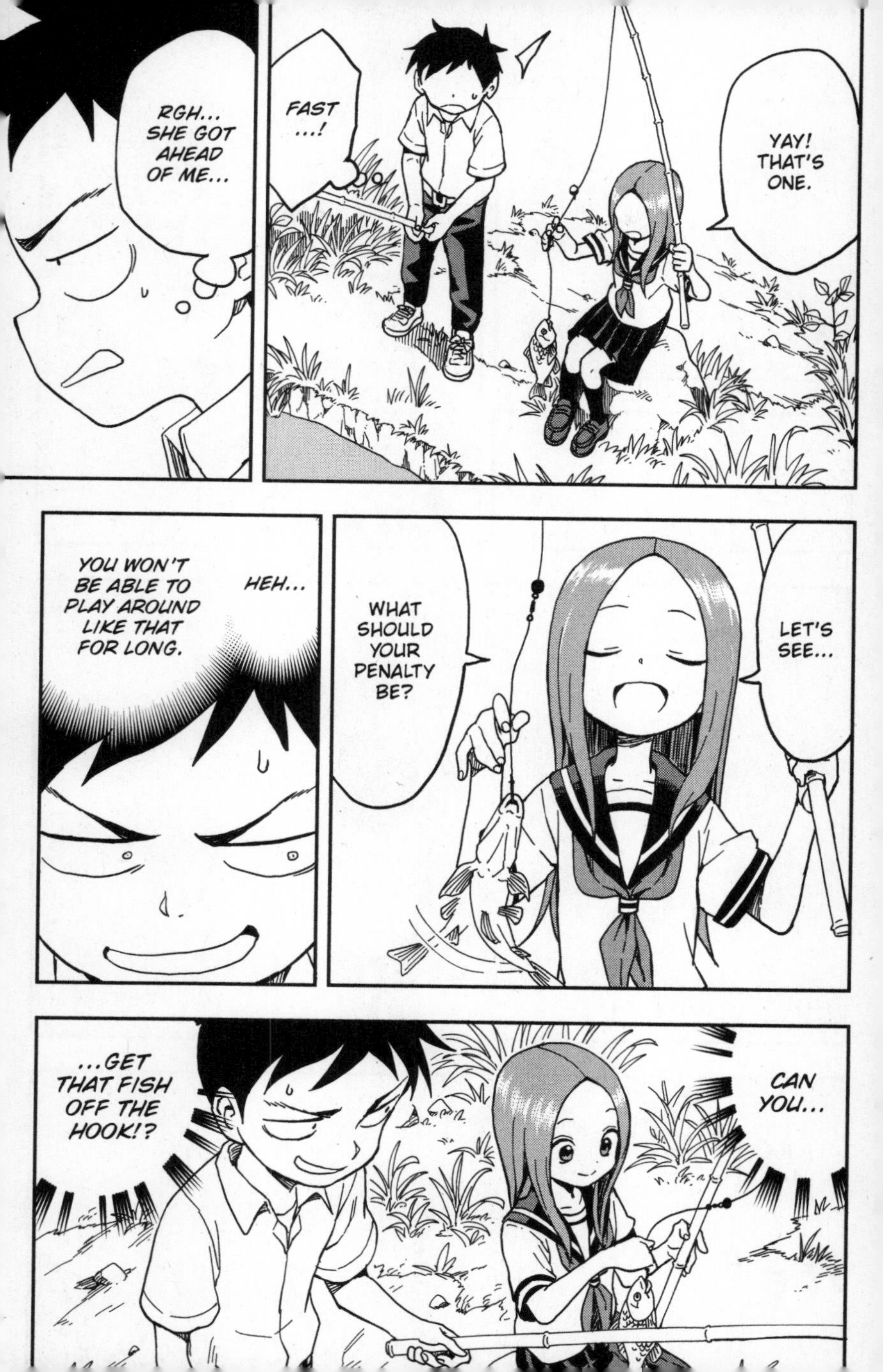
YAY! THAT'S ONE.
FAST ...!
RGH... SHE GOT AHEAD OF ME...
LET'S SEE...
WHAT SHOULD YOUR PENALTY BE?
HEH...
YOU WON'T BE ABLE TO PLAY AROUND LIKE THAT FOR LONG.
CAN YOU...
...GET THAT FISH OFF THE HOOK!?

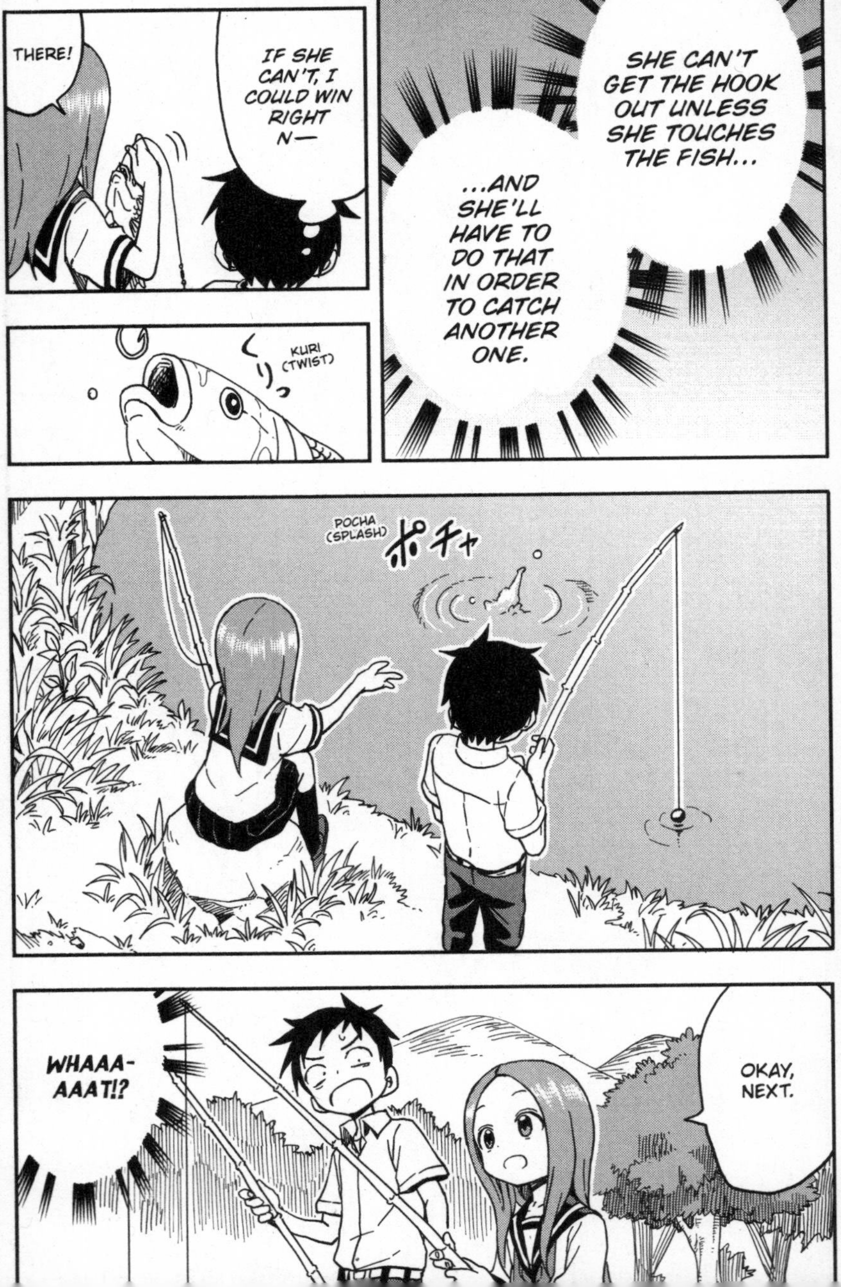
SHE CAN'T GET THE HOOK OUT UNLESS SHE TOUCHES THE FISH...
...AND SHE'LL HAVE TO DO THAT IN ORDER TO CATCH ANOTHER ONE.
IF SHE CAN'T, I COULD WIN RIGHT N—
THERE!
KURI (TWIST)
POCHA (SPLASH)
OKAY, NEXT.
WHAAAA-AAAT!?

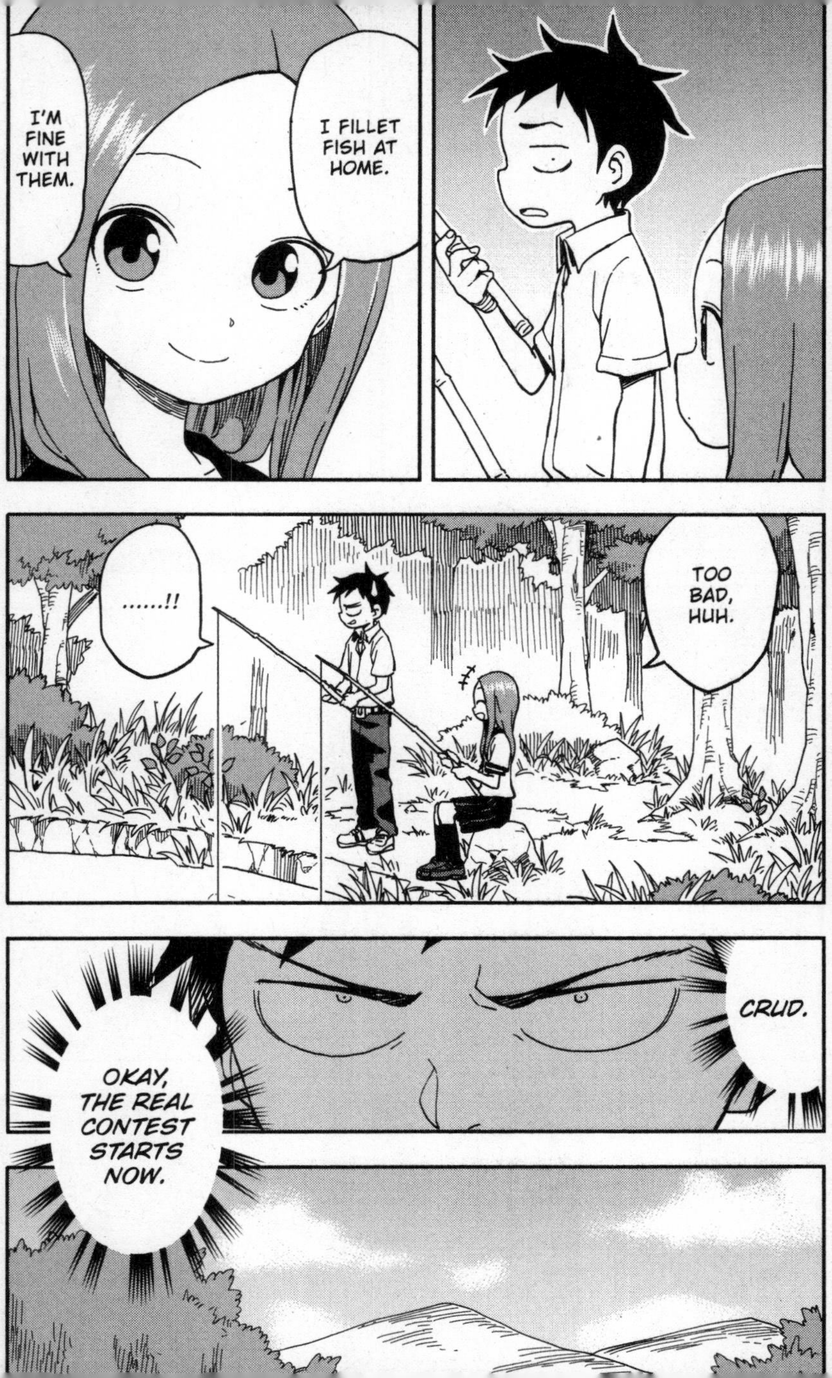
I FILLET FISH AT HOME.
I'M FINE WITH THEM.
TOO BAD, HUH.
......!!
CRUD.
OKAY, THE REAL CONTEST STARTS NOW.

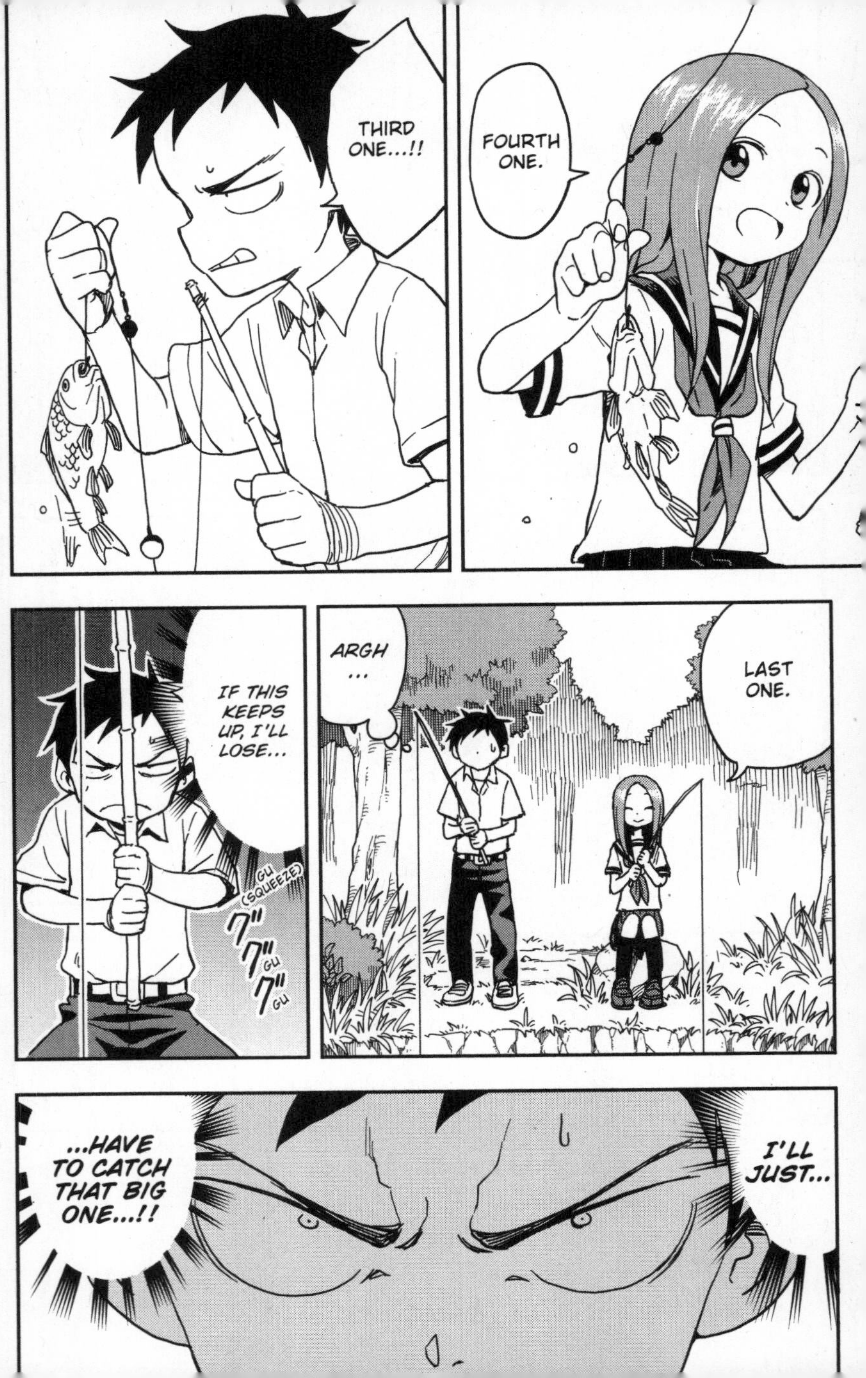
FOURTH ONE.
THIRD ONE...!!
LAST ONE.
ARGH ...
IF THIS KEEPS UP, I'LL LOSE...
GU (SQUEEZE)
GU
GU
I'LL JUST...
...HAVE TO CATCH THAT BIG ONE...!!

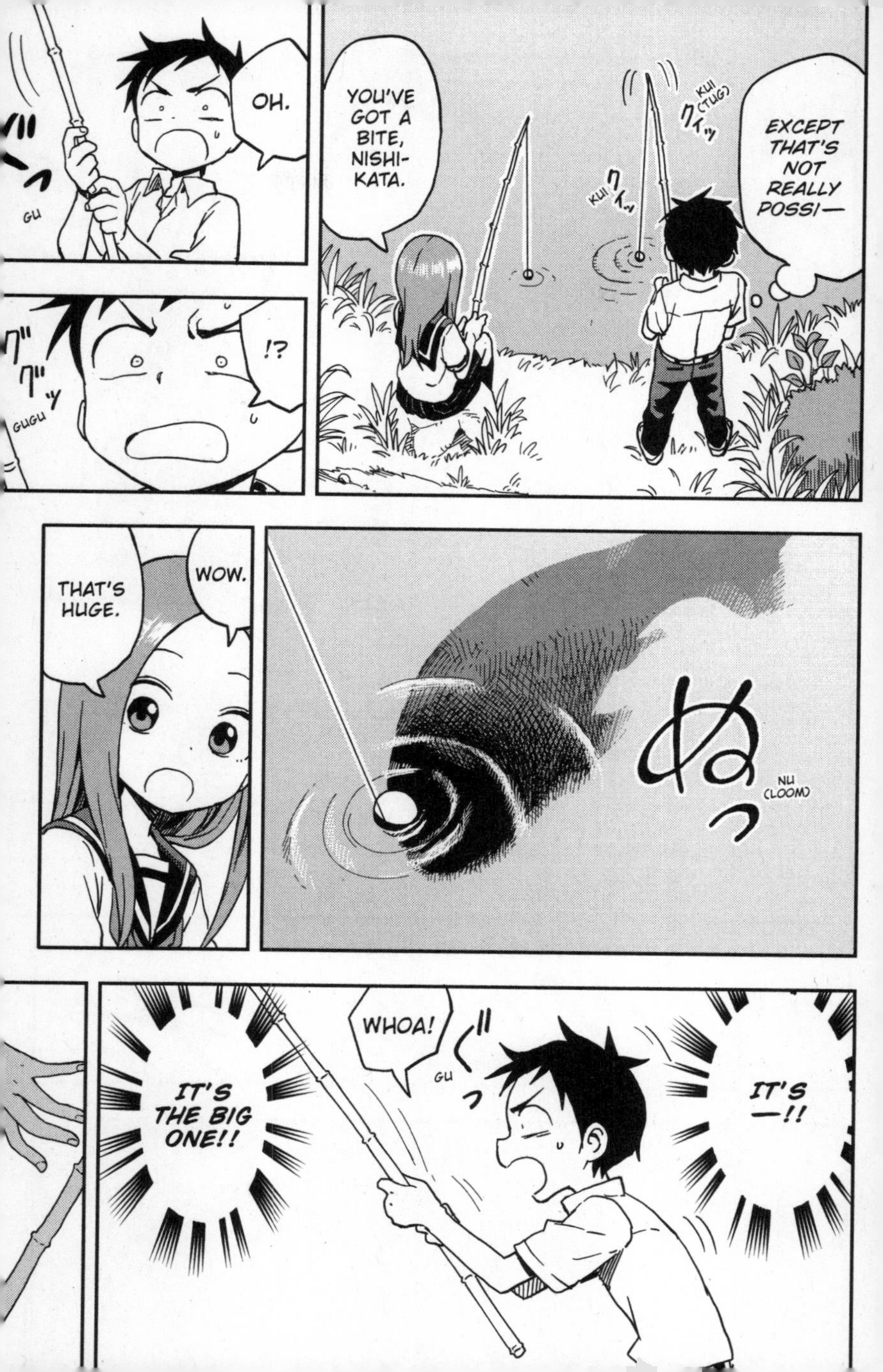
EXCEPT THAT'S NOT REALLY POSSI—
クイッ KUI (TUG)
クイッ KUI
YOU'VE GOT A BITE, NISHI-KATA.
OH.
グッ GU
!?
ググッ GUGU
ぬっ NU (LOOM)
WOW.
THAT'S HUGE.
IT'S —!!
ぐっ GU
WHOA!
IT'S THE BIG ONE!!

HUH?

と
TO
(TMP)

キュ
KYU
(SQUEEZE)

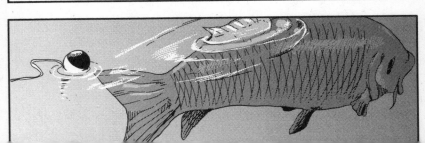

ブリ
BUCHI
(SNAP)

フリ

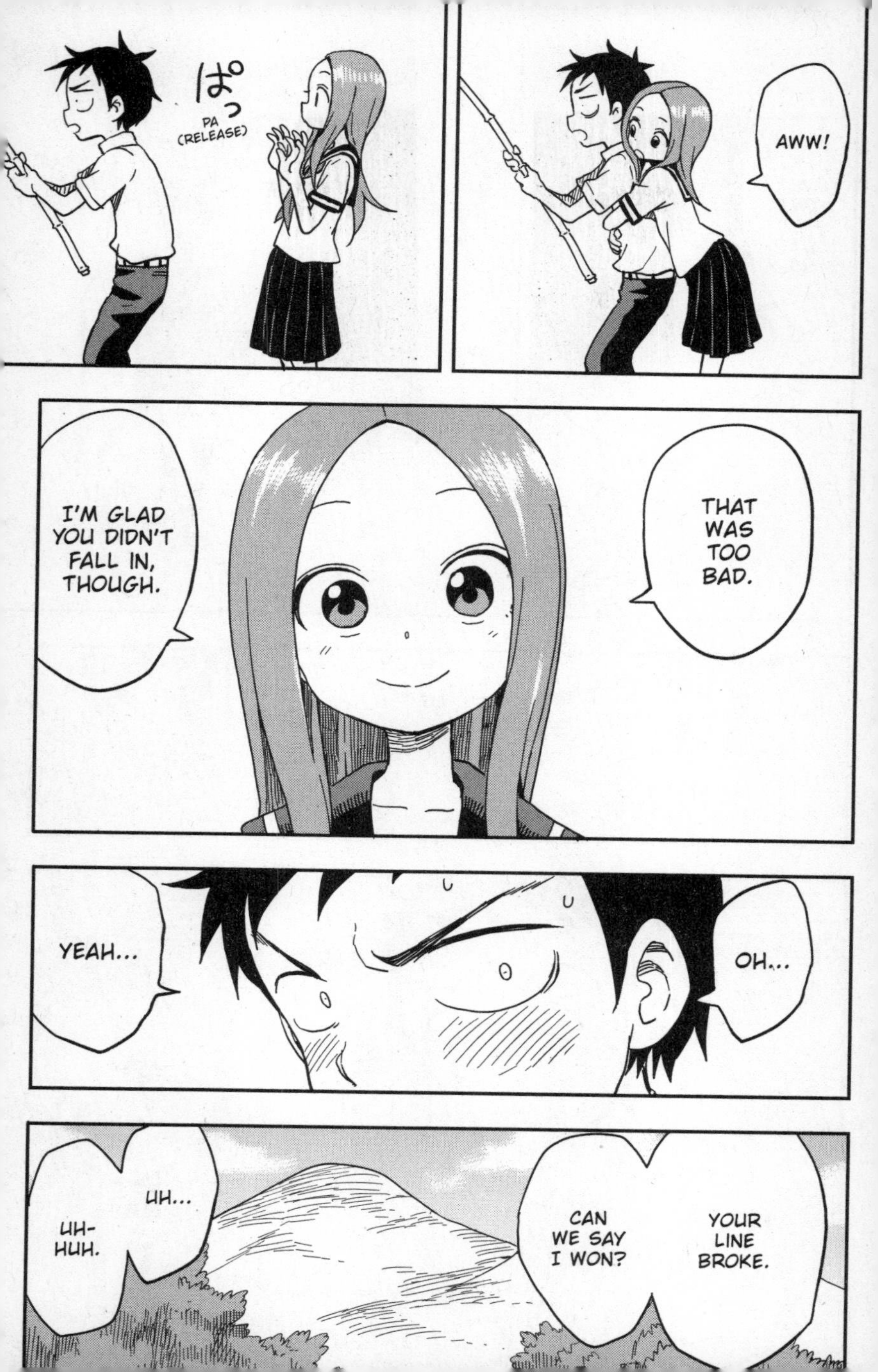
AWW!
ぱっ
PA (RELEASE)
THAT WAS TOO BAD.
I'M GLAD YOU DIDN'T FALL IN, THOUGH.
OH...
YEAH...
YOUR LINE BROKE.
CAN WE SAY I WON?
UH...
UH-HUH.

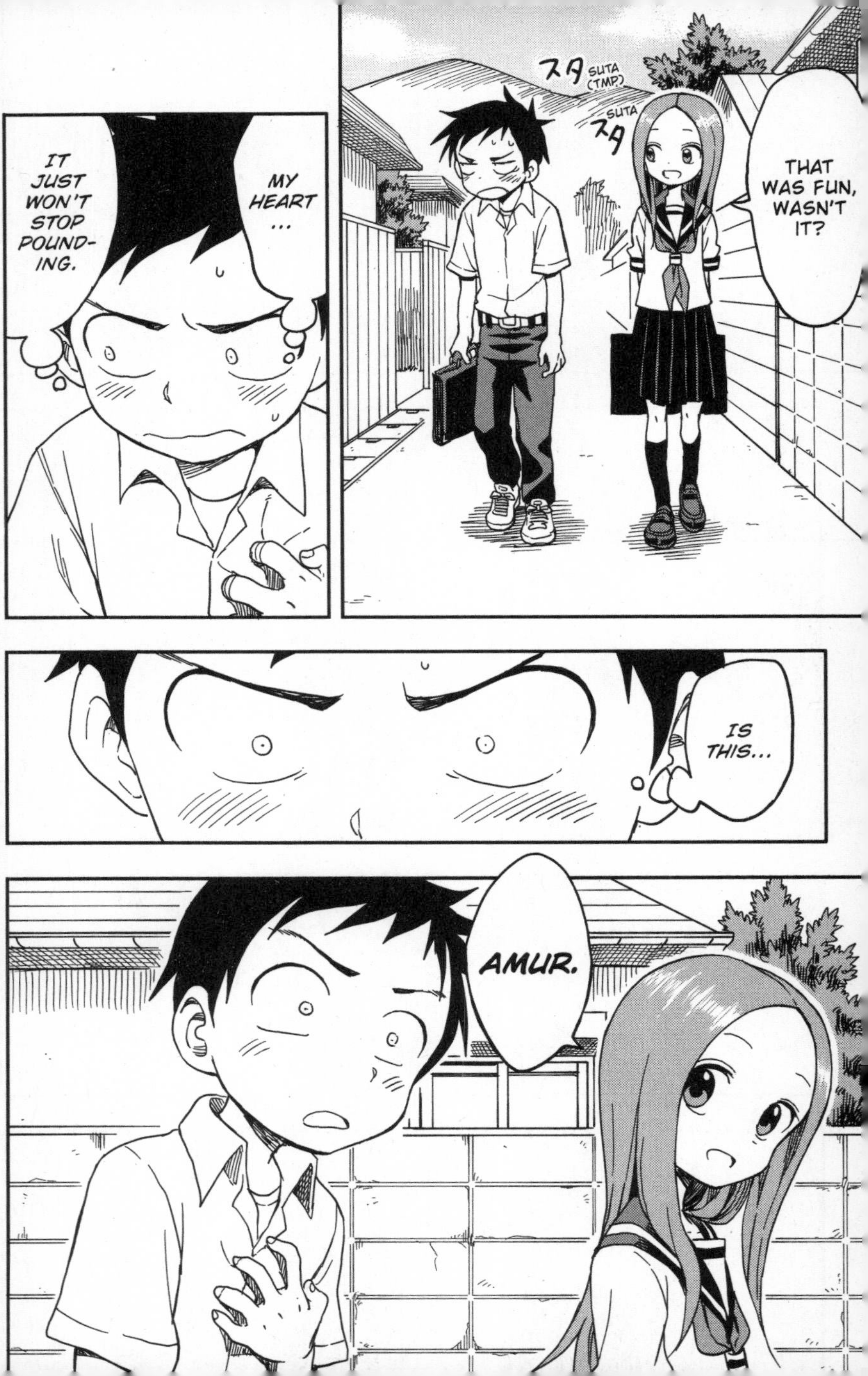
THAT WAS FUN, WASN'T IT?
スタ SUTA (TMP)
スタ SUTA
MY HEART...
IT JUST WON'T STOP POUNDING.
IS THIS...
AMUR.

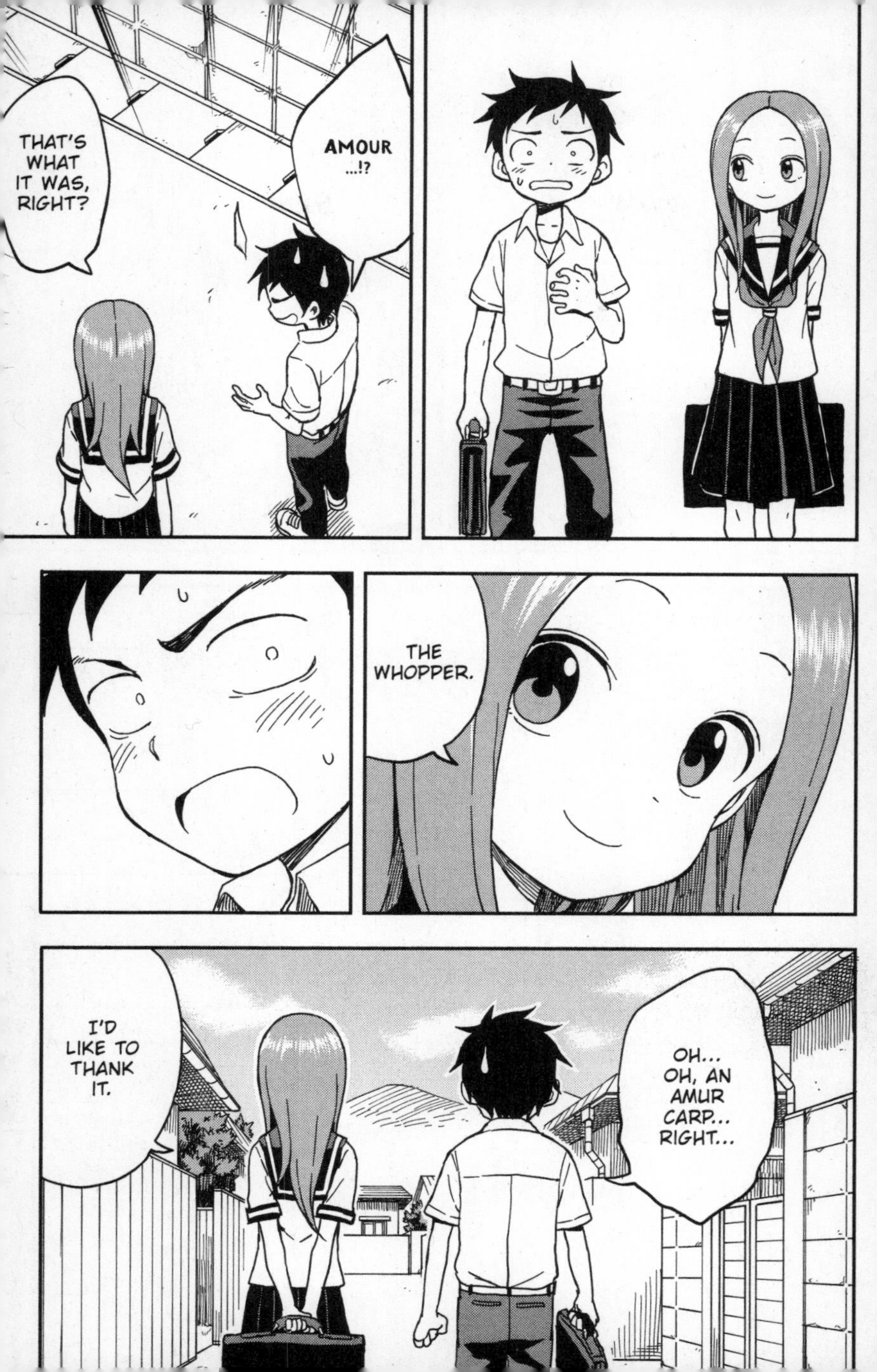
AMOUR ...!?
THAT'S WHAT IT WAS, RIGHT?
THE WHOPPER.
OH... OH, AN AMUR CARP... RIGHT...
I'D LIKE TO THANK IT.

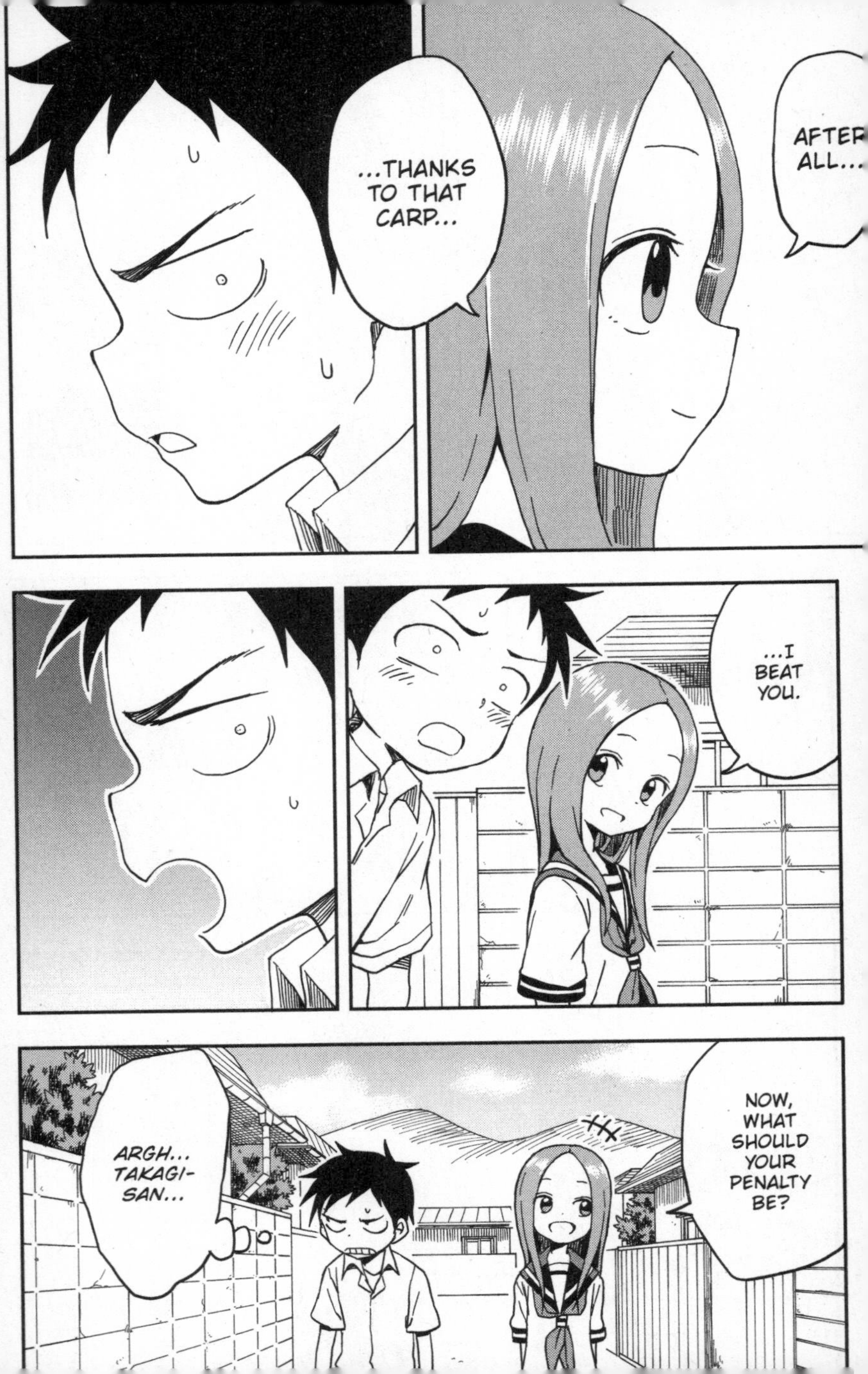
AFTER ALL...
...THANKS TO THAT CARP...
...I BEAT YOU.
NOW, WHAT SHOULD YOUR PENALTY BE?
ARGH... TAKAGI-SAN...

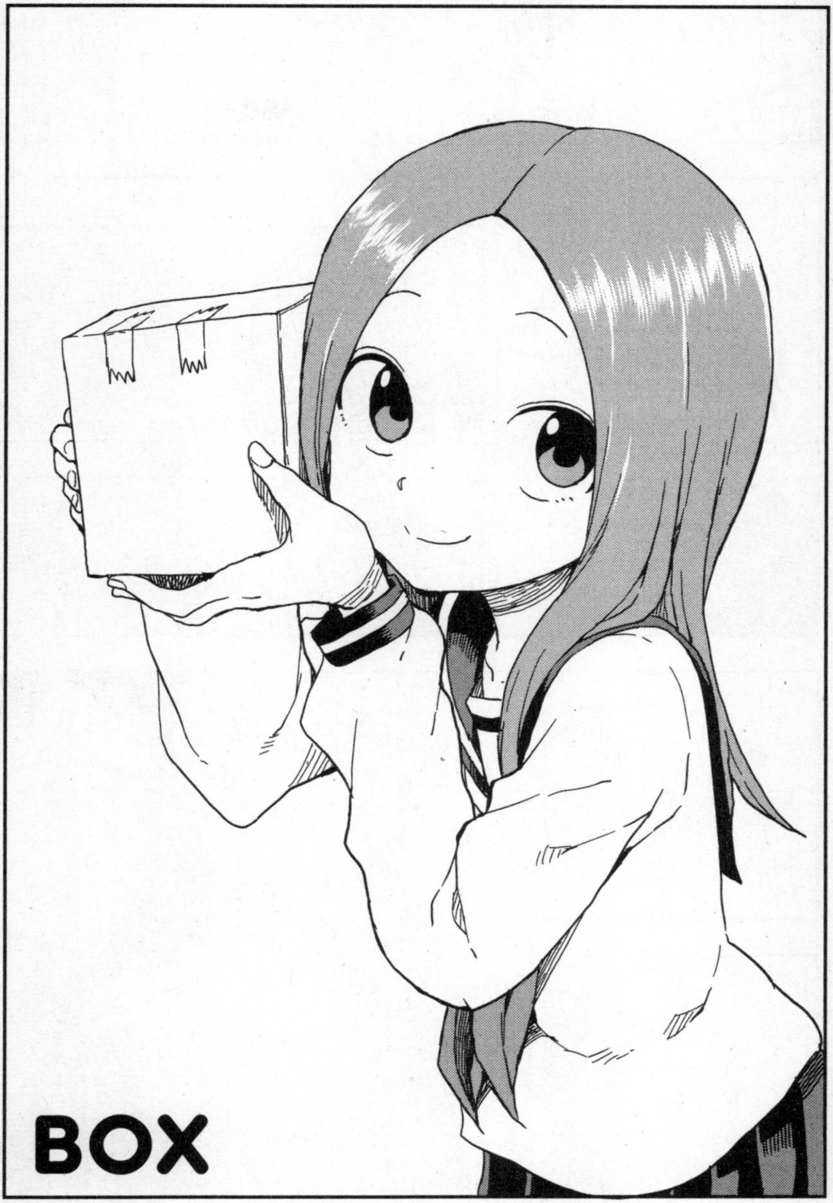
BOX

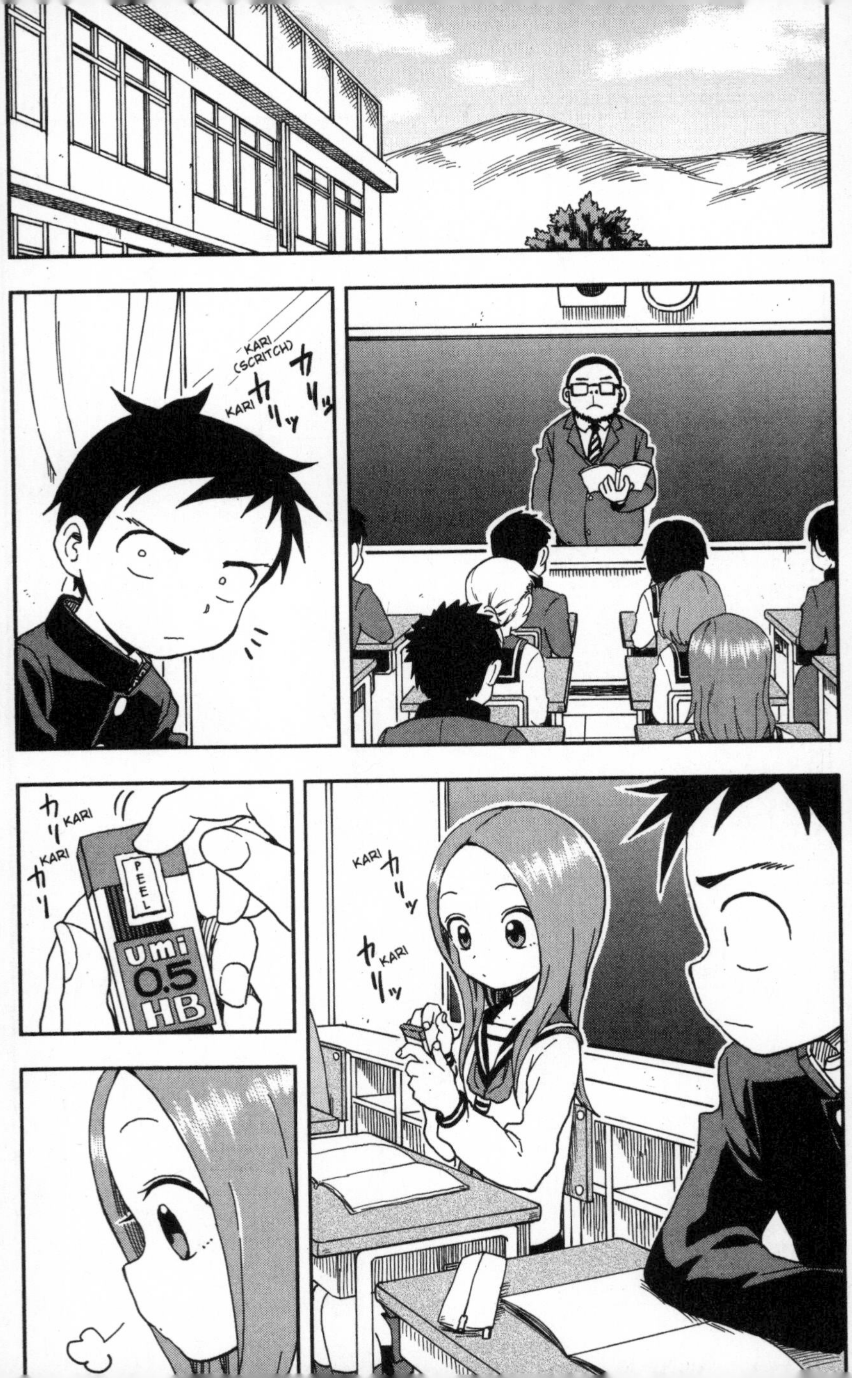
KARI (SCRITCH)
カリッ
KARI
カリッ
KARI
カリッ
KARI
カリッ
KARI
カリ
KARI
カリ

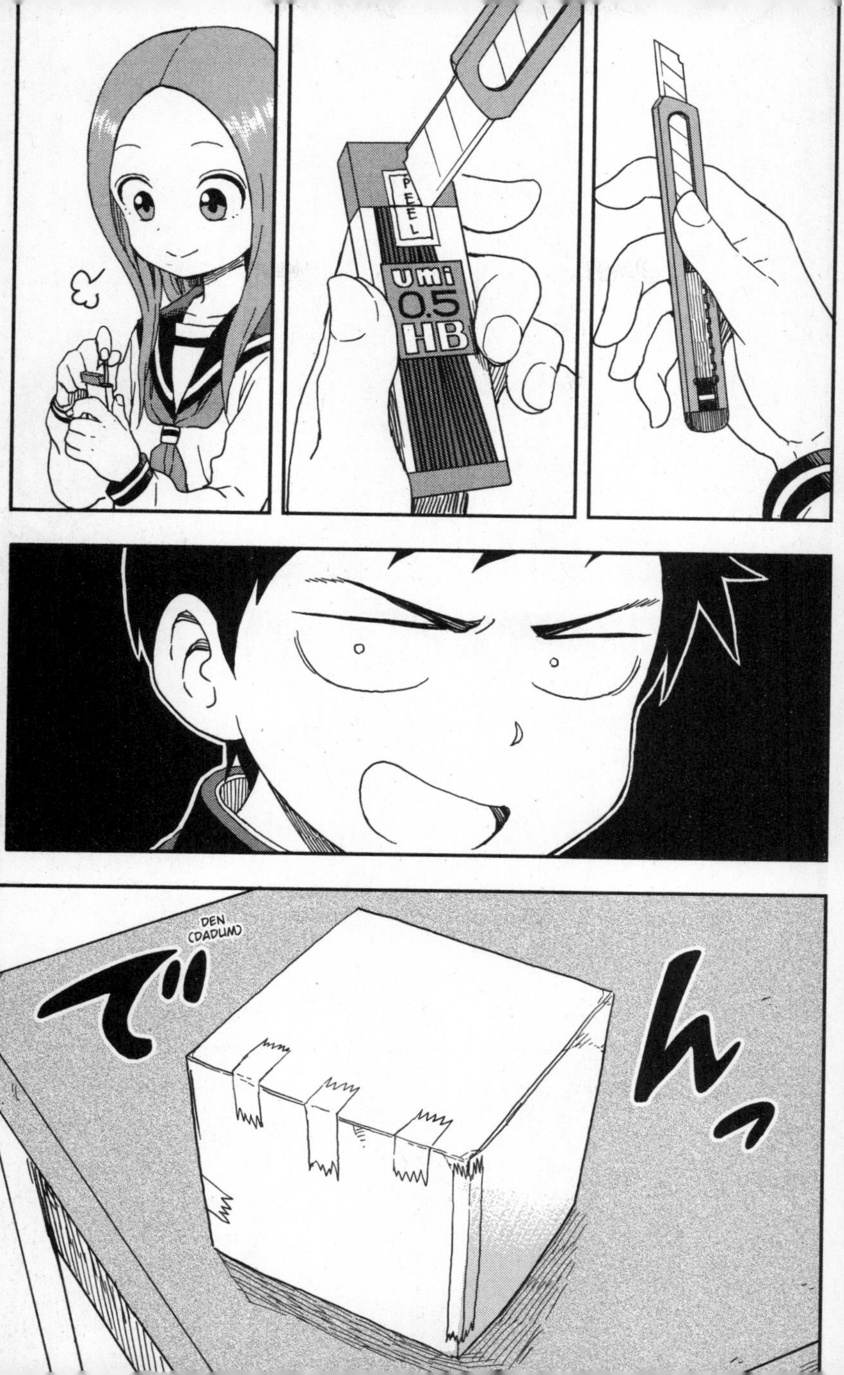
PEEL
umi
0.5
HB
でん
DEN
(DADUM)

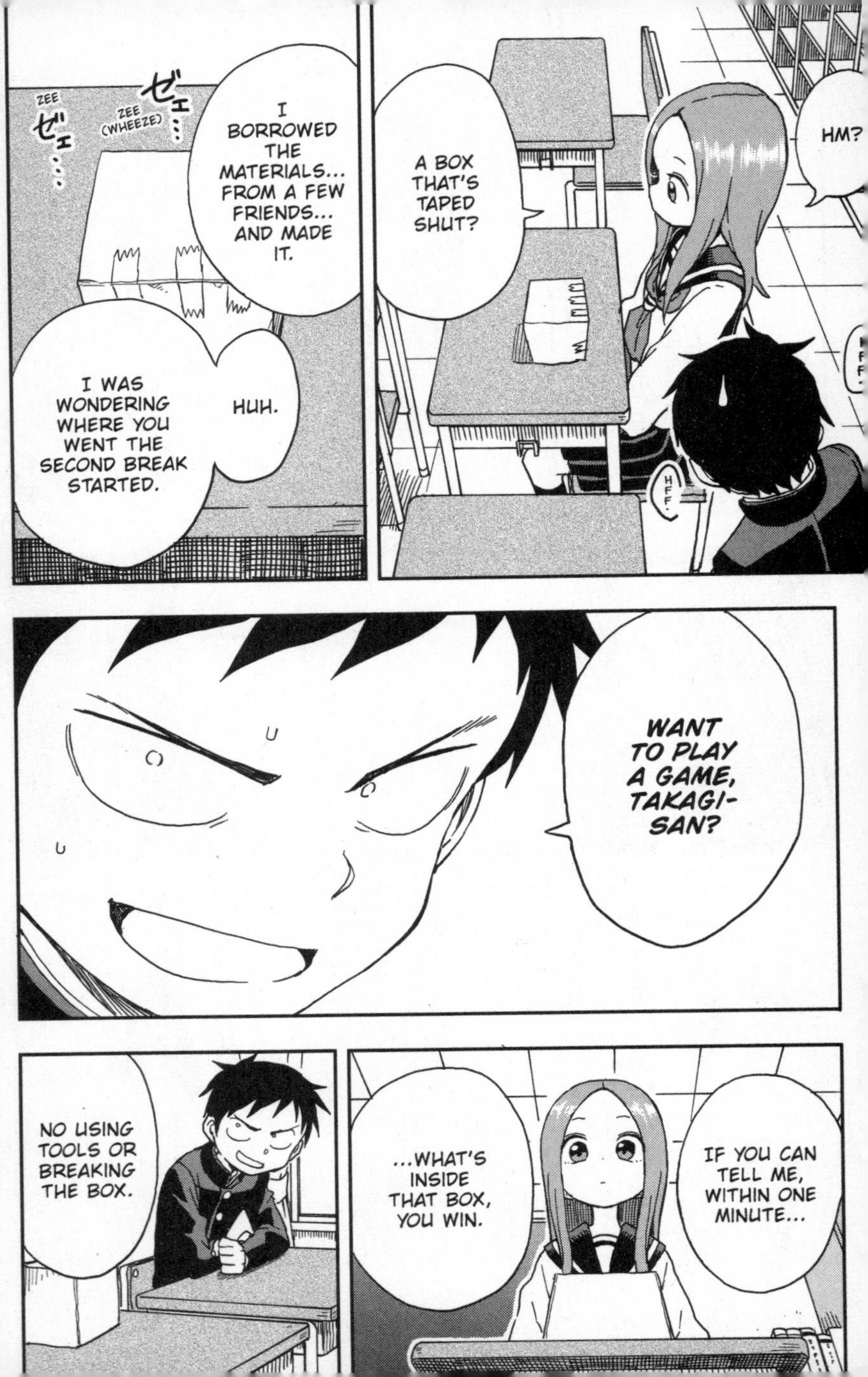
HM?
A BOX THAT'S TAPED SHUT?
HFF.
I BORROWED THE MATERIALS... FROM A FEW FRIENDS... AND MADE IT.
ゼェ…
ZEE (WHEEZE)
ゼェ…
ZEE
HUH.
I WAS WONDERING WHERE YOU WENT THE SECOND BREAK STARTED.
WANT TO PLAY A GAME, TAKAGI-SAN?
IF YOU CAN TELL ME, WITHIN ONE MINUTE...
...WHAT'S INSIDE THAT BOX, YOU WIN.
NO USING TOOLS OR BREAKING THE BOX.

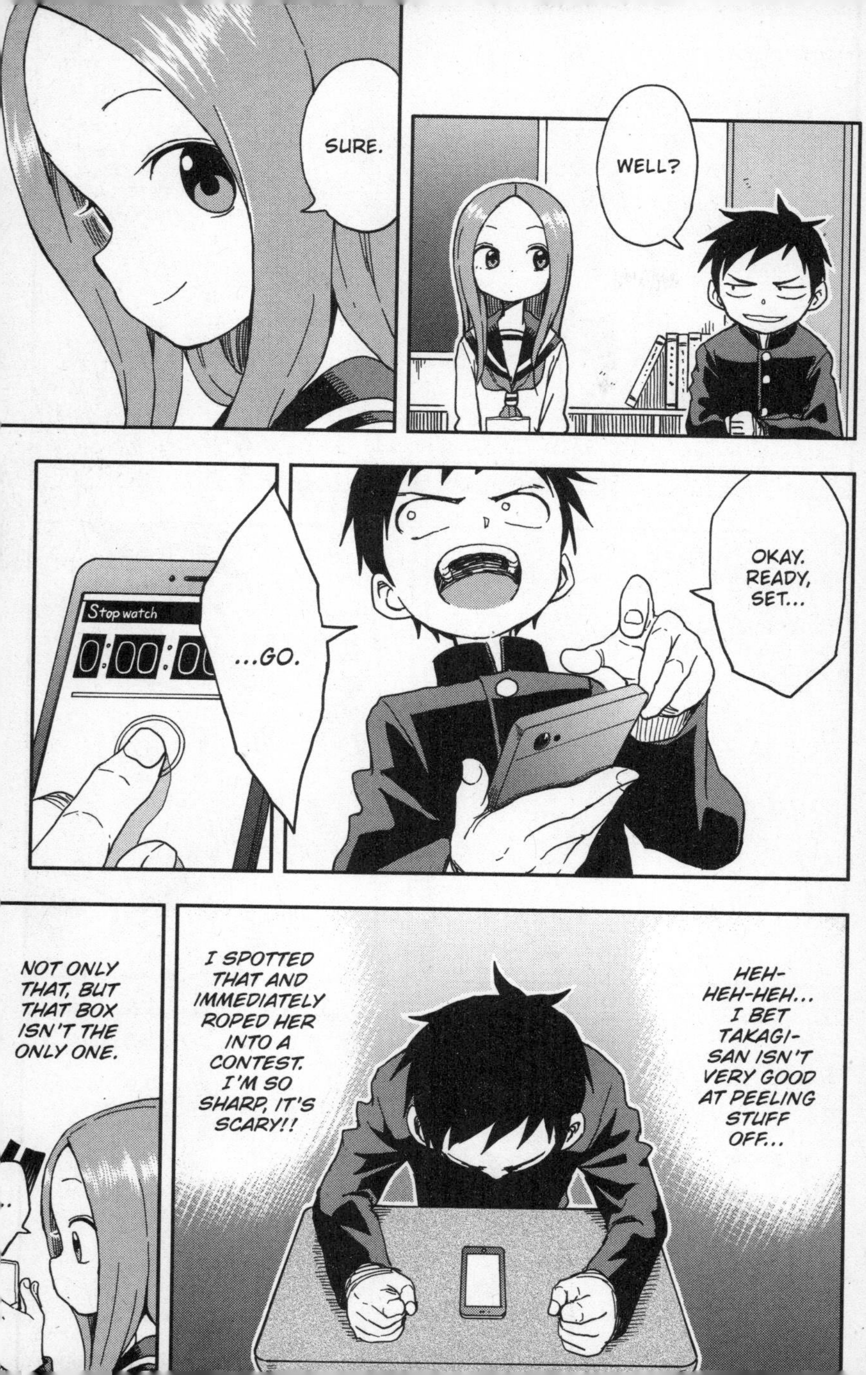
WELL?
SURE.
OKAY. READY, SET...
Stop watch
...GO.
HEH-HEH-HEH... I BET TAKAGI-SAN ISN'T VERY GOOD AT PEELING STUFF OFF...
I SPOTTED THAT AND IMMEDIATELY ROPED HER INTO A CONTEST. I'M SO SHARP, IT'S SCARY!!
NOT ONLY THAT, BUT THAT BOX ISN'T THE ONLY ONE.

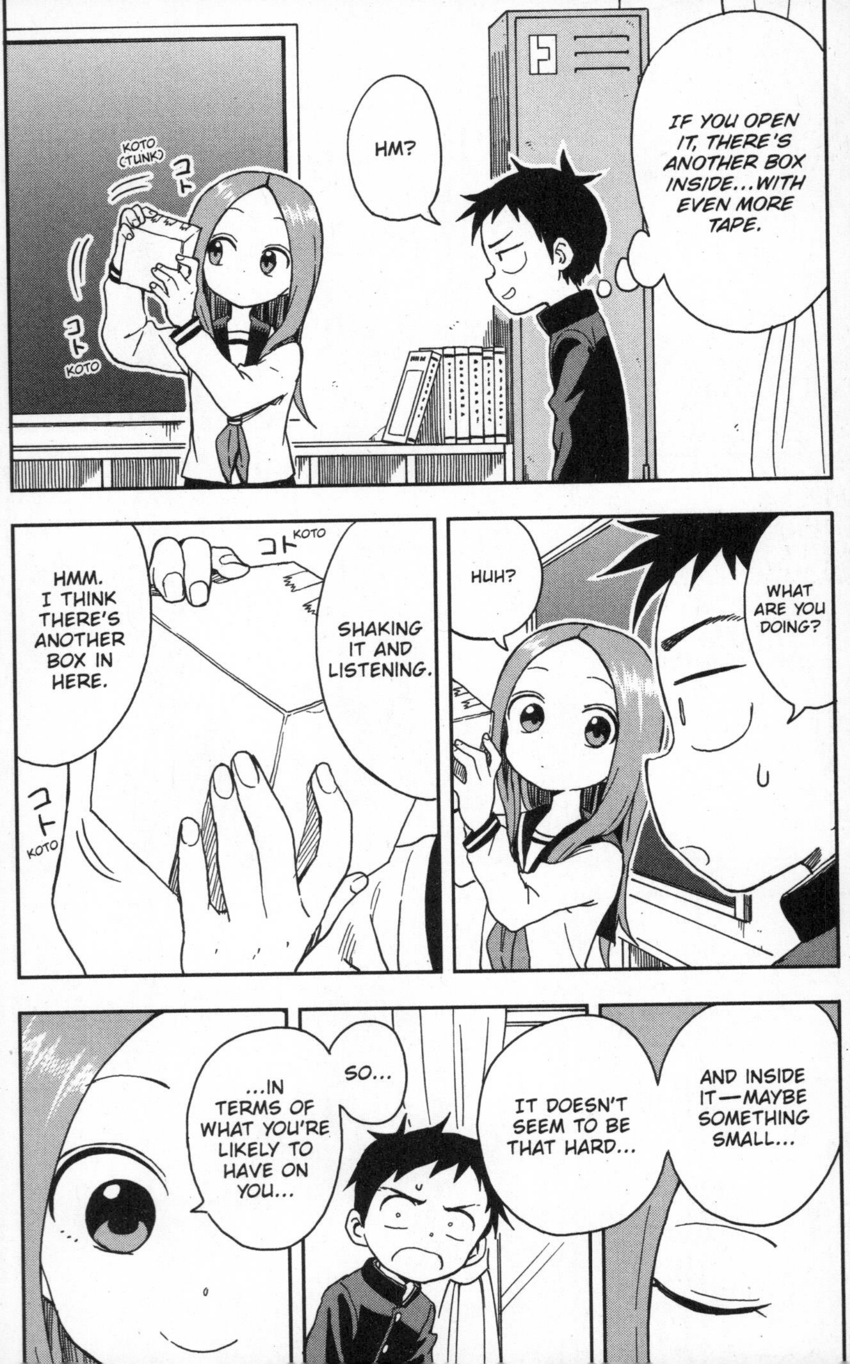
IF YOU OPEN IT, THERE'S ANOTHER BOX INSIDE...WITH EVEN MORE TAPE.
HM?
コト KOTO (TUNK)
コト KOTO
WHAT ARE YOU DOING?
HUH?
SHAKING IT AND LISTENING.
コト KOTO
HMM. I THINK THERE'S ANOTHER BOX IN HERE.
コト KOTO
AND INSIDE IT—MAYBE SOMETHING SMALL...
IT DOESN'T SEEM TO BE THAT HARD...
SO...
...IN TERMS OF WHAT YOU'RE LIKELY TO HAVE ON YOU...

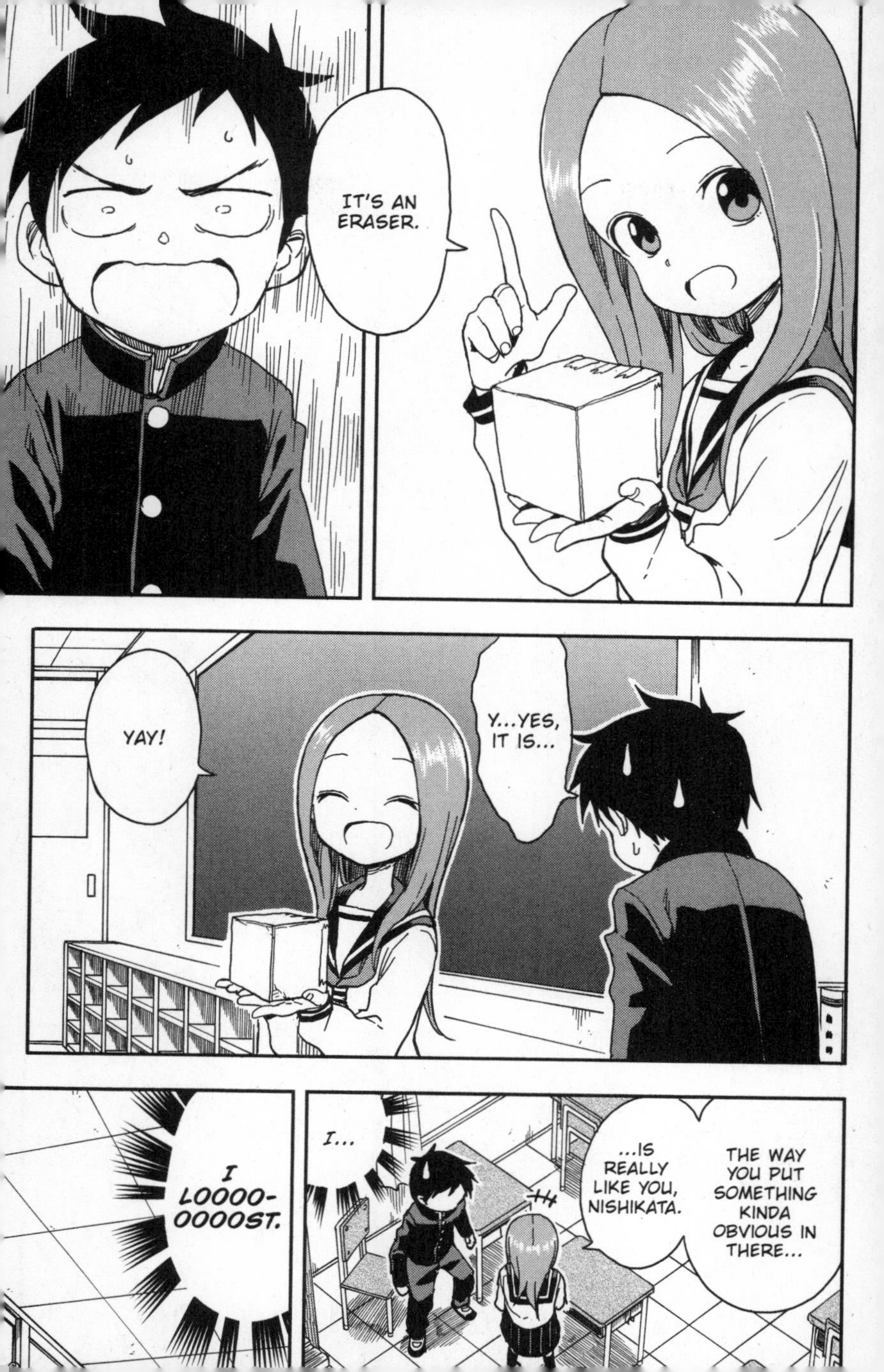
IT'S AN ERASER.
Y...YES, IT IS...
YAY!
THE WAY YOU PUT SOMETHING KINDA OBVIOUS IN THERE...
...IS REALLY LIKE YOU, NISHIKATA.
I...
I LOOOO-OOOOST.

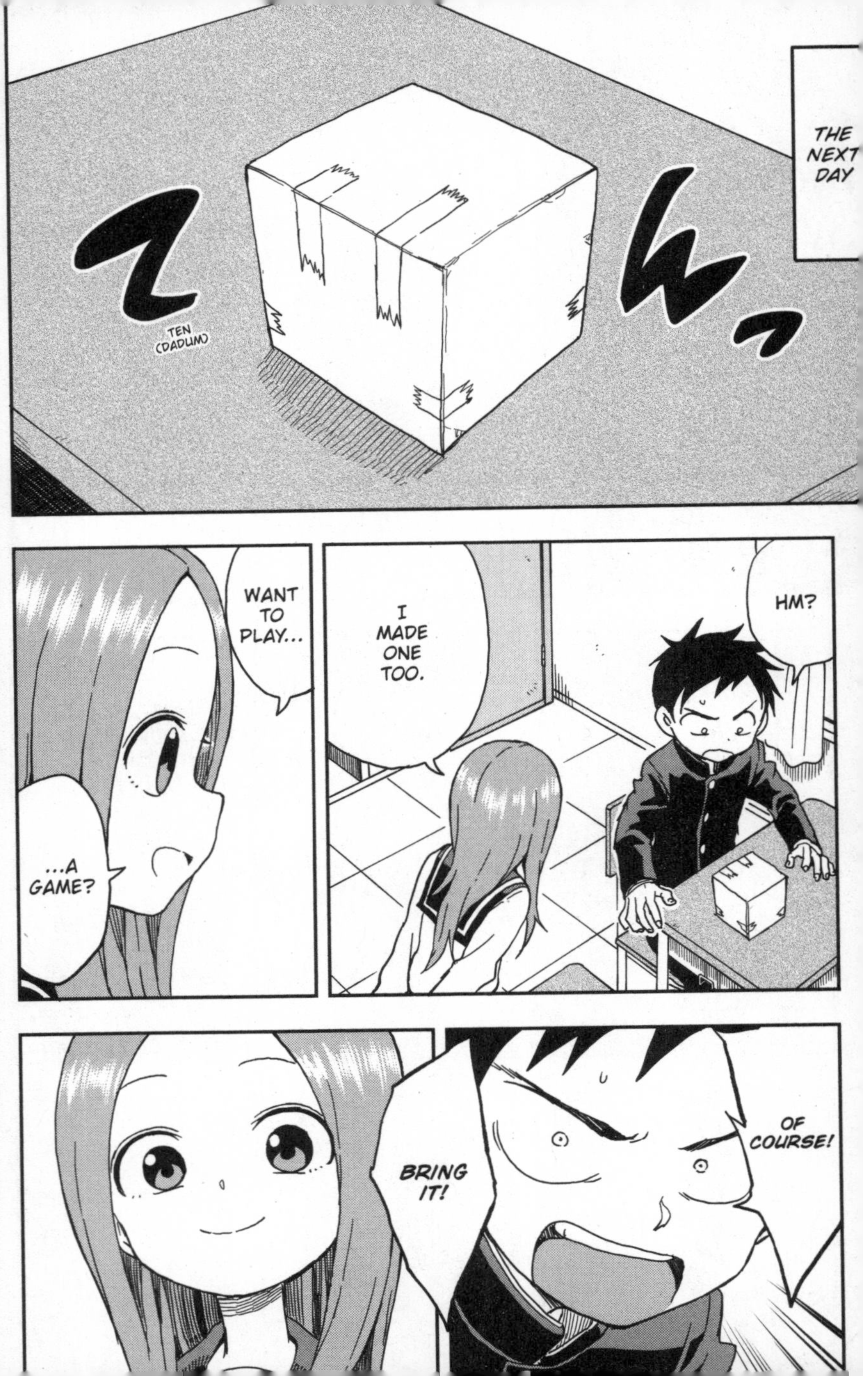
THE NEXT DAY
TEN (DADUM)
HM?
I MADE ONE TOO.
WANT TO PLAY...
...A GAME?
OF COURSE!
BRING IT!

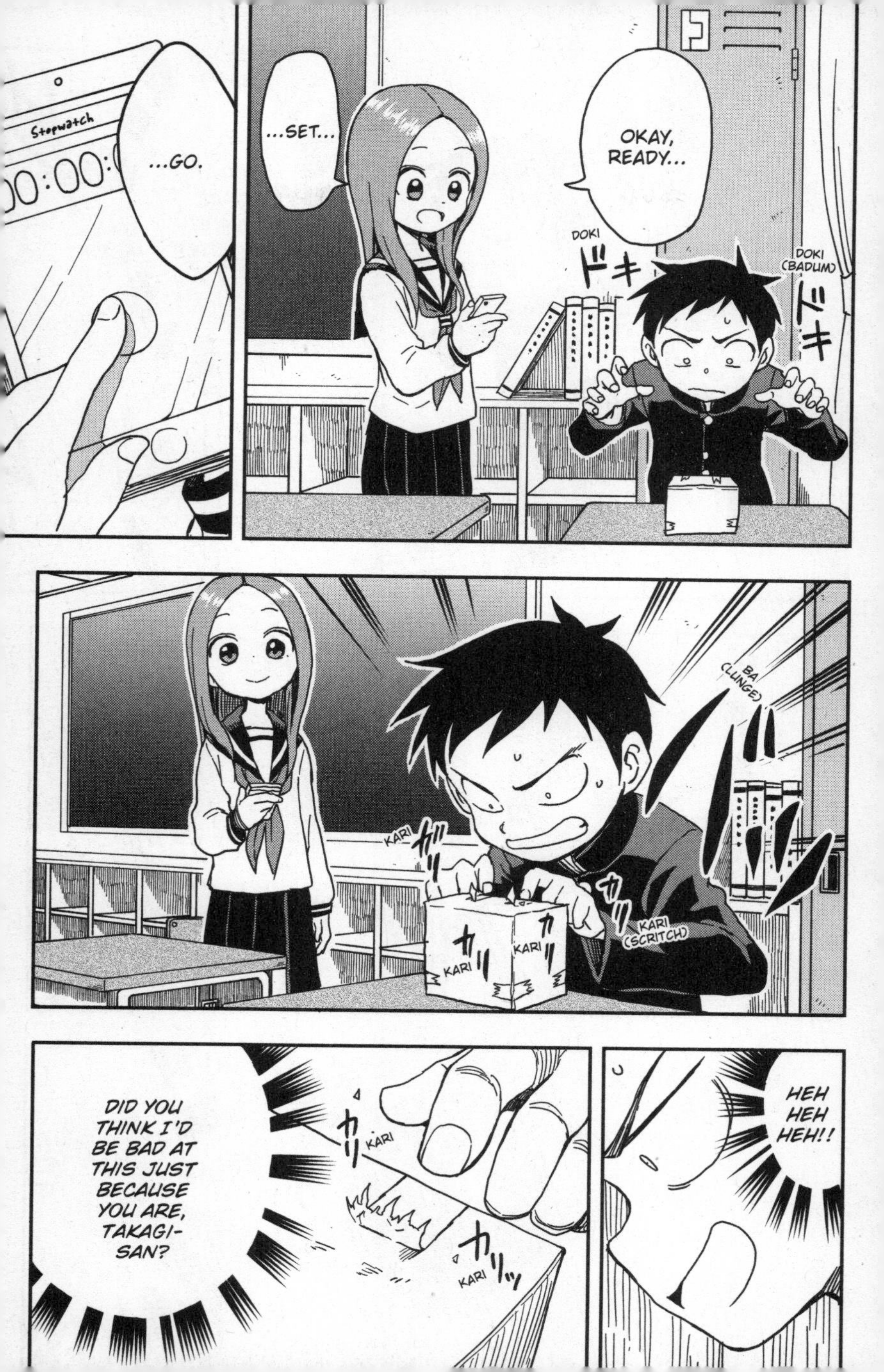

OKAY, READY...
DOKI
ドキ
DOKI (BADUM)
ドキ
...SET...
Stopwatch
...GO.
BA (LUNGE)
KARI
KARI (SCRITCH)
KARI
KARI
HEH HEH HEH!!
DID YOU THINK I'D BE BAD AT THIS JUST BECAUSE YOU ARE, TAKAGI-SAN?
KARI
KARI

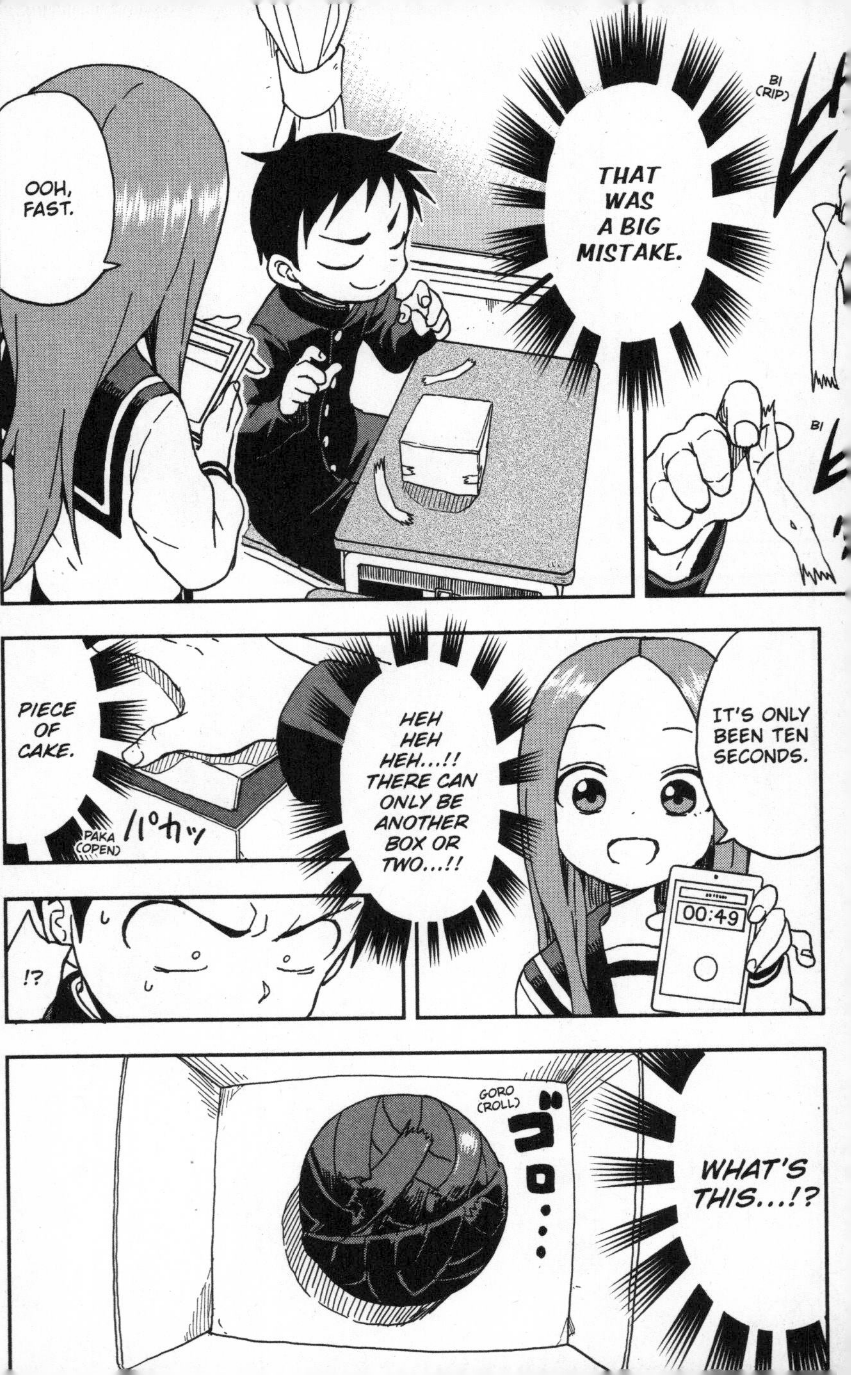
BI (RIP)
BI
THAT WAS A BIG MISTAKE.
OOH, FAST.
IT'S ONLY BEEN TEN SECONDS.
PIECE OF CAKE.
HEH HEH HEH...!! THERE CAN ONLY BE ANOTHER BOX OR TWO...!!
PAKA (OPEN)
パカッ
!?
WHAT'S THIS...!?
GORO (ROLL)
ゴロ…

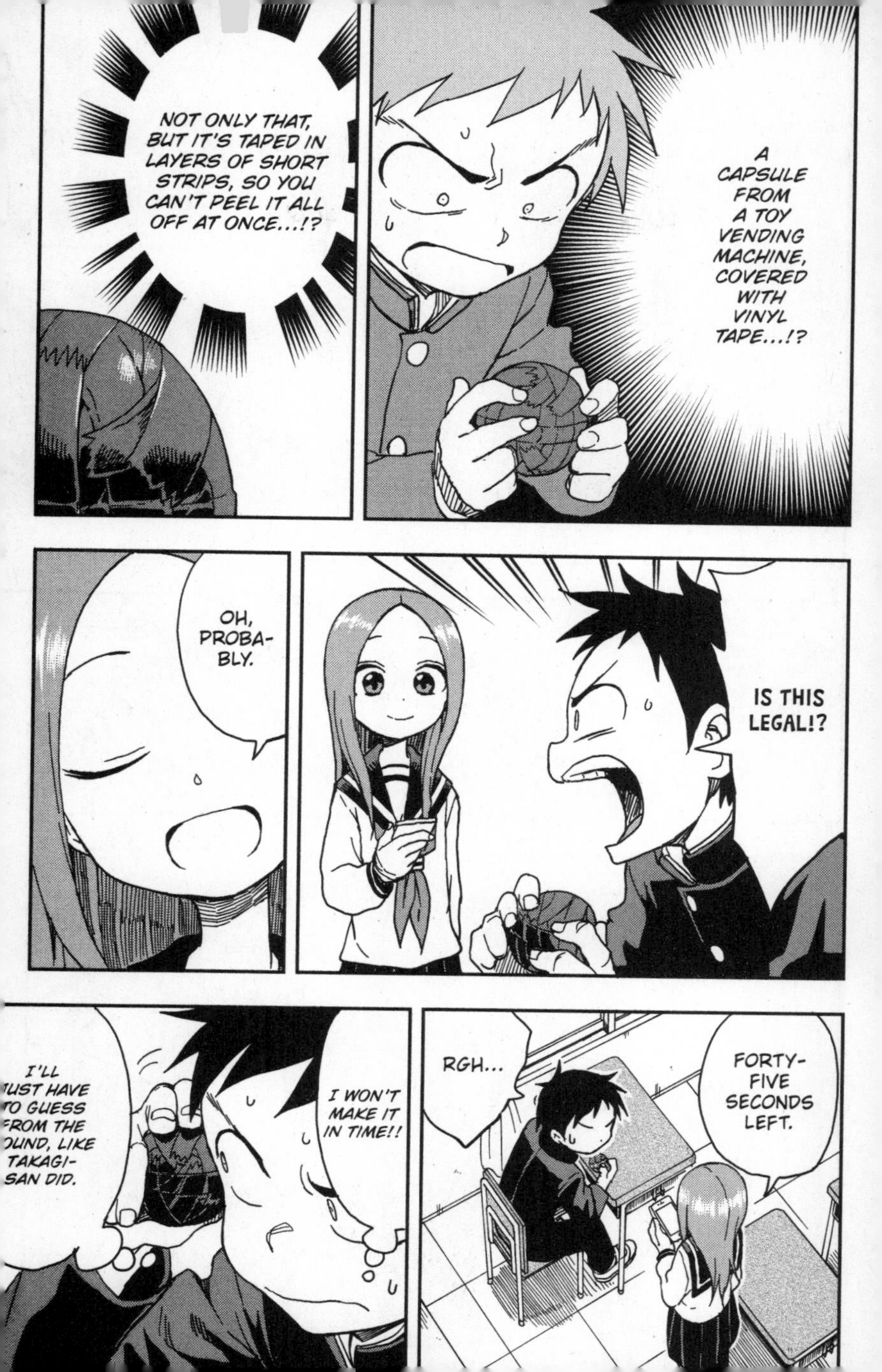
A CAPSULE FROM A TOY VENDING MACHINE, COVERED WITH VINYL TAPE...!?
NOT ONLY THAT, BUT IT'S TAPED IN LAYERS OF SHORT STRIPS, SO YOU CAN'T PEEL IT ALL OFF AT ONCE...!?
IS THIS LEGAL!?
OH, PROBA-BLY.
FORTY-FIVE SECONDS LEFT.
RGH...
I WON'T MAKE IT IN TIME!!
I'LL JUST HAVE TO GUESS FROM THE OUND, LIKE TAKAGI-SAN DID.

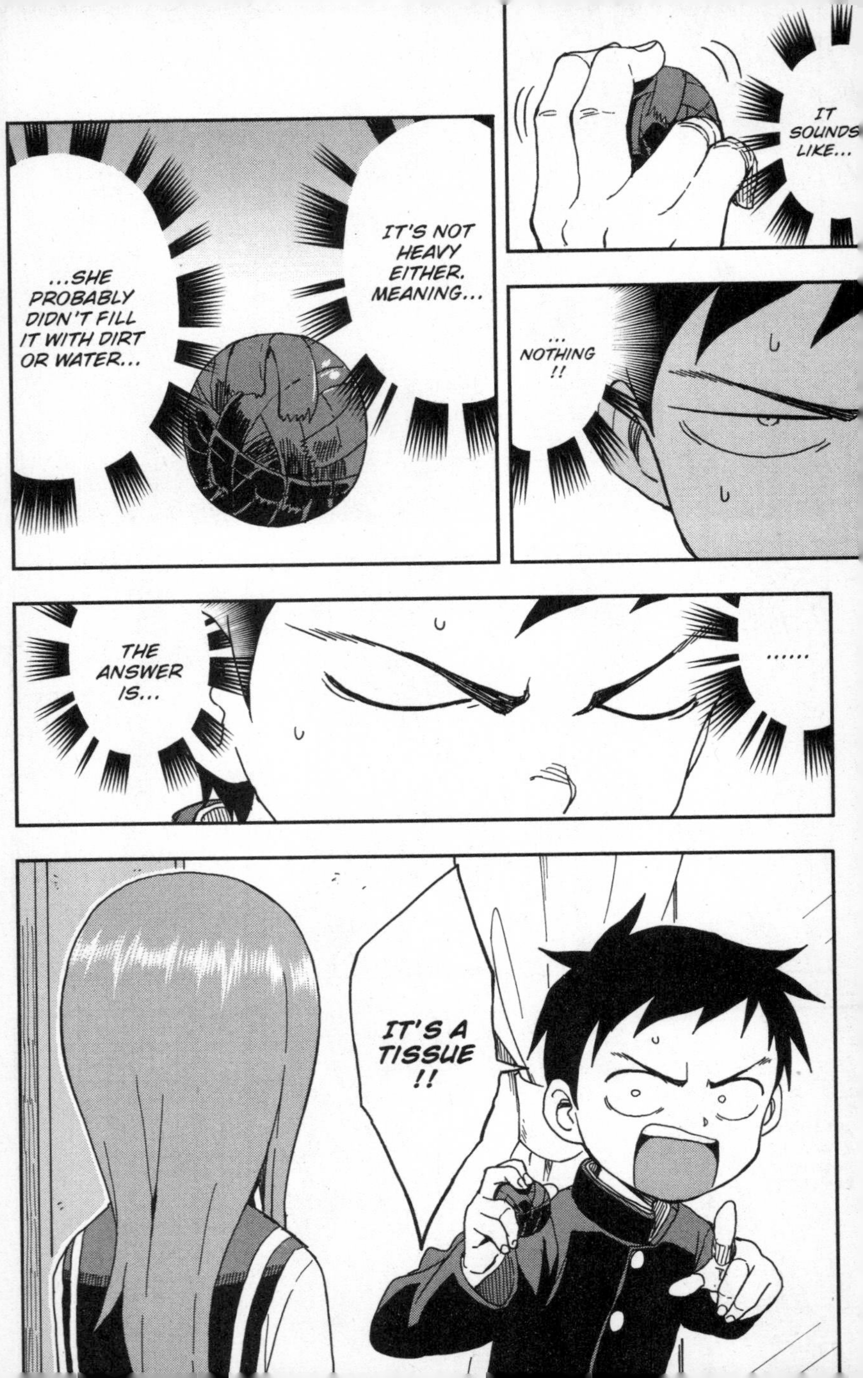
IT SOUNDS LIKE...
...NOTHING!!
IT'S NOT HEAVY EITHER. MEANING...
...SHE PROBABLY DIDN'T FILL IT WITH DIRT OR WATER...
......
THE ANSWER IS...
IT'S A TISSUE!!

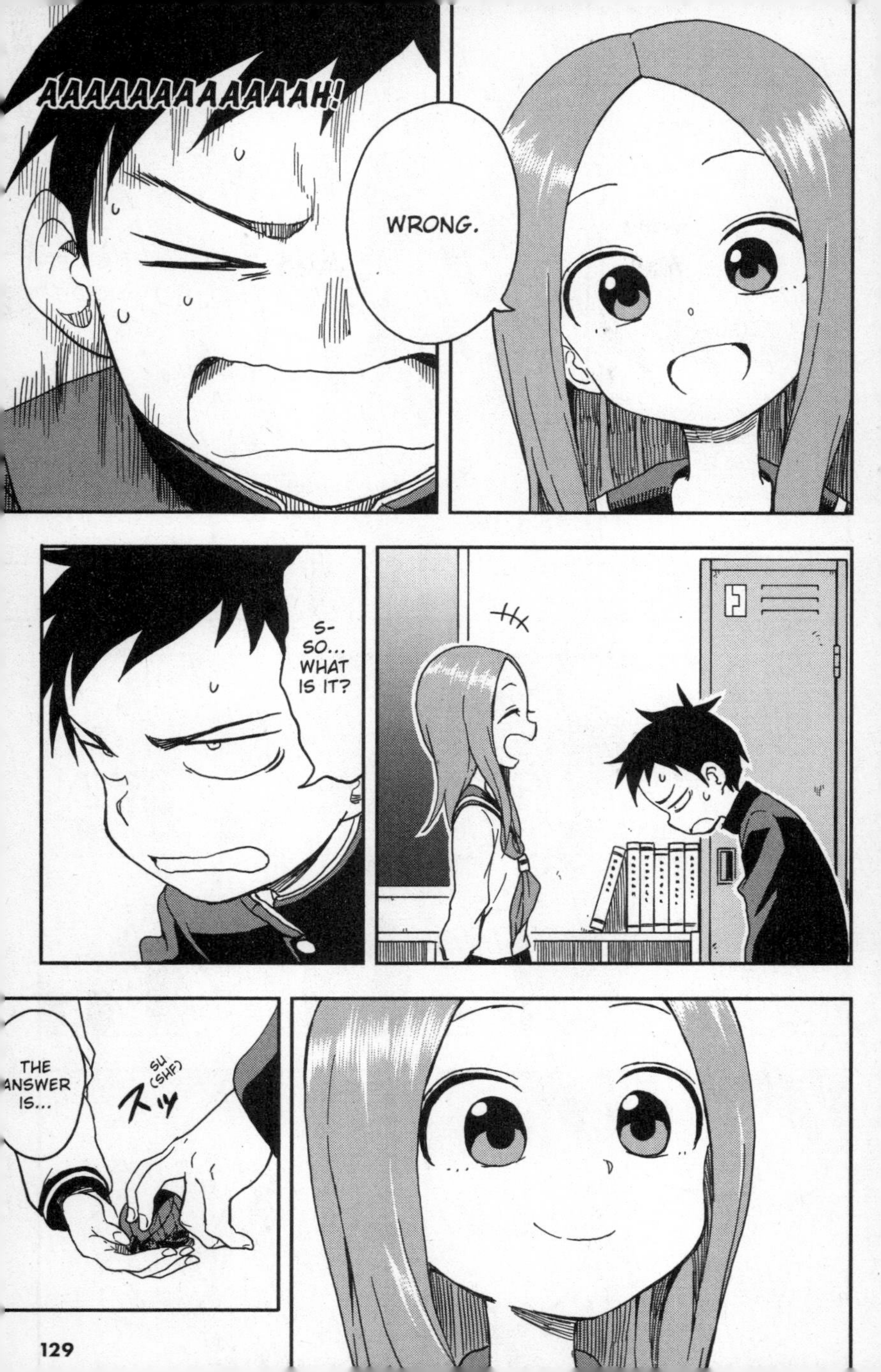
WRONG.
AAAAAAAAAAAAH!
S- SO... WHAT IS IT?
THE ANSWER IS...
スッ SU (SHF)

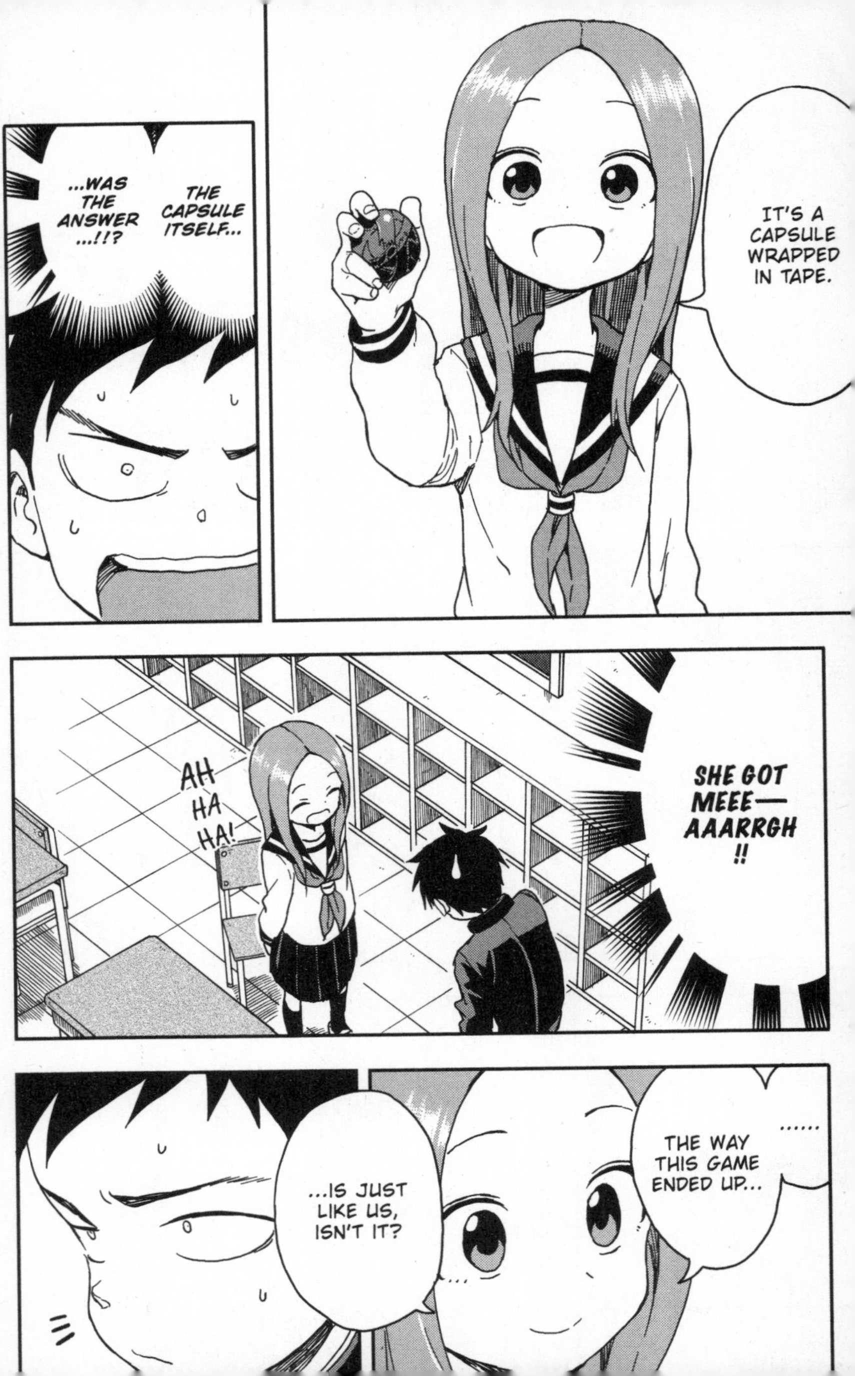
IT'S A CAPSULE WRAPPED IN TAPE.
THE CAPSULE ITSELF...
...WAS THE ANSWER ...!!?
SHE GOT MEEE—AAARRGH !!
AH HA HA!
......
THE WAY THIS GAME ENDED UP...
...IS JUST LIKE US, ISN'T IT?
...

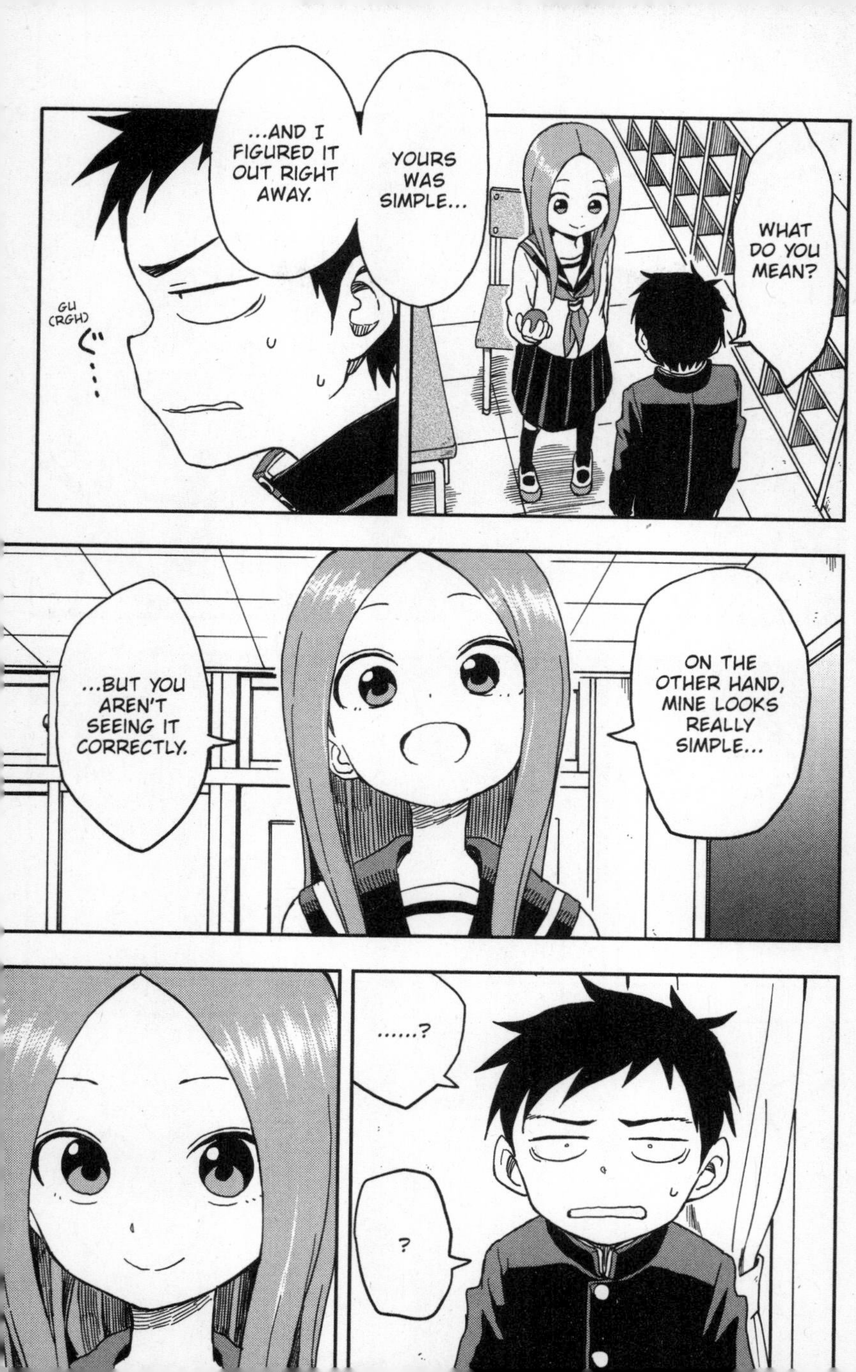
WHAT DO YOU MEAN?
YOURS WAS SIMPLE...
...AND I FIGURED IT OUT RIGHT AWAY.
GU (RGH)
ON THE OTHER HAND, MINE LOOKS REALLY SIMPLE...
...BUT YOU AREN'T SEEING IT CORRECTLY.
......?
?

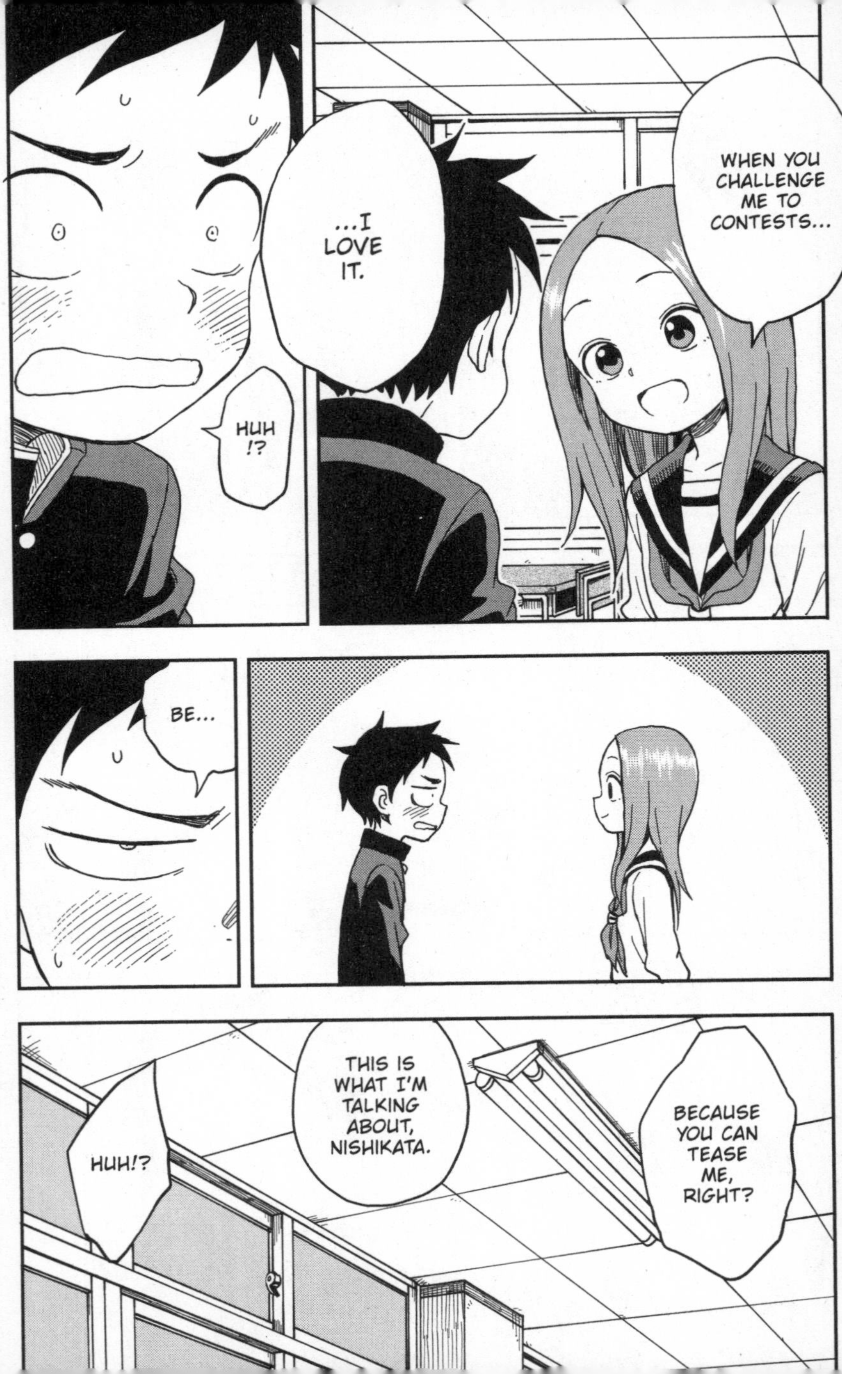
WHEN YOU CHALLENGE ME TO CONTESTS...
...I LOVE IT.
HUH!?
BE...
BECAUSE YOU CAN TEASE ME, RIGHT?
THIS IS WHAT I'M TALKING ABOUT, NISHIKATA.
HUH!?

Teasing Master
Takagi-san

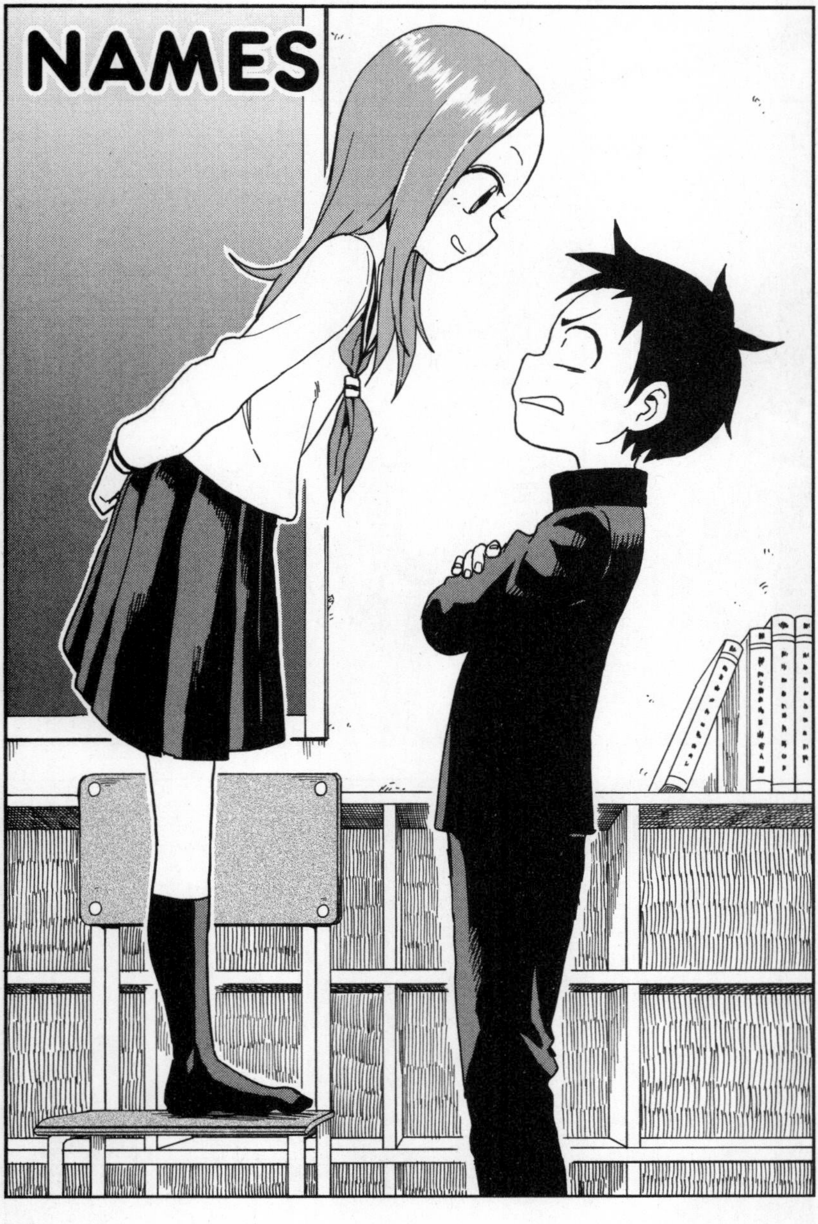
NAMES

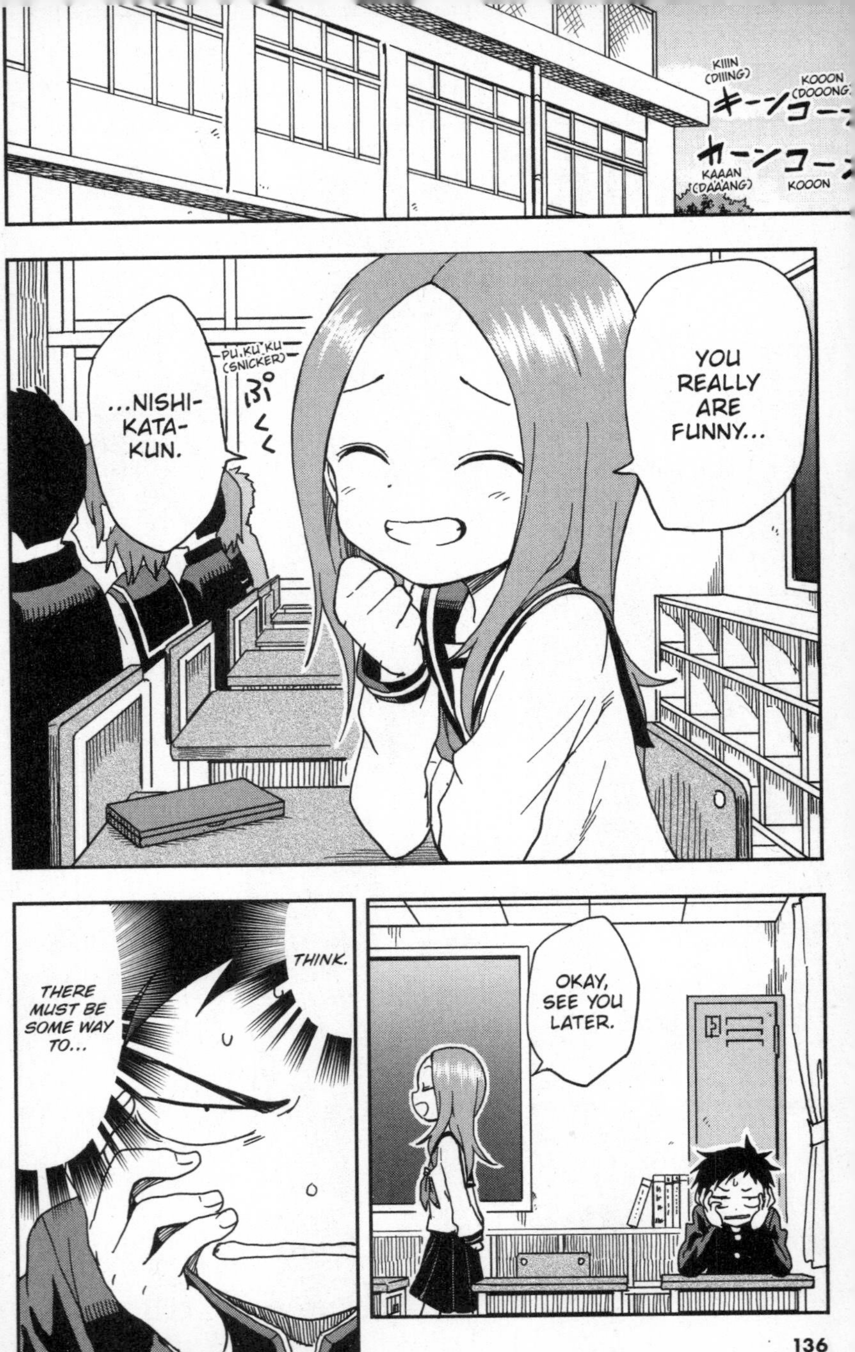
KIIIN (DIIING)
KOOON (DOOONG)
キーンコーン
カーンコーン
KAAAN (DAAANG)
KOOON
YOU REALLY ARE FUNNY...
PU KU KU (SNICKER)
ぷくく
...NISHI-KATA-KUN.
OKAY, SEE YOU LATER.
THINK.
THERE MUST BE SOME WAY TO...

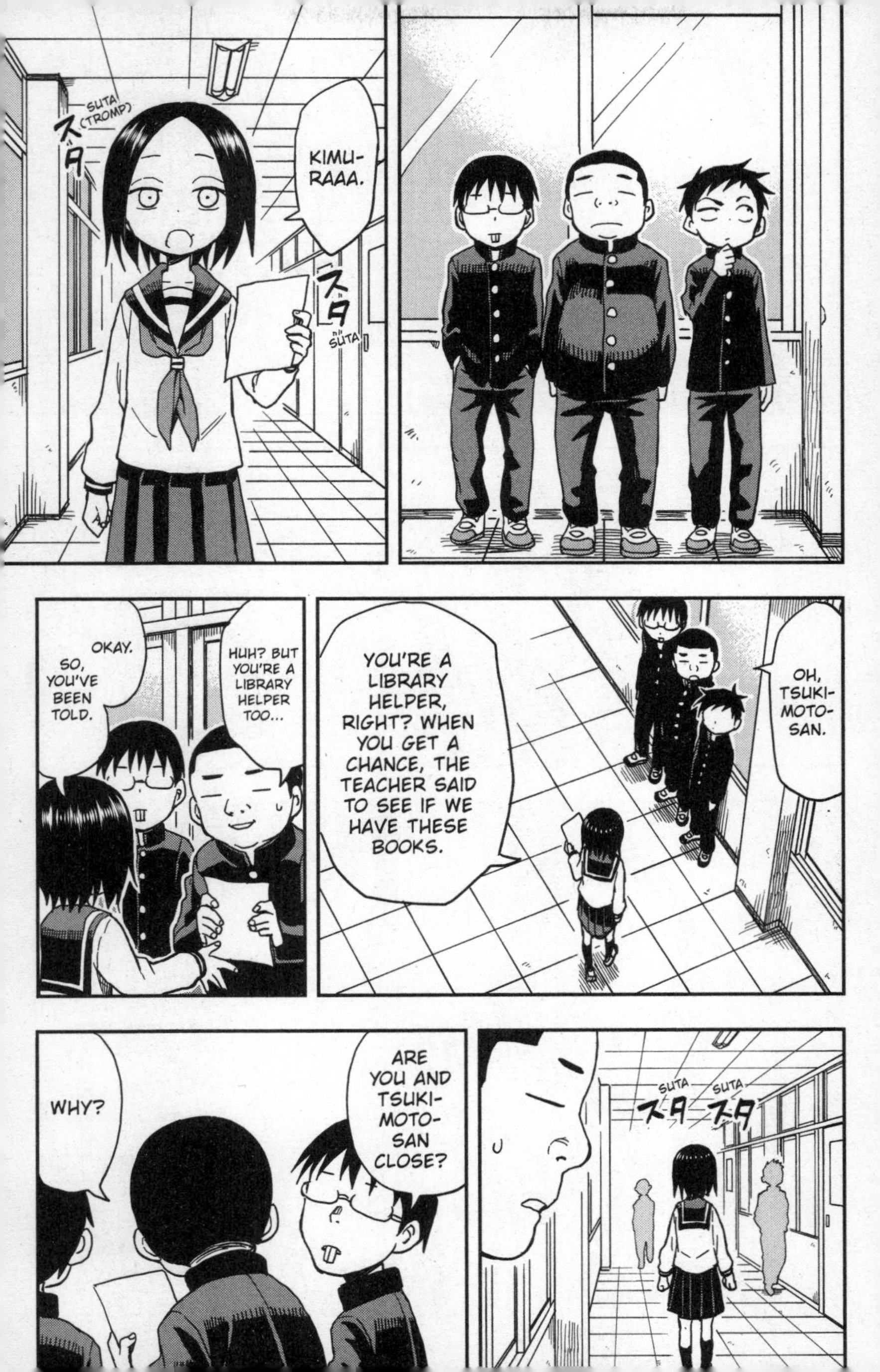
KIMU-RAAA.
SUTA (TROMP)
スタ
スタ
SUTA
OH, TSUKI-MOTO-SAN.
YOU'RE A LIBRARY HELPER, RIGHT? WHEN YOU GET A CHANCE, THE TEACHER SAID TO SEE IF WE HAVE THESE BOOKS.
HUH? BUT YOU'RE A LIBRARY HELPER TOO...
OKAY. SO, YOU'VE BEEN TOLD.
SUTA SUTA
スタ スタ
ARE YOU AND TSUKI-MOTO-SAN CLOSE?
WHY?

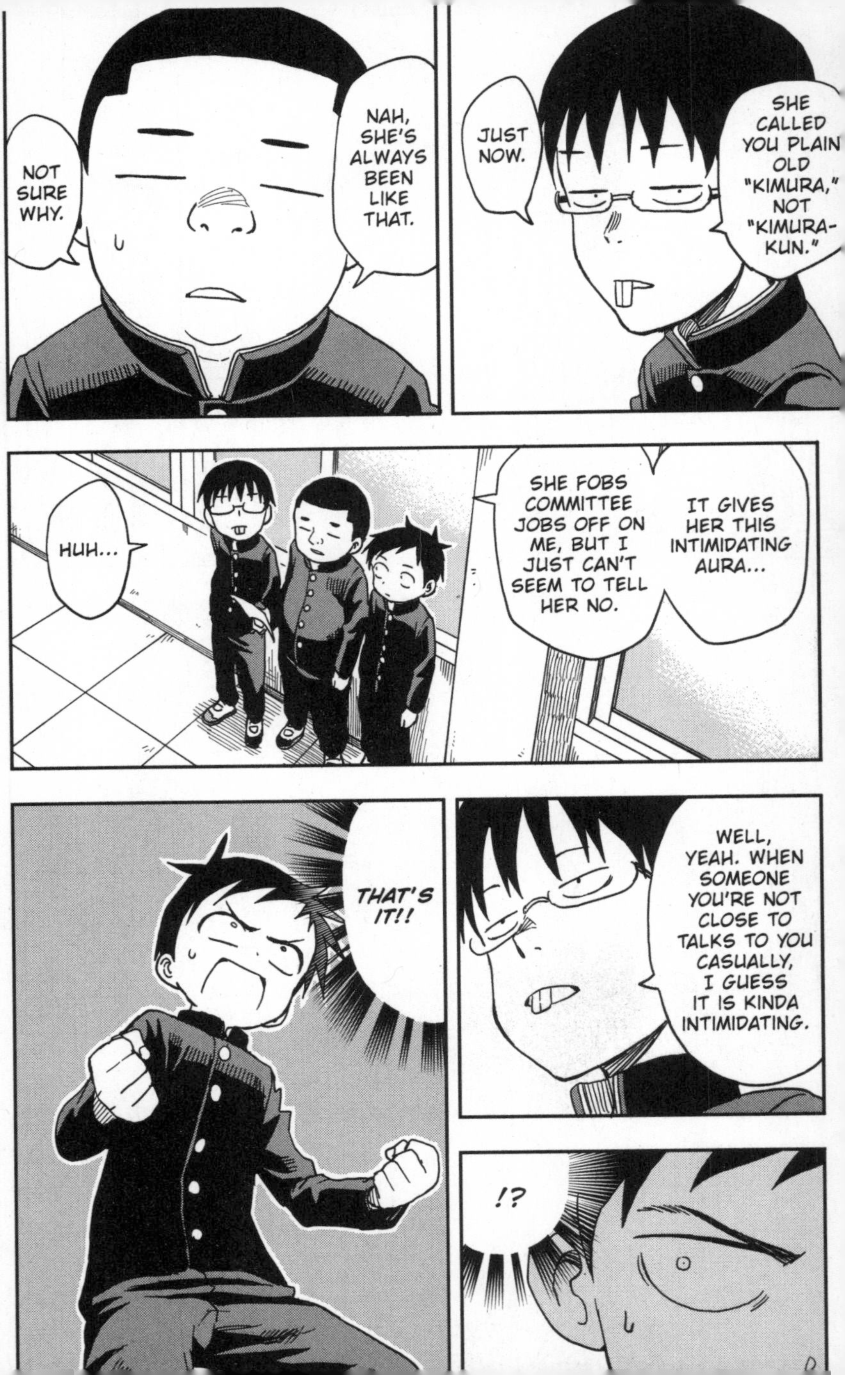
SHE CALLED YOU PLAIN OLD "KIMURA," NOT "KIMURA-KUN."
JUST NOW.
NAH, SHE'S ALWAYS BEEN LIKE THAT.
NOT SURE WHY.
IT GIVES HER THIS INTIMIDATING AURA...
SHE FOBS COMMITTEE JOBS OFF ON ME, BUT I JUST CAN'T SEEM TO TELL HER NO.
HUH...
WELL, YEAH. WHEN SOMEONE YOU'RE NOT CLOSE TO TALKS TO YOU CASUALLY, I GUESS IT IS KINDA INTIMIDATING.
!?
THAT'S IT!!

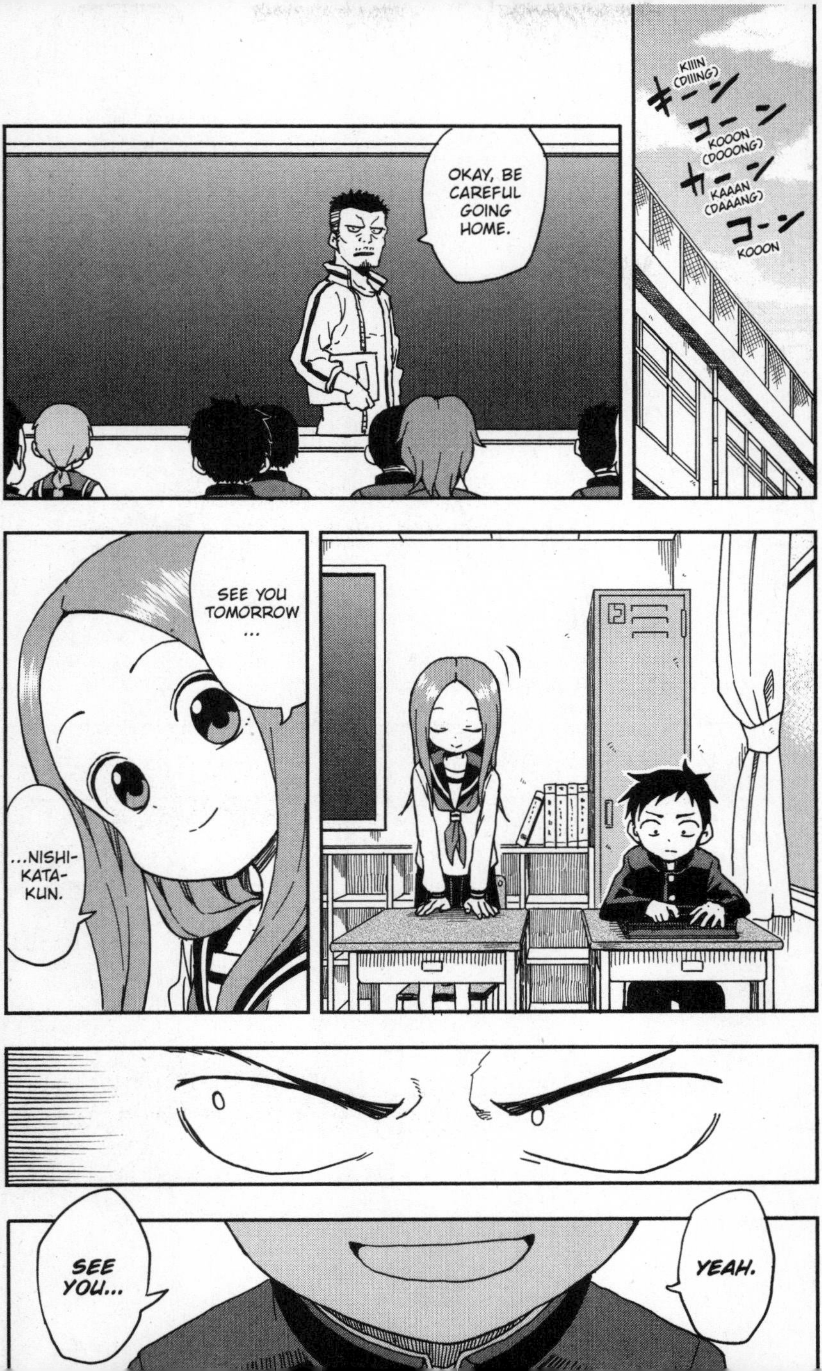
キーン
KIIIN (DIIING)
コーン
KOOON (DOOONG)
カーン
KAAAN (DAAANG)
コーン
KOOON
OKAY, BE CAREFUL GOING HOME.
SEE YOU TOMORROW ...
...NISHIKATA-KUN.
YEAH.
SEE YOU...

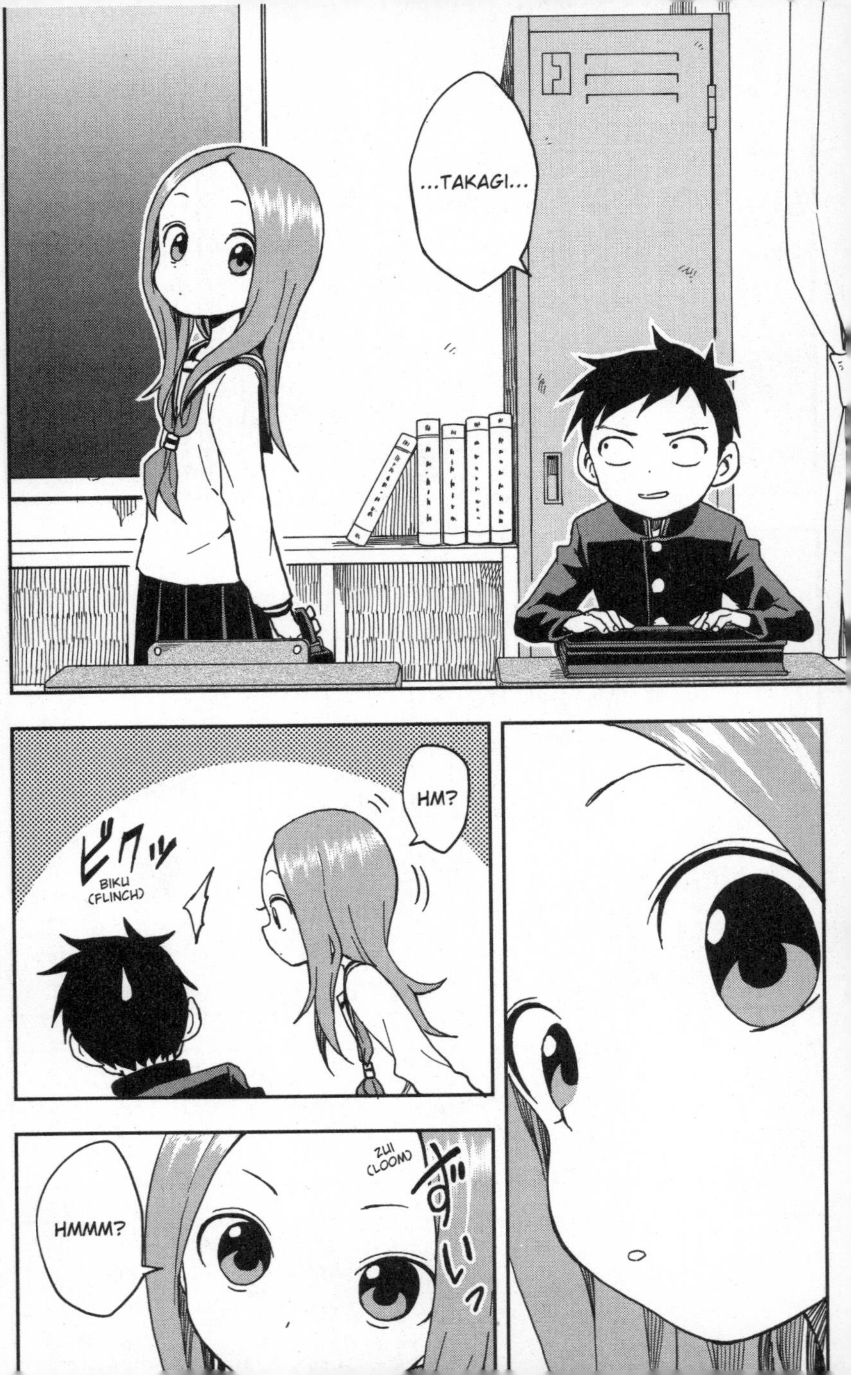
...TAKAGI...
HM?
ビクッ
BIKU (FLINCH)
ずいっ
ZUI (LOOM)
HMMM?

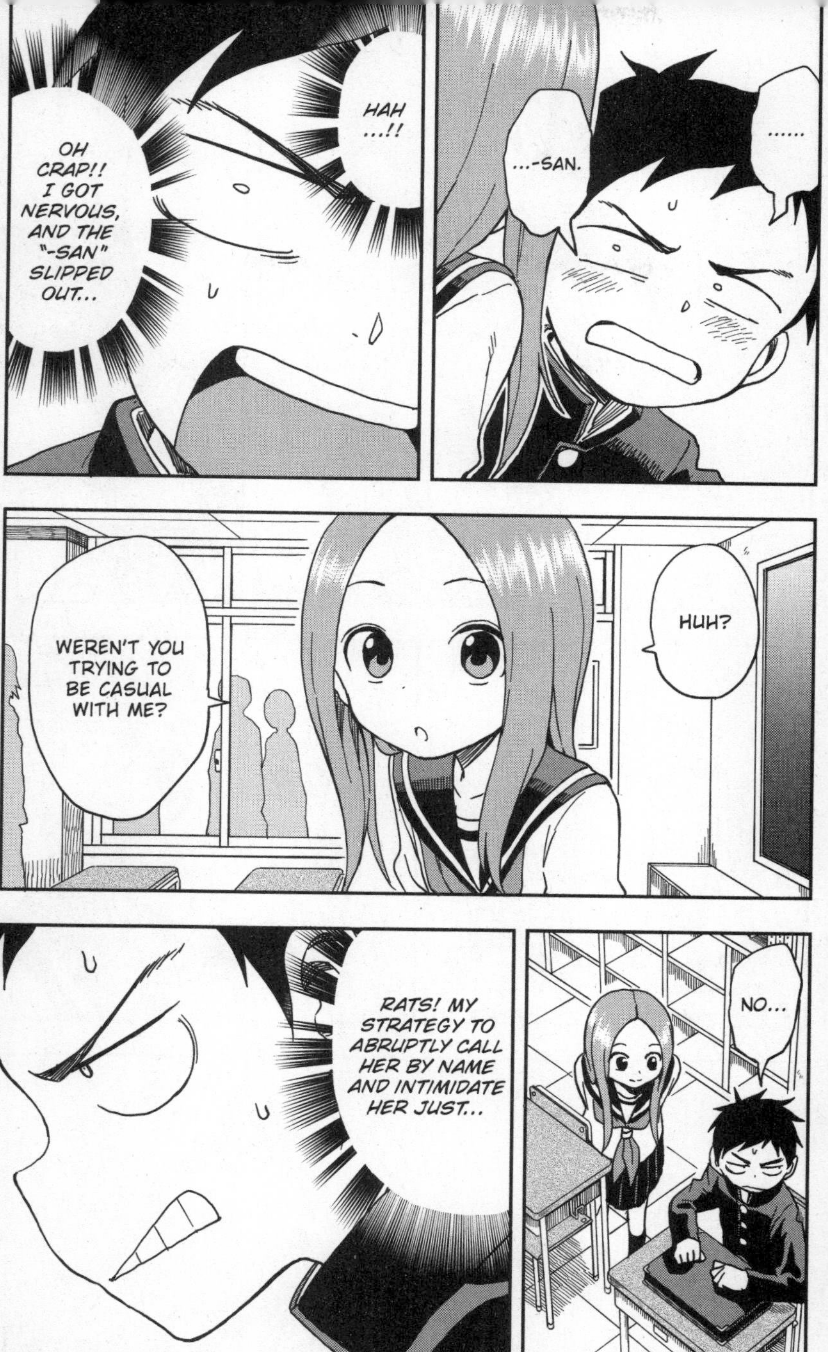
......
...-SAN.
HAH ...!!
OH CRAP!! I GOT NERVOUS, AND THE "-SAN" SLIPPED OUT...
HUH?
WEREN'T YOU TRYING TO BE CASUAL WITH ME?
NO...
RATS! MY STRATEGY TO ABRUPTLY CALL HER BY NAME AND INTIMIDATE HER JUST...

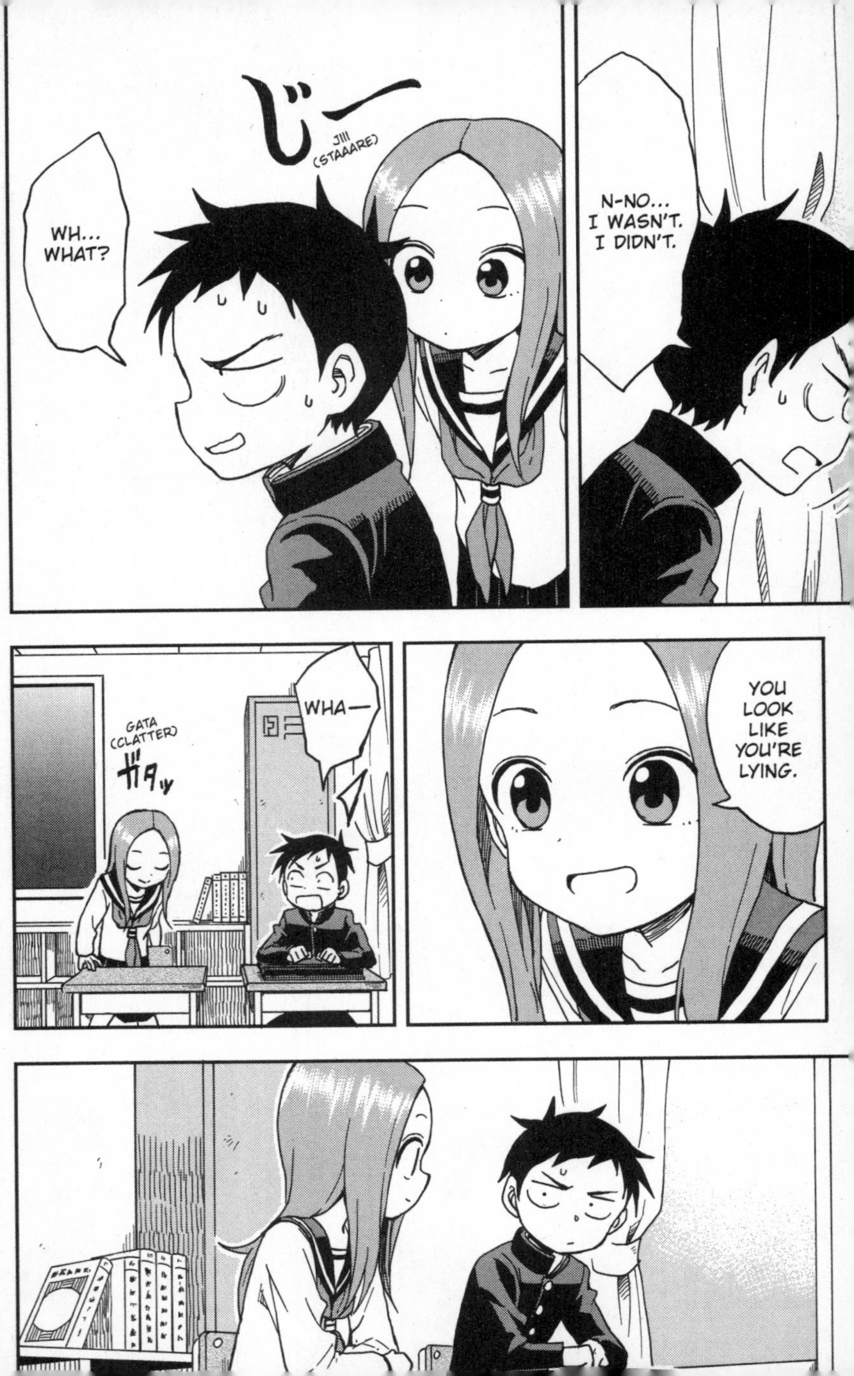
N-NO... I WASN'T. I DIDN'T.
じー
JIII (STAAARE)
WH... WHAT?
YOU LOOK LIKE YOU'RE LYING.
WHA—
GATA (CLATTER)
ガタッ

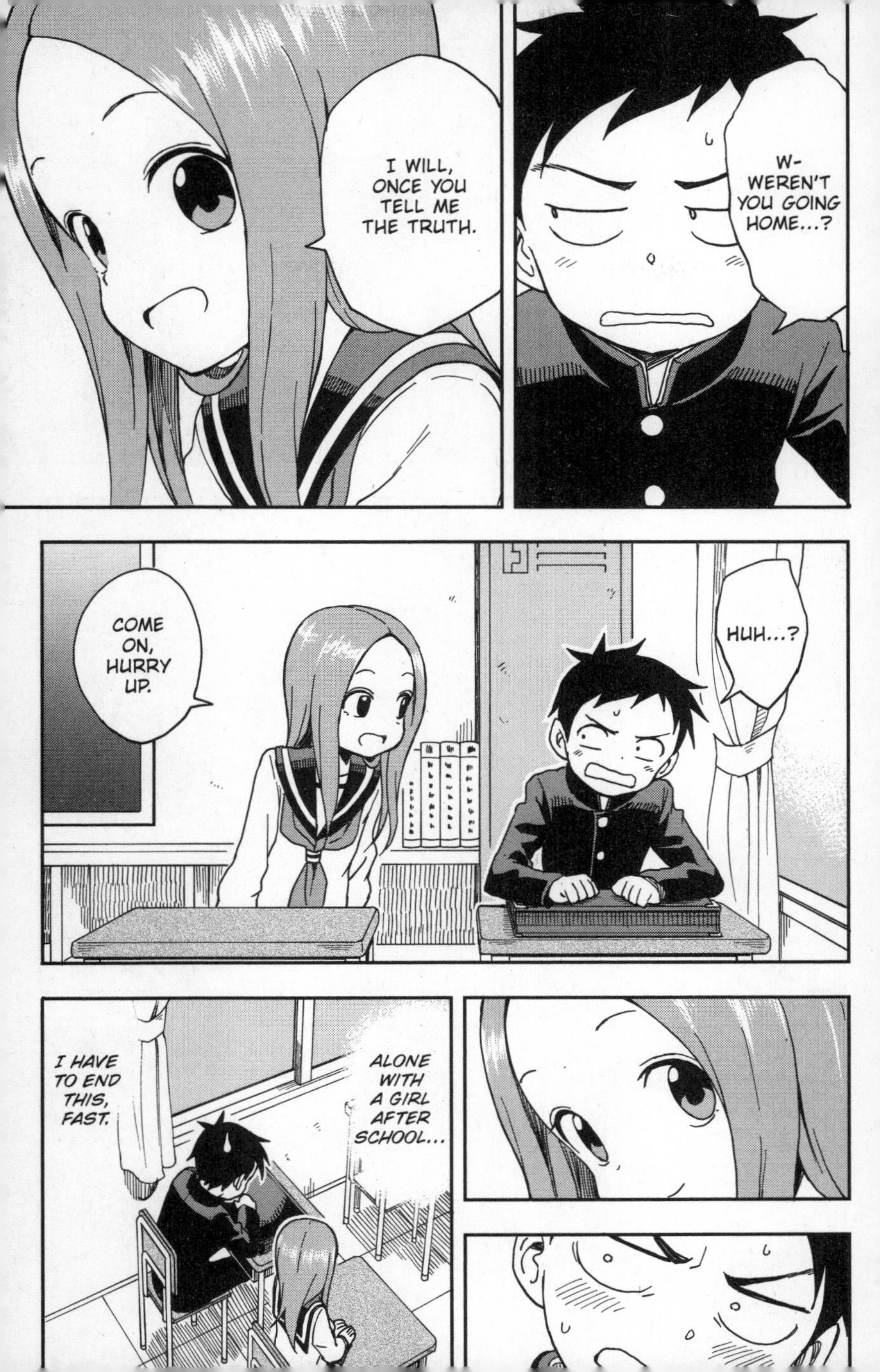
W-WEREN'T YOU GOING HOME...?
I WILL, ONCE YOU TELL ME THE TRUTH.
HUH...?
COME ON, HURRY UP.
ALONE WITH A GIRL AFTER SCHOOL...
I HAVE TO END THIS, FAST.

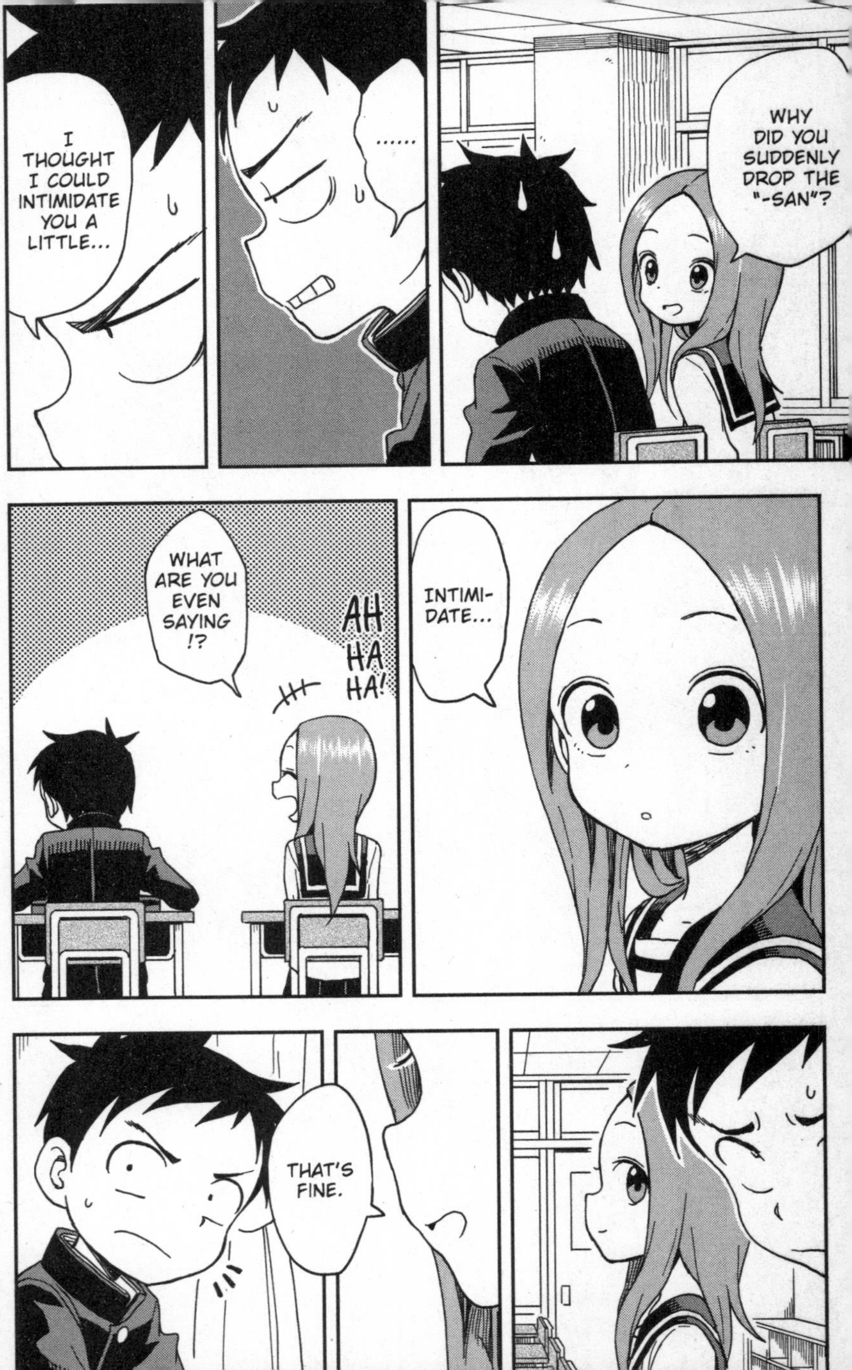
WHY DID YOU SUDDENLY DROP THE "-SAN"?
......
I THOUGHT I COULD INTIMIDATE YOU A LITTLE...
INTIMI-DATE...
WHAT ARE YOU EVEN SAYING !?
AH HA HA!
THAT'S FINE.

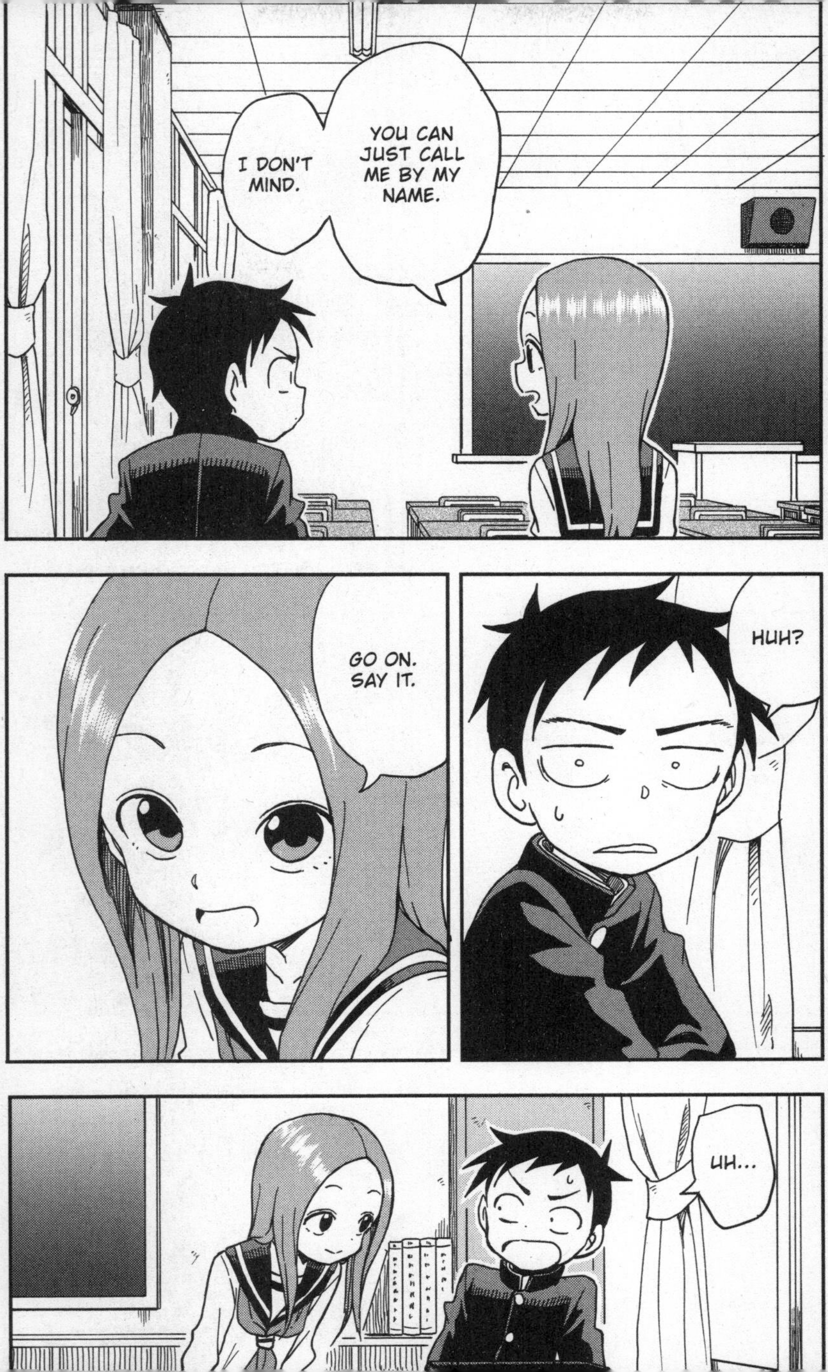
YOU CAN JUST CALL ME BY MY NAME.
I DON'T MIND.
HUH?
GO ON. SAY IT.
UH...

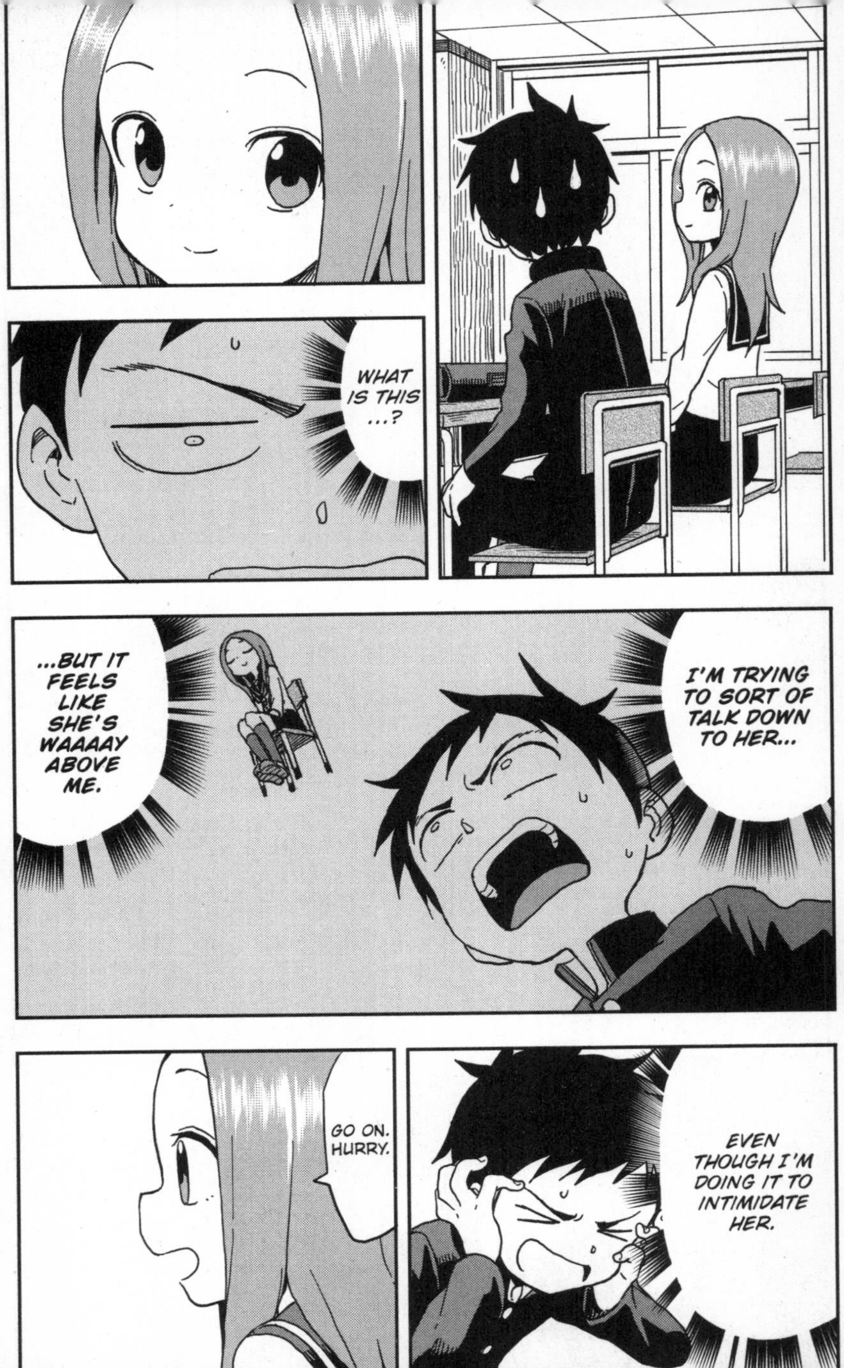
WHAT IS THIS ...?
I'M TRYING TO SORT OF TALK DOWN TO HER...
...BUT IT FEELS LIKE SHE'S WAAAAY ABOVE ME.
EVEN THOUGH I'M DOING IT TO INTIMIDATE HER.
GO ON. HURRY.

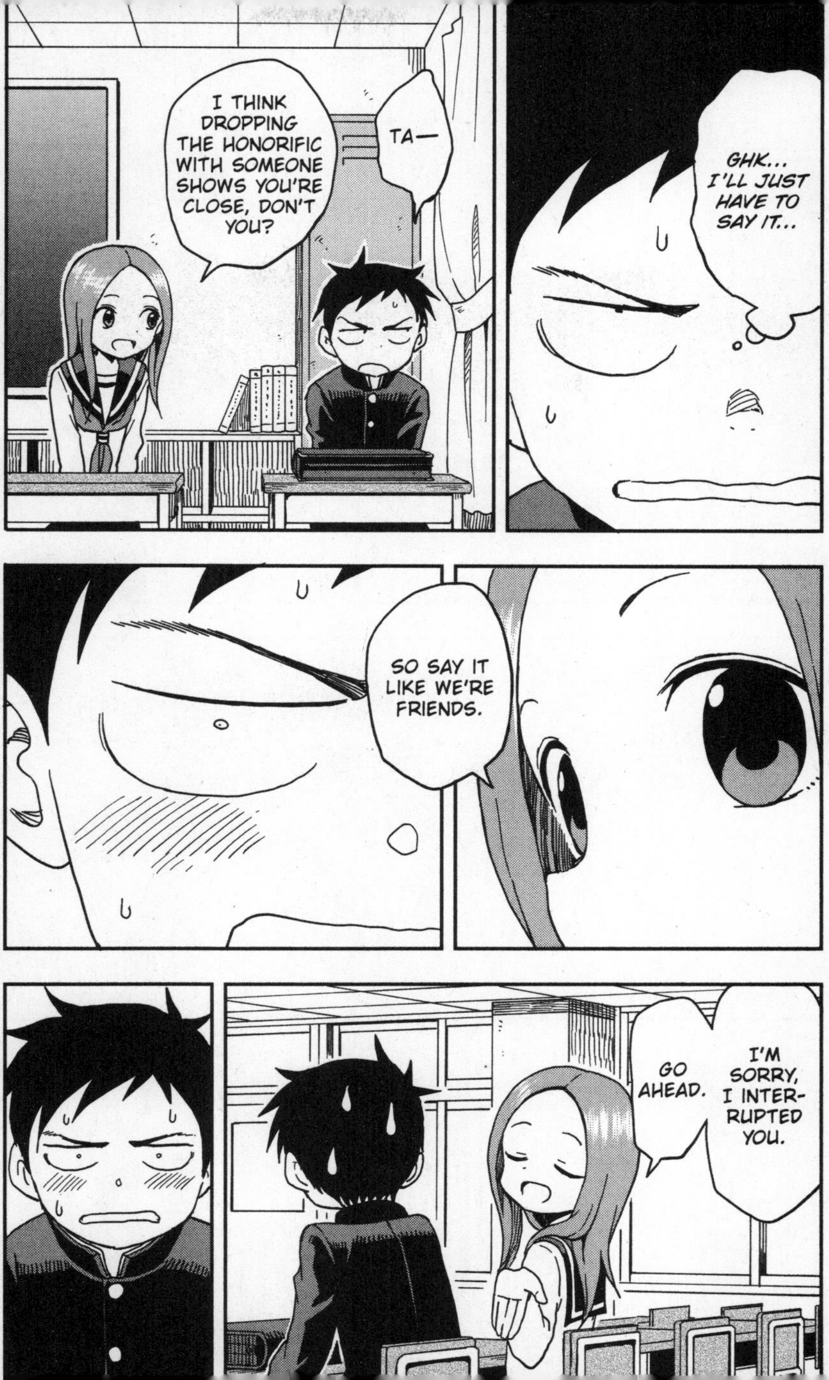
GHK... I'LL JUST HAVE TO SAY IT...
TA—
I THINK DROPPING THE HONORIFIC WITH SOMEONE SHOWS YOU'RE CLOSE, DON'T YOU?
SO SAY IT LIKE WE'RE FRIENDS.
I'M SORRY, I INTERRUPTED YOU.
GO AHEAD.

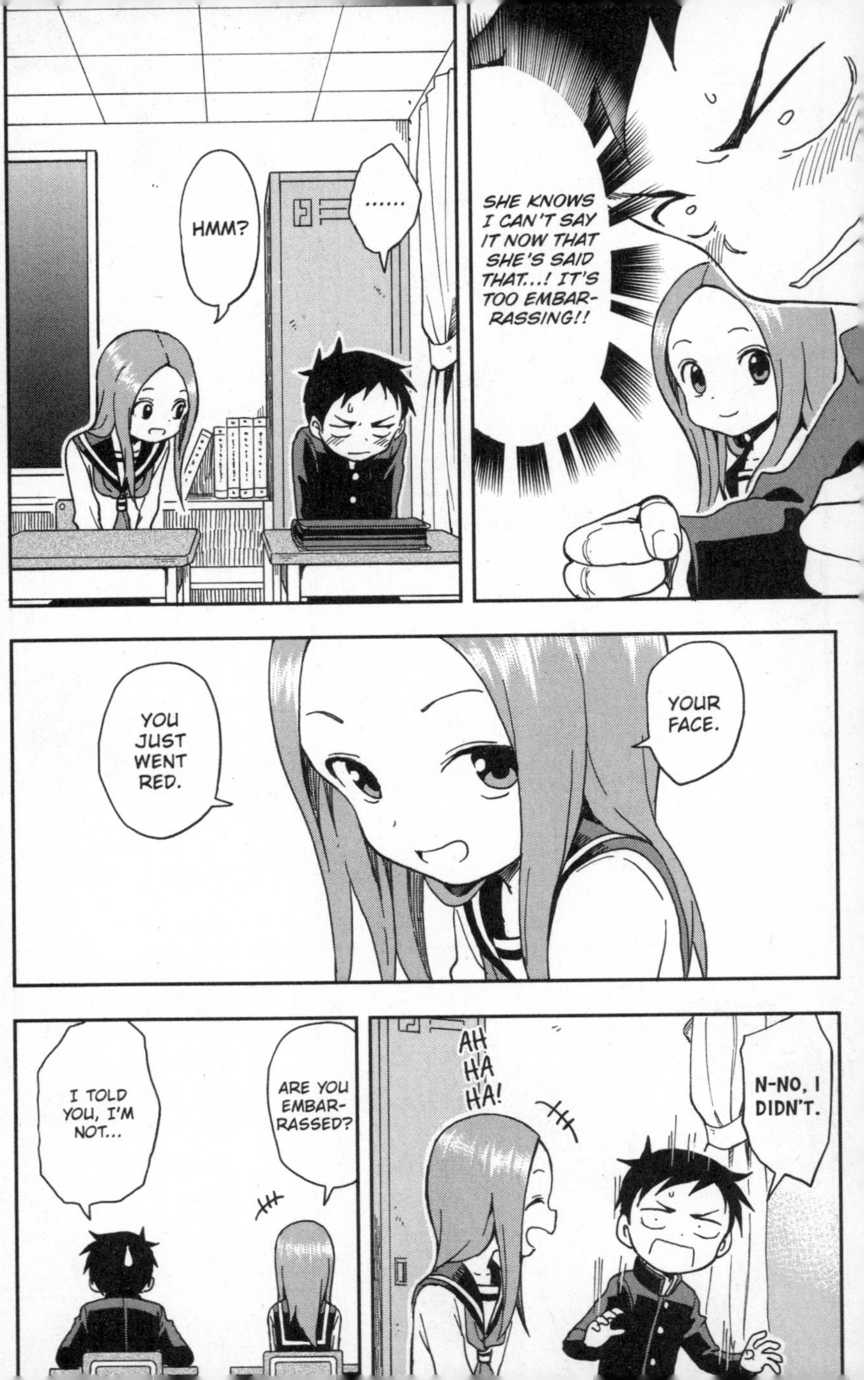
SHE KNOWS I CAN'T SAY IT NOW THAT SHE'S SAID THAT...! IT'S TOO EMBAR-RASSING!!
......
HMM?
YOUR FACE.
YOU JUST WENT RED.
N-NO, I DIDN'T.
AH HA HA!
ARE YOU EMBAR-RASSED?
I TOLD YOU, I'M NOT...

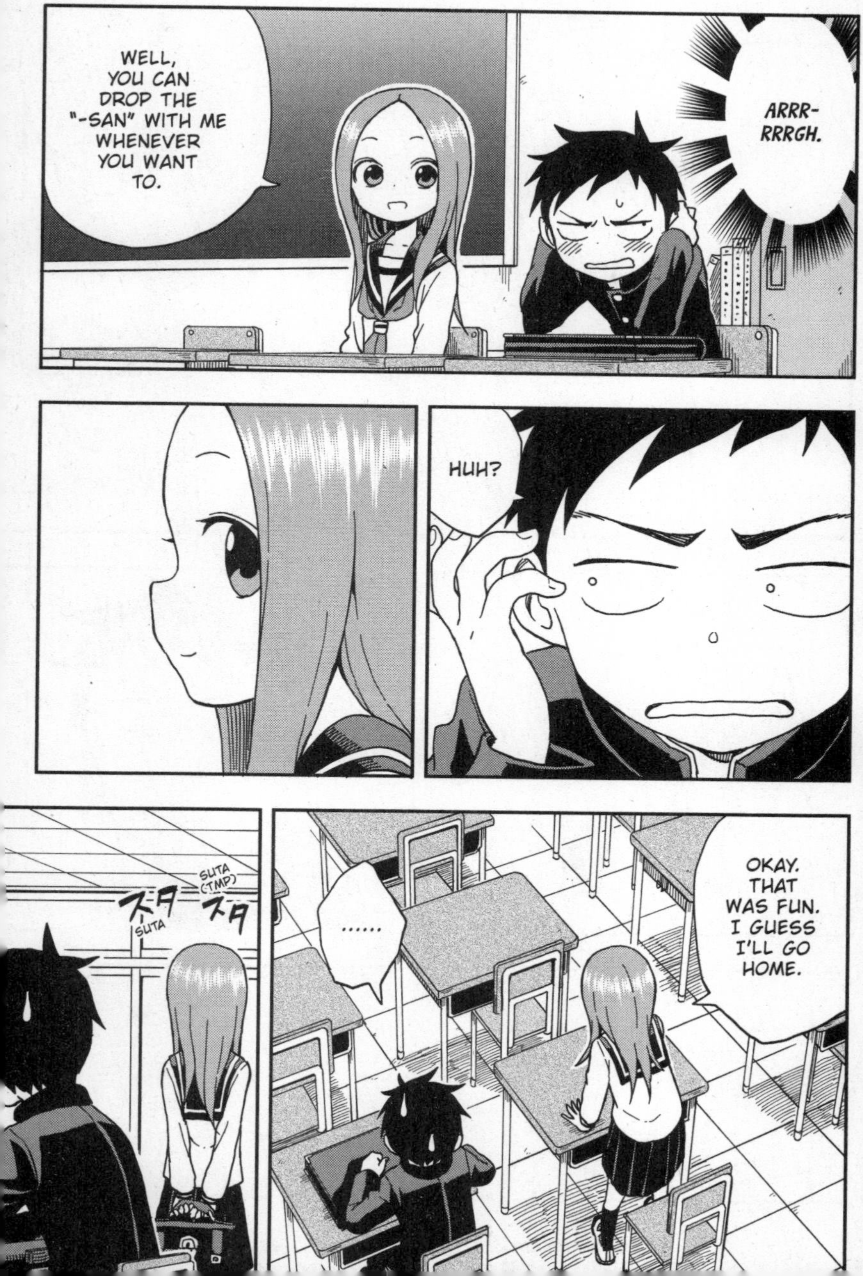
ARRR-RRRGH.
WELL, YOU CAN DROP THE "-SAN" WITH ME WHENEVER YOU WANT TO.
HUH?
OKAY. THAT WAS FUN. I GUESS I'LL GO HOME.
......
スタ
SUTA (TMP)
スタ
SUTA

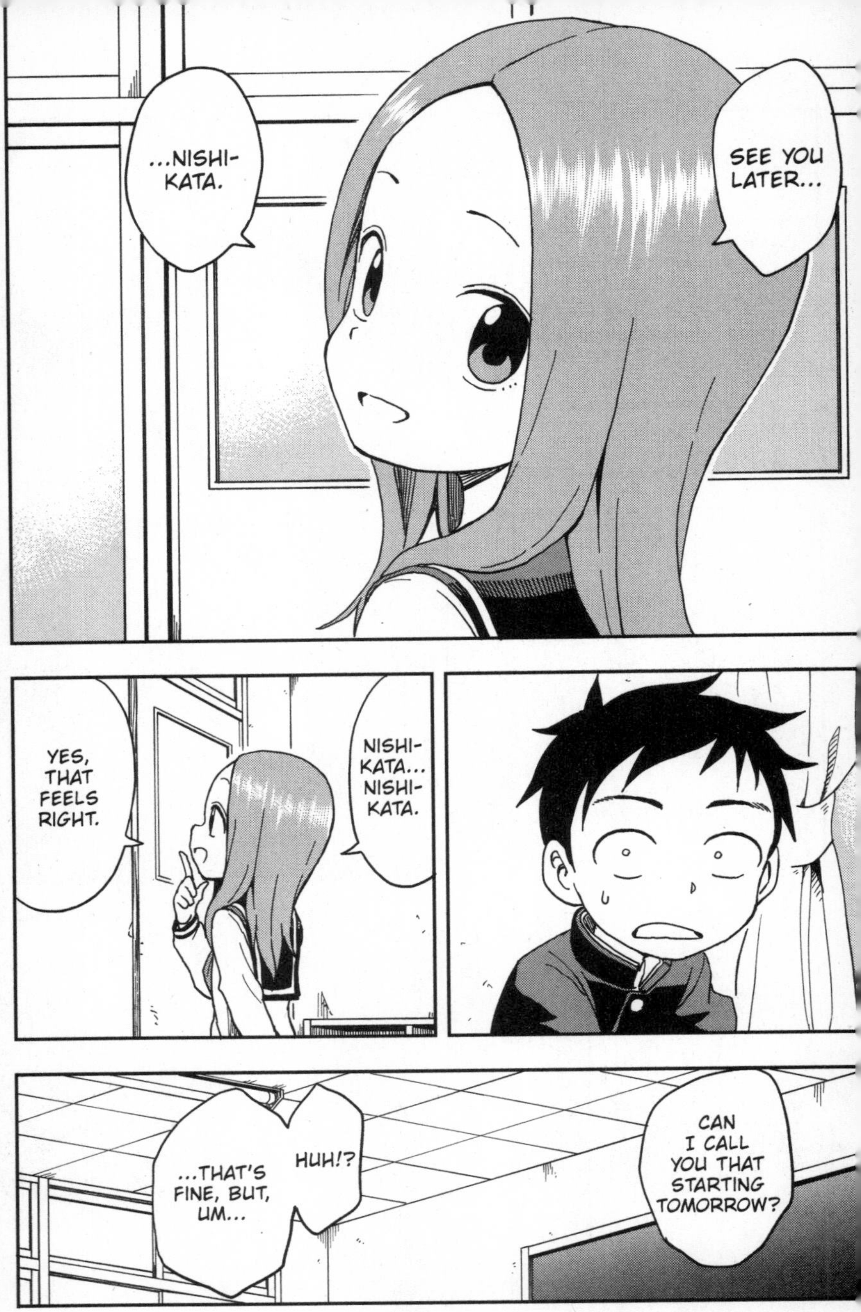
SEE YOU LATER...
...NISHI-KATA.
NISHI-KATA... NISHI-KATA.
YES, THAT FEELS RIGHT.
CAN I CALL YOU THAT STARTING TOMORROW?
HUH!?
...THAT'S FINE, BUT, UM...

TEASING MASTER TAKAGI-SAN 10 / THE END

BONUS

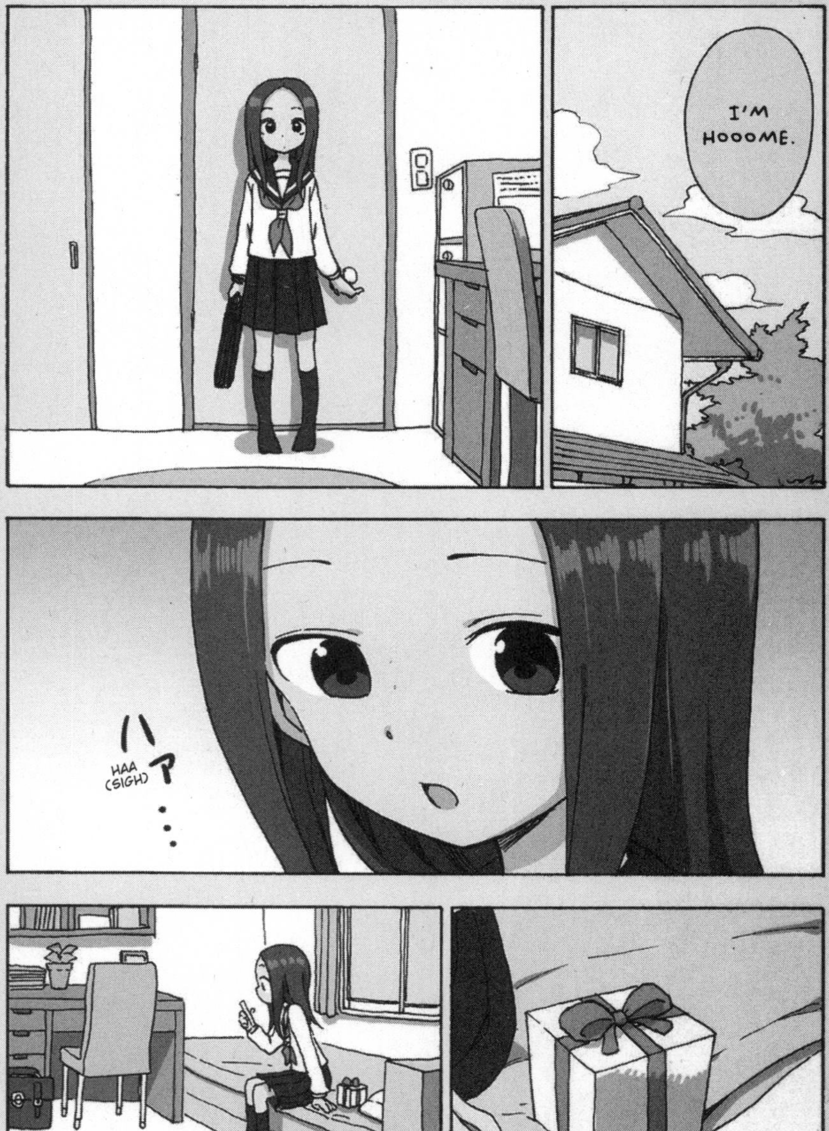

I'M HOOOME.
ハア
HAA (SIGH)
...

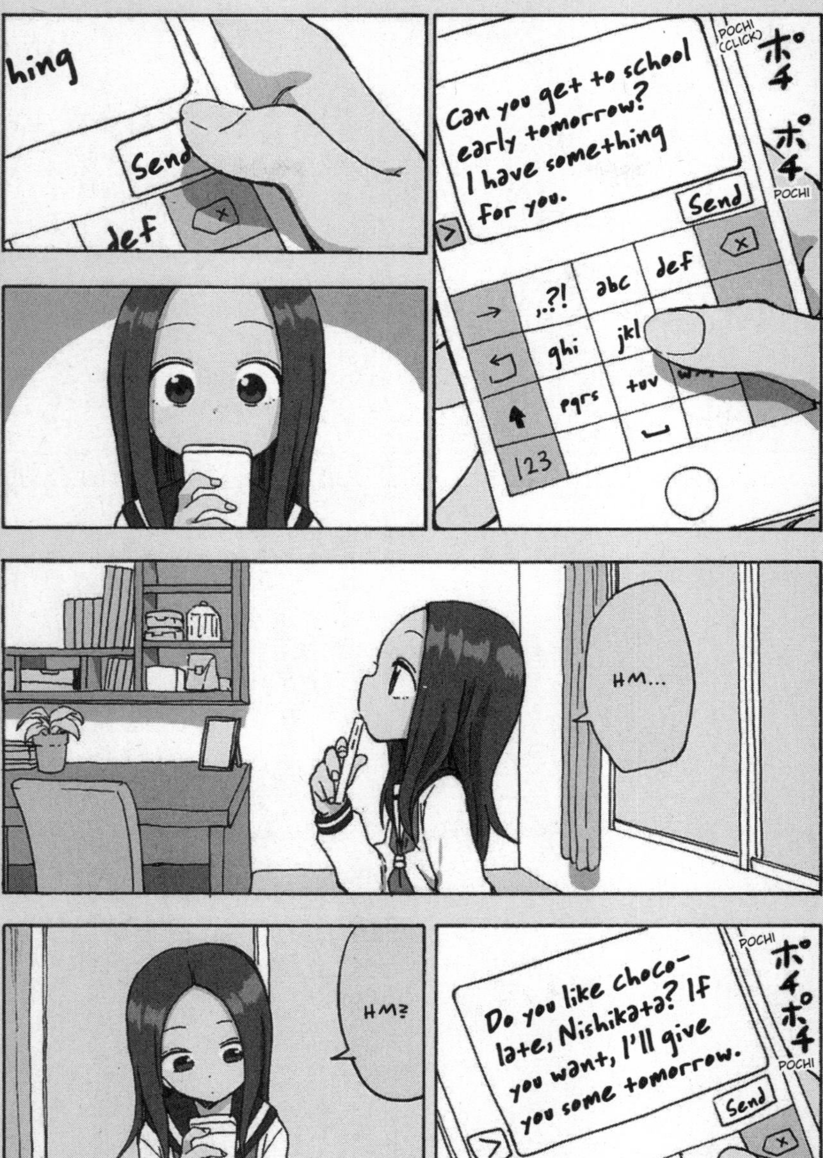
ポチ
POCHI (CLICK)
ポチ
POCHI
Can you get to school early tomorrow? I have something for you.
Send
,.?! abc def
ghi jkl
pqrs tuv
123
hing
Send
def
HM...
ポチポチ
POCHI
POCHI
Do you like choco-late, Nishikata? If you want, I'll give you some tomorrow.
Send
abc
HM?

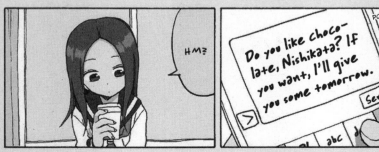

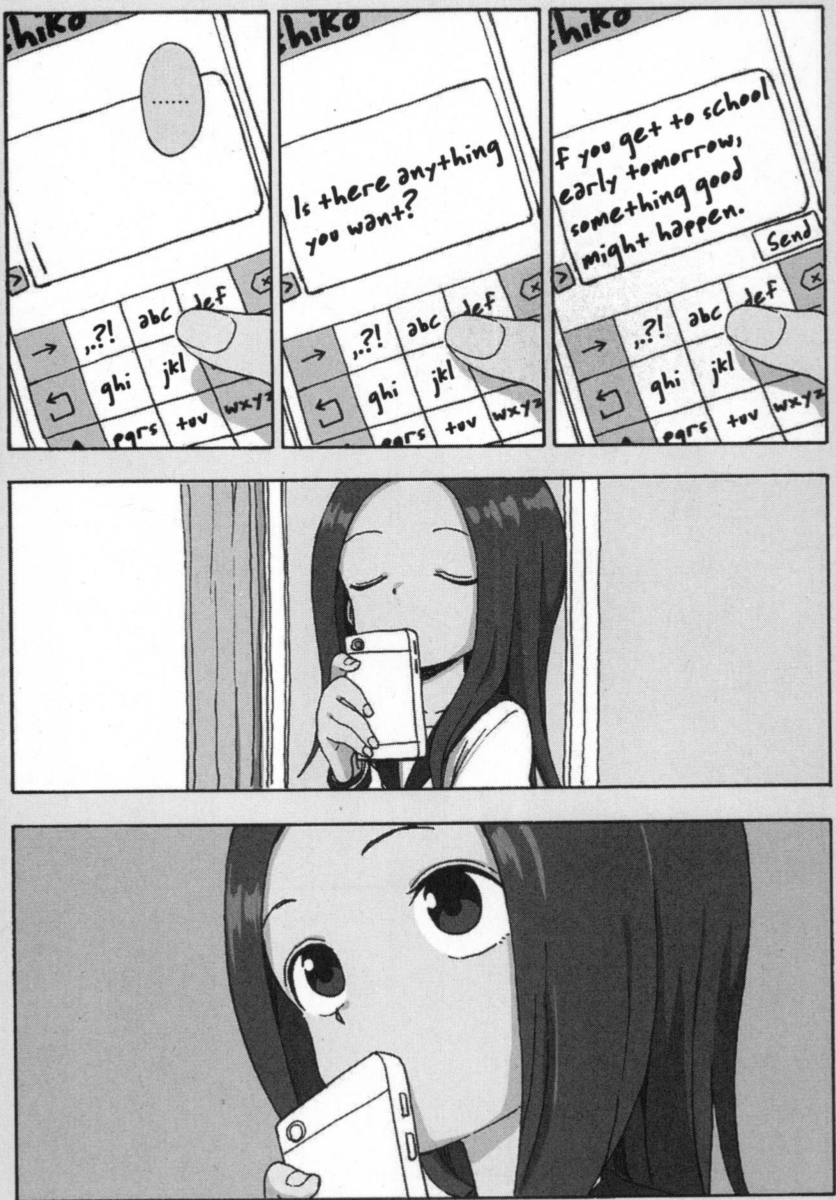f you get to school early tomorrow, something good might happen.
Send
Is there anything you want?
......

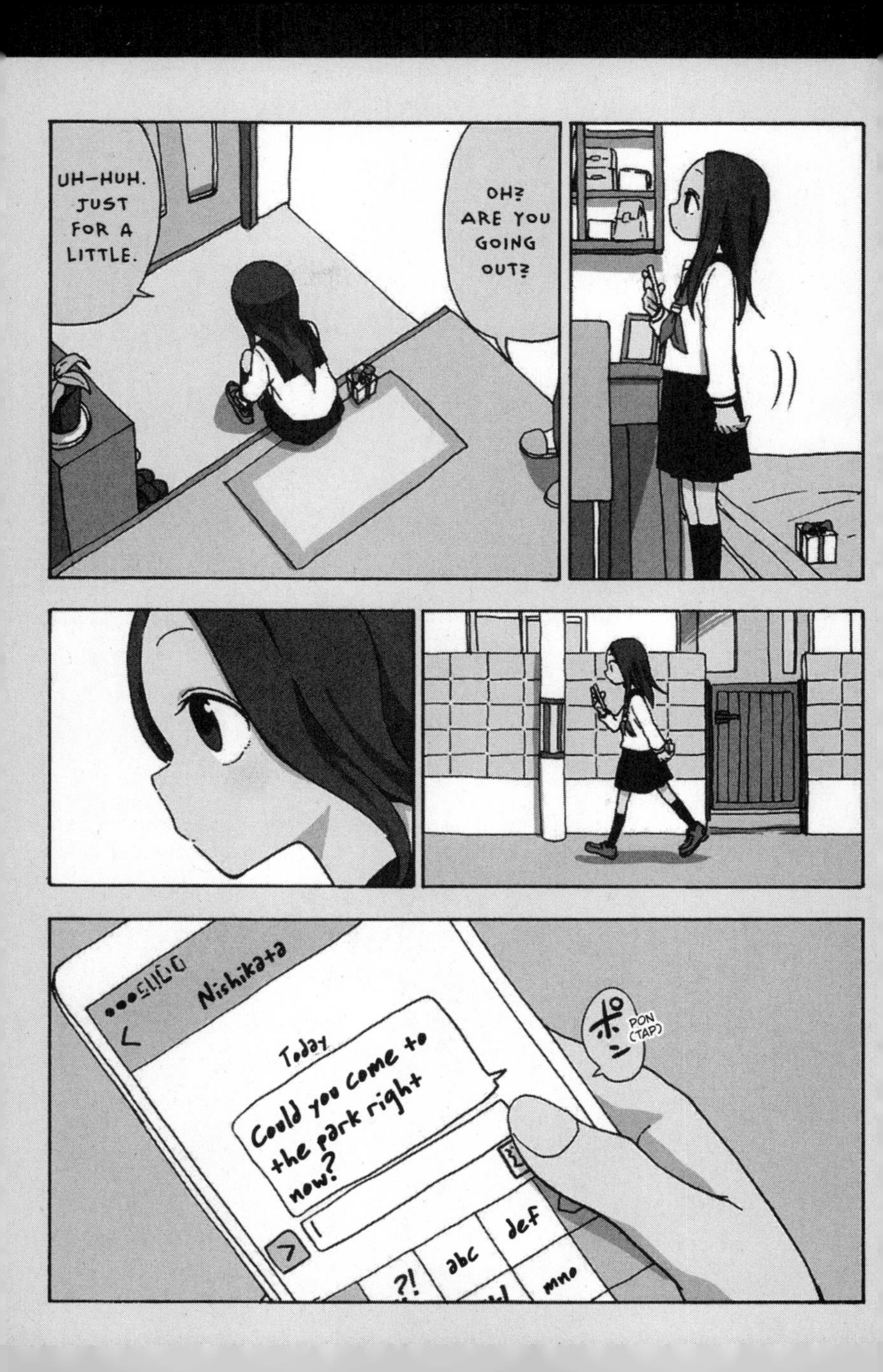
OH? ARE YOU GOING OUT?
UH-HUH. JUST FOR A LITTLE.
Nishikata
Today
Could you come to the park right now?
PON (TAP)
def
abc
?!
mno

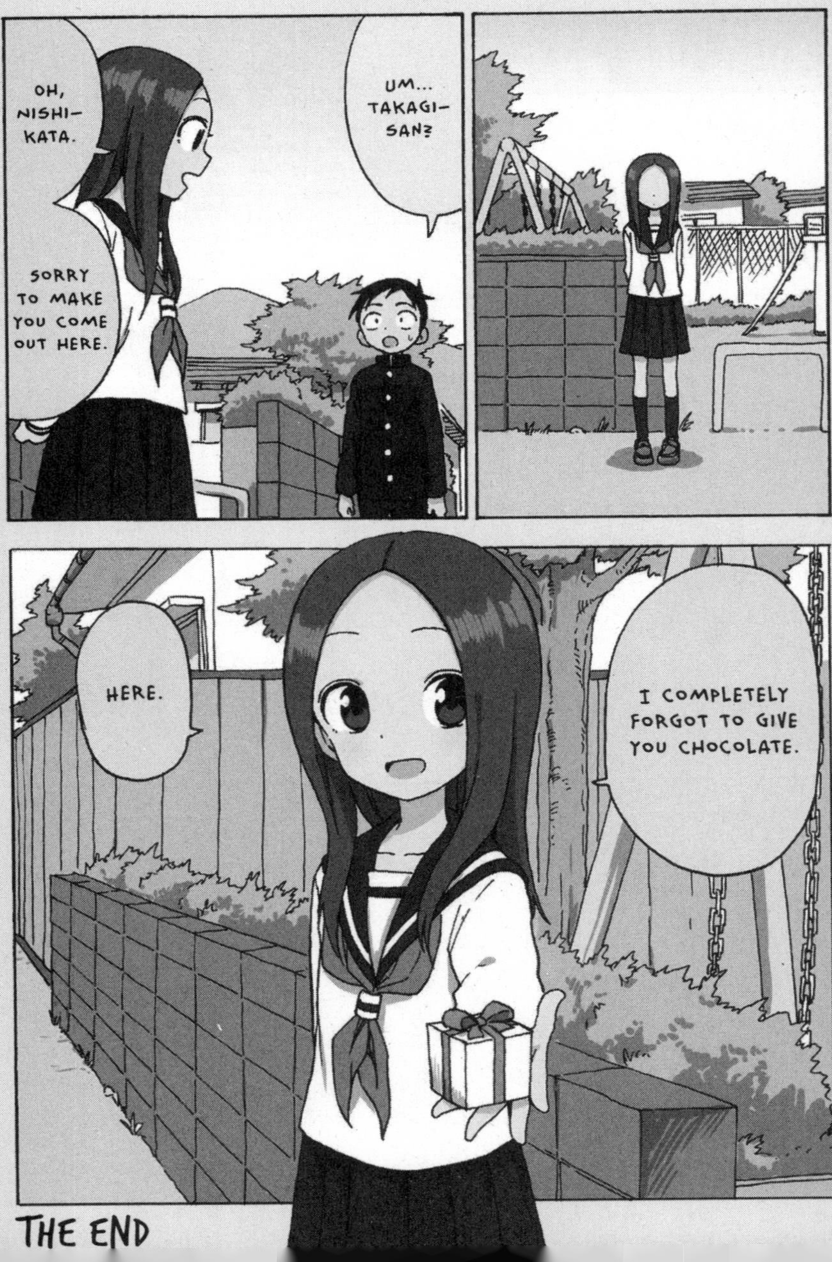
UM... TAKAGI-SAN?
OH, NISHIKATA.
SORRY TO MAKE YOU COME OUT HERE.
I COMPLETELY FORGOT TO GIVE YOU CHOCOLATE.
HERE.
THE END

Translation Notes

COMMON HONORIFICS

no honorific: Indicates familiarity or closeness; if used without permission or reason, addressing someone in this manner would constitute an insult.

-san: The Japanese equivalent of Mr./Mrs./Miss. If a situation calls for politeness, this is the fail-safe honorific.

-kun: Used most often when referring to boys, this indicates affection or familiarity. Occasionally used by older men among their peers, but it may also be used by anyone referring to a person of lower standing.

-chan: An affectionate honorific indicating familiarity used mostly in reference to girls; also used in reference to cute persons or animals of either gender.

-senpai: A suffix used to address upperclassmen or more experienced coworkers.

-sensei: A respectful term for teachers, artists, or high-level professionals.

Page 84
Sports tests are similar to physical education tests in America, in which students are scored throughout various athletic events on their flexibility, strength, and agility.

Page 114
In Japanese, the word for this particular kind of carp and romantic love are both *koi*. Since Nishikata's been thinking about that hug, when Takagi says the word, he automatically picks the wrong meaning.

WE'RE ON VOLUME 10 ALREADY. THANK YOU VERY MUCH.

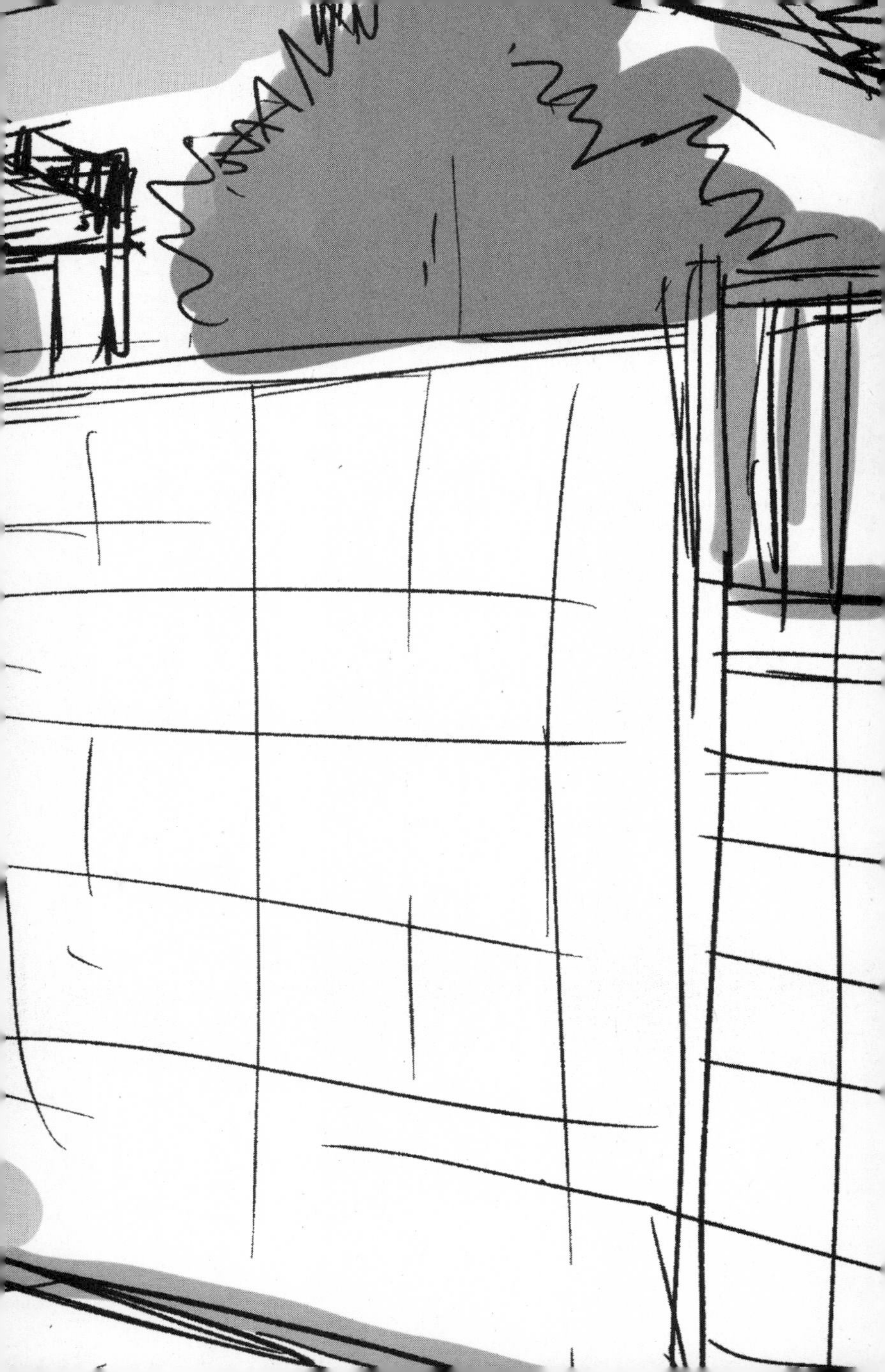

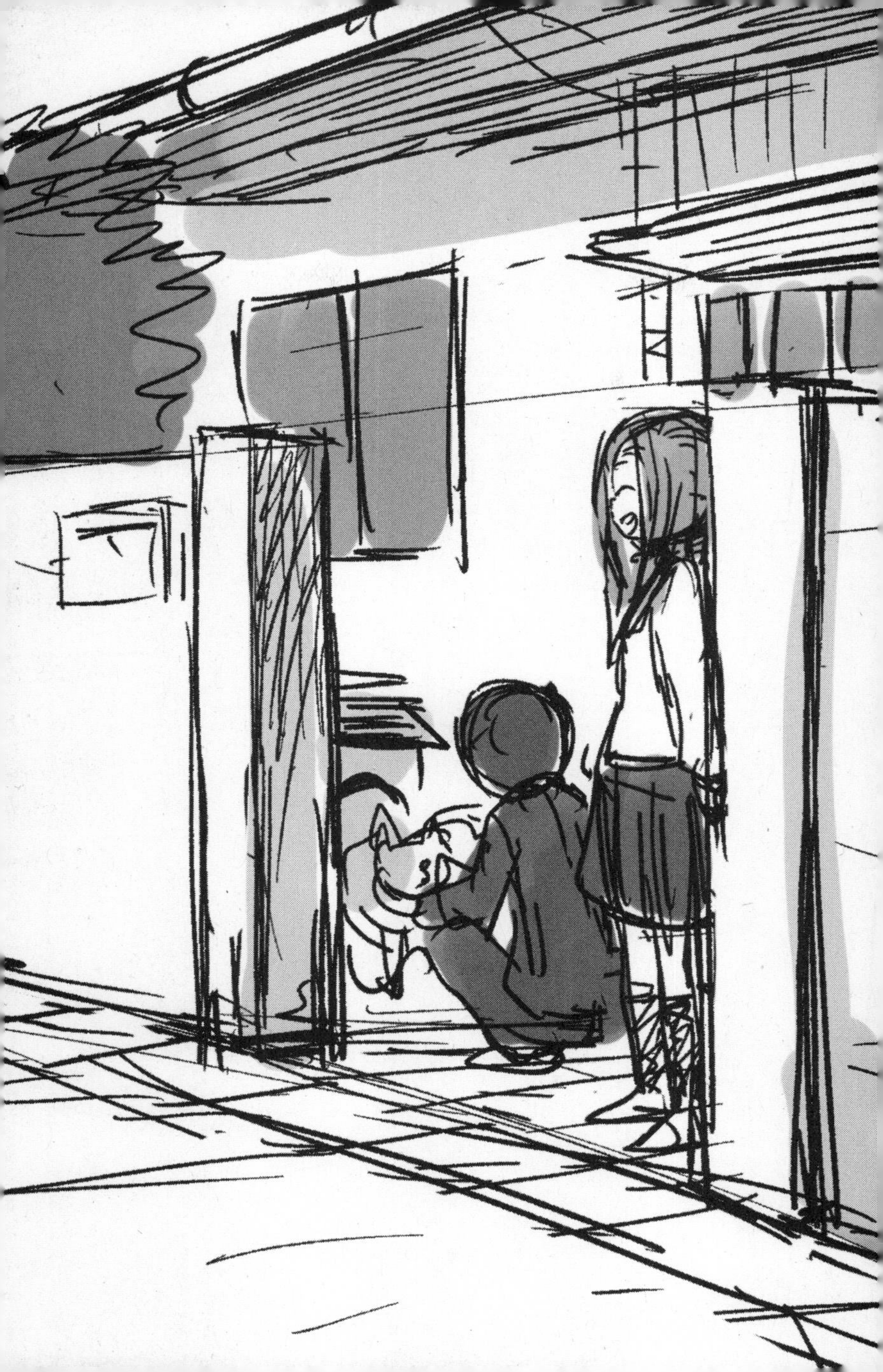

Teasing Master Takagi-san ⑩

Soichiro Yamamoto

TRANSLATION: Taylor Engel ♦ **LETTERING:** Takeshi Kamura

This book is a work of fiction. Names, characters, places, and incidents are the product of the author's imagination or are used fictitiously. Any resemblance to actual events, locales, or persons, living or dead, is coincidental.

KARAKAI JOZU NO TAKAGI-SAN Vol. 10
by Soichiro YAMAMOTO
© 2014 Soichiro YAMAMOTO
All rights reserved.
Original Japanese edition published by SHOGAKUKAN.
English translation rights in the United States of America, Canada, the United Kingdom, Ireland, Australia and New Zealand arranged with SHOGAKUKAN through Tuttle-Mori Agency, Inc.

English translation © 2020 by Yen Press, LLC

Yen Press, LLC supports the right to free expression and the value of copyright. The purpose of copyright is to encourage writers and artists to produce the creative works that enrich our culture.

The scanning, uploading, and distribution of this book without permission is a theft of the author's intellectual property. If you would like permission to use material from the book (other than for review purposes), please contact the publisher. Thank you for your support of the author's rights.

Yen Press
150 West 30th Street, 19th Floor
New York, NY 10001

Visit us at yenpress.com

facebook.com/yenpress
twitter.com/yenpress

yenpress.tumblr.com
instagram.com/yenpress

First Yen Press Edition: October 2020

Yen Press is an imprint of Yen Press, LLC.
The Yen Press name and logo are trademarks of Yen Press, LLC.

The publisher is not responsible for websites (or their content) that are not owned by the publisher.

Library of Congress Control Number: 2018939489

ISBNs: 978-1-9753-5941-6 (paperback)
978-1-9753-1476-7 (ebook)

10 9 8 7 6 5 4 3 2

GRA

Printed in Italy